THE SHADOWED SPRING

Books by Carola Salisbury

THE
SHADOWED
SPRING

Carola Salisbury

DOUBLEDAY & COMPANY, INC.

GARDEN CITY, NEW YORK

1980

ISBN: 0-385-14958-1
Library of Congress Catalog Card Number 79-7808
Copyright © 1980 by Doubleday & Company, Inc.

For George Behrend, of Jersey, C.I.,
who has been in the business of studying
comfortable railway travel for fifty years.

THE SHADOWED SPRING

PART

ONE

Chapter One

THE YEAR 1878, WHICH WAS THE YEAR ALL THESE THINGS happened in my life, began like any other for me: bland and quite unpromising. True, I was engaged to be married to Richard Neale, who, as the Reverend Mr. Richard Neale, was curate to St. John's parish church in St. Errol, stalwart of the local cricket XI, a notable baritone both in the sacred and secular persuasions. But, then, I exaggerate, for Richard and I were not *exactly* engaged; there was no betrothal ring, no general announcement of our state to friends and relations. There was between us—an understanding. Poor Richard, with his miserable stipend of £22 per annum and little chance of advancement and preferment, save that of stepping into dead men's shoes, was in no position formally to bind a woman by promise of matrimony. We merely existed in a state of hope that some near-miracle—as for instance the windfall of an inheritance from some forgotten relation, or an unexpected preferment from some powerful patron of the Church—would raise Richard to the state where he was able to lead me to the altar.

I have to make this quite plain—to myself as much as to others —in view of Richard's subsequent conduct: I was not bound to him, nor he to me, by any other than a mutual esteem and a slender hope for the future.

South Cornwall, in the year of 1878, was an enchantment. After an exceedingly hard winter, which had filled the grave-yards from Falmouth to the Tamar and killed off two newborn lambs out of three, spring burst upon the duchy with all its thrilling promise, blinding the eyes in the glory of flame-headed rhododendron, lordly azalea—all the exotic flowering shrubs and trees with which the southwest peninsula is so richly blessed. In that spring, the towering palm tree in the garden of Mrs.

Mount's School for Young Ladies sent forth a single yellow flower, the first time in living memory. Palms are fairly abundant in south Cornwall, but I never did see one flower before or since.

I had taught French and German at Mrs. Mount's since I was sixteen, after my mother passed away; making the difficult transition from pupil to teacher in midterm of 1869. My competence in these two languages stems from the fact that my father was French and our family had lived in Le Havre till his death, when Mother brought us—my two older sisters and myself—to live in her birthplace, which was the cathedral town of St. Errol in the duchy of Cornwall. Father had been a commercial traveler before settling down to run a hotel in Le Havre, and had gained a great knowledge of languages in the course of his wanderings. From infancy, I was obliged, together with my sisters, to speak English and German, at all mealtimes.

My sisters perished from the scourge of influenza within a few weeks of each other, and Mother went soon after. At sixteen, I was alone in the world. It is fortunate that I possess the capacity to look after myself and stand on my own two feet. I have no complaints about my blessings in that direction, but I would sorely have wished for a better complexion, better looks. My face is freckled and stubbornly *healthy looking* (and this in a time when the cornerstone of female beauty is reckoned to be an interesting pallor), and my nose is turned-up, my mouth too big. But I have large and clear blue eyes, and I tell myself that my auburn hair is my crowning glory. Unhappily, I also have the temper to go with the hair.

The events of the year 1878, insofar as they concerned me and wrought such a great change in my life, truly began with my excursion to the Music Hall with Daisy Marchmain, a fellow teacher at the school and my best friend. Daisy was a merry bundle of berry-black-eyed mischief, who only retained her position at the school because of her undoubted competence as a teacher of mathematics and needlework, for her ways were the despair of Mrs. Mount, our headmistress and employer. Daisy had an elder brother named Ned, who was "down" from Oxford after Hilary term.

"Clarrie, my dear," she said to me. "It's Ned's birthday on Friday, and he's taking us both to the Music Hall. No, I'll not listen to any protests, for 'tis quite respectable for a pair of ladies to go to the Music Hall in company of a gentleman—particularly when he's 'family.' So there. The Music Hall it is, and then an eel-pie supper at that nice chop house in Frobisher Street, by the church, you know."

Mention of St. John's parish church, if nothing else, prompted my instant response to my friend's invitation,

"Daisy, I can't go," I told her. "Richard wouldn't approve of it. Not to the Music Hall."

Daisy folded her hands on her lap and contrived to look pious —a difficult feat for one of her looks and proclivities.

"Richard will not know," she responded, "for ain't he in Truro, attending the choral festival there? Nor is he due back till Tuesday next."

I frowned. "Daisy, you're not suggesting that I don't tell him?"

"That I'm not," she responded blandly. "But he'll not know in advance, so that won't hurt him. And 'twill be a waste of time for him to repine afterward." Daisy, as I had grown to accept, was not excessively fond of Richard.

"We-e-el . . ." I hesitated, and was lost. To tell the truth, I did not entirely share Richard's feelings against all manner of theatrical performances—as, indeed, I did not share his views in many other directions. My intended, a Cornishman born and bred, was as austere in his life as he was in his religion, looking upon such flummeries as the Music Hall as snares and delusions devised by Old Nick to lure the unwary down to hell-fire.

And Tuesday—the day of his return to St. Errol, when I should in all conscience have to tell him of my escapade—was almost a week away . . .

"Thank you both for the invitation, Daisy," I said. "I accept with much pleasure."

And, so saying, changed my whole life.

St. Errol, dominated by the steep-sided, flat-topped hill known as "Old Billy" that lies on the edge of the town, boasts a fine modern cathedral in the Gothic style, built by Mr. Butterfield on the site of the original medieval edifice which was burned down in the civil disturbances during the corn riots of the 1790s. I knew the cathedral and the precinct quite well, for some years previously I had attended the residence of the Dean, Dr. Millhench, to tutor his daughter Felicity in French. Felicity Millhench—delicate as a flower, beautiful as she was spoiled and overindulged—was three years younger than I, and latterly never deigned to acknowledge me in the street: I—a poor spinster teacher.

At one end of the long high street that leads westward to Truro is the cathedral and the lower slopes of "Old Billy," at the other, eastern, end is the market cross, the Sir Bevill Grenvile tavern, most of the shops and emporia, several eating houses of the poorer sort frequented by fishermen and sailors. And the Globe Music Hall. It was to the Globe, on a spring eve of balmy, pink-and-violet-tinted delight that, in company with my friend Daisy and her brother, Ned, I directed my steps.

Ned was in a gay and amusing mood, determined to please us if it killed him. Oxford had not greatly extended the rather shy young boy who had departed thence a year before—save that the eye of faith could discern, on his upper lip, the ghost of an ambitious military-style moustache. He had also taken to the wearing of velvet suiting and long hair, which, as he explained, was the badge of the aesthete. It seemed that the leader of the Oxford aesthetes was a certain Mr. Oscar Wilde, who was at Magdalen College with Ned, and was tipped to win the Newdigate Prize for poetry. That Ned Marchmain could attempt to combine the style military with the style aesthetic was Ned all over.

The velvet suiting and the long hair notwithstanding, Ned was all the military man that evening as we progressed, arm-in-arm, Daisy in the middle, down the high street. He was leading off about the troubles in the Balkans.

"Mark it, ladies," he declared, "we shall be at war with the Russkies before Easter. It's as inevitable as death. By gad, but I wish I could be in at the kill!"

"I'm glad, at least, that father's iron hand, not to mention the persuasive charms of your Mr. Wilde, will happily prevent you from being skewered on the end of a Russian bayonet," responded his sister.

Ned thrust out his lower lip, an expression that I had seen him employ since boyhood. "Don't you be so sure, Daisy my girl," he said. "A man of honor, an Englishman and a gentleman, can't stand by when duty calls. If the need arises, I'll cut Oxford and enlist, see if I don't."

"You'll do no such thing!" declared Daisy.

I could see our birthday outing turning into a Marchmain family squabble, so I sought to pour oil on the troubled waters by calling their attention to the poster outside the Globe, which we had just reached.

"There's the treat we have in store," I said, pointing.

> CHANG HI—*Juggler Extraordinary*
> MISS BETTY SUGDEN—*Chanteuse de Luxe*
> MR. ARTHUR MAGINNIS—*Songs and Patter*
> THE MISSES ERMYNTRUDE & EMILY WITH
> THE PERFORMING GOATS
> *Direct from His Triumphant Tour of*
> *Europe, the One and Only—*
> MR. HARRY "THE TOFF" TAFT *with his*
> *Repertoire of popular ballads.*
> *Etc., Etc., Etc.*

The interior of the Globe dated from the beginning of the century, when it had been a theater proper—presenting the plays of Shakespeare with sundry sensational embellishments such as fireworks, cannon fire, flying ballets—but had fallen on evil times during the Hungry Forties when it had been turned into a cattle and sheep market. Some signs of its fall from thespian grace still remained. The cattle stalls, still with their half-doors, were made to serve as lower tier boxes when the building became a theater again. And I declare that neither the Misses Ermyntrude's and Emily's performing goats, nor the closely packed audience of town- and countryfolk, could have entirely accounted for the distinct odor of the stable that permeated the auditorium. For all that, the Globe was bravely got up with a wealth of gold leaf, red plush, and engraved glass. And the great chandeliers, each with its cluster of hissing gas mantles that touched a finger of brightness on every eager, upturned face, were reflected from the gilded cherubs that lined the balcony wall and made the crowded space so intolerably warm that we were obliged to take off our coats.

The performing goats were the first to be presented, after the orchestra had bowed and scraped its way through an overture. They proved to be charming in manner, but limited as to tricks. Daisy whispered to me how greatly Miss Emily resembled our headmistress and employer, and was seized with a fit of the giggles in consequence. The Chinese juggler was quite diverting, likewise Miss Betty Sugden, *chanteuse de luxe*. Mr. Arthur Maginnis I personally found rather vulgar. The last turn of the evening, the undoubted star of the enterprise, the reason why folk had journeyed from the four corners of the duchy to be present, was Mr. Harry Taft, known to all as "The Toff," pride of the English music hall, whom even I, a sheltered spinster schoolteacher living in remote Cornwall, knew by fame and repute as well as I know our sovereign lady, Queen Victoria.

"Bravo, Toff!" They cheered him from the packed seats up in the roof. "Give us 'By Jingo,' Toff!"

He was tall and thin as a crane, dressed in a tail coat with a carnation at the buttonhole, gleaming top hat, white gloves and cane—the epitome of the aristocratic man-about-town that was his stock in trade. He acknowledged the applause of the audience with a flourish of his cane and a tip of his hat, then, signaling to the conductor of the orchestra to follow him, launched into a popular ballad.

He had a pleasing, strong voice that carried over the limelights and must surely have been heard quite clearly in the back row of the gallery. Furthermore, his repertoire was—unlike that of the egregious Mr. Arthur Maginnis—quite above reproach as to propriety.

At least, till he came to his closing song . . .

I had heard it many times in the last few weeks, ever since the news burst upon the nation that British ironclads had forced the straits of the Dardanelles and anchored off Constantinople in defiance of the invading Russian armies who were advancing to take that famous city of the sultans. Delivery lads whistled it in the streets of St. Errol. Down by the quay, one could hear the fishwives singing it as they gutted the day's catch. Sometimes it seemed that that lilting tune, those braggardly words, were part of the very air that one breathed in that spring of 1878.

Mr. Harry Taft waved hat and cane as he sang it, strutted like a soldier from one end of the stage to the other and back and called upon his audience to join him in the choruses—which they did, full-throated. I stole a glance at Ned, and saw a patriotic tear course down his smooth cheek, so affected was he by the sentiments contained in the words that he bawled with the rest:

> "We don't want to fight,
> But by jingo if we do,
> We've got the men,
> We've got the ships,
> We've got the money too . . ."

Daisy was sitting the other side of her brother. She made a moue at me and rolled her eyes as Ned threw back his head and delivered the defiant declaration that closed the chorus:

> "The Russians shall not have Constantinople!"

Nor was that the end of it. Out onto the stage came a bevy of befeathered and beribboned ladies of the chorus, all bearing quiversful of small Union Jacks, which they then proceeded to throw, like darts, into the audience, where they were snatched at and flourished with abandonment. From his advantageous seat in the fourth row, Ned was one of the first to win a flag, and was caught up in the waving and the shouting, the ferment of popular patriotic fire-eating. And the song began again:

> "We don't want to fight,
> But by jingo if we do . . ."

Well for the good folk of St. Errol and the fair duchy of Cornwall to brag, safe in their dreamy backwater, where the scent of summer flowers already lay upon the springtime air. Well for silly Ned Marchmain to wave his red-white-and-blue. Back to Oxford he would go for Trinity term, and the terrible confrontation in far-off Constantinople between the Russian armies ashore and the gray-walled ironclads at the anchorage would be resolved, one way or the other, long before Ned Marchmain could take the Queen's shilling and the coat of scarlet, and be trained for a soldier.

"The Russians shall not have Constantinople!"

The Globe Music Hall echoed and re-echoed to the final flourish, and the very chandeliers jounced and tinkled in time to the stamping of many feet and the clap of many hands. Suddenly I wished that I had not allowed myself to be persuaded to come to the Music Hall after all, for I had no sympathy with the wild and unreasoning emotion about me and could only think of the coming reproach in the eyes of my half-intended when he came to hear of Ned Marchmain's birthday outing and my part in it.

Richard returned from the choral festival at Truro on the following Tuesday. I knew this because Mrs. Bowers, who was the daily cleaner at the school, told me that she saw him riding in the high street on his bicycle on that day. I was puzzled, and somewhat hurt, when he did not come to see me immediately upon his return, or soon after. In the event, it was not till the Thursday evening following that Lizzie, the maid-of-all-work, tapped on the door of the staff room, where I was correcting essays, to inform me that the Reverend Neale was attending me in the front parlor. I went to him at once—or as soon as I had smoothed back my hair and dabbed a little rice powder on my unfashionably wholesome cheeks.

The front parlor had a glazed roof and walls and was more like a conservatory, with a tiled floor and large pots of palms and pampas grass. My heart gave a treacherous lurch, to see the well-made figure in clerical black and twice-around collar seated on one of the wrought-iron chairs with a Testament upon his knee, his smooth, blond head bowed over the open page. He looked up and rose to his feet at my approach, pocketing the volume.

"My dear Clarissa," he murmured in his sonorous baritone, "I trust you are well."

"I am very well, thank you, Richard," I replied, trying hard to keep the tremor from my voice. "And you?"

"As you see me," he replied. And implanted a chaste kiss upon my proffered right cheek.

I saw him plainly: as handsome as a Greek god—a nose as straight as Hermes' and eyes as blue and clear as the waters of the Aegean that lap the Attic shore; mouth chiseled by the hand of Praxiteles, and hair of purest gold that lay in clustered curls across his brow and gathered in profusion behind his perfectly shaped ears which lay so closely to his sculptured head. In her more teasing moments, Daisy Marchmain insisted that Richard's hair owed something to the ministrations of the curling tongs, a declaration I had always stoutly denied; though it has to be said that I had no evidence one way or the other and had never dared to broach the subject with my intended.

"You are looking—very well," I faltered feebly. "Was the choral festival the success you had hoped?"

He smiled. "In modesty, I have to say yes, Clarissa."

"You won one of the prizes? Oh, Richard, I am so pleased for you."

His smile broadened, to reveal his perfect, white teeth.

"Better. I won no fewer than three prizes," he said. "But I will tell you more of that later. There is another matter I must speak to you about also, Clarissa. What would you say to a walk as far as the quay? The weather is quite clement, and I will bring you back in time for supper and prayers."

"That will be lovely," I said. "Give me just two minutes to fetch my bonnet and shawl."

"And your parasol," he advised. "The low-cast sun is ruinous to a lady's complexion."

"Yes," I replied meekly. Oh, my Richard! Do you not see that my complexion is already ruined? With my sudden joy over-clouded, I went to get my belongings.

The act of tying the ribbon of my bonnet meant that I must gaze upon my imperfections in the looking glass once more, and also meet my guilty eyes. Soon, perhaps within minutes, and at least before Richard walked me back to the school, I must confess about the visit to the Music Hall; must see the distaste and disapproval in those splendid blue eyes. Would it—should it—be sooner or later? On all counts, I decided that I would postpone the evil moment for as long as possible by allowing Richard to do all the talking.

"I am ready, Richard," I told him, re-entering the front parlor.

"Then let us go, my dear Clarissa," he replied, extending his arm for me to take.

"A handsome couple—they make a handsome couple." That was the phrase which, with more hope than conviction, I always repeated to myself, like a talisman, when we were out together, imagining in my wild optimism that passers-by applied the declaration to the pair of us. I never had doubt that plenty of eyes fell upon Richard in appraisal, and always gave my reflection an anxious glance in every shop window we passed, to make sure that, complexion or no, I was not disgracing him by having a turned-down hem, an ill-tied bonnet ribbon, or by wearing a sullen and uncomely expression.

We walked down the high street toward the line of gray-blue water and the forest of masts and rigging at the end of the town. Richard talked, and I listened. He told me about the music festival. It had been well-attended. Dr. Millhench, the dean of St. Errol Cathedral had been there. And his daughter, Felicity.

"An admirable young lady," declared my intended, "possessing an excellent soprano voice and a virtuous disposition to match. She spoke very warmly of you, Clarissa."

"How kind," I murmured. Then why did she always look through me, I thought?

"Very warmly indeed," he said. "Told me that she owes her command of the French language entirely to your excellent teaching."

"She is too generous," I said, remembering that, for all my teaching—excellent or otherwise—Felicity had never been able to commit even the rudiments of French grammar and syntax into her silly, empty head.

"Yes, she has a generous heart," he said. "For instance, we were entirely thrown out of countenance and very nearly had to withdraw from the quartette competition when our soprano Mrs. Eveleigh was taken on a quinsy, but Miss Felicity stepped into the breach at less than an hour's notice and sang the soprano part."

"With success, I hope?" I ventured.

"With resounding success," said he.

"Well, that was a blessing," I said. "What luck."

"Rather more than luck," said Richard. And he smiled the tight little smile that I always intercepted when he regarded his own reflection in shop windows. "Rather more—how to put it?—a team effort. She and me."

"How nice," I heard myself say faintly.

"With less than an hour to spare before the competition," said Richard, "we were able to secure, through the influence of Dr. Millhench, the loan of a pianoforte. Which done, I was able to coach Miss Felicity in the soprano part of the quartette, myself accompanying her upon the pianoforte."

I thought of the long and wasted hours I had spent trying to drill French irregular verbs into Felicity Millhench's unaccommodating brain. "And you accomplished it in less than an hour, Richard?" I asked him in astonishment.

"I do not say that I am anything out of the ordinary as a teacher," he admitted. "Nor Miss Felicity a notably outstanding pupil. All I will say is that there sprang up between the two of us, master and pupil, an immediate—ah—*rapport*."

"Oh—a *rapport?*"

"A *rapport*." He nodded sagely. "By the way, the sun is shining full upon your right profile, my dear Clarissa. I beg you to incline your parasol slightly so as to shade yourself."

I obeyed without comment. By then we had reached the edge of St. Errol quay. Through the harbor entrance, under the small stone lighthouse on the end, and watched by a group of barefoot urchins who were fishing with rods and lines, a herring boat glided in on the flood tide, its kipper-brown sails flapping lazily in the evening breeze. The womenfolk in their sacking aprons were waiting, bare-armed, to clean and gut the catch as soon as it was landed, for the fisherfolk of south Cornwall work all hours and in all weathers—men, women, and children all.

Richard wrinkled his nose with distaste as the reek of the empty fish baskets that the women carried was brought to us along the quay, and I was reminded that it was he who had prevailed upon the aged and weak-willed vicar of St. John's to discontinue the custom by which the fisherfolk were encouraged to attend the Harvest Festival Service, together with such of their gear—nets, baskets, lobster pots, and the like—as could conveniently be displayed in the church. Richard's argument had been that the stink of rotten fish offended the carriage folk who rented the best pews.

His arm guided me away from the scene of the approaching herring boat and the waiting women. "Let us go and sit at the far end of the quay," he said. "And I will tell you my news. I may say, my most promising and encouraging news."

There was a stone block abutting from the wall at the end of the quay, which had served as a seat since time immemorial. And it was there that my intended and I took our places, side by side, and he removed his tall hat and laid it on the rough-hewn granite flagstones by his feet. The onshore breeze gently ruffled the still golden curls that framed his nobly shaped brow, and I thought how I would do anything—anything—to keep him for myself; would be as attentive to my person, to my hair, my linen, my fingernails, shoes, the hem of my skirts, as I knew he would wish me to be. And yet, at the same time, I despised myself for the thought: that I could contemplate marriage with a man who could impose such a tyranny upon me. But what can a woman do when she is twenty-five and without a fortune? And he so beautiful to look at and—most of the time—so gentle and attentive.

"Touching upon the events of the Truro choral festival," said Richard, "the outcome serves to illuminate the truth of such sayings as 'mighty things from small beginnings grow.'" He looked at me quizzically.

"I—I'm afraid I don't follow you, Richard," I said.

"I will enlighten you, Clarissa," he said. "My small efforts in coaching Miss Millhench, together with my personal success in carrying off three prizes in the solo competitions, did not pass unnoticed by the Dean. It is common knowledge that, so far as singing is concerned, the lesser clergy of the Cathedral simply do not pull their weight. No fault of theirs. The canons are all men in their sixties and seventies, hanging on to sinecures. The deacons are beneath contempt, mere place servers. It is the Dean's wish to raise the Cathedral to the eminence it knew in the last century, as one of the great centers of choral music."

I looked at him, this godlike but oddly flawed man who, for

reasons unknown, had condescended to enter into an "understanding" with a homely schoolma'am without fortune or beauty.

"Richard!" I breathed. "You don't mean . . ."

"The Dean's eyes have lit upon me," he said simply. "To carry out his wish."

"A place in the Cathedral?"

"Bishop's chaplain," he said. "A humble role, another sinecure. But a place at the center of power. Beyond that, in swift order, I see a continuous rise in eminence. Deacon. Archdeacon. Somewhere, not far hence, a deanery awaits me. And somewhere beyond that—a bishop's palace."

I hung breathless upon his words, marveling at the wonder of it.

"And so you have gained the place at the Cathedral?" I cried.

"Almost," he said. "Yesterday, I spent the whole day at the deanery and was brought to luncheon with the bishop, who sized me up and did not seem to find me wanting. Mark you, Clarissa, it is not yet signed, sealed, and delivered. The bishop is a man of stern and unbending principles. And so is his wife. If I know my man, he will at this moment be taking a straw vote around the diocese to ensure that the chaplain-elect is beyond reproach in all respects. And that brings me, my dear Clarissa, to our own personal relationship."

"Yes?" I whispered. "What of that, Richard?"

The wonderful, Aegean-blue eyes avoided mine. "Taking all things into consideration, Clarissa, and in view of the fact that we are not officially affianced, I did not think it—er—prudent to make too much of our relationship in my conversations with the dean and the bishop. Other than to mention that we were friends."

"Did you not?" I said. And, closing my eyes, "Please go on."

"You must be reasonable, my dear Clarissa," he said sharply. "If the appointment of bishop's chaplain is indeed confirmed, there will be nothing in it for the pair of us. For me there will be a Spartan accommodation at the Palace. Bachelor accomodation, I would add. For you, my dear—nothing. Marriage, for us, will continue to be out of the question for some time hence."

"I see," I whispered. And thought I saw very clearly.

"Clarissa, Clarissa," he murmured. And he treated me to a brilliant smile, for which I would have walked for him on my hands and knees from Land's End to John o'Groats. "Don't take on so. You have yet to hear the best of it."

"And what's that?" I asked, without much enthusiasm.

"Why, we have *both* been invited to the Bishop's Palace, to dinner on Monday next," he said.

I actually sensed my jaw dropping open, and could not have prevented it for the world. I gazed at my intended, unable to speak.

"Do you not hear me, Clarissa?" he said. "You have been invited to accompany me to the Palace."

"I—I couldn't possibly!" I breathed. "Not dine—at the Palace." As lief dine with Her Majesty at Buckingham Palace as at the seat of the Lord Bishop of St. Errol.

His brow furrowed with small annoyance at me. "Tsk! How absurd, my dear," he chided. "Why not?"

"Why not?" I cried. "Because I have nothing to wear for a start, and that's good enough reason for *any* woman."

"You have your Sunday best," he retorted. "No one will expect any other than that from you." He smiled at me kindly. "You are a poor schoolteacher with no fortune of your own. To attempt to create the impression that you are anything other would be vainglorious and prideful."

"I confess to the sin of pride," I retorted tartly. "But I have no wish to sit at the bishop's table looking like a woman who's come up from the country to sell eggs. A fine figure I should cut beside Felicity Millhench, who'll be there in a dinner gown of silks and laces straight from Paris I shouldn't wonder."

"That is possible, indeed probable," he conceded. "But, then, Miss Felicity is a young lady of fortune, a deceased relation having left her half a million, as I have been informed. Your positions are not to be compared."

"Are they not?" I breathed, and felt my eyes prickle with tears.

Richard did not notice my distress. By his looks, he appeared to have satisfied himself that he had overcome my arguments. He took my hand and smiled his blue-eyed, frank and open smile. I was lost on the instant.

"Come now, Clarrie," he said. He seldom used my pet name;

indeed, he had several times spoken of it as lacking in dignity. "We'll have no more of this. You *shall* come to the Palace as my loving friend, and I shall be proud of you. My dear, you simply cannot let me down, nor throw back in her face the good intention of she who proposed to the bishop that you should accompany me."

Once again, I was surprised!

"And who was this lady who proposed me?" I asked.

"Why Miss Felicity," he replied. "Who else?"

"Oh!" I exclaimed. And, again, "Oh!"

The reek of fish was creeping in waves along the quay, as the baskets were filled by the efforts of the women's deft fingers. Richard got to his feet and replaced his tall hat.

"I think it is time that I walked you back to the school, my dear," he said.

I rose and followed him, my mind a battlefield of disturbing thoughts. As we drew abreast of the fishwives, some of them bobbed and smiled, and some of them murmured asides to each other, eyeing Richard's tall frame admiringly. He treated them to no more than a brief tipping of his hat—and this without removing the handkerchief that he held to his nose. By the time we left the quay, I had resolved some things in my mind. Firstly, I would indeed accompany my intended—my handsome and fastidious Richard—to the bishop's table, and not merely to assist my intended's career in any small way I could. I could scarcely credit that Felicity had put my name forward as a dinner guest for reasons of her high regard for me. She had been a surly and difficult pupil and a distant and haughty ex-pupil. I had the notion—and it was no more than a nagging imp at the corner of my imagination—that the dean's rich and beautiful daughter had some special reason for wishing me at the bishop's dinner table in company with the handsome Richard Neale. And, much as I viewed the prospect with unease, nothing on earth would have kept me away.

And the second thing I had decided was this: I was *not* going to wear my old Sunday best, my dowdy maroon velvet with the bedraggled lace at cuffs and throat that had been unfashionable when I had inherited it from my deceased eldest sister.

Thirdly, in view of the delicate position Richard was in concerning his appointment as chaplain to the stern and unbending Lord Bishop of St. Errol, I determined to say nothing, after all, about the visit to the Music Hall.

Daisy Marchmain cheerfully supported my decision about the Music Hall.

"Richard will not thank you for your frankness," she declared, "and the poor fellow will be in a tizz for ever after in case the bishop finds out. Though why your comings and goings should concern *him* is beyond all belief. You want to borrow a gown, then? Well, I don't see why not. We're both of a size, and a few temporary stitches will soon make up the difference."

"You're very kind, Daisy," I said. "I wouldn't ask, but I simply couldn't face Felicity Millhench's expression if she set eyes on my maroon velvet."

"It's a pleasure to deprive that stuck-up minx of an opportunity to sneer," said Daisy. "So you've a suspicion that she's set her cap on your Richard?"

"I don't know," I admitted, "but he is certainly very smitten with her. He gave her a singing lesson in Truro and speaks of a *rapport* that sprang up between them."

"I like it less and less," said Daisy. "There is something indefinably sinister about mixed singing lessons. I was going to offer you my blue taffeta, which is pretty and modest, but in view of what you have just told me, I am now inclined to suggest the ivory-white satin with the suggestion of a *décolletage*."

She riffled through the rack of garments hanging in her wardrobe. Daisy, whose people were well-off and indulgent, only worked as a schoolteacher because she had a lively mind and was bored by what passed for high society life in mid-Cornwall. She had clothes galore, most of which remained unworn.

"*Eh, voila!*" she exclaimed, holding up a shimmering creation of satin, stiff and creamy-white, and sewn all over with tiny pearls. "This will knock the precious *rapport* into a cocked hat, or M. Worth of Paris grossly defrauded my poor papa. Yes, this is worth a singing lesson or two. Put it on, Clarrie."

"It's beautiful," I cried. "Quite beautiful."

It fitted me excellently well, though Daisy, shaking her head and clucking her tongue, insisted in pinning a couple of small tucks in the waist.

"Your figure is my despair," she said. "Sometimes, when I look at you, I am almost half inclined to forego cream cakes and sweet chocolate."

"How can you say that, Daisy?" I protested. "And to a perfectly ordinary person like me, with a turned-up nose, mouth too big, figure nothing to write home about, and . . ."

Turning, I saw a total stranger: a regal-looking woman in shimmering white satin, regarding me with slight, frowning disapproval from the shadowed far end of Daisy's bedroom. Some trick of light and shade for a few moments puzzled my eyes, and it was with a shock that I saw the vision to be only myself reflected from a pier glass.

All unbidden, there came to my mind that well-known fragment from Robert Burns—the expressed desire to see ourselves as others see us—and I wondered if that gift, that vision, had momentarily been granted to me.

A moment's examination, and I dismissed the idea as ridiculous.

The Bishop's Palace, which lies within the ancient cathedral precinct and a stone's throw from Mr. Butterfield's great edifice, is part of the original, medieval foundation and had once been the most resplendent ecclesiastical residence in the West Country, famed for munificent hospitality. The great hall, which was scarcely less impressive in size and richness of decoration than the nave of the cathedral, and into which, on the night of the dinner party, Richard and I were ushered and announced by the bishop's butler and majordomo, was lit by candelabra and chandeliers, whose massed pinpoints of bright flame shone out dramatically against the mysterious gloom that rose almost beyond the range of vision to the dark, hammer-beamed roof high above, where gilded angels spread their wings, and naked putti bore shields emblazoned with the armorial devices of past bishops of St. Errol. The effect was dramatic in the extreme, but it has to be said that the burning of so many candles filled the air with the sickly smell of wax, though this had the advantage of masking the heavy odor of mold and mildew that hung in every corner of the vast chamber.

"This way, please." The butler gestured for us to follow him down the great hall, past a long refectory table set with silver and napery, to where, beyond a tall screen of pierced and fretted stonework, another, smaller, chamber could be discerned. In it, several people were already gathered.

Our footsteps rang loudly upon ancient flagstones worn hollow in some places by the tread of past generations. Halfway down the hall, was a fireplace large enough to roast the carcass of a whole ox, where the trunk of a mighty oak burned sullenly with touches of blue lights, showing that, April or no, there was still frost about. Despite the huge fire, despite the massed candles, it was penetratingly cold in the great hall of the Bishop's Palace, and I was glad to have brought with me my mother's Paisley shawl, to wear across my nearly bare shoulders.

"The Reverend Mr. Neale and Miss Clarissa Herbert," intoned the butler at the entrance to the antechamber where the others were assembled. I was aware of half a dozen pairs of regarding eyes turned upon us. They were seated about an elegant Dutch-tiled stove in the center of the circular chamber. One of them rose. I recognized the tubby figure of the bishop of St. Errol; round and plump as a butterball in his black frock and knee breeches, with domed head rising from a frill of white hair that stuck out all around and was curled under at the ends like a Florentine page boy's. His eyes, behind thick-lensed spectacles, were mild and amiable. Shy, even.

"Ah, Neale!" said the prelate. "And Miss Herbert, eh? Delighted to make your acquaintance, ma'am. But have we not met before, eh?"

I timidly offered him my hand. "No, my lord, but I was at Mrs. Mount's School when last you presented the annual prizes for work and conduct."

"Ah, yes. Thought I had seen you before. Excellent establishment, Mrs. Mount's. So you teach there, hey?"

"French and German, my lord," I replied.

"Very commendable," he pronounced. He gestured to the others assembled. "May I introduce you to my lady wife, the

Dean and Mrs. Millhench, Archdeacon the Honorable David de Tracey. And Miss Millhench, whom I think you know."

"How do you do."

"How do you do . . ."

I bobbed a brief curtsy to the bishop's and the dean's wife, both ladies of formidable mold, who could have passed for sisters, and whom I knew, by reputation, to be the sort who expect such small marks of homage from lesser womenfolk. Felicity Millhench did *not* receive any curtsy from me, but I shook hands with her, and enjoyed a most unworthy *frisson* of triumph to see the nakedly jealous glance that she threw at my beautiful, borrowed gown.

"Sit with me, my dear, and tell me about yourself." The suggestion—it was more like a military command—was addressed to me by the bishop's wife Mrs. D'Arcy, whose massively corseted bulk was encased in a dinner gown of black bombazine embellished with jet ornaments, and whose shock of hennaed hair was surmounted by a black osprey plume. She smelled strongly of peppermint and patchouli.

I obeyed, which put me between our hostess and Mrs. Millhench, who, despite the fact that I had in the past tutored her daughter, knew me hardly at all. The dean's lady, in dramatic contrast to Mrs. D'Arcy, wore bright pink: a girlish pink that sat ill upon her. She, too, wore a plume: a spray of bird-of-paradise feathers that gave her the appearance of a very stout cockatoo. She treated me to a long examination through her lorgnette. The interrogation began:

"Are your parents alive, my child?" demanded Mrs. D'Arcy.

"No, ma'am. They have both passed away."

"That is a pity. A young gel needs the support of her parents. Do you have siblings, or other relations?"

"My sisters are also deceased, ma'am. But I have distant cousins in the duchy."

"You are greatly to be pitied, child. What was your father's occupation?"

"He was a commercial traveler for many years, and after that . . ."

"A *commercial* traveler?" interposed Mrs. Millhench, bringing her lorgnette into play. "In what *commerce* did your father travel?"

"In—corsets, ma'am," I replied.

"In *corsets?*"

"For both ladies and gentlemen, ma'am," I offered, by way of mitigation.

They both stared at me. The conversation about us had ceased. By this time, I was the object of everyone's attention.

"Indeed?" commented the bishop's wife in a faint voice.

"And after that," I said, "he kept a hotel in Le Havre till his death."

A silence followed, and then:

"We have stayed in Le Havre," said Mrs. Millhench. "Do you not recall, Dean? At the Hotel Royale et Diplomatique. It was very smart." She looked at me encouragingly and with a touch of hope.

"That was not our place," I admitted. "Father kept a small establishment on the waterfront called the Pension Petit Bel-Air. It was not very smart or very grand. But it was clean and respectable."

"Indeed?" said Mrs. D'Arcy again.

I tried to sink lower in my chair, glimpsing as I did so Felicity Millhench's malicious glitter and Richard's expression of agony. How embarrassing for him, and he with all his high ambitions, to be revealed as a man whose lady friend's father had been a traveler in corsets and the owner of a small hotel on the Le Havre waterfront. And before such exalted company!

"Pray correct me if I am mistaken, Dean. But is not *your* family background of the military persuasion?" A drawlingly affected voice drew the attention from me. The speaker was the archdeacon, a man of about Richard's age, with a profile like a well-bred horse and a smooth mane of butter-yellow hair. A monocle glittered in his right eye, held there as if part of his anatomy, with no visible means of attachment.

"Not military, Archdeacon, but naval." Dean Millhench's voice boomed like the bass bell up in Mr. Butterfield's high tower.

"Is that so? I had thought it was military," drawled the young archdeacon. He took a silk handkerchief from his breast pocket and dabbed the tip of his long, aristocratic nose.

"Naval. Very decidedly," boomed the dean.

"I always allude to the dean as 'The Captain,'" interposed Mrs. Millhench. "Of a ship, you know."

At this the dean, tall and thin as a crane, even when seated, cracked his massive, knobbly fingers and grinned wolfishly.

"The comparison is very apt," he declared. "If one likens the cathedral to a flagship and the diocese to a fleet, my lord archbishop, here, is the admiral of the fleet and I am captain of the flagship." He treated the prelate to his vulpine grin. "I trust you will not chide me for my presumption, my lord, but, like every ship's captain, I regard the cathedral in every way as *my* cathedral."

"Ah, quite so, Dean. Quite so," responded the bishop, who did not look as if he ever had, or ever would, summon up the courage even to chide the forbidding Dean Millhench for selling Mrs. D'Arcy to Barbary pirates.

"Which brings me to the question of next Tuesday's Chapter meeting. While your lordship and the archdeacon are both present . . ."

The talk drifted to cathedral matters, with the dean firmly at the helm, and the womenfolk keeping a respectful silence. I was grateful for my respite, for which I had to thank the Hon. Mr. de Tracey. Not that it could have been his deliberate intention to save me from further interrogation, for I was nothing to him and he had not spared me a glance.

I sat and watched them, those men of the church. The dean: loud and forceful, master of the company; even master of the lordly bishop himself, who scarcely said a word, and that word was always "yes." But I did notice that even Dr. Millhench deferred to the Hon. Mr. de Tracey when that languid aristocrat occasionally interposed a remark. And I remembered being told that the archdeacon was heir to a viscountcy and a considerable fortune. My own intended treated him with a certain wistful respect. Poor Richard! How he would have wished to have been born rich, titled, and privileged, instead of poor and ambitious—for what a canker is ambition without means. And how the presence of the Hon. Mr. de Tracey—still only in his mid-twenties and already an archdeacon—must be casting a shadow over his own modest prospect of becoming the bishop's chaplain.

I let my gaze wander around the circle of the company, till it fell upon Felicity Millhench. She was looking at Richard in a sidelong, regarding manner, from under her unbelievably long eyelashes, and I thought I recognized the look of a female predator contemplating her prey. She must have sensed my eyes upon her, for she turned to meet my gaze, colored up most becomingly, and swiftly looked away.

I felt a sharp pang of unease. With barely a few minutes of the evening gone, poor Richard had been embarrassed and humiliated by the company's snobbish reactions to my humble background, and it augured badly for the rest of the evening. Without raising her elegant little finger or uttering a word, Felicity had been able to mark up a minor but palpable hit against me. What might be in store for me when she herself started to probe at my defenses? Suddenly, I felt the vulnerable nakedness of being poor, undistinguished, not very pretty, and wearing borrowed clothes. And next time I could not rely upon the languid archdeacon to switch attention from me.

It was then that the butler sidled into the antechamber with the announcement that dinner was served.

"Will you take my arm, Mrs. Millhench, ma'am," said the bishop, "and we will lead the way to table."

Two by two, with Richard and me bringing up the rear, we filed into the great hall, where silent servitors stood in ranks, two behind each tall-backed chair.

The aroma of rich meats now quite overpowered the reek of candle wax and the musty stench of decaying fabric. Despite my unease, I felt my appetite stir. I glanced up at Richard's face. He smiled down at me.

"I am sorry for what happened, Clarrie," he murmured. "But you bore yourself with some credit. Mark you, I do not think it was *absolutely* necessary for you to have been *quite* so forthcoming with your answers."

I looked at him in surprise. "Richard, you don't mean that I should have lied about my father's occupations?" I asked.

"Oh, no, no," he said. "I mean nothing of the sort. But, my dear, there is such a thing as tact. There is such a thing as the diplomatic answer. You need not, there is no call in some circumstances, to blurt out the *whole* truth from the very housetops."

"Oh, I see," I replied, remembering the matter of my visit to the Music Hall, and taking some comfort from his philosophy. "Do you like the gown I'm wearing, Richard?"

"Nothing wrong with it at all," he replied. "You see? I told you that your Sunday best would be quite adequate for the occasion. What would be the object of trying to compete with Miss Felicity on her own ground?"

I think I could have hit my intended then, for, as I have already admitted, I have the temper that goes with the red hair.

The sheer whiteness of the linen tablecloth was almost totally obscured by dishes, plates, *épergnes*, silverware of all kinds from candelabra to such conceits as a life-sized representation of a swan, between whose arched wings reposed a nest of fresh fruits.

"What will modom desire for her first course?" A liveried servitor loomed over me, bowing low. His breath smelled of beer. "There is spring soup, or there is *soles à la crème*. There is fried smelts, or there is fillets of mackerel."

"I—I think I would like the soup," I murmured.

"As modom pleases." He dipped a ladle into the great silver tureen.

"Wine, modom?" Another servitor hovered at my elbow, in his hand a tall, napkin-wrapped bottle.

"No thank you." I had no wish to befuddle my wits at the bishop's table, not with Felicity Millhench as an opponent. I picked up my soup spoon, glancing sidelong as I did so. At the far end of the table, across from me and seated on Mrs. D'Arcy's right, Felicity was watching me, her slanting, catlike eyes veiled by her long lashes.

We were eight at table, with the bishop at one end and his lady at the other. Our hosts were flanked by their most senior guests, leaving Richard and me facing each other in the middle. I had the dean on my left and Mrs. Millhench on my right, and felt like a castle under siege.

By the end of the soup and fish, the talk was all of the threatened war with Russia, with the dean, as usual, making all the running. As dictator of the table, he had the unswerving support of his wife, and also of Mrs. D'Arcy, who constantly roused her husband to do likewise, which the bishop had no hesitation in doing. Dr. Millhench, one gathered, was of the pro-Russian faction who wanted Britain to have no part in preventing the Tsar's armies from overthrowing the ramshackled regime of Sultan Abdul Hamid and occupying Constantinople. The archdeacon appeared to have no opinions one way or the other, but addressed himself to his fish and wine. My poor Richard's views were not sought.

The soup and fish having been cleared, entrées were brought to the table. There was curried lobster, lamb cutlets, oyster patties, and a whole ham garnished with broccoli. I partook modestly of the lamb cutlets. The serving of the entrées, the fussing of the servitors, and the diners' attention upon their own needs, caused conversation to tail away.

And then, clear and high above the rattle of cutlery, Felicity Millhench's penetrating little voice,

"Miss Herbert, I do declare that I have not complimented you upon your gown, which is very fine."

I took a breath. "Thank you, Miss Millhench," I replied evenly. "And may I return the compliment?" She was wearing a creation of dull gold embellished with lace. It was exceedingly pretty, but it did not have the style of my borrowed plumes.

"This is only an old thing," she replied, flicking the material dismissively. "While yours, I perceive, is from Paris. Worth, is it not?"

"Yes," I admitted. "But it's not . . ."

"Not—*what*, Miss Herbert?"

From the corner of my eyes, I saw the dean's wife pause in the act of lifting a forkful of curried lobster to her lips, while across the table Richard was staring at me—and the gown—with incredulity. And I remembered his words about not blurting the truth, the whole truth, from the housetops.

"It's not new," I said feebly.

I hoped that the matter would rest there, but it was not to be. Felicity returned to the attack.

"New or old, how lucky you are to be able to flit over to Paris for your shopping," she said. "The pension in Le Havre must have been more profitable than your description suggests. I think you must be a very modest person at heart, Miss Herbert."

"You are quite mistaken," I declared. "The fact is, I . . ."

Mrs. Millhench's sonorous contralto drowned me. "My dear Felicity," she said, "you are well able to go to Paris at any time you choose, since you are a young lady of fortune"—she threw me a puzzled glance through her raised lorgnette—"as Miss Herbert also appears to be."

"Mrs. Millhench, I'm afraid that you are . . ." My words were quenched by the booming bass bell of the dean, who was beaming at me with something approaching approval, showing his great fangs.

"Ah, I find it most commendable, most encouraging, a salutary lesson to all of us—and I do not except you, Felicity my dear, for you are very remiss in this particular—when one hears of a young lady of fortune who, while having no need to work for her living, nevertheless devotes herself to raising the cloud of ignorance from young minds in the noble calling of teacher."

"Very commendable, indeed," commented the bishop. "You put it very well, Dean." His weak and watery eyes peered at me appraisingly over the top of his spectacles.

"My lord. Dr. Millhench . . ." I tried again to speak out and dispel the tissue of falsehood that was being woven about me, but Felicity had not finished with her sport. She interrupted me,

"You are quite right, Papa," she said. "Miss Herbert is a treasure. A saint in human guise. How well I remember her kindness and patience when she was my tutoress in French. And all the time I thought she was doing it only for pecuniary gain, instead of which she was lavishing all that care and attention, all that skill and devotion, in the interests of learning. As you said, Papa —in raising the cloud of ignorance from my mind."

"It behooves the privileged to serve others," intoned the bishop.

"All those hours of devoted teaching," cried Felicity. "And I have to admit that I was a most unrewarding scholar. Yet Miss Herbert persisted with me, in patience uncomplaining, while all the time she could have lived in cosseted idleness."

"Please . . ." I begged.

Then came the drawling voice of the aristocratic archdeacon, "I rather fancy Miss Herbert is trying to say something."

Silence.

I met poor Richard's eye across the table. There was a private agony there, and an entreaty.

I took a deep breath and said, "Miss Millhench is quite mistaken. I have no fortune. I work for my living at one of the few occupations open to a woman who, though poor, has been decently reared by loving parents."

The dean's wife, lorgnette still trained upon me, made a fussy gesture toward the gown, the Worth gown which had provided that minx Felicity with the means to weave her malicious fantasy.

"But—but? . . ." She scarcely knew how to put it.

"Borrowed, ma'am," I told her.

Poor Richard's eyes closed in agony.

Silence. And then,

"Reverting to the question of the Balkan problem," drawled the Hon. David de Tracey, "are you then of the opinion, Dean, that the Royal Navy should withdraw from Turkish waters?"

The misfortunes of Clarrie Herbert were blessedly forgotten for the while. The table was listening to the dean delivering his views on the Balkan question, while Clarrie herself ate humble pie and kept her peace, grateful to be released from causing Richard any further embarrassment. Felicity Millhench threw me the occasional, tight-lipped, slanting-eyed, feline glance of triumph. Two palpable hits to me, was her message. And dinner scarcely halfway through.

Entrées over, we were at the second course, which comprised a choice—or some of each—of forequarter of lamb, larded guinea fowls, boiled chickens and asparagus peas, and some conceit or other with neck of veal and vegetables. I have a very clear recollection of the fare at that nightmare dinner, for the reason that I kept my menu and place card till very recently, when they were lost while moving house. The fine viands and rich wines, translated into a like value of bread and cheese and small beer, the bishop's table that night could have fed the entire poor population of his sprawling diocese.

"I put it to you, my friends," boomed the dean, "that the issue, for a churchman, is simply that of Christian against pagan. And when one recalls the atrocities committed by Turks against

Christian Bulgarians in seventy-six, there can be no doubt as to where one's conscience dictates one. Christian Russia must not be dissuaded from her Crusading course by fainthearts."

The archdeacon shook his head. "One must remember, Dean," he said, "that the Tsar's troops, in their advance through the Balkan passes and the Thracian plain, showed equal cruelty to people of the Mohammedan faith." He dabbed the tip of his nose with his silk handkerchief. "As Her Majesty remarked to my father and the Prime Minister t'other month—I wish I had brought Papa's letter with me so that I might have read it to you: 'It is not for Christianity, for the Russians are quite as cruel as the Turks, but for conquest, that this cruel, wicked war was waged.'"

"Did she now?" exclaimed the dean, with the wind quite spilled from his sails. "Did the Queen say that, then, Archdeacon? And to your father?"

"That she did, sir," responded the archdeacon blandly. He took from his eye his monocle and polished it carefully with his white silk handkerchief, never once shifting his gaze from the dean's face. "And now, by the humiliating Treaty of San Stefano, which the Tsar has forced upon the sultan almost literally at bayonet point, the Turkish Empire in Europe is virtually dismembered, and the Balkans lie open to Russian domination. And for that reason, Dean, I believe that the British fleet should remain off Constantinople, for, while our brave fellows are there, the Tsar will stay his hand."

In the silence that followed this pronouncement, the slightest sound—the rattle of a spoon, the squeak of a servitor's shoe—would have been an intolerable intrusion. In short and simple terms, the effete young aristocrat-cleric had stated what sounded to me like a cast-iron case for our fleet to remain in Turkish waters.

The bishop appeared to share my view. After a respectful interval, he tapped lightly on the table top with his pink, plump hand.

"Hear, hear!" mumbled the prelate. "You are quite right, Archdeacon. I never heard it more plainly stated: the justification of a show of force as a deterrent against the greater evil of a general war. Well said, sir. Well said."

The dean's countenance was a picture of baffled fury. Two

bright pinpoints of color appeared on the pallid skin drawn tautly over his prominent cheekbones, and he showed his grave-yard teeth in something like a snarl. The Very Rev. Dr. Mill-hench, Dean of St. Errol, obviously did not take kindly to those who disagreed with his views, and the archdeacon—aristocrat or no aristocrat, be his noble father a confidant of the queen or not—was clearly no exception.

"There may be much truth in what Mr. de Tracey says," commented Mrs. Millhench. "Do you not think so, my dear Mrs. D'Arcy?"

Mrs. D'Arcy gazed fondly upon the archdeacon. Here was a lady who loved an aristocrat, and was prepared lovingly to give closer examination to the views of an aristocrat than she would have given to the views of a lesser mortal.

After a moment's reflection, she said, "I see a great truth in what Mr. de Tracey says. The British fleet is the civilized world's bastion against tyrants of the Tsar's sort. Let *Pax Britannica* prevail!" she concluded in ringing tones, so that one felt almost constrained to rise to one's feet and sing the National Anthem.

The effect upon the dean was very noticeable. A choleric hue suffused his pallid cheeks, extending to the scraggy neck imprisoned in its tight bands. Here was he betrayed not only by his fellow clerics and by his own wife, but—far worse—by the true power behind the episcopal throne of St. Errol, the bishop's wife herself. One could see it in his eyes and in the way his bony knuckles stood out from his clenched fists; how the sense of betrayal, adding fuel to his fury, drove him to indiscretion.

"I think," he declared in his loud, bass boom, "I think that you must all be—Jingos! Like the absurd people who sing the appalling Music Hall ditty!"

A gasp of horror went around the table. Somewhere, as if from far off, I heard again that catchy, lilting tune, those brash and braggardly words—rudely trespassing over the hallowed, ancient threshold of my Lord Bishop of St. Errol from time immemorial:

> *"We don't want to fight,*
> *But by jingo if we do . . ."*

One could see that the dean instantly perceived that he had gone too far. The unspeakable had been spoken. At the bishop's own table, he had likened him—and his wife—to the mindless rabble of the music halls. Dr. Millhench's suddenly frightened eyes flickered around the table, trying to gauge what effect his thoughtless declaration had made upon the company. He did not have long to wait.

"Bishop! I have never been so insulted!" This from Mrs. D'Arcy, who was quivering with rage, so that her black osprey plume bristled like the comb of a fighting cock.

"Gervase! How *could* you?" It was the first time that Mrs. Millhench had addressed her husband by name.

Across the table from me, Richard swallowed hard and looked down at his plate. I chanced a glance toward Felicity Millhench, and was surprised to note that her eyes had taken on a steely glitter of something oddly like triumph—and I experienced a slight sensation of unease on that account. Only the archdeacon seemed entirely unmoved by the dean's outburst. He sat back in his chair and, taking up his wineglass, twirled it round and round between his white, slender fingers, smiling to himself the while.

"Madam—my Lord Bishop . . ." the dean's voice was hoarse with the profound emotion of a strong man struck down in his hour of pride.

"At my own table!" cried the bishop's wife.

"Mrs. D'Arcy—Madam—it was a slip of the tongue, merely," pleaded the unhappy man. He spread his great, bony hands as if in a blessing, and his singularly unaccommodating features took on a smile of seraphic benevolence. "How could you think that I, my dear friend—I think I may still call you friend—would mean such a slur in earnest?"

"I can speak for Dr. Millhench and attest to the truth of his declaration!"

All eyes turned to Richard, as he delivered these words in ringing tones. And with what style! He had risen to his feet, and stood, one hand on hip, the other extended, palm outward, as if throwing a gage upon the table in defense of his superior. What a splendid figure he made, with one curly lock falling carelessly across his fine brow, blue eyes steady and earnest. We all hung, breathless, upon his next words.

"A slip of the tongue, as Dr. Millhench has said," continued my intended, "delivered by a sincere man in the passionate sincerity of his convictions. But I can attest, ladies and gentlemen, that nothing was further from the dean's mind than to connect anyone present with the abomination of that dreadful doggerel that is chanted daily in that unholy of unholies, the so-called 'Music Hall.'"

(Oh, my Richard! I thought. If only you *knew* . . .)

"I am given to understand," said Mrs. D'Arcy, and from the changed tone of her voice, it seemed that she was inclined to bend before Richard's advocacy and take a more reasonable view. "I am given to understand that, this very week—indeed, this very night, as we sit here—the rites of the abominable Music Hall are being perpetrated within this very cathedral town, not half a mile from this spot."

(Oh, Richard! . . .)

"That is so, ma'am," confirmed my intended. "And I have it from Dr. Millhench's own lips that he and the cathedral Chapter have striven with might and main to close that den of depravity, but to no avail."

"The mammon of unrighteousness is too strongly entrenched within the ramparts of that ungodly place," declared the dean, his courage returning, and smiling benevolently at the champion who had leaped to his defense in his hour of need. "My letter of protest to the management of that den of iniquity went unanswered, and the young curate who delivered it by hand was subjected to the lewd importunities of painted women of the stage."

"Appalling!" cried Mrs. D'Arcy.

"Such so-called entertainments, for the base passions they arouse in the breasts of the ignorant and drunken unfortunates who frequent them, should be banned by Act of Parliament!" declared Mrs. Millhench, looking with more benevolence upon her husband.

"Hear, hear!" mumbled the bishop, tapping the table top.

"I would go further," said Richard (Oh, Richard! be careful what you say!). "I would go further, and give my testimony, which is this: that all who frequent the abominable institution of the Music Hall should be cast into the outer darkness, where, shunned by all decent folk, they should remain till they have purged their wickedness by true and abject repentance."

His—for me—terrible words were greeted by a chorus of approval from those who had been most closely concerned in the discussion, though I noticed that the archdeacon remained aloof from it all, and continued to smile privately to himself, as if enjoying some secret confidence. My eyes slid guiltily toward Felicity Millhench, to see how she was taking it all. One look into her face and I knew why she, of all people, had proposed me as a guest at the bishop's table.

"I wonder, Miss Herbert," she said in a loud, clear voice that must have carried the entire length of the great hall, "if you have purged *your* wickedness by true and abject repentance yet?"

"Is it true, Clarissa? Tell me, I beg you, that there is some mistake!"

Before them all, Richard was interrogating me publicly. Before the scandalized gazes of the bishop, the dean and their ladies; with Felicity Millhench's gloating smile somewhere at the edge of my tear-misted vision. And heaven knows what the archdeacon was thinking.

"There's no mistake," I whispered.

"*Again!*"

"No mistake," I said, louder. "It's true that I went to the Music Hall."

"*Alone?*"

"No," I said. "With Daisy Marchmain." I looked around their faces, seeking for some expression of sympathy or understanding. "Daisy's a fellow teacher at Mrs. Mount's. And her brother, whose birthday treat it was."

"And you never thought to mention it to me, about this—birthday treat?" Richard almost spat out the last two words.

"I—I thought you wouldn't approve."

"And how right you were!" he cried. "Happily, your deceit has come to light"—he looked down the table to where Felicity was sitting, her delicately pretty face wearing the expression of a kitten that has made free with a whole bowl of cream—"thanks to the intercession of a true friend."

"I didn't see her coming out of the place," said Felicity. "It was my maid who saw her and reported it to me. So embarrassing! The wretched gel was quite rude to me. She remembered, you see, that Miss Herbert used to come to the deanery and teach me French."

"Evil frequently rubs off on to the innocent," declared Mrs. D'Arcy. "I have often said so, have I not, Bishop?"

"Yes, my dear," confirmed the prelate.

"But I didn't think at the time that it was wrong!" I cried, adding, with some defiance, "and I don't think so now!"

"Nor is it, or was it, Miss Herbert," came a drawling voice.

"Mr. de Tracey!" exclaimed the bishop's wife.

"Sir!" cried the dean, appalled. "Will you be so good as to explain yourself?"

"With the greatest of pleasure, Dean," responded the young archdeacon, who appeared to be enjoying the situation in which he had placed himself. He reached out and, taking an apple from the *épergne* before him, proceeded to peel and quarter it with devastating expertise.

"Firstly, you must know that only by laying myself open to the sin of hypocrisy can I condemn the Music Hall. My great-great grandmama, you see, was a singer of ballad songs at Vauxhall Gardens, when that dubious pleasure haunt was favored by the Prince Regent and his set. Great-great grandmama so delighted Prinny that she was summoned, after her performance, to be presented to him. Two years later, when he became king, Great-great grandmama found it expedient to marry a complaisant gentleman much older than herself, who was immediately given a viscountcy by his lady wife's royal patron." He skewered a segment of his apple on the end of a knife and transferred it to his mouth. "So, you see, when one considers the manifest advantages that the singing of ballad songs has brought to my family, I would be a hypocrite indeed to cavil at the Music Hall. Or at those who frequent it."

The archdeacon's astounding revelation put an end to my persecution. No more was said. The rest of the dinner limped on in oppressive silence. I suppose that the remaining courses were served. I certainly recall, from the missing menu card, that there were ducklings and cabinet pudding, raspberry cream and Victoria sandwiches. I have no remembrance of eating any of them, nor do I seem to remember any one else but Mr. de Tracey partaking—which he did with every appearance of enjoyment, occasionally flashing me glances of amused encouragement—of which I was greatly in need.

Richard refused every dish, kept his eyes bowed to his plate, and I saw a small muscle working in his cheek, as he chewed the bitter cud of humiliation.

We left the Palace together, arm in arm, in the moonlight after a formal display of stilted thanks to our host and hostess and a "good night" to our fellow guests. I stepped out of the august portals, knowing full well that I should never in all my life be invited to re-enter them.

Not till we were out of sight of Mr. Butterfield's twin towers did Richard release my arm and, taking a pace to one side, stare down at me from under the brim of his tall hat.

"How could you, Clarissa?" he demanded. "In view of all that was at stake—my warm friendship with the dean and his family, my future prospects, the understanding that lies between us—how could you commit such a folly and, having committed it, keep silence?"

It was his reference to the dean and his family, that stung me to rebellion.

"If that minx Felicity Millhench hadn't seen fit to show her spite, no harm would have been done," I told him.

"How can you speak so of that fine and upstanding young woman?" he cried. "When one considers that, having gravely offended our hosts this evening, you may have cost me my hoped-for advancement. And it will be only through the good graces of the dean and his wife—aye, and Miss Felicity—that I have any chance of recovering my position with Mrs. D'Arcy—I mean, with the bishop."

"I am *quite* sure that your position was never *really* in hazard," I told him. "Only mine. And that was what Felicity intended. That was why she had me invited. Don't worry—dear Felicity will bend every effort to reinstate you in the good graces of the bishop's wife. Now that she has rid herself of *me!*"

He stopped in his tracks and stared at me with what I could only imagine to be genuine puzzlement, and in that instant I think I saw Richard Neale—the real Richard Neale—stripped of all his manly beauty, his smooth phraseology, and his inspiring presence—for the first time.

"What do you mean?" he cried. "How *can* you slander that innocent girl? Clarissa, Clarissa, I am afraid that I have been greatly mistaken about you all this time."

"And I you, Richard," I replied, as calmly as I was able. "And I never realized it before this moment. Whether you are truly self-deceived or merely two-faced, I have no way of telling, but there is one thing I have learned from my careful observation of you across the dinner table."

"And what is that, pray?" he demanded stiffly.

"You definitely use a curling iron on your hair! Good-bye!"

With that, I left him, picking up my skirts and fleeing along the high street, past the Globe Music Hall—object of my downfall—past the shops and the Sir Bevill Grenvile tavern and the market cross, not pausing in my flight till, breathless, I reached the gates of Mrs. Mount's School.

Chapter Two

"DAISY, I'VE GOT TO GET AWAY FROM HERE. AWAY FROM ST. ERROL. Away from the memories. Away from any chance of meeting him again."

Daisy was understanding, as a true friend is always understanding; not seeking to impose her viewpoint, merely probing at the edges of one's resolve, pointing out the inconsistencies, and laying them out for one's consideration.

"There's no hope that you'll make it up with Richard?" she asked.

I shook my head. "Impossible," I declared. "Even if he were to come to me, open-handed—which he won't—it could never be the same between us again."

"At the risk of being depressing, dear, there never was much between you," said Daisy. "He had you on the end of a piece of string because it suited his vanity to have the best-looking woman in St. Errol dancing constant attendance upon him."

"Oh, Daisy! Give over, do!" It irritated me when she was so fulsomely flattering. Not that I am against flattery, but it ill accorded with my present state of being in a limbo of uncertainty and self-doubt.

She shrugged. "If you can't believe the evidence of your own looking glass, that's your misfortune," she said. "In any event, it seems that he has now set his cap on La Millhench, or she's set hers on him, which amounts to the same thing. So, we discount any question of a reconciliation between you. And I agree that you must leave St. Errol. Where will you go? I shall miss you, Clarrie."

"And I shall miss you, Daisy," I told her. "As to where—I want to go far away. France, I think. Back to where I began."

"And what will you do—teach? Try for governess?"

"What else?"

"Mmm. Well, you know how things are, Clarrie."

"Yes." I knew well enough. The copy of *The Times*, to which we of the staff of Mrs. Mount's contributed, and which arrived daily in our cramped little staff common room, always contained at least three full columns of small advertisements relating to teachers and governesses, but the traffic was all, or nearly all, in one direction. The staff of Mrs. Mount's always scanned the advertisements in the hope of improving their positions. It was a futile hope in the face of such appeals as: *"Superior Day School Mistress . . . unexceptionable references . . . wages and locality immaterial,"* or, *"A Lady of Rank wishes to recommend an accomplished Governess who has just finished the education of her daughter . . ."* which meant that Lady Muck, having ground every last ounce of use out of some poor governess, was salving her conscience by spending a few shillings on an advertisement before throwing the discarded creature out into the street.

"Hey-ho!" said Daisy cheerfully. "Let's then see what *The Times* has for you today." And she took from the staff common-room table, from among the detritus of the staff's midmorning tea things, our communal copy, opened it at page two, where the advertisements relating to employment invariably began, and ran her forefinger down the closely printed columns.

Miserably, I recalled my present condition. Gone, my best, my only, chance of marriage, with all the advantages which that desirable state held out to a woman of no fortune or prospects. I was twenty-five and unwed. Given my circumstances, it was unlikely that in our modern society another suitable chance would ever occur again. Daisy might praise my looks, but my looks, such as they were, could bring me nothing but trouble in the marriage market. What use for looks, save to win for oneself the role of a rich old man's plaything? No, I told myself, I would resign myself to a useful spinsterhood. And France beckoned. France, the land of my upbringing, home of my childhood . . .

"Well, I do declare!" Daisy's exclamation broke in upon my somber reverie. "Clarrie, it is as though the very gods of Olympus, bored with sitting on clouds and doing nothing all day, have contrived this very advertisement for your benefit and their amusement. Look . . ."

She handed me the newspaper. The item under her thumb was, as she had implied, tailor-made for Clarissa Herbert, spinster of St. Errol:

> TITLED ENGLISH GENTLEMAN (WIDOWER)— Resident in PARIS, requires a LADY capable of instructing his little girl in English, French, German & Music. She must be of respectable family and not under 25 years of age. Salary £40 per annum. Apply with TWO REFERENCES to Gerrard, 29a Sloane Square, London.

"Well, what do you think?" Daisy's lively, dark eyes danced with delight. "Isn't it just what you were looking for?"

"Mmm. I'm a bit dubious about the music part, though."

"Fiddlesticks! You play the pianoforte like an angel, and you're quite well versed in theory. You may be sure that you'll be more than adequate in that department. Now, my gel—take up your pen and write. Now. Immediately."

A bell rang in the downstairs corridor. It was followed by the rushing of many feet, the hubbub of girlish conversation. Through the window, I could see a stream of Mrs. Mount's Young Ladies moving out into the garden for their midmorning recess, two by two, in their blue pinafore dresses. And I suddenly felt the pangs of parting. Eight years is a long time. To leave the school that had been my home for so long would not be easy when it came.

"I shall have to tell Mrs. Mount straightaway," I said, "for I'll need an immediate reference from her."

"Two," said Daisy. "You'll need two. Now, where shall you get the second, Clarrie?" Her eyes twinkled with mischief. "From the dean, perhaps? Or the bishop?" I had told her the whole story of the disastrous dinner at the Palace.

"I think not," I responded wryly. "But—wait—you have given me an idea, Daisy. There is someone who might give me a reference. I have a—certain feeling—that he might well . . ."

Mrs. Mount's severe countenance softened when I told her of my intention. I pleaded "personal reasons" for my decision, and she did not question me further. It occurred to me that all and sun-

dry probably knew more about my relationship—my past relationship—with handsome Richard Neale than I had ever imagined. She wrote a very complimentary letter of reference there
and then, kissed me for the first time ever, and told me that I
should greatly be missed. It then only remained for me to obtain
my second reference.

At six o'clock that evening, a time when, I judged, a single
gentleman might well have had his tea and be between the activi-
ties of afternoon and evening, I wended my way—rather nervously, and looking around every corner—to the cathedral Close,
where the various dignitaries of the diocese kept house. Walking
very quickly past the front of the Palace, and hideously aware
that Mrs. D'Arcy might be watching me from behind any of the
lace-curtained windows, I bent my hasty footsteps to the small,
stone-built house, the last in a terrace on the east side of the
Close, where lived the object of my enterprise. I had several
times seen the polished brass plate on his oaken door and, never
having made his acquaintance before the fateful dinner party,
had always pictured him as a white-haired churchman in his dot-
age.

> *Venble. and Honble. D.C.R. de Tracey, M.A.*
> *Archdeacon*

My knock summoned a pinched-faced housekeeper, who
looked me up and down and demanded to know my business
and, when I told her, demanded to know if I had an appointment with the archdeacon. No, I did not, I informed her. The
matter had arisen suddenly and was urgent. She gave a doubtful
sniff, asked me to enter and wipe my boots, and left me in a
white-paneled hallway that smelled of wax polish and was heavy
with the slow ticking of a long-case clock.

"Miss Herbert! What a delightful surprise. To what happy
chance do I owe the honor?"

Mr. de Tracey came out into the hallway, all smiles. He was
wearing a dark blue riding-out coat, breeches, and tall boots, but
still retained his clerical twice-around neckcloth.

I offered him my hand. His was cool and dry. "Mr. de Tracey,"
I said. "I have no right to be here, and no right to make any
request of you, but . . ."

"But you are here, nevertheless." He smiled. "And, you will

make your request notwithstanding. Excellent, Miss Herbert. That is just what I would have expected of you, with your honest and forthright style. Come into the drawing room, do. That will be all, Mrs. Settle."

"Yes, sir," muttered his housekeeper, glancing me up and down again, before sniffing and making her exit.

The drawing room had a deeply recessed window that looked out on to the back of the house, where an ancient mulberry tree sprawled its knobbly branches across a flagged courtyard in the center of which a circular fishpond splashed a jet of crystal water from the mouth of a green-bronze dolphin. The room was simply and tastefully furnished in the manner of the previous century, with masculine touches that revealed much of its occupant's tastes. There was a fox's head mounted on the wall, group photographs of college boat crews, crossed fencing foils and mask, a heavily autographed cricket bat. No sign, anywhere, of the appurtenances of the archdeacon's vocation.

"Will you take some tea?" he asked. "Or a glass of sherry wine, perhaps?"

"No, thank you."

"Please then be seated, Miss Herbert, and tell me of this strange request that intrigues me so greatly. I, myself, will take a glass of sherry, as I generally do at this hour."

I took a button-back chair by the window, while he poured himself a glass of straw-colored wine from a crystal decanter. When he had done this, he turned to face me again. Smiled. His eyeglass winked in the reflected sunlight from the window.

"Well?" he left the question hanging, silent, in the air.

I took a deep breath. "I—I am leaving my present employment at Mrs. Mount's and seeking a post abroad. And I wondered if, on such short acquaintance, you would please provide me with a reference."

He took a sip of his wine, sat down opposite me.

"Leaving—because of Neale?"

"Yes," I breathed.

"You have broken your attachment?"

"Yes."

"I see. You know, of course, that his appointment as bishop's chaplain was announced after the Chapter meeting this morning? Or perhaps you do not."

"I didn't know," I replied. "I wouldn't have expected—Richard —to inform me. I'm very glad, for him. Glad that my behavior at the dinner party didn't spoil his chances, after all."

"Your behavior—as you are pleased to call it, Miss Herbert— might well have," said the archdeacon bluntly. "The appointment was very much in the balance. I tipped the balance by casting my vote in his favor."

"You?" I stared at him in puzzlement. There was no accounting for this surprising young cleric. To my knowledge, he had not exchanged a word with Richard throughout the evening of the dinner party. He had given me the impression that he considered my then intended as being beneath his notice. "Why did you do that, Mr. de Tracey?"

"For a host of reasons," he replied. "Not the least important being that I consider Neale to be the stuff of which senior churchmen—some senior churchmen—are made. Oh, he is this, Miss Herbert, and he is that, but it takes all sorts to make up the ministry, and there is a place for us all." He gave a wry, self-deprecating smile. "There is even a place for fox-hunting great-great grandsons of ballad singers. There is another reason why I gave him my vote, but by your leave, I will refrain from telling you that till we are better acquainted. However, if you are hoping to take up employment abroad, our acquaintance may tend to wither by neglect—which is a pity. To where do you hope to go?"

"To Paris," I told him.

"Paris is very fine," he declared. "And well worth a letter of recommendation. Let us then see to it." Taking his wineglass, the archdeacon crossed over to a spindly legged writing table of papier-mâché and, seating himself there, picked up a pen and eyed me quizzically. "Now—how to begin? How's this?—'To Whom It May Concern, the applicant, Miss Clarissa Herbert, is known to the writer as a lady in whom one could repose one's total trust and confidence.' How does that read, eh?"

"That is very generous, Mr. de Tracey," I murmured.

"I can do better than that," said the archdeacon. "Mark my words, Miss Herbert, I've only just begun to give my summation of your character." The butter-yellow, smooth head bowed over his pen as he scribbled the lines, read them with visible satisfaction, and eyed me again. "As to your honesty and probity and so forth—'Miss Herbert is fearless in her defense of Truth and Right. She is Faithful to a fault, and Compassionate in shielding others from hurt.'"

I shook my head, knowing what he was at, and to what he referred. "It wasn't like that, Mr. de Tracey," I told him. "I concealed my visit to the Music Hall for the very base reason that I was ashamed to tell Richard."

"Initially, perhaps," he conceded, "but later, when you found out that he was intriguing to get himself made bishop's chaplain —oh, don't bother to protest, my dear Miss Herbert, there is no advancement without effort, and the ministry is no different from any other occupation in that respect. Intrigue is simply another form of effort for advancement. When you found this out, you kept silence to protect him because despite the excellent exterior, which will carry him far in his vocation, he is a weak man and easily put down. True?"

How he—whom I had at first thought to be an effete and pampered aristocrat and a placeman—saw into my very mind! I nodded.

"Yes. And will he marry Felicity Millhench, do you think?"

"In all probability," said the archdeacon. "I do not think he realizes that he is chasing her, but I am sure she will presently catch him. May I ask if that eventuality will hurt you greatly?"

"No," I said, and in all honesty. "Not now."

"Miss Herbert," he said, "will you marry me?"

In the long silence that followed, I distinctly heard the longcase clock ticking out in the hallway beyond the closed door, and the sound of the fountain splashing in the shadowed garden outside. The archdeacon's head bowed once more over the letter, the pen scratched away to the end of it, closed with a flourish of a signature. He folded up the sheet of paper, rose, and came across the room toward me. I took the letter from his outstretched hand and thanked him in a whisper.

"I wish you every good fortune with your application," he said. "And, having secured the appointment, trust that you will be very happy in Paris."

"Thank you," I said, rising. "Mr. de Tracey, before I go I must . . ."

"No need to give me an answer to my question—my most indiscreet and ill-timed question," he said. "In my defense, I would point out that it was the act of a desperate man, who, faced with the sudden knowledge that our brief acquaintance must soon be terminated, seized his last, his one and only, chance of declaring himself. Perhaps—perhaps if there had been the opportunity for our acquaintance to blossom and to flourish. A summer season. Time for unfortunate first impressions to fade. Or am I being too optimistic? Answer me honestly. You are always honest."

I avoided his eye; looked down at my hand.

"I—I esteem you greatly already, Mr. de Tracey," I murmured. "You have shown much kindness to me."

"But your esteem, under any circumstances, will remain—esteem?" he asked.

I met his gaze. His eyes—the one uncovered and the other behind the circle of glass—were unwavering.

"I am answered," he said.

"Good-bye," I said.

"Good-bye." He took my hand.

I spoke to no one, not even to Daisy, of Mr. de Tracey's astonishing proposal, but with a mind awhirl of conflicting emotions, sat down immediately upon my return to school and wrote my letter of application to the mysterious personage Gerrard in Sloane Square, London, which done, I posted it, together with the two letters of reference enclosed. And then I walked down to the quay, where I had last walked with Richard.

I stood for a long time on the rim of the breakwater, in the shadow of the lighthouse. The fishing fleet was at sea. With the eye of faith, one could faintly discern their brown topsails on the southern horizon. Beyond that horizon lay France, where, with every hope, I would soon be journeying, leaving Cornwall behind —perhaps forever.

What lay ahead for me? One doleful prospect had been considerably lightened by the archdeacon's proposal: Though twenty-five and without a fortune, I was demonstrably not completely "on the shelf" as the saying goes, and might yet meet someone with whom I could share our mutual lives in a special enchantment whose quality I could only dimly comprehend. Perhaps, somewhere beyond that gray-green horizon of sea, carrying out his ordinary daily life, and all unaware of me as I was of him, was the man for whom I had been fashioned, and who had been fashioned for me.

I sighed, and went back to help Daisy and the other teachers supervise the girls' suppertime.

A reply to my letter of application came by return mail and was postmarked London. I could scarcely bring myself to open it; but raced upstairs to my room and contemplated it for a long while, as it stood propped up against my washbasin, willing the contents to be favorable, fearful that they would not. Finally, I broke open the seal, and out fell a square of pasteboard, which, upon puzzled examination mounting to joyful release, I discovered to be a combined steamer-and-rail ticket—*to Paris!*

I had got the job!

Fingers trembling with excitement and haste, I unfolded the letter and read the contents:

> 29a Sloane Square
> London
> 10th April, 1878

Dear Miss Herbert,

Following upon your application, your qualifications, experience and references commend themselves, and I have the pleasure to inform you that the position is yours.

Lord Audubon is at present in Paris and you must repair there to take over the education of his lordship's 6 year-old daughter the Hon. Jane Audubon. I have enclosed a steamer-and-rail ticket to Paris for Monday next, the 15th April, and I trust you will be able to meet this date. Also enclosed is a bank draft for £5 to cover your incidental traveling expenses.

The General Steam Navigation's ship leaves London Bridge Wharf for Calais at 10 A.M. on that day. Upon arrival in Paris, you must present yourself at the British Embassy in the rue du Faubourg St. Honoré, number 35.

Pray telegraph me if you are unable to meet the date of sailing.

Yours sincerely,

> Nigel J. Gerrard
> Private Secretary to Lord Audubon.

On a day of scudding clouds, high blue sky, and scattered showers, I took the railway out of Cornwall and traveled east to the capital. A rainbow stretched across the sky from sea to moorland when we clattered over Mr. Isambard Kingdom Brunel's great bridge over the River Tamar and into Devon. And the rainbow seemed to beckon me: a promise up in the illimitable blueness, forever there, forever receding.

I was on my way. On the rack above my head, all my worldly possessions, which had been augmented by the present of a traveling clock from the staff and pupils of Mrs. Mount's School for Young Ladies, and also by the gift of two gowns from my dear friend Daisy. To her, also, I was indebted for the smart tweed traveling costume which I wore for the occasion. I had protested at her overgenerosity, but she had brushed it all aside. What use had she for all those clothes? she asked me—and she stuck in the backwater of St. Errol. We both wept at the railway station when the time came to say good-bye. And the party of sixth-form girls, who were also seeing me off, sang the school song as the train pulled out in clouds of smoke and belching steam, the song that had been composed the previous year by the music mistress, Miss Gladys Potts, on the occasion of Her Majesty being proclaimed Empress:

> *"From Afric's darkest mountain*
> *To Greenland's farthest floe,*
> *Staunch Daughters of the Empire,*
> *In Duty's call we'll go."*

My traveling companions included a gentleman of bucolic complexion, who, though it was barely midmorning, was already partaking of a picnic basket containing a whole roast capon, a game pasty, a large spiced sausage, together with a bottle of claret and a flask of brandy. He sat opposite. Next to me was a lady of quality. I knew this because she had been escorted into the carriage by a lady's maid, who had fussed around her mistress, tucking a plaid traveling rug about her knees with almost maternal solicitude, inquiring of the rest of us if we minded the windows being tightly closed, because "Madam" was susceptible to drafts; afterward herself retiring to the more modest comforts of a second-class carriage when the whistle blew for departure. On my right, a clergyman in tall hat and bands nodded away in the limbo between sleeping and waking throughout most of the journey, thereby sparing me from the possibility of conversation with him, and the almost certain revelation on my part (so hopeless am I at any sort of concealment or dissembling) that I was acquainted with the members of the St. Errol Cathedral hierarchy. The other two seats were unoccupied. It was, of course, a first-class carriage. My combined steamer-and-rail ticket, priced at the unbelievable sum of 29 shillings, from St. Errol to Paris direct was augmented by another ticket, priced at 14 shillings, which gave me access to a saloon cabin on the steamer from London to Calais. I, who had never in my life traveled other than by second class at the best, felt like Cinderella on her way to the ball in her glass coach.

Toward midday, we drew into Reading, where I delved into my carpet bag and took out a napkin containing a Cornish pasty of chopped beef, onions, and diced potatoes encased in pastry that the school cook had put up for me. As I took my first mouthful, I met the eye of the bucolic gentleman seated opposite. He, who had recently eaten his way through a midmorning repast that would have fed a family of four, actually had the gall to watch me greedily. A little of an hour later we passed through the outskirts of the great city, capital of the Empire.

My expedition had been well planned by Daisy. She, more conversant than I with the teeming world beyond Cornwall, had devised an itinerary which included an overnight stay at a hotel in Bayswater that was favored by her family, a booking that she had secured by telegraph. She had also made a list of things I must do and places I must see before catching my boat on the following morning. I regret to say that I neither saw nor did any of those things, but went straight to my hotel—which I found to be very comfortable—and wrote the first long and highly particularized entry into the new diary with which I had provided myself. I had never kept a diary before in my life, and the abrupt change in my circumstances seemed as good an opportunity as any to begin. It was dusk when I had finished writing, and I went down to the hotel dining room for an excellent supper and was in bed by nine.

Next morning, I settled my bill (seven and sixpence, which I thought to be exorbitant), ordered a hansom cab, and directed the driver to take me to London Bridge wharf. My great adventure had truly begun.

The City at nine on a weekday morning, London Bridge, with the reek of Billingsgate fish market, the endless teeming multitudes passing to and fro, a sea of bobbing hats and horses' ears, was as alien to me as if I had alighted fresh from the moon. My cabbie put me down at a floating wharf on the edge of the dirty gray river, and my baggage with me. There were several ships of all sizes tied up there, and an enquiry of a passing sailor gave me the information I needed: The Calais packet was a large paddle steamer right in front of me, and she was called *Hermione*.

"Good morning, ma'am. I am the purser. Ticket if you please. Thank you, ma'am." A remarkably spry young fellow in brass-buttoned jacket and jaunty peaked cap greeted me at the top of the gangplank, examined my ticket, and upgraded his manner from casual politeness to positive unctuousness when he perceived that I was a first-class passenger with a saloon cabin; himself guided me to the saloon deck, which was at the rear end of the vessel, and showed me to a large and pleasant compartment furnished with an armchair and sofa, and a made-up bunk. I thanked my guide and settled myself in a seat by the window to watch our departure.

And it was then that I saw—*her*.

In all my life, I have never beheld a woman who exuded such a powerful impression of hauteur and arrogance. She was tall, exceedingly so, straight-backed, and head held erect. She walked with pantherine grace, gloved hand resting lightly on the crook of a white parasol that she used as a walking stick. On her wealth of dark hair, which she wore in a chignon, was a wide straw bonnet tied under her firm chin with a green bow. The casual effect of the straw bonnet was echoed by a simple traveling costume of black velvet heightened only by a diamond brooch at her corsage. Her skin was as smooth and white as the finest marble, and her eyes—as they flashed imperiously toward the two porters who were struggling after her with her trunks— were large and emerald-green. A few moments, only, I saw her quite clearly and close at hand, and then she passed from my sight. But not out of my life.

I had taken off my coat, and was ridding my hands of London grime in the washbasin, when there came a knock at the door. It was my friend the purser. He looked embarrassed and unhappy. I soon learned why.

"Ma'am," he said, "I wonder if you would mind changing your cabin for another?"

"Why, pray?" I asked, surprised.

"Because this is *my* cabin!" It was the green-eyed pantheress I had espied coming aboard. She stood two paces from me. The voice was all of a piece with her appearance and manner: haughty and domineering.

"But—I have a ticket," I said, being determined not to be overawed. And I produced the cabin ticket and held it out for her to see, fourteen shillings printed there and all.

"Given in error," she responded distantly, scarcely troubling to give it a glance. And, to the officer, "Will you kindly show this— person—to another cabin and have them bring my things here?"

The man eyed me nervously. "You'll be quite comfortable, ma'am," he said. "The other's not quite so big, but it's well appointed, and . . ."

"I'm glad to hear it," I replied tartly. "I wouldn't wish this lady to be uncomfortable. And I haven't the slightest intention of vacating my cabin for her or anyone else."

"Yes, ma'am," he mumbled, and turning to she of the green eyes, "You see, ma'am, I'm afraid . . ."

"This cabin is mine!" she said, ignoring him, and giving me the full benefit of her haughty stare. "I will explain, since it is apparent that one's simple word is not sufficient. I gave most particular instructions that I be given the cabin furthest away from the noise and vibration of the engine and the paddle wheels, and was assured, quite unequivocally, that the cabin in question was vacant and that it would be booked in my name. And now, will you please vacate my cabin? I have a headache coming on, and I should like to rest."

I might have backed down then, for the woman was clearly quite convinced that she was in the right, and after all, it mattered little to me to shift my traps to another cabin, even if it was smaller and nearer the engine and paddle wheels. But my adversary made the mistake of thinking that the matter was settled to her satisfaction, and made as if to brush past me and into the compartment. She was brought up short by my outstretched arm as I seized the jamb of the door.

Her eyes flared dangerously.

"Will you let me pass?" she hissed.

"No," I replied.

"Ladies, ladies . . ." the purser was at his wit's end. "Might I suggest that . . ."

"*You* will hear more of this!" snapped the woman with green eyes, silencing him with a look. "I shall report *your* conduct to the owners."

She treated me to a stare—quested me from head to foot, taking in the details of my appearance and dress, pricing everything I wore, estimating my station in life—and no doubt found me inadequate in all respects. For a moment, I thought that I, too, would be threatened with some dire reprisal, but having weighed me up, no doubt with a view to remembering me if our paths ever chanced to cross again, she turned on her heel and strode off, elegant and pantherine to the last, her parasol tap-tapping down the corridor.

I raised my eyebrows to the unhappy purser, gave him an encouraging smile, and shut the door.

We sailed on the stroke of ten, with the chimes of St. Paul's still in the air as the ropes were thrown into the sluggish water. The great paddle wheels began to thunder, and the *Hermione* nosed her way out into the London river. I went out on deck to see the last of the old country, and was still there when the gong was sounded for luncheon. We were in the broad estuary, with the county of Essex a smudge in the mist to the northward, as the ship hugged the Kent shore, where children waved from willow trees, and a field full of cows took flight at the sight and sound of the passing juggernaut with its tall chimneys gushing black smoke.

The dining saloon was almost empty. I lunched alone and in silence at a long table that ran the length of the compartment. Blessedly, there was no sign of my adversary, the lady with the green eyes—a circumstance for which I was profoundly grateful. Brown Windsor soup, lamb cutlets and green peas, tapioca pudding, and custard whiled away a pleasant hour. The ship was rounding the North Foreland and dipping her stem into the choppy waters of the English Channel when I went out on deck again. I wondered—since she so objected to the noise and vibration of the engines and paddle wheels—if she of the green eyes was perhaps a bad sailor, and enjoyed the unworthy speculation that a rough Channel crossing might well avenge me for the quite considerable annoyance her arrogance had caused. With which thought, I went to my cabin and whiled away the rest of the afternoon by writing up my diary and then losing myself in my favorite Dickens, *A Tale of Two Cities*.

The *Hermione* docked in Calais at eight o'clock that evening. I had taken high tea in the saloon, again without seeing my late adversary, but I had no sooner secured my place in a corner seat in the Paris train when she swept past in all her glory, followed by the ubiquitous porters with her luggage. Our eyes met, and her fine chin went up a perceptible inch. That was all. She scorned, even, to give me a second glance.

The train was late in starting, and had gone no farther than Boulogne before it hissed to a halt and remained there for another hour. The moon was up when we set off again through the silent countryside of northern France, past villages and homesteads with eyeless, shuttered windows, and rivers like ribbons of beaten silver. I dozed fitfully, and a small girl who sat next to me slept with her head upon my shoulder. Dawn was breaking over the tall gray blocks of stately houses as we steamed into Paris.

Nine-thirty, I decided, would be a proper and suitable time at which to present myself at the British Embassy (why the British Embassy, neither Daisy nor I had been able to fathom, save to speculate that my new employer, Lord Audubon, must be some sort of diplomat). Accordingly, I breakfasted on coffee and *croissants*, gave my best French accent an airing for the benefit of a friendly waiter, who opined, in answer to my enquiry, that I might well reach the rue du Faubourg St. Honoré within twenty minutes in a *fiacre*.

I set off just after nine, rattling through the long boulevards behind a high-stepping horse and a driver wearing a jaunty tall hat who whistled all the way. A policeman at the impressive gates of the British Embassy scarcely spared me a glance as I nervously entered, carrying my luggage, crossed an imposing cobbled courtyard, and addressed myself to a gentleman in a wealth of gold lace and brass buttons, who unbent sufficiently to inform me that I should see the duty secretary, and led me through a marble doorway, down an endless corridor, and into a large, sparsely furnished room that was dominated by the ticking of a clock on the chimneypiece. He left me with the assurance that someone would presently attend to my needs. The hands of the clock stood at twelve before I saw another soul.

He was a vague-looking young man in a frock coat. An Englishman. He looked at me very dubiously over a pince-nez.

"Governess to Miss Audubon, you say? Well, that's very odd."

"Please, why is it odd?" I asked him.

He spread his hands. "Why, because the child was sent back to England only yesterday, to stay with her grandparents while Lord Audubon's away."

I suddenly felt empty. "You mean—neither the child nor her father is here?" I faltered.

"Lord Audubon's in Paris," said my informant. "He'll not be leaving till tonight. Or so I'm told."

"Then, please, can I see him?" I asked. "To ask him what he intends of me?"

My companion thought for a few moments and replied, "That shouldn't present any problems, I don't suppose. I think the best course for you, Miss—er . . ."

"Herbert," I supplied. "Clarissa Herbert."

"The best thing, Miss Herbert, is for you to see Colonel Grant. He's the new military attaché, and traveling with Lord Audubon tonight. He'll straighten out your little problem, for problem it is, and that's for sure. Very odd, to have sent you over here the day after the child went back to England. Very odd indeed. Make yourself comfortable, Miss—er—Albert. I'm sure the colonel will see you presently." And with that, he walked out and left me.

Another hour ticked past. Surely, I thought, everyone in the Embassy, Colonel Grant and all, would now be having luncheon. It might be another two hours or more before I was summoned —always supposing that the vague young man in the pince-nez had even remembered to pass on the news of my arrival. At that moment, the door opened. It was the functionary in uniform who had admitted me.

"Be so good as to follow me, please," he intoned.

Meekly, I obeyed. He led me down the corridor to an impos- ing staircase, whose walls were lined with portraits in massive gilt frames; portraits of impressive-looking gentlemen, some of them in uniform, all of them full of the pride of birth and posi- tion. At the head of the stairs, my guide paused before double doors, upon which he gave a discreet tap. A voice from within bade us to enter.

"Miss Herbert, sir."

"Yes, yes. Show her in and leave us." A harsh, testy voice.

"Very good, sir."

The man seemed glad to be gone. He was at the other side of the door in a trice, and I was alone with the owner of the testy voice.

It was a large room, furnished with a desk and a few chairs, and a row of bookshelves. Maps of all shapes and sizes were pinned to the walls, and a large map was spread over the entire desk top. Poring over it, standing, hands extended across it, was he whom I took to be Colonel Grant. All I could see at the mo- ment was the top of his head—which was thatched with dark, curly hair, close-cut—and broad shoulders and powerful arms. And the hands: oddly delicate hands, splayed over the map, revealing well-tended fingernails, and a pelt of fine black hair covering the backs of them. There was a sandwich lying on a sheet of wrapping paper close by his hand: a long sandwich, made of a whole French bread, with ham. Without looking up, he reached for it, took a savage bite and chomped it with evi- dent satisfaction. Next, he reached for a glass of red wine that also stood on the map. The act of drinking it brought the upper part of his face to my view. Our eyes met. His eyes were gray like the stormy waters of the English Channel.

He lowered the glass, but not without taking a long draft of the wine, during which time his glance never wavered.

"What is all this nonsense?" he demanded. "I'm told that you've been sent from England to teach the Audubon child." He had a scar on the angle of his right cheekbone, and it looked like a dueling scar. I also saw that he was in uniform: a dark blue tunic unbuttoned at the neck, pantaloons of the same material.

"That is correct," I said evenly. "Do I take it that I am addressing Colonel Grant?"

"I'm Grant," he conceded gruffly. He straightened up and contrived to moderate the surly look he had about his mouth, but it was with an effort. I would have sworn—it sprang to my mind immediately—that the gallant colonel was somewhat the worse for drink. His voice, though firm, was hesitant. And when he moved around the desk to confront me, his step was decidedly unsteady.

"How do you do?" I murmured.

"How do you do?" he countered, and took my proffered hand. I was reminded, with a wayward pang of tenderness, of an elegant drawing room back in far-off St. Errol. Like Archdeacon de Tracey's, the colonel's hand was cool and dry, but with a hint of steely power which had been entirely absent from that of the churchman.

"Regarding my situation as governess . . ." I began.

"Miss Herbert, do you have some form of documentary evidence?" he demanded. "A letter of appointment, perhaps?"

I took Mr. Gerrard's letter from out of my reticule and passed it to him without comment. He read it through, with two deep frown lines between his dark eyebrows deepening as he progressed down the page. When he had finished, he gave me back the letter and strode over to the window, where he stood for some time, his hands clasped behind his back. Silent. Brooding.

Presently, he said, "Miss Herbert, you are an embarrassment to me, and I frankly confess that I don't know what to do with you."

"I—I don't understand," I murmured unhappily.

He turned, the cold gray eyes playing over me dispassionately. I might have been a piece of furniture, something without feelings, something which, having been condemned as inadequate or inconvenient, could be thrown aside and forgotten.

"It is not necessary that you should understand, Miss Herbert," he grated, and began a perambulation of the room, pacing to and fro like a caged leopard, pausing now and again to glare up at a map of Europe which hung close by the fireplace.

"Sir, may I see Lord Audubon?" I cried at length.

"No, ma'am, you may not!" he replied. "Lord Audubon is—he is busily engaged upon preparations for a long journey which we are taking tonight. The outcome—when his lordship returns, when his daughter comes back to Paris—all these considerations are entirely speculative. On balance, I think the best thing is for me to send you back to England, to the child, where you can teach her needlework and deportment, or whatever, till the present crisis blows over and she returns to her father in Paris."

"I do not teach needlework and deportment," I said coldly. "My subjects are French and German—at the highest and most proficient levels." This insufferable man was not to run away with the notion that I was some little ignoramus. Needlework and deportment, indeed!

"German?" He paused in his stride and regarded me. "Did you say German? And French? Both fluently?"

"Yes," I told him.

A short pause—and he then threw at me an exceedingly colloquial piece of German, spoken quickly, so as to confuse me I do not doubt, and in what he imagined to be the accent of a Berliner. I all but laughed aloud at the clumsy trap that had served only to betray his own deficiencies in the niceties of the language, and proceeded to put him right. This I did as tactfully as possible: firstly commenting upon his remark and capping it with another, and then—I blush to look back on it!—giving him a short lesson on the finer points of pronunciation.

To give credit where credit is due, my "pupil" took it in very good part . . .

"By jove, I do believe that you have been sent to me by the hand of providence, Miss Herbert," he cried, interrupting me.

And he actually smiled, an enterprise that greatly transformed his severe, harshly chiseled countenance, so that he looked much younger than I had placed him, surely no more than thirty or thirty-five at most.

"At the risk of repeating myself," I told him, "I must again say that I don't understand."

"Oh, but you shall, my dear, my most providential Miss Herbert," he declared. "Now, tell me this, in the pursuance of your employment for Lord Audubon as governess to his daughter in French and German—and these at the highest and most proficient levels, as you have convinced me—are you willing to journey anywhere within reason at your employer's requirement?"

I answered, but guardedly. What was this man about?

"Of course."

"To—say, for the sake of argument—Russia?"

Russia sounded a very long way, but,

"Yes."

"St. Petersburg. That's the capital city, you know."

"I possess a smattering of geography, Colonel Grant," I said stiffly.

"Tomorrow," he said.

"Tomorrow?" I echoed.

He gestured over the map that lay upon the desk, sweeping his well-kept hand from west to east across the colored terrain.

"To St. Petersburg," he said. "We leave by special train from the Gare du Nord at midnight, or as soon after midnight as possible, contingent upon the prompt arrival of all our passengers. In any event, we leave when we please, for this will be a very special train, journeying upon a very important—I may say a vital—mission, and the entire resources of the French, Belgian, and Prussian railways are ours to command. I cannot speak of the Russian railway system," he added.

"This vital mission of which you speak, sir," I said, "would it be impertinent to ask the nature of it?" Something in his voice, in the way he narrowed his piercing gray eyes, had sent a small *frisson* of alarm through my frame.

"It *is* impertinent," he conceded gruffly. "But I will tell you nevertheless. We are journeying to St. Petersburg to save the peace of Europe!"

After this surprising statement, upon which he did not enlarge, Colonel Grant crossed over to the bookcase again, and took down a leather-bound volume tooled in gold.

"Are you willing to accompany us to St. Petersburg?"

I nodded. "Yes."

"Then take the book in your hand," he said, "and repeat after me: 'I'—then state your full name . . .'"

"I—Clarissa Thérèse Herbert . . ."

". . . 'swear by my allegiance to Her Majesty the Queen'"—he cocked a dark and forbidding eyebrow at me—"You *are* one of her subjects, I presume?"

"My—my father was French," I said, "but my mother was a Cornishwoman, and I have always so regarded myself."

"Mmm," he grunted. "To continue: '. . . Her Majesty the Queen, that I shall speak to no unauthorized person concerning the mission to St. Petersburg, and that I shall, as a true subject of Her Majesty, carry out such duties as are presented to me.'"

I repeated the rather daunting declaration, wondering all that time what I—humble Clarrie Herbert, late of St. Errol—could possibly find to do that would affect in any way the fortunes of the little woman who already ruled over more than half of the world.

The colonel thought for a moment, then added something that brought a gasp to my lips,

"'No matter what the hazards to me personally.'"

I gasped again—"Oh!"

"I require it, Miss Herbert," he said evenly. "If you do not feel equal to completing the oath, you may leave this room and no more will be said on the subject between us. But I shall still require the discretion that you have already promised to exercise."

I took a deep breath and, "No matter what hazards to me personally," I said.

"Excellent," he said. "Excellent, Miss Herbert." He then sat down heavily in the chair behind his desk and passed a hand across his brow, smoothing aside a stray lock that hung there.

And all at once I knew that I had been mistaken about this man. Not alcohol, but sheer weariness accounted for the occasional, slight hesitancy of his speech, the almost imperceptible unsteadiness of his walk. And with that knowledge, my heart went out to him in sympathy, even compassion, though in all my life I had never before made the acquaintance of a man who appeared to stand less in need of either.

A knock on the door. Colonel Grant called "come in." A sturdy, florid-faced soldier entered. Of middle age, he wore sergeant's chevrons on his dark blue tunic. His hair was a brighter red than mine and cropped like a scrubbing brush. One watery and appraising blue eye took me in and returned to the figure behind the desk.

"Is all in readiness, Gumble?" demanded the colonel.

"All ready—sah!"

"Read your report."

Bringing himself even more stiffly to attention, the man Gumble read out from a piece of paper attached to a board. "In accordance wiv instructions, the special train will be at Platform Three in time for midnight departure, and will be made up as follows: one locomotive, two day carriages, first class. One luggage van. One sleeping car of the—er—Companee Internationalee dez Waggons-Litts, serial number 15, comprising three compartments wiv . . ."

"There is no need, Gumble, to particularize in such excruciating detail," interposed his officer. "Proceed with the arrangements for the predeparture reception."

"Sah! The manager of the station was prevailed upon to lend his suite for the reception, comprising one large room wiv long table, cut glass chandelier, fine mirrors, chairs, etcetera. One smaller retiring room, wiv . . ."

"More briefly, Gumble, more briefly." Grant passed his hand across his eyes. "What of the victuals?"

"Wittles, sah, have been arranged by Messrs. Fauchon, provenders, of the *Place dee lar Madeleine*, who will also provide waiters, etcetera."

"And the final list of passengers?"

"Sah! Sleeping car passengers will include yourself, sah. My Lord Audubon. Princess Bibescu and maid . . ."

"*And* maid?" Grant frowned. "Isn't it enough that the lady presumed upon an old acquaintanceship to gain herself a free ride to St. Petersburg, without the added encumbrance of her maid? Still, I suppose the services of a lady's maid will relieve the rest of us from having to dance hand and foot upon the princess. Proceed."

". . . er—Miss Augusta Scrase . . ."

"*No!*"

I gave a start of surprise at the vehemence of his interjection. Sergeant Gumble blinked and went very red indeed.

"Strike Miss Scrase's name from the list. She will not be accompanying us after all. Miss Herbert, here, will be the fifth, and last, sleeping-car passenger."

The watery blue gaze slid to take me in again from head to foot. A rubbery mouth sketched the ghost of a grin.

"Yes, sah! 'Ow shall I designate Miss Herbert, sah?"

"'Interpreter,'" said Grant, meeting my eye. "Put down: 'Interpreter in German.' Now—briefly—the remaining passengers?"

I did not listen to the list of names and functions that the sergeant then read out. My mind was racing with a hundred vivid thoughts inspired by the colonel's astonishing statement. I, in the space of a few short minutes, had metamorphized, like chrysalis to butterfly, from a mere governess to an Interpreter in German. And so designated by a military attaché at the British Embassy in Paris. And that elevated gentleman—had he not told me only a few minutes before that the enterprise upon which we were about to depart was for no less reason than to save the peace of Europe? Whatever would they say back in St. Errol?

I was dragged back to the there and then by the close of the sergeant's peroration.

"That will be all, Gumble," said Grant. "Dismiss."

"Sah!" The sergeant stamped both feet and gave a most violently exaggerated salute, but made no move to depart.

"What the devil now?" growled Grant.

"Permission to speak—sah?"

"No!"

"Permission to repeat request, sah?" Gumble was not to be moved. My admiration went out to him for his courage and perseverence. It was not misplaced.

"Proceed," said Grant with heavy resignation.

Did I observe the sergeant's befrogged and bebuttoned chest relax a hairsbreadth? And did that cropped head, set so stiffly on the tightly collared neck, ever so gently incline to one side? The barking voice certainly softened,

"Sah, wiv respect, will you not now get some rest? You've been on your feet ever since we bin 'ere, ever since this business blew up. Not a wink of sleep 'ave you 'ad for . . ."

"Mind your confounded business and get out!" said Grant without heat.

"Sah!" The sergeant was not one bit put out, but gazed at his officer with an expression of renewed respect, as if for all the world he would have been disappointed and disillusioned by any other response. He gave another salute, spun around, stamped to the door, and went out.

"That will be all, Miss Herbert," said Grant, rising. "You have heard the general drift of it. Please present yourself at the stationmaster's suite in the Gare du Nord at, say, eleven o'clock this evening. There will be a reception, a champagne buffet supper. You will meet your fellow passengers and hear a brief statement about our mission to St. Petersburg, and then we shall depart. As you heard, you will have a berth in a sleeping car. The cars of the Compagnie Internationale des Wagons-Lits are, so I am informed, luxurious to a degree as far as railway travel is concerned."

I got up and offered him my hand.

"Colonel Grant, I . . ."

"Yes, Miss Herbert?" A sudden new weariness came into his eyes. I almost sensed the thought flitting through his tired brain, "What is this silly woman going to waste my time on now?"

"Oh, it's nothing," I said, even though there were a hundred things I wanted to ask him, not least of all: should I need extra, warm clothing for the Russian steppes? Did the steppes begin at St. Petersburg? I scarcely knew.

"Then, till this evening." He bowed. It was a dismissal.

"Till this evening, Colonel."

I left him. I had not gone ten steps down the sumptuous staircase, on my way to the waiting room where I had left my luggage, when I remembered one thing I simply had to say to Colonel Grant. I had to thank him for what was surely a considerable honor that he had conferred upon me by taking me with him to St. Petersburg. I hastily retraced my steps. Tapped lightly upon his door and, receiving no reply, peeped in. He was slumped across his desk, arms spread wide, his cheek resting upon the map, eyes closed. Fast asleep upon the instant amid the detritus of his hastily bolted luncheon of a ham sandwich and a glass of wine—a slender repast that he had not even had the opportunity to finish.

I tiptoed slowly into the room. I need not have taken so much trouble, for nothing in the world would have awakened him but Gabriel's horn. I took a small pillow from an extremely uncomfortable-looking straight-backed sofa (no wonder he had preferred to slump where he sat) and brought it over to the desk.

Gently, oh so gently, I took his cheek in my palm and slowly lifted his head from the desk, then slid the cushion underneath and allowed his head to descend upon the yielding softness. His cheek felt strangely taut and firm to my touch, and the unaccustomed texture of shaven, male skin was—oddly disturbing.

A curling lock of his glossy, black hair lay over his ear. I had an impulse to smooth it back—but instantly quenched the impulse.

He never stirred from first to last, as I tiptoed out again, closed the door quietly, and went out to see what Paris offered me in the hours till my next encounter with the disturbing Colonel Grant.

Chapter Three

PARIS HAD MUCH TO OFFER. IT WAS TWO-THIRTY WHEN I LEFT the Embassy, encumbered by only my carpet bag (the doughty Sergeant Gumble had encountered me in the entrance hall, had taken charge of my remaining traps and winkingly informed me that he, too, was traveling to St. Petersburg and would ensure that they would be delivered to the train), walked down the rue du Faubourg St. Honoré to the Rue Royale, where I found an excellent and reasonably priced restaurant. Here, after an unaccustomed *apéritif*, I enjoyed a *sole bonne femme*, an ice, and some fruit. I am tremendously drawn to great ecclesiastical buildings, particularly of the Gothic style, so my steps naturally turned toward the looming bulk of Notre Dame, standing like a great ship on its own island in midriver. On the way, I was courteously greeted, smiled upon, and had innumerable hats doffed at me, by menfolk of all ages and persuasions. I have to say that I found the experience not unpleasant, for, as I soon learned, your Parisian *boulevardier* does not have the irritating persistence of your average Englishman, but is concerned merely to express his admiration of a passing lady. And who is averse to admiration?

Notre Dame was a revelation. For a long time, I sat in the mysterious blue gloom, under its soaring columns and arches, and let my mind drift where it willed—wending through my past life, my many disappointments and griefs, the joys that had illuminated some golden days. It was approaching dusk when I went out, and a bank of cloud over the heights of Montmartre betokened the coming of a storm. I found a small, decent hotel by the riverside, where the proprietress was not averse to making a modest profit from a respectable-looking young woman who wished to rent a room and use of a bath just for the evening. I paid her in advance with an English half-sovereign, which she bit between her teeth and, finding it to be of true gold, conducted me to a decent room on the second floor, afterward instructing a chambermaid to heat Madame a bath of water.

I lay in the cosseting warmth of my bath, and thought of poor, weak, self-deluded Richard back in St. Errol, and how wretched a figure he cut in comparison with Colonel Grant, a man of ruthless power and dynamism who could hardly have known a moment of self-doubting in his life. Having disposed of this speculation, I rose, dried myself, and, mindful that I was attending a champagne buffet supper in the company of an English nobleman, a—had I heard it aright?—Russian princess, and Colonel Grant, I put on one of the gowns that Daisy had given me: a pretty evening gown of wild white silk sprigged with small pink roses. At half-past ten, Mme. the Proprietress summoned me a *fiacre*. It was streaming with rain, and lightning was etching a silhouette of Paris's rooftops and chimneys, when my conveyance lumbered and rattled under the archway of the Gare du Nord.

The great station, at that hour, was almost deserted. A few faceless figures stood like wraiths in the pools of lamplight. Somewhere in the dark, I could hear the hissing of steam, and far off, at the end of an echoing vault of iron and glass, I could see the ruddy glow of a furnace.

" 'Evening, Miss 'Erbert, ma'am."

I turned to see and receive the salute of Sergeant Gumble. The good sergeant was tricked out in his full-dress regimentals, with fur-collared dolman slung jauntily across his left shoulder, a saber and sabretache clinking at his calf, and a hussar's plumed busby perched on the side of his cropped head.

"Good evening, sergeant," I responded. "Am I late?"

Most of his reply was lost in a lowering crash of thunder accompanied by a lightning bolt that momentarily illuminated the vast station hall, while a new onslaught of rain thrummed down on the arch of glass high above us. However, I managed to gather that though some of the party had already arrived I was by no means the last. Gumble lent me his arm and guided me, through lamplight and shadow, to the far end of the station, where stood a train with its locomotive muttering steam, and a long stretch of red carpet connecting it to an imposing doorway opposite.

The sergeant guided me through the door, where a flunkey in white wig and knee breeches relieved me of my cape. A functionary—the same brass-buttoned and gold-laced fellow, I took him for some kind of majordomo—who had first greeted me at the Embassy, bowed me through another door and announced my name in stentorian tones.

The reception chamber was of imposing size and loftily ceilinged, with pier glasses along every wall, so that one had useful glimpses of oneself from every angle. There was a table set in the center, which was piled high with surely every comestible known to man. I saw the hundred eyes of a peacock surmounting the centerpiece; a boar's head, glazed and iced; and puddings, and jejaws of all description. A white-gloved waiter approached me with a tray of tall champagne glasses. I took one, and cast a glance about me for Colonel Grant. I espied him almost immediately. He was with a lady, and had already seen me, doubtless having had his attention drawn by the announcement of my arrival. He looked toward me over his companion's shoulder—she was holding him in conversation—and treated me to a brief nod. I wondered if he had slept well.

"Good evening, ma'am." A voice made me turn. The speaker was a young man at my elbow. I had an instant impression of a stiff quiff of sandy hair, a freckled face, amber-colored eyes full of good humor, a nose a trifle too short for comfort, a mouth of exceeding generosity. With an air of effortless ease, he was dressed—unsuitably for the occasion—in a tweed Norfolk jacket and tweed knickers tucked in woolen stockings, like a man going out for a day's pheasant-shooting. I liked him on sight, and could not place his unfamiliar accent.

"Might I be so bold as to present myself, ma'am?" he said. "Ralph Orwell, of the *Baltimore Advertiser and Examiner*. Your servant, ma'am." And he took my proffered hand and implanted upon the air an inch above my knuckle a kiss styled for a duchess.

"Ah! You are an American journalist?" I said, conscious of not having made a notable feat of ratiocination.

"That's right, ma'am," said Mr. Orwell. "And may I compliment you on your gown, ma'am? I doubt, I greatly doubt, if your gracious lady Queen Victoria is looking finer, is cutting a better dash, in Windsor Castle this night. No, ma'am."

Despite my instant liking for Mr. Orwell, I suddenly felt a little out of my depth. "Thank you, sir," I said.

"And I hope and trust," said Mr. Orwell, "indeed, I pray, that you, ma'am, are a member of the party departing for St. Petersburg this night?"

"Yes, I am," I told him.

He made a sweeping gesture. "If the whole venture were an abysmal waste of time," he said, "if we were to traipse all the way to the Ultima Thule, only to come traipsing back empty-handed, this will be my consolation: you were there, Miss? . . ."

"Herbert," I supplied. "Clarissa Herbert."

He took a long draft of his champagne. "Clarissa!" he declaimed. "Clarissa. Clarissima. And to extend it into Latin, we have Clarissae, which is 'of Clarissa,' or 'to or for Clarissa.' And we have Clarissa in the Ablative, which is 'by, with, or from Clarissa.' I hasten to add, Miss Herbert, that before the rigors of the Fourth Estate quenched the fire of scholarship in my soul, I was a Classicist of Harvard, and sometime of Oxford. Miss Herbert, I do not appear to have your undivided attention. What has taken you, Miss Herbert? Why are you staring toward yonder looking glass? Why have your cheeks turned pale?"

I took a deep, shuddering breath. During my new friend's airy meanderings, my attention had gone in search of Colonel Grant again. I had swiftly found him, reflected in the pier glass beyond Mr. Orwell's broad shoulder. The colonel's back was now turned toward me. Not so—as formerly—that of his lady companion . . .

I saw her clearly in the looking glass: dark-haired and arrogant, the magnificent head held high, pale skin like the finest porcelain, green-eyed, pantherine. My erstwhile adversary from the cross-Channel packet. And here—at the St. Petersburg pre-departure reception!

I shifted so that *she* should not see me, interposing the American's stalwart frame between our line of vision.

"Mr. Orwell," I whispered, "please don't look now, I beg you. But that lady with the dark hair. The one in gold, talking to Colonel Grant. You know Colonel Grant?"

"Sure, I've met the colonel," he replied, good humoredly. "And I've been introduced to the lady with him. Pheeew! What a female, that! Treated me as if The Boston Tea Party had never happened, as if it was George Washington who had died instead of brother Lawrence, as if we hadn't won the war and were still around to wave the Union Jack for that little lady in Windsor. Sure, she treated me like the wild colonial boy with straw in my hair. What worries you about *her*, Miss Herbert, Clarissa, Clarissima? What worries you about—what's her name again?—Miss Scrase, Miss Something Scrase."

"Augusta Scrase!" I whispered, remembering the exchange that had taken place between Colonel Grant and the sergeant. "Thank heaven. *She* isn't coming to St. Petersburg after all. So all I have to do is to avoid her this evening. Difficult—but not impossible, not if I keep the buffet table between her and me . . ." I was talking to myself, almost unconscious of my companion; till that freckled face, that pair of humorous eyes, swam into my view, and Mr. Orwell took my chin gently between finger and thumb and directed my gaze to meet his.

"Miss Herbert, lady," he murmured. "Clarissa, Clarissima, I don't know what this is all about, but I have doleful news to impart. Miss Augusta Scrase is indeed coming with us to St. Petersburg, for she told me so herself."

"Oh, no!"

"Oh, yes. With her own lips. And that is not a lady who says one thing and means another. Behind that damask cheek is a mind with the unswerving drive of a steam hammer."

"What am I going to do?" I breathed.

For answer, he deftly removed another brimming glass of champagne from a passing waiter, tipped half of the pale amber liquid into his own part-empty glass, the rest into mine. And then, "First, Miss Herbert, lady," he said, "I suggest you tell me what you have *already* done."

And so, in brief terms, I told him of my encounter aboard the Channel packet, and of the green-eyed Miss Scrase's overbearing arrogance. He listened without comment—he was a good listener —and when I had done, he nodded his head.

"The situation is impossible," he declared. "The affront given and the affront received, taken in conjunction, make impossible any future, continuous congress between you and the person in question. I cite the example of a lady and gentleman, both at that time fresh acquaintances of mine, the lady obviously some twenty years older than he, and both named Cadwallader. I introduced them to the assembled company as mother and son. As Mrs. Cadwallader hissed bitterly into my ear a moment later, they were—husband and wife!"

"What a dreadful story!" I exclaimed, appalled, despite my own problem. "But then, you weren't afterward cooped up with this Mr. and Mrs. Cadwallader on a long journey to St. Petersburg."

"Worse!" he said, raising his eyes in agony to the elaborate plasterwork of the ceiling. "We were immediately afterward cooped up together on a small steam yacht from Boston to Charleston, South Carolina. And the Cadwalladers' eyes scarcely ever left me in all that long voyage—she with hatred at my having penetrated powder and rouge and determined her real age, he with shame at having been detected in the state of being married to a rich older partner."

"What am I going to do?" I repeated, casting another glance over his shoulder. "Goodness! Colonel Grant's looking this way and gesturing. I do believe he's going to bring that woman over here to introduce us both."

"Clarissa, Clarissima," whispered my new friend. "Let me call a cab. I will take you anywhere, anywhere. My life is yours to command . . ."

"*You* have drunk too much champagne, sir," I told him.

"Yes. Alas, yes," he admitted.

I again peeped over his shoulder into the pier glass. The colonel had taken his companion's arm and was steering her toward where Mr. Orwell and I stood close by the buffet table. The wildest thoughts of escape or concealment commended themselves to me: to dart around the towering mass of comestibles and take shelter behind the nodding plumes of the peacock; to assemble a facial expression so unlike my own that Miss Scrase—who, after all, had only seen me for a few moments in the uncertain light of a cabin doorway—might not recognize me. And then I said to myself, silly goose, it was she who offered the affront, and not you, albeit you answered her roughly. And remembering my self-respect, I swung around to meet my late adversary, chin high and defiant.

I have to say it, I give her her due: Miss Augusta Scrase, though she recognized me instantly, did not by so much as a tremor of her well-tended eyelashes betray her surprise. The English upper classes have much to commend them.

"Miss Scrase," began Colonel Grant, "may I present . . ."

"I have met the lady!" said she in a voice frozen by a long passage over arctic wastes.

There was no mistaking her tone. Even a man could have detected it. Grant's shrewd eyes flickered from one to the other of us.

"Oh," he murmured, and, "I see."

"I made the lady's acquaintance on the boat," she said, "but it did not come to the exchanging of names."

"Miss Augusta Scrase," said Colonel Grant, "Miss Clarissa Herbert."

"How do you do?" I said.

"How do you do," she replied. We did not extend hands, either of us.

"This is the lady of whom I was speaking," said Grant, who had quite recovered from his momentary surprise and was eyeing us both quizzically.

"The 'Interpreter in German'?" She had a way of saying it that sounded like an insult, and her aristocratic lip curled ever so slightly. "The lady must be very—competent—to have graduated so quickly from schoolma'am to interpreter for the Foreign Office."

"Why do you not test the lady, Miss Scrase?" said the colonel smoothly. "Your competence in the language is greater than mine."

A voice in my ear—that of Mr. Orwell, "Fifteen rounds and no holds barred—and *I'm* putting my money on the redhead."

"Be quiet!" I whispered back.

At that same moment, Miss Scrase directed to me a remark in German; gabbled quickly, with slurred vowels and consonants, and in highly idiomatic phraseology of the sort that only a fluent speaker could possibly either deliver or understand. Due to Mr. Orwell's interjection, I missed it, and asked her to repeat what she had said, a request that caused her to glance at Colonel Grant with a raised eyebrow.

At that, I nearly lost my temper. But not quite. Instead, I threw some German at her, as fast, slurred and idiomatic as hers had been, and well-larded with slang words and phrases of the native Berliner that I had learned from my much-traveled father.

I said to her, in effect, "Madam, no one is more sorry than I about the ridiculous scene on the boat, but you must grant faults on both sides. You treated me like dust under your feet, and I responded with my habitual stubbornness. Since we are to travel together, can we not bury our differences?"

The large green eyes widened with surprise. She had understood every word—no mean German speaker, she, either. And for one moment I thought she was going to unbend. Glancing at Colonel Grant—who must have followed the drift of my outburst —I saw the corners of his firm mouth crinkle in the ghost of a smile—quickly erased. But the unbending was not to be. The green eyes remained icy, her mood intransigent.

"Nevertheless, the cabin was booked in my name," she said.

I had no wish to reopen the argument. "Such a pity it had to happen," I countered. "And such a remarkable coincidence. I mean—you and I . . ."

"Not such a remarkable coincidence," she responded, and she picked up the hem of her long evening gown of shimmering *tissue d'or* and draped it expertly over a slender, white-gloved wrist. "Both tickets—and my cabin reservation—were made out for the same voyage by the same fool clerk at the Foreign Office. And he sent you *my* reservation! Colonel Grant, I think I should like some supper. Shall we find seats?"

They left us, she on his arm. I had the distinct impression of having lost the contest, a feeling not shared by Mr. Ralph Orwell.

"Fight temporarily discontinued in the second round," he said. "With the redhead leading by a narrow margin of points. How about some supper, Miss Herbert? And I'd like you to meet a couple of my colleagues of the Fourth Estate."

There were perhaps a dozen guests already present at the reception, though the abundance of servants greatly increased one's sense of being in a large crowd. Some of the guests, by the shyness of their bearing and the modesty of their attire, I took to be merely junior functionaries from the Embassy. They huddled by the buffet and ate swiftly and with an air of collective guilt of all that was offered. There was no one who could possibly have been Lord Audubon, and no one remotely resembling a Russian princess. Ralph Orwell told me that both were expected imminently.

We were provided with chairs and tempted with food. A fellow in an absurdly tall chef's cap presented before me an enormous dish containing conceits of shellfish made into tiny tarts and garnished with piped sauces that looked like icing. I took two. And was introduced to the American journalist's colleagues.

The first was an Englishman. He was tall, exceedingly thin, with thick-lensed pince-nez and an air of desperate academism, who shook my hand vigorously and announced himself as Henry Martin, of the *London Courier,* and was I not fascinated and intrigued by the prospect of journeying all the way to St. Petersburg by rail? he asked, with considerably more vehemence than the question demanded. I meekly said that I was.

"Martin's a railway fanatic," said Ralph Orwell, in an aside. "And a thundering bore. Watch you don't get caught alone with him."

The next of Mr. Orwell's colleagues was small, stout, and flamboyantly attired in the manner of the self-conscious bohemian, in flowing cravat, flowered waistcoat, heliotrope spats. He addressed himself to me in the accents of the *Ile de France* and said he was Jules Charlot, political correspondent of *L'Observateur de Paris.* M. Charlot, whose perfume was quite overpowering, bowed low over my hand, revealing that the hair at the crown of his head was augmented by a rather obvious wig.

"Miss Herbert's presence is both a delight and a surprise," he purred. "And, considering the composition of the personages departing for St. Petersburg tonight, by no means the only surprise."

"What do you mean by that, Jules?" demanded Orwell. "That's a very odd observation."

"Is it so, *mon ami?*" countered the other, and his berry-black, shifty eyes slid sidelong, this way and then the other. "Think about it for a while, my dear Ralph. A little later in the evening, maybe, if you have not solved my little riddle, I will enlighten you."

A roll of thunder crashed out from somewhere not far distant, causing a dramatic hush in the hubbub of conversation all around us. Above my head, the crystal droplets of the chandelier briefly shimmered and jangled together. The thunder, the silence, the tiny tinkling, and the Frenchman's cryptic and indefinably sinister remark all contrived to send an involuntary shudder through my body.

There came a sudden stir, a ripple of whispered comment. All eyes turned to the door.

"Here comes Princess Natasha," murmured Ralph Orwell. "And, by Jupiter, she's everything they told me she'd be!"

Princess Natasha Bibescu, *née* Romanoff ("Niece of the Tsar, and favorite niece at that," was Ralph Orwell's aside. "Married a millionaire Rumanian count and widowed at twenty."), descended upon the gathering like a bird of paradise alighting amid a group of farmyard chickens. She floated rather than walked, lacy fragments of her train and her ermine pelisse drifting insubstantially in her wake. With breathtaking economy of effort, she received the company, giving brilliant attention to everyone whom Colonel Grant presented to her. A graceful inclination of the head for Augusta Scrase's formal curtsy; dazzling smiles and an extended hand for the menfolk; a pat on the cheek for me—to my complete embarrassment.

"So charming, so pretty," was her comment. I felt like a child brought before a matriarch, and she could not have been a day older than I.

Embarrassment in plenty for Colonel Grant. Addressing the entire company, as well as him, she cried, "Ah, my hussar, my *beau sabreur!* Do you remember our first meeting at the summer palace at Tsarskoye Selo? The summer gardens and the fountains playing, and I—an untried chit of a thing, unused to the ways of the world. Lost! Lost in adoration of the handsome Englishman. Do you remember, *mon cher colonel?*"

Grant, whose stern face was a picture—taut, stiff-lipped, brick red, unwavering of expression—gave a brief bow.

"I recall the pleasure of our meeting at Tsarskoye Selo, Princess," he replied.

"Fond reminiscences must attend upon other events," said the princess, and looking about the ring of awestruck faces, she made an extravagantly despairing gesture with a small, plump, beautifully shaped hand that was almost hidden in glittering diamonds—as was her throat, and the wealth of flaxen hair that framed her lovely, pink-and-white complexioned face. "My friends, I have to tell you that, somewhere between here and Nantes, my entire luggage has been lost!" she cried.

"Oh, surely not, ma'am," said Grant.

"Yes, yes!" said the princess. "Jewel case and all. Did I not dispatch it in advance, in charge of my maid?" She turned and, tapping me gently on the wrist with her fan, whispered to me confidentially, "A new creature, my dear. A helpful willing little thing, but a trifle *folle*. You know the sort. Oh, I am quite despairing!"

"Your maid traveled by road, ma'am?" demanded the colonel.

"By diligence, yes," said the princess. "And so did I."

"Then I will immediately telegraph every posting station between here and Nantes," said Grant. "Your maid's coach may have had a small mishap, calling for a repair at some village blacksmith's . . ."

"A mishap!" The princess' voice rose musically. "How can you speak of a mishap, Colonel? My little Pepé!"

Colonel Grant's face grew suddenly more taut, more set, less florid. "I am afraid I do not understand, ma'am," he said in the tones of a strong man who has been tried very close to his limit. "*Who* is Pepé?"

Before the princess could answer, there was a commotion over by the door. The majordomo from the Embassy, in the act of announcing newcomers, was thrust unceremoniously aside by an intense-looking young woman dressed all in black after the manner of a Continental lady's maid. In one arm she carried a large crocodile-skin jewel case, in the other a small white poodle, whose frizzed top-knot was tied with a large pink bow.

"*Madame la Princesse!*" cried the newcomer. "I have arrived at last!"

"Pepé—my darling!" Princess Natasha swept forward and, gathering the little dog from the maid's arm, she showered it with kisses. "How will you forgive your wicked mistress for abandoning you all day to that stupid girl? Be kind to your poor mistress and forgive her. No—you see?—he is not pleased." She gave me a despairing glance of tear-filled, baby-blue eyes as the little dog snapped at her hand and wiggled to get free. "My dear, will you have them bring him some caviar? He dotes on caviar. That, and a sip of champagne. A little light collation will quite restore his good spirits."

I gestured to one of the waiters and made the princess' wants known. He came back with a silver dish. After him, another man bearing a saucer and a magnum of champagne wrapped in a white napkin.

"Is it ikra caviar?" demanded the princess. "My Pepé will abide no other."

The waiter respectfully confirmed that this was so. The dish was lowered to the ground, the dog with it. The small, bearded face descended upon the pile of limpid granules. The docked tail commenced a brisk wagging.

"Put the saucer of champagne beside him, so that he can take a sip when he pleases," said the princess. She smiled at me, dabbed at her eyes with a lace handkerchief, an action which caused the jangling, jeweled bracelets at her wrist to catch against an elaborate diamond necklace that lay across the upper slopes of her generous *poitrine,* so that one of the tear-shaped pendants fell with a tinkle at her feet. Clicking her tongue with slight annoyance, she stooped to pick it up, and slipped the diamond droplet into her reticule as if it had been a piece of loose change. I had noticed, with some surprise, when she was bending down, that the hem of her white lace dress was none too clean.

"My dear," she said to me—she appeared to have adopted me

as friend and confidante—"try some of the ikra caviar. Do you know it? No? It is quite excellent. It can only be made in winter and is excruciatingly difficult to preserve. *Garçon*, bring more, much more. And leave the bottle of champagne. My father had a supply raced by *droshky* from Astrakahn to our estate in the Ukraine every January. This must surely be the last of the ikra caviar that they will see this year in France. Excellent, is it not? Are you enjoying it, my dear? Do you know, I never did catch your name . . ."

The caviar really was very good. I had eaten quite a lot of it, and drunk more champagne than I would have believed, and the poodle Pepé, having gorged himself, had fallen asleep close by his mistress's skirts, when the majordomo announced: "The Right Honorable, the Lord Audubon of Monsfield, Emissary Extraordinary to the Court of St. Petersburg."

Lord Audubon was—in a word—impressive. Not impressive in the way that Princess Natasha Bibescu was impressive, with her total unselfconsciousness, her casual way with priceless diamond droplets, her total disregard of the fact that the hem of her gown was muddied. That sort of impressiveness came, surely, from being a member of a dynasty that had ruled Russia for more than a quarter of a millennium. I had no knowledge of Lord Audubon's ancestry, but I know that upper-class Englishmen, with or without titles, stalk the earth as if it had been fashioned by the Creator exclusively for their benefit. Archdeacon de Tracey possessed some of that quality, though lightly borne; Lord Audubon had it all, and carried it with ostentation.

He was tall. Half a head taller than Colonel Grant, and broader in proportion. Mid-brown hair smoothed sleekly behind his ears, and a silky, military-style moustache of slightly darker color. His complexion was excellent: The healthy pallor of a gentleman of leisure who, nevertheless, is no stranger to physical activity—as breadth of shoulder and spareness of flanks provided evidence. Lord Audubon was dressed in evening tail-coat and searingly white shirt front and cravat, a somberly tasteful attire relieved only by the glittering star of some order of chivalry pinned to the left breast of his coat. His eyes were mid-brown disposed to hazel. I would have put him something short of thirty years of age, which might have been somewhere between the ages of Colonel Grant and myself.

Like a well-rehearsed actor, he moved forward to an advantageous position in the center of the gathering, looked about him with that reserved, tight-lipped smile which betrays nothing save civility, glanced toward Colonel Grant, and said,

"Well, now, Colonel. Are we all assembled? Has the princess arrived? In which case . . ."

"Princess Natasha is here, my lord," said Grant, advancing. "Ma'am, may I present Lord Audubon?"

The princess flicked fragments of ikra caviar from her fingertips, laid aside her champagne glass, and extended her hand toward the Emissary Extraordinary to the Court of St. Petersburg.

"How do you do, my lord," she said. "It is very civil of you to take me with you to St. Petersburg, and when you present your credentials to darling Uncle Alex, I shall certainly accompany you and tell him of your great kindness."

I saw Lord Audubon exchange a glance with Colonel Grant, and it struck me that, assuming "darling Uncle Alex" to be Alexander II, Tsar of All the Russias, it had been a considerable feather in the colonel's cap to bring along the ruler's favorite niece.

"You are too kind, ma'am," said Audubon, bowing.

"I am presuming that you have never visited St. Petersburg before, nor been presented to the Tsar," said the princess.

"I have not, ma'am," replied Audubon. "Nearly all my time in the diplomatic service has been spent in the Balkans and the Near East, and latterly in Constantinople—from whence I was recalled to carry out this present mission."

"Constantinople—ah!" The princess's blue eyes lit up with great interest. "Do you know the sultan, my lord? Is it true that his discarded concubines are bundled into sacks and thrown at night into the Bosphorus?"

Lord Audubon smiled. "I promise you, ma'am, that the sultan is an extremely civilized man, and such stories are greatly exaggerated."

"Oh, dear," said the princess, disappointed.

"But I am assured that such practices were carried out in quite recent reigns," added Audubon, by way of consolation.

"Ah," said the princess. "It is a great comfort to know that one has not nursed untruths for a whole lifetime. But what of yourself, my lord? I am told that you are a widower. I am very sorry to hear of your poor wife's passing. I trust it was not a painful end. And your child—you have a child?"

"A daughter, ma'am," murmured Audubon. "My wife died in bearing her."

Awakened by another clap of thunder, little Pepé rose and went over to sniff reflectively at Lord Audubon's highly-polished elastic-sided boots. Diplomatically, Colonel Grant seized upon the slight distraction to change the subject.

"Sir, may I present Miss Herbert?" he said, indicating me. "As I told you in my note, Miss Herbert was appointed by your secretary in London as governess to Miss Jane. But in view of the lady's high qualifications as a linguist, I took the liberty of temporarily appointing her *ad hoc* interpreter."

"Very enterprising of you, Colonel," said Audubon. "How do you do, Miss Herbert. My daughter's loss is our own inestimable gain." He took my hand, held it a trifle longer than etiquette required, and his eyes swept over me, searchingly. If a widower, then a very susceptible widower, I thought.

"Thank you, my lord," I said. "Nevertheless, I look forward to meeting Miss Jane at an early date."

"Quite so, quite so," he replied. "Upon our return from St. Petersburg."

"If I may interject, sir," said Grant. "Speaking of St. Petersburg, time is now pressing. Might I suggest that the room be cleared of all save the principal parties, so that a brief statement may be made concerning our mission?"

"Just so, my dear Grant," assented Lord Audubon.

Somewhere in the vast glass and iron vault outside, a steam whistle shrilled out, and died away like a banshee's wail.

Before departing, the waiters passed around more champagne and fresh temptations of the gastronomic art. With their departure went the minor functionaries who were also journeying to St. Petersburg, but who were not privy to the inner secrets of the mission. Remaining were Lord Audubon and the colonel, the three journalists, Miss Scrase, and—unbelievably—Clarrie Herbert, raised in one astonishing day from schoolma'am to diplomats' interpreter.

Curled up in an armchair, nibbling at ikra caviar like a pretty, contented pussy cat, was Princess Natasha Bibescu. She had not offered to leave with the rest, and it is certain that no one had dreamed of asking her.

"Will you attend to the preliminaries, Colonel?" said Lord Audubon.

"Yes, sir." Grant stalked to the front of the buffet table, stood there with the peacock's tail spread, fanlike, behind his dark-maned head. He was wearing the full-dress regimentals of a hussar officer, and—Lord Audubon or no Lord Audubon—entirely dominated the gathering with his lean height, his quietly masterful bearing. A moment's pause, so that the very air was still and I could hear the ticking of a pulse in my temple, and he began,

"In brief terms, ladies and gentlemen, it is Her Majesty's wish to preserve the peace between her Empire and Imperial Russia. My Lord Audubon, as the subject of Her Majesty most fully conversant with Balkan affairs, has been instructed to convince His Imperial Majesty the Tsar that Britain and Russia must not go to war over Constantinople."

"I wish you every success, my lord!" cried Princess Natasha, raising her champagne glass to the Emissary. "And be assured that I will use every bit of my influence with darling Uncle Alex to further your mission, for I think it would be truly awful if our two empires went to war over silly old Constantinople." She hiccuped and smiled amiably around the gathering.

"I thank you, ma'am," said Lord Audubon, bowing.

Colonel Grant paused a respectful moment, cleared his throat, and resumed:

"The remainder of the party comprises myself. As former assistant military attaché to the Court of St. Petersburg, it will be my duty to advise my lord on the more arcane details of Russian protocol. Also . . ."

"Ah, you should have seen him then!" All eyes turned to Princess Natasha, who was gazing in rapture upon Grant. "A mere lieutenant he was, but already marked for high office. The ladies of the court were swooning for him. *Quel beau sabreur!* I quite lost my heart, I can tell you, though only a child."

Another pause—more painful this time. Another clearing of the throat, and the colonel continued,

"Acting as private secretary to the Envoy Extraordinary will be Miss Augusta Scrase. Miss Scrase, I need hardly add, was private secretary of several successive British Ambassadors to Russia."

"We never met, I think, Miss Scrase," Princess Natasha interposed yet again. "Were you often at the Winter Palace, or at Tsarskoye Selo?"

"My duties took me mostly to Moscow, Princess," came the frigid reply.

"Only the interment of near and dear relations ever takes me to Moscow," said the princess. "Moscow is unbelievably *bourgeois.*"

"*I* did not find it so," responded Miss Scrase, who was not to be put down—she a member of the English upper class—by a mere foreigner, princess or no.

The colonel broke in hastily. "Miss Clarissa Herbert will act as interpreter in German—an important function, since by far the greater part of our journey, from the Rhine to the Russian frontier, will take us through Prussia. Finally, we have the distinguished political correspondents, Messrs. Orwell, Charlot, and Martin, from the United States, France, and England respectively. The special role of these three gentlemen in this mission will be explained by Lord Audubon, who will now address you. My lord." He gave the Emissary a brief bow, turned, and walked in my direction. I felt my skin prickle all over as he passed close by me—so close that the fur trim of his dolman brushed my bare shoulder—and took up a position just behind my chair. To my considerable unease.

In marked contrast to the colonel's, Audubon's delivery was informed by overbearing arrogance. Hand on hip, a sheaf of notes held negligently in the other, he addressed us like a crowd of the no doubt silent and overawed tenants and servants back at his stately home and boundless acres.

"Constantinople is a powder barrel," he boomed, "which, if ig-

nited, will set all Europe ablaze. If the Russian artillery ashore
fire upon the British fleet anchored off the Golden Horn, our
ships will return the fire. The reverse is true also. My task, as
Emissary Extraordinary, with my deep and special knowledge of
Turkey and my close personal friendship with Sultan Abdul
Hamid, is to convince the Tsar that if he orders the withdrawal
of his troops from the gates of Constantinople, the British fleet
will withdraw also, and in return, the sultan will be obliged to
relinquish his Balkan territories of Hungary, Rumania, Bosnia,
Serbia, Bulgaria." He paused, and swept us with his haughty
gaze. "Any questions?" he snapped.

The challenge could only have been intended for the newspapermen. It was quickly taken up.

"Sir, that's a very large assumption you've made," came the
quiet drawl of my new friend Ralph Orwell. "You say that Sultan
Abdul Hamid will hand over all that territory—just like—that?"
The American snapped finger and thumb.

"He will be—persuaded," replied Audubon.

"By you, sir?" asked Orwell. "By reason of your—what was
the phrase—'close personal friendship'?"

"By me—and others," replied Audubon.

"You'll—persuade—him to hand over most of his Balkan pos-
sessions. In return for the Russians not taking Constantinople?
Do I have it aright? And you're going to sell this deal to the
Tsar."

"Precisely!"

The American rubbed his jaw, pinched the tip of his too-short
nose, screwed up his amber-colored eyes, and squinted at the
English aristocrat.

"You'll pardon my mentioning it in passing, Lord Audubon,"
he drawled, "but, speaking as just another wild colonial boy, I'd
say that, with close personal friends like *you* around, Abdul
Hamid sure don't need any enemies. No suh!"

Instantly, the atmosphere in that room was charged with danger. Lord Audubon's pale countenance took on two bright spots
of color, one on each aristocratic cheekbone, and I saw his
fingers tense on the papers that he held. The savage stillness was
broken, and the hideous tension dispersed, by the matter-of-fact
voice of Colonel Grant from behind my left shoulder,

"The matter of the Balkan settlement is irrelevant to our present mission, Mr. Orwell," he said. "We are concerned with preserving the peace of Europe at a time when one salvo of guns could destroy it for a generation! Any further—*relevant*—questions?"

"Yes, sir." It was the Englishman, Martin. Martin the railway enthusiast. "You spoke of the special role that we three correspondents will play in this mission. What, pray, is this role?"

It was Grant who answered. "You, gentlemen, will be privileged to be present at a historic occasion, in return for which privilege, you are put on your honor to divulge nothing about this mission till we have reached St. Petersburg and saved the peace. Then you will have the exclusive right to shout the joyful news from the rooftops of the world. Gentlemen, I well know there will be temptations along the way. On our frequent halts, you will have easy access to telegraph offices, by means of which you will be able to send advance news to your papers. If you value the peace of Europe, gentlemen, you will do no such thing."

The directness, the honest simplicity, of his statement brought the deserved response of a respectful silence. It was the Frenchman Charlot who broke that silence, addressing Lord Audubon.

"Milord," he said, "it is no secret between us, I take it, that there are many who would not wish your mission to succeed?"

"That is so, monsieur," replied Audubon. "There are pro-war parties in your own country, in Prussia, and in Russia." The haughty countenance assumed a contemptuous smile. "In England, we call them 'Jingos,' after a vulgar Music Hall song they have adopted as their war-cry. Yes, there are many who would wish my mission to fail."

"One more question, sir!"

It was Ralph Orwell again . . .

"Yes?" said Audubon.

"Aside from a few flag-waving Jingos, as you call them, and aside from a few more of their ilk on the Continent, are there any real, hard, serious opponents of your peace move?" Orwell paused for a moment. "The sort of people who—who might make a real, serious attempt to prevent you from reaching St. Petersburg?"

Audubon did not reply, but looked down at the papers in his hand.

I seemed to hear again the words of the strangely disturbing oath that Colonel Grant had made me repeat after him in his room at the Paris Embassy:

"I shall . . . carry out such duties as are presented to me . . . no matter what the hazards to me personally."

It was Grant who spoke for Lord Audubon. I looked up to see him there, standing close by my shoulder, his face harsh and impassive.

"No, sir," he said. "We are not anticipating any such move. We are simply taking a pleasant railway journey of some sixteen hundred miles. And no one—no one, sir—is going to stop us!"

A sleepy voice from the edge of the group: We all turned to look at Princess Natasha, who was stretching herself like a newly awakened pussy cat and beaming at us all.

"I do declare, I must have dozed off. When does the train leave?"

The reception over, we trooped out to the waiting train. Princess Natasha in the front, one hand tucked in Lord Audubon's arm, the other holding a pink silk cord at the other end of which trotted her pet poodle.

She called to her maid, who curtsied as her mistress passed through the outer door and onto the red carpet that swept toward the train. "Hortense, go back in there and bring some caviar and a bottle of champagne for darling Pepé's breakfast."

I slid a furtive glance behind me, and could see no sign of Colonel Grant, but Mr. Martin, who was walking behind me, met my eye and was encouraged to quicken his pace.

"You will be most interested in your sleeping car, Miss Herbert," he informed me.

"Indeed?"

"Yes. It was originally built by an American engineer named Colonel Mann, whose initial may still be seen engraved upon the windows, even though the car now bears the livery of the Compagnie Internationale des Wagons-Lits. Now, what d'you think of that, hey?"

"I scarcely know what to say, Mr. Martin," I said, in truth.

"Thought that would surprise you," he declared.

"It does. Oh, it does."

Mr. Martin warmed to his subject. "The present fifty-three sleeping cars," he said, "of which yours is number fifteen, were originally run as Mann's Railway Sleeping Carriage Company Limited. But then Colonel Mann had to sell out . . ."

We were half way down the red carpet. Something—a conjunction of events, the lamplight and the shadows, the soaring roof of the great station, the pedantic voice at my side, the champagne—conspired to give a curiously strange sense of unreality to everything, as if I were not Clarrie Herbert in the there and then, but someone quite different, who was watching, hearing, and feeling through Clarrie Herbert's senses. The sensation, though profoundly disturbing, had overtones of euphoria. I smiled up at my companion.

"What you are telling me is quite fascinating, Mr. Martin," I said. "Please go on. What happened, pray, to Colonel Mann?"

"Well . . ." began the Englishman. But I was not fated to hear the rest of the story. Someone came up behind me, and a pair of hands laid something warm and heavy—a cloak—across my shoulders.

"Miss Herbert." A voice at my ear. It was Colonel Grant. "I almost forgot that I'd brought along for you my old cavalry cloak, since you are departing for Russia at such short notice and the nights can get very cold there, and the wind blows chill off Lake Ladoga, even in the spring."

I looked up at him. His face was in the deep shadow cast by his hussar's fur busby, so I was unable to read the expression in his eyes.

"Thank you, Colonel," I whispered. "I—I will take good care of your cloak."

"No need to return it," he said. "You will put it to good use, I'm sure. Now—this will be your compartment. As you see, there are three such compartments in the *wagon-lit,* and each sleeps two persons. Lord Audubon and I will share one, Princess Natasha and her maid another, and you will share the third compartment with . . ."

"Oh, no!" I cried.

I distinctly felt my jaw fall open, involuntarily, from sheer shock and dismay. His face, now turned to lamplight, showed a tight smile at the corners of his lips. Was he mocking me?

"I'm afraid so," he murmured.

"Not—Miss Scrase!" I pleaded. "Please, Colonel Grant."

"Would that be so awful?" he asked.

"Of course," I told him. "After what happened . . ."

"Your only alternative," he said, "will be to journey in one of the day coaches. They are first class and not uncomfortable, but of course, it would mean that you would have to have a compartment of your own, and since we did not budget for a lady in the day coaches, no fewer than eight men will then have to squeeze into a compartment planned for four, and . . ."

"Please forget what I said, Colonel," I whispered contritely. "I don't want to put so many people to so much trouble. I—I'll share with Miss Scrase."

"The experience might prove to be—not unrewarding," he said. And then I knew for *certain* that he was mocking me.

"I doubt it, Colonel," I replied.

"You might discover that Miss Scrase is a human being after all," he said.

"I know that already," I replied. "Unfortunately, she doesn't seem to be *my* kind of human being!"

He bowed his head then, so I had no means of telling if he was angry or amused.

"Good night, Miss Herbert," he said. "Sleep well. Our first halt will be beyond the Belgian frontier tomorrow morning, at Liège, where we shall all take breakfast, by prior arrangement with the Belgian railways, in a private suite at the station. I do not suppose that we shall get a decent English meal, but have to make shift with the general and austere fare of the Continentals, viz: bread and coffee. You look uncommonly fine in that old cloak of mine, Miss Herbert—I bid you good night." He was gone.

Gone, also, was my late informant, the pedantic Mr. Martin. He was deep in conversation with one of the minor functionaries from the Paris Embassy, by the open door of one of the first-class day coaches, and no doubt regaling him with esoteric railway lore. I looked into the compartment that I was to share with the appalling Miss Scrase, and was agreeably surprised. The furnishings were of maroon plush, with a richly piled carpet of the same hue, and flouncy white curtains drawn across the windows. Two comfortable-looking bunks or cots, set one above the other, occupied one wall of the compartment. Both cots were capable of being discreetly screened by curtains which had been looped back to show brilliant white sheets, suavely quilted covers, pillows surely of swansdown.

The train's whistle screeched. Looking to left and right, I saw that others were entering their compartments. These were the last to mount; Princess Natasha and her maid (and the poodle Pepé), Lord Audubon, and Colonel Grant were already aboard.

Grant . . .

Mounting into the compartment, I touched the smooth, dark blue broadcloth of his old cloak. The tall collar was faced with black Astrakahn fur. A thick band of time-faded gold lace was sewn around the whole, crinkled edge of the garment. It was lined with dark red taffeta. A heavy, warm, lived-in garment which, for a reason that I was not able to define, had become on the instant oddly dear to me.

I was snatched from my reverie by the arrival of Augusta Scrase, who showed by her manner that she was no more pleased with our mutual sleeping arrangement than I. Her luggage—and my own considerably humbler traps—had been placed in the center of the compartment. Her green gaze made a swift calculation of their number, then turned to the two bunks set one above the other.

"I shall have the lower sleeping berth," she said in tones of finality.

I shrugged. "As you like," I said, for it was all the same to me.

Other appointments, screened by a curtain opposite the bunks, included a washbasin and a large pitcher of warm water. An oil lamp hung from the ceiling, and there were candle brackets on both interior walls. A few moments' consideration of our traveling abode revealed that the top bunk let down for daytime and that the lower one served also as a day sofa, and there was a folding table set against the wall. There was also a big brass cuspidor, ashtrays for gentlemen, and the usual minor offices. All in all—Miss Augusta Scrase excepted—the accommodation was in some respects no worse, and in some a very great deal more commodious, than my own narrow room under the eaves back at Mrs. Mount's School for Young Ladies in St. Errol.

In silence, Miss Scrase laid a small valise on her bunk and snapped open the lid to disclose a frilly pink night-shift and a peignoir to match. The train had not yet departed, and the silence and inactivity was oppressive. I made an attempt at conversation.

"Princess Natasha is a very colorful personality. Something of an eccentric, don't you think?"

Coldly, she replied, and without looking up or turning around, "She is Russian aristocracy. What more to say? They ape the English and the French. Scorn to speak their own language, but at bottom, they are no better than their own *moujiks,* the common peasantry. Idle. Incompetent. Inefficient. Filthy."

That seemed to dispose of Princess Natasha! I could not but smile at her sweeping dismissiveness.

There came a tap on the window of the door. It was Colonel Grant. He opened it and, saluting us gravely, said, "We are just about to depart, ladies. We may from time to time stop during the night at various out-of-the-way places, depending upon the exigencies of the service, so I should advise you to lock both of the doors. Our estimated time of arrival at Liège is just before ten o'clock in the morning. I wish you a good night's sleep."

"Thank you, Colonel," I murmured.

Miss Scrase merely nodded coldly. I had the notion that she disapproved of him.

Moments later, to the accompaniment of screeching whistles and the gushing of steam, the special train for St. Petersburg slowly started forward. Taking my place by the window, I watched the dark interior of the great station slide past me with ever increasing rapidity, till we burst out into the night of streaming rain and the tall, lit-up buildings of Paris. The storm still raged. Away in the distance, beyond rooftops and chimney pots, the ragged crest of Montmartre was picked out, in a blinding instant—just as I had identified it on the skyline, in the afternoon of my first unforgettable day in Paris, with the church of Sacre Coeur, stark-white as an iced wedding cake—and was then returned to the concealing darkness.

"I hope," said Miss Scrase, "that it is not your intent to stay up all night. I have had a most tiring day. I may say, a most fraught day. And I wish to retire immediately. Moreover, I cannot sleep with the light on."

"I'm weary, too," I told her. "By all means let us retire."

"I shall now prepare myself for bed," she declared. And, taking her night attire and wash bag, she went behind the curtain. With a shrug, I took out my own things from my old carpet bag, sat down on the edge of her bunk, and waited for madame to complete her ritual of retirement. I had quite a while to wait. The train was out of Paris and stealing across dark and mysterious French farmland by the time she re-emerged: face shiny with white-lead cream, lustrous dark hair concealed within a nightcap, her stately form wrapped in a delectable peignoir.

"I will leave you to extinguish the light," she said, adding, "after not too long an interval, I hope."

My own preparations took very little time, for I had bathed that evening. Nor do I sleep with cream upon my face, reckoning that the summer suns of twenty-five years have put my complexion beyond all repair. Miss Scrase was asleep—or feigning sleep —by the time I came out from behind the curtain, and lay like a beautiful corpse upon a bier, with pale hands folded on her breast, and a ball of cotton wool laid upon each eye.

I whispered my prayers, turned down the lamp, and climbed up into the upper bunk, slipping between suave and deliciously warm sheets (someone had had the forethought to lay a hot-water bottle in there), and pulling Colonel Grant's cavalry cloak over me as a bed cover. In the cosy darkness, I could detect the faint scent of the cloak's former owner: a disturbingly male smell, compounded of well-oiled leather, macassar oil, and the slightest hint of fine cigars. The scent of him prompted me to remember that he was near at hand. Two compartments farther along—for Princess Natasha and her maid were our next door neighbors. I pictured him lying there, awake, perhaps, a late-night cigar clamped between those firm lips. Thinking of—what? Or of whom? Not of the common little chit of a woman on whom as a kind afterthought he had carelessly bestowed an old garment, that was for sure.

With a sigh, I turned over and closed my eyes. The last thing I remember before drifting off was an unfamiliar sound coming from below.

Upper class she might be, haughty lady she might be, but Miss Augusta Scrase snored like any fishwife.

I was riding a fast horse over what must surely have been the Russian steppes, which in my thoughts was a boundless plain of waving grassland, all under a full moon as bright as day. And I was being pursued. This was the hazard of which Colonel Grant had warned me, and my duty was—as I had sworn—to evade my would-be captors and bear news to the Tsar at St. Petersburg.

Bent low over my mount's streaming mane, I cast a swift glance back over my shoulder. There were three of them: faceless men in tall hats. Well mounted. And gaining on me with every stride.

I dug my booted heels into my horse's flanks, whispered into his ear to give me more. More speed. More chance of life. It seemed that he responded, but when I looked back again, the faceless ones were closer still. I cried out in despair.

We fell, then; horse and rider, in a tangle of flying limbs. The ground came up and struck my head, stunning me to unconsciousness, yet, through the darkness, I sensed that all was well. Someone—not the faceless ones—was gathering me up and bearing me away in his arms. I caught the tangy, male scent of leather and macassar oil mixed with cigar.

He bore me up onto his own mount and rode away, leaving the enemy far behind. I was safe. Not wishing to hasten the moment, I delayed opening my eyes to look into his face, savoring the thought of meeting his gaze.

Slowly, sleepily, I opened my eyes. In the stupefying stillness that followed, in the intolerable silence that I was unable to shatter because I could not draw breath to scream, I found myself looking up, not into the face of Colonel Grant, but into the image of death: an eyeless skull.

Still fighting for breath to shape a scream, I woke up, bathed in my own sweat, and sat bolt upright.

It was the sudden stillness that had awakened me, that and the silence. The train had stopped. With a sigh of relief, I made to compose myself again, but as I did so, a shadowy figure passed in front of the window opposite, turned, and looked into the compartment.

I screamed. I was still screaming when the train gave a jolt and began to move again. The sound and the movement woke Miss Scrase. Her white face, a blur from out of the darkness below me, looked up.

"Will you be so good as to cease that vulgar caterwauling at once? Have you taken leave of your senses, woman?"

"Someone—someone was peering in on us!" I faltered.

"Looking in on us?" All the contempt in the world, all the yawning gulf of birth, riches, opportunity, that lay between us was expressed in the inflection of those words. "How in heaven's name could anyone possibly look into this compartment when the train is moving? You *must* be deranged."

I did not argue, but lay back on my pillow. Nor did I sleep again that night. The storm had abated, and the night must have advanced considerably during my disturbing dream, for it seemed no time at all before dawn was pinkly illuminating the ceiling above my head and explaining the shape of Miss Scrase's sable cape that hung at the far side of the compartment.

Later, in the early morning, I lay huddled in my bunk, with the fur collar of Colonel Grant's cavalry cloak pulled closely about my ears, while we curved through mountainous countryside of a mysterious enchantment full of dramatic slopes bristling with pine trees, peaks still bearing the winter's snow, sudden gorges, and unexpected cascades. At full daylight, I lowered myself carefully so as not to wake my companion, washed myself in cold water, cleaned my teeth, plaited my hair up into a chignon, and dressed to face a new day.

At close on ten o'clock, just as the colonel had promised, we steamed into a large station: Liège. And a glimpse through the curtains at the bustle of the workaday world almost—but not completely—banished the feelings of disquiet that my nightmare, and its sinister aftermath, had kindled in my imagination.

Chapter Four

IMMEDIATELY AFTER ARRIVAL, OUR TRAIN MOVED SLOWLY TO A remote part of the station: a quiet backwater, on the one side overhung with newly flowering chestnut trees, and the other commanding a view down to a broad river—which I took to be the Meuse—where quite large vessels plied to and fro, their paddle wheels making complex patterns of herringbone on the still surface of the water.

There came a knock on the door. Unlocking it, I opened it a crack, to reveal the bucolic countenance of Sergeant Gumble, who looked as if he had spent all night polishing his buttons and brushing every last speck of Paris dust from his immaculate blue tunic. He saluted violently.

"The colonel's compliments, ma'am, and will the ladies kindly repair to that building yonder"—he pointed to a quite large house with high gables, green shutters, and flaking cream plasterwork that stood hard by the railway line—"where breakfast will be served."

"Thank you, sergeant."

"Your servant, ma'am!" Another staggering salute, and he was gone.

Something stirred behind me. Turning, I saw Augusta Scrase's eyes regarding me crossly over the edge of her sheets. In the morning light, her greasy face, habitually so marble white, was unhealthily tinged with green in the hollows, and for almost the first time in my life, I was grateful for possessing a complexion like a homely apple—and was instantly contrite when I remembered that I had disturbed her sleep and in all probability given her a bad night.

"Who was that?" she demanded. "And where are we?"

"It was the sergeant," I said, "and we've just arrived in Liège. Breakfast is being served, so I'll leave you alone to get ready. Don't hurry, for I'm sure we've plenty of time." And I smiled.

She frowned. "Did you not call out in the night?"

"I—think I may have," I said.

"Mmmm. I seem to remember your waking me," she said. Another disapproving frown. "Well, will you be so kind as to vacate the compartment so that I can get up in peace?"

I departed. There seemed no profit in trying to ingratiate myself with my traveling companion.

I took my shawl, but it was warm in the morning sunlight. I had descended from the carriage and was crossing the open stretch of cobblestones that led to the cream-colored house with green shutters, when a voice hailed me.

"Young miss! I forget your name. Wait for me!"

It was Princess Natasha. She was dressed in a tartan day gown with a handsome bonnet trimmed in the same material. Her pretty face was radiant with good health and good humor.

"Good morning, ma'am," I said.

"First let me attend to my darling Pepé's needs," she said. "Hortense!"

"*Madame la Princesse* desire? . . ." from the carriage.

"Hortense, you will give the remainder of the caviar to Pepé, together with some champagne."

"Yes, *Madame la Princesse*. How much champagne, *Madame la Princesse?*"

The princess rolled her eyes at me. "*Quelle folle*, as I have told you, my dear," she murmured. "Why, a little less champagne than the little darling demands, you silly creature!"

"Yes, *Madame la Princesse*. I only asked, *Madame la Princesse*, because *le petit* is not himself this morning, and one does not want to . . ."

The Princess rolled her eyes. "Attend to me, Hortense," she said. "After he has fed, you will take him for his constitutional. A quarter of an hour at least, stopping whenever he desires. Then you will tie him up by his lead in a comfortable spot in the shade where he can take a nap. And then you may get yourself some breakfast."

"Yes, *Madame la Princesse*. Thank you, *Madame la Princesse*."

"Come, my dear." The princess took my arm, and together we went to breakfast. "Did you sleep well?" she asked.

"Not very well," I said. "And you?"

"As ever, perfectly," she replied. "And I rose at six o'clock to do my calisthenics. My maternal grandmother, who greatly resembled me in physique and appearance when she was my age, performed calisthenics night and morning, and swam in the River Neva, regularly, in all weathers, till she died at the age of ninety-seven. Now, what do you think of that?"

"Do you do likewise, ma'am?" I asked.

She laughed and squeezed my arm. "I do not," she said. "I am the laziest creature alive, but from time to time I think of grandmama, and then my conscience dictates that I do my calisthenics. Only for five minutes, that's enough. *Too* exhausting!"

"And your maternal grandfather, ma'am, did he, also live to a great age?" I asked her.

"Alas he did not," she replied shortly. "Grandmama was widowed at twenty-three. He was assassinated by a bomb outside the opera house and died in her arms. Ah!—do I smell real Scottish kippers? And in Belgium of all places?"

Upon entering the house, we were greeted by an obsequious servitor in a swallow-tailed coat, who bowed deeply and ushered us into a large chamber, in the center of which an enormous cooking stove glowed redly, and a small army of aproned and white-capped acolytes tended a myriad of saucepans and skillets, cooking pots and frypans, with careful frenzy. The princess and I were the first of the special train's passengers to arrive, and were presented with menus the size of broadsheets. Clearly—and despite Colonel Grant's gloomy prognostications—the Belgian railways had taken most extraordinary trouble to cater for the appetites of their distinguished guests, for there was kedgeree, deviled kidneys, whitebait, Dover sole, and—as the princess had discerned from afar—kippers.

We both settled for the latter: plump fillets of young herring, smoked and salted to perfection and cooked in butter. The coffee, also, was excellent. As we breakfasted, we talked. Princess Natasha's laconic statement about the appalling end of her grandfather had shocked me into the realization of the tremendous disparity of our positions—I and the effervescent and unselfconscious creature who sat by my side, chatting gaily between hearty mouthfuls of her kipper.

Had others of her family suffered the same fate as her grandfather? I asked. Oh, yes, she said airily. Did I not know that no less than three Romanoff Tsars had perished in blood? And even darling Uncle Alex—whose reforms had not been equalled since those of Peter the Great; who had liberated the serfs, brought in trial by jury, and heaven knows what else—even he walked in constant fear of assassination by extremists and revolutionaries. But then, she opined, swallowing the last mouthful of her kipper and sighing with happy repletion as she mopped up the melted butter from her plate with a morsel of fresh-baked bread, were the evils visited upon we Romanoffs any worse than the evils that we Romanoffs have visited upon ourselves—for did not even Peter the Great have his own son, the Tsarevich, flogged to death in the Troubetzkoy jail? I was digesting this morsel of horror when Colonel Grant and Lord Audubon entered the breakfast room, preceded by the bowing servitor.

"Ladies," said the Emissary, "may we join you at table?"

"Do by all means, my lord," said Princess Natasha. She waved a shapely little hand at the nearest acolyte. "And *I* will have another kipper. On second thoughts, I think I will not."

"Good morning, Miss Herbert," said Grant, who seated himself opposite me. "Did you sleep well on the journey from Paris?"

"Yes, Colonel," I lied. For how to begin to explain about a dream involving himself that ended in horror and an apparition which, on reflection, must surely have had a perfectly rational explanation (say, the train stopped at a small, wayside station and was inspected by a railway worker, who just happened to glance into the *de luxe wagon-lit*, to reassure himself that his betters were comfortable)?

I would dearly have wished to have continued my conversation with the colonel, but throwing aside her screwed-up napkin, the princess rose to her feet.

"Come, my dear," she said to me, "there simply *must* be hot water for washing available in this establishment. Let us leave these gentlemen to their breakfast—gentlemen, the kippers are excellent—and avail ourselves. At what hour do we depart, Colonel?"

"At eleven-thirty o'clock, or as near to it as possible, ma'am," said Grant, rising from his seat in concert with the Emissary.

"Or at *your* convenience, ladies," added the latter, fixing Princess Natasha with an intensely ardent glance, which, it not being received, he instantly transferred to me.

The servitor-in-charge, having overheard the princess' remark, bowed deeply and indicated for us to follow him.

The princess took my arm, murmured in my ear, "I grow to like Lord Audubon less and less. The English nobility, you know, are quite insupportable. I could not bear that man's company an instant longer. Do you know, while you were conversing with Colonel Grant, the creature had the effrontery to reach out his foot under the table and touch mine? Would you believe it? They are all alike!

"I remember, when I was a gel, reading of that dreadful Dashwood and his Hellfire Club, all those devilish goings-on. The English aristocracy, you see, my dear, have not constantly been purged of their evil humors. In France, a hundred years ago, their *aristos* were decimated by the brisk medicine of the guillotine. My own family, for all their faults, have never hesitated to cut down the dissolute, the weak, the unreliable members of the *boyar* caste by means of the block, the gallows, secret poisoning, *lettres de cachet,* etcetera.

"Nevertheless," she continued, "it has to be said that I wish Lord Audubon every success in his mission to darling Uncle Alex. Ah!—I think that at last our estimable guide has brought us to hot water. My dear!—a bath! And brimming with hot water! What joy!"

The servitor bowed her into a chamber on the second floor of the house. In it, a couple of smiling maidservants stood, towels in hand like priestesses of some arcane cult, at each side of an enormous copper bath tub, from whose pellucid depths the heady aroma of attar of violets pervaded the entire chamber.

"Till later, my dear," said the princess, squeezing my hand. The door closed upon her. Our guide beckoned me on.

I do not know by what means—save by the obvious disparities of our dress, manner, and deportment—the Belgian railways had discerned the social gulf that lay between Princess Natasha and me, but the distinction was very nicely made. No brimming bath for me; only a handbasin and brass taps of running hot and cold water—but none the less welcome for that—in a sunny room overlooking the station yard, where our train stood sighing occasional gusts of white steam, and the driver and his mate sunned themselves upon the stack of bright coal behind the locomotive. I stripped to my shift and had a good, hot-water wash, and was in the act of drying myself when I glanced out and saw Ralph Orwell and his two colleagues coming over the cobbled yard toward the house for breakfast. They were laughing together, and looked rather crumpled and disheveled, after the manner of men who have slept in their clothes and not washed or shaved. I smiled to myself, wondering if Orwell had quite recovered from all the champagne he had drunk the night before.

With plenty of time before the train's departure, I finished my *toilette* in a leisurely fashion and went out into the station yard by a side exit. My intent was to cross over to where I should have a good view down into the river below and the other part of the city beyond. I had not gone more than a dozen paces before I was brought short by a wail of distress.

"Mam'selle! Mam'selle! Je vous en prie . . ."

It was Hortense, the princess' maid. The "crazy one," as her mistress had unkindly dubbed her. Certainly Hortense fitted the description on this occasion, with her bonnet awry, hair coming down, shawl slipping off, and eyes wild.

"What is it, Hortense?" I demanded of her in her native French. "Calm yourself, girl. Take a deep breath and tell me what ails you."

"It is Pepé!" she cried. "He has broken his lead and run away. Oh, what will the princess say? She will never forgive me if the little one comes to harm—never!"

"Show me where," I told her. "He can't possibly have gone far in this short while. When did you last see him?"

"Five minutes—ten." She had no way of knowing, and was too distraught to think clearly, but she still retained just enough composure to lead me to a bank of trees at the side of the house, where, tied to a new spring shoot growing from the bole of one of them, was part of the pink silk cord that served as the little dog's lead.

"He has broken it, you see, mam'selle," cried Hortense. "Or chewed it through. And now where has he gone, I ask you?"

I stooped and picked up the end. With a sudden unease, coupled with a presentiment of tragedy that was quite unaccountable, I saw quite clearly that the strong silk cord had not been broken or chewed through, but had been cleanly cut, as with a sharp knife.

There did not seem any point in further disturbing the maid by telling her *that*.

"Hortense, go and find Colonel Grant," I ordered. "Tell him to come quickly."

Dry-eyed and entirely in command of her emotions (for centuries of usage instills an inherited iron self-control in those of high aristocratic birth), the princess stated quite flatly that the train was not continuing its journey till Pepé was found, or, alternatively, she, Princess Natasha Bibescu, was not continuing with the train should they be so heartless as to order its departure. And she offered them the option by not going into her compartment, but by perching herself upon a packing case some distance from the train, where she sat, perfectly composed, plump hands resting upon the crook of her parasol, looking into the middle distance.

The Emissary and Colonel Grant were in a quandary that did not keep them guessing for long: on a mission of great delicacy to the Tsar of All the Russias, one does not leave His Imperial Majesty's favorite niece sitting in a railway yard. The two men exchanged a grim glance, a nod.

"Start searching, everyone!" snapped the colonel. "Look in the yard and in the building where we had breakfast. Beat those bushes over there."

All of us, the train's passengers, made to obey. The princess continued to sit where she was, no doubt content that the whole entourage was sufficient to restore to her her beloved pet. Ralph Orwell met my eyes, grinned.

"You've got to admire Natasha's style," he said. "I'm laying ten to one that we leave here with the dog, even if she has to call out the entire Liège police force to help find him."

"He'll not be found. This is simply a show of good intent." The speaker was Colonel Grant. Casting a glance toward the princess, he went on, "Miss Herbert's right. The lead was cut with a knife."

"The dog was stolen, you mean?" asked Orwell.

"It's a valuable animal," said Grant. "And did you not see its collar? Studded with diamonds. The thief will be miles away by now. We'll make a good search. After that, I'm sure the princess will be reasonable and allow us to proceed." He frowned. "I hope."

"Come, Miss Herbert," said Orwell. "Let us search together."

The American and I walked to that part of the yard which overlooked the river. I felt his eyes on me.

"You look as if you slept well, Clarissa," he said.

"Moderately," I replied. "And you?"

"I and my fellow members of the Fourth Estate sat up and addressed ourselves to a very excellent bottle of French brandy," he replied. "And discussed certain odd features of this expedition. While diverting in the extreme, it was not conducive to what you would call a good night's sleep."

I looked at him sharply. The good-humored eyes were watchful, and I had the impression that he was trailing his cloak for an exchange of confidences. So I obliged him.

"What odd features, in particular, did you discuss?" I asked him.

"Mainly, the composition of the party," he said. "This stemmed from a remark that Jules Charlot made at the reception last night. I think you were with us at the time."

I remembered. "He spoke about me and others of the party," I said. "He put it to you as a sort of riddle. Did he provide the answer to that riddle?"

"He did not," said Orwell. "But he defined the questions more clearly. And we still do not have the answers. Not even after a long night over a bottle of excellent brandy."

"And what are the questions?" I asked him.

We had reached the end of the yard, and the top of the bank that fell gently away to water meadows, full of fat cattle, that lined the river far below. Previously hidden from view by the slope of the ground, we could now see that the limit of the railway property was bounded by a high iron fence with spikes on top. No man, and not even a small dog, could have squeezed through that barrier.

"I reckon we'd best go across to the other side and help the colonel search the bushes yonder."

We retraced our steps.

"The questions?" I prompted him.

"The first is easy," he said. "The second you aren't going to like."

"Indeed?" I said, puzzled. "Please go on."

"This was Charlot's first question, and it's a good one," he said. "Now, it's perfectly normal, on a diplomatic mission of this kind, to invite accredited political journalists to accompany the party. What is odd—and unusual—in this present case is that not one of us, not Martin, Charlot, or I, have any knowledge or experience whatever of Russian affairs, since all of us are specialists in the politics of western Europe and America. And not one of us speaks a single word of Russian. It's almost as if we were hand picked for our—in this case—unsuitability for the job. And the same goes for you, Clarissa, Clarissima!"

"Oh, *does* it?" I cried, and I felt my redhead's temper rise.

"Which brings me to the second question," said Orwell. "Why are you, of all people, picked as interpreter, little Miss Herbert? Are you telling me that the might and majesty of the British Empire doesn't have a team of highly trained interpreters in all languages at one of their most prestigious embassies in Europe, but that they have to fall back on the services of a little schoolma'am who happened along to teach the rudiments to Lord Audubon's six-year-old?"

I faced him. "Sir, you are very rude!" I snapped.

He grinned his lop-sided grin. "Not unintentionally, Clarissa," he said. "For, as one of your countrymen said, 'A gentleman is never rude, save by deliberate intention.'"

"I doubt if the definition embraces you, nevertheless, Mr. Orwell!" I retorted, and turning on my heel, I swept away with as much dignity as I could muster, and remembered to keep my head high. "Little schoolma'am," indeed. A fig for him. And, besides, I told myself ruefully—it was too near the truth for comfort.

I came upon Colonel Grant, who was treading through knee-high grass in the bushes at the far side of the station yard, among stunted rhododendron bushes. As much to gain some protection from more of the American's frank speaking as deliberately to seek the company of the man I found both fascinating and disturbing, I went closer to him. And saw him suddenly start, stare at the ground ahead of him, and exclaim aloud.

"By heaven! Who could do such a thing?" he cried.

I gasped and stepped forward the few paces that separated us. Looking down into the grass where Grant's gaze was directed, I caught a brief glimpse of a scrap of white fur dabbled with bright carmine—before Grant's broad shoulder was interposed.

"Don't look, Miss Herbert," he said. "It's not for a woman's eyes!"

"Oh, how awful!" I choked. "Why would *anyone* . . ."

But he had already dismissed me from his mind.

"A warning! My God—it's begun already!"

He said it softly, so softly that I might have mistaken the words if I had not been so close to him.

Then he stooped, and, a moment later, handed me the little dog's diamond-studded collar.

"Break the news to her, please, Miss Herbert," he said. "With —reservations."

"But what happened to him, my dear? You say my darling Pepé met with an accident. What *sort* of accident?"

"Well, ma'am . . ." I looked out of the carriage window, but found no inspiration from the passing countryside.

"No, do not tell me!" she interposed, holding up an imperious, plump hand. And her diamond bracelets jangled. "I am too tenderhearted. Too, too susceptible in sensibility to bear the awful truth that I see in your face. Tell me only, my dear, that my darling did not suffer. Tell me that, do." The lovely blue eyes, now that uncertainty had given way to knowledge, now that she was alone with me and her maid, were brimming with tears.

"I'm sure he did not suffer," I said.

She closed her eyes and sat back in the sofa that we shared.

"I thank St. Andrew and St. Gregory," she breathed.

The news that Pepé had been killed, when I had broken it to

her, had called from her the simple request that I share her compartment for the next stage of our journey, which was to Cologne. It was a request—accompanied, as it was, by a tender, impulsive squeeze of hands—to which I was glad to agree. And now we were sitting side by side on the lower bunk, made up into a sofa, while the maid, Hortense, was in an armchair opposite, sewing a patchwork quilt and eyeing us from time to time—grateful, no doubt, that she had been absolved from all blame for the little dog's death.

"Travel is so boring," said the princess presently, opening her eyes. "And I must put darling Pepé's sad end from my mind. Divert me, my dear Miss Herbert. Tell me of yourself. Your personal life, not the boring details of where you were born, where educated, etcetera, etcetera." She tapped my arm with her fan. "Tell me, I beg you, of your *amours*."

The maid Hortense giggled, changed it to a cough, and readdressed herself to the patchwork.

Amused despite myself, I replied, "Princess, I'm afraid the story of my *amours* would scarcely divert you for longer time than it would take to tell—which is a very short time indeed."

Her blue eyes widened in surprise. "But you have received—and rejected—offers of marriage, surely?" she said. "I have in my time rejected no less than eleven suitors, and I except my late-husband, Count Bibescu. Why, I was married and a widow by the time I was twenty. And you are? . . ."

"Twenty-five," I admitted. "An old maid, already. Left upon the shelf."

She stared at me for a moment, then pointed at me.

"I have it!" she exclaimed. "I see it in your eyes, my dear. You have loved and you have lost, as the phrase is. What happened, my dear? Did your beloved die? Was he taken from you by the cruel hand of war, like so many? Tell me, do! I sense a great tragedy here. We Romanoffs have the gift of being able to pierce beyond the veil and perceive things that are hidden from the common ruck of human kind."

There was no evading the issue. The princess was too persistent, too warm of heart, to be denied. But I could have done without the maid's presence when I was about to bare my hurts.

We had been speaking in French. It was in English that I responded to the princess' invitation to confidences—a language totally incomprehensible to Hortense.

"There was—someone," I admitted. "We were affianced—almost."

"And what happened, my dear?" breathed my confidante, touching my hand. "Did he forsake you for another? Tell me quickly. I am breathless with concern for you."

I thought back to Richard. Did he indeed leave me for another, in a sense? Had he already half-decided, before that disastrous dinner party at the Palace, that his happiness—not to mention his fortune—lay with Felicity Millhench, rather than with me?

"There *was* someone else," I admitted. "Though the actual break between us was brought about by my own folly."

"Folly—why folly?"

I thought for a few moments, trying to assemble it properly.

"Well," I said presently, "considering my attributes—considering that I have no fortune, am not particularly good to look upon, and am already twenty-five, an age, in the society in which we live, that is tantamount to being an old maid—taking all those things into account, some would think that I threw aside my chances too soon, and delivered him up to the other woman too readily, without a fight."

The princess shook her head sadly. "You suffer many grave disadvantages, my dear," she said. "In a world dominated by men, a woman of no fortune can scarcely hope to be more than chattel. As for your age and your looks"—she made small, fussy gestures with her hands, and I could see that the good-hearted soul was trying to think of comforting things to say, small white lies—"twenty-five is a *nice* age. I have known many suitable marriages contracted where the lady was twenty-five, or even older. Touching on your looks—why, my dear, the very goodness shines through you. Your eyes are very fine, and your hair—most striking. And your complexion"—she reached out to touch my cheek, my rosy apple cheek, seemed about to make some definitive comment, but changed her mind—"charming. Quite charming."

"So that's my story," I said. "You have heard it all, ma'am—the true account of my *amours*."

Her eyes twinkled, and she smiled archly. "Ah, but that is not the end of the story, eh, my dear? There is more, is there not?"

I looked at her in blank astonishment.

"Princess—I—you have the advantage of me," I murmured.

She wagged her finger, as one does to a teasing, recalcitrant child. "Come, come, Miss Herbert," she chided. "You can trust me. I, who have eyes to see for myself. And I a Romanoff, who can perceive much that is hidden from others."

"Ma'am, I don't know what you're talking about," I told her.

"Have I not seen your looks?" she cried.

"My—looks?"

"The first time I saw you together," she said. "I *knew!* I saw it written in your eyes!"

"Knew—*what?*" I cried.

"Knew that you loved him to utter distraction," she replied. "Now, do not deny it."

"Loved—*who?*" I cried.

"Why—Colonel Grant!"

"Colonel Grant?"

"You are in love again," she said. "But you may be sure, my dear, that your tender secret is safe with me."

I stared at her, between despair and bewilderment. "It's not true!" I breathed. "I scarcely know him, and I'm not the sort to fall like a silly schoolgirl for . . ." I broke off, appalled.

She smiled, shrugged. "I accept the mild rebuke, my dear," she said. "I, myself, was a silly schoolgirl, scarcely more, when I also fell in love with Jack Grant at first sight. But, my dear, like all silly schoolgirls, I grew into a woman, with duties and responsibilities. A princess of the blood Royal, furthermore, whose duty lay in furthering the interests of our dynasty, to which end, I was on offer to the most eligible bachelors among the Royal families and higher nobilities of Europe. Do you know, your own dear Queen would not have been averse to my marriage with either Prince Arthur or Prince Leopold, but I fancied neither. I think— I think I might have accepted the Prince of Wales, though he is ten years older than I, and more. But he was already married. Such a jolly fellow."

"Ma'am . . ." I began.

"Our cases are *quite* different, my dear," she continued. "I was a headstrong, impulsive gel at the time. You are a woman of mature tastes and some experience—though, from what you have told me and implied, not a great *deal* of experience—of the world. I was, and am, a person circumscribed by blood and rank. While you, yourself . . ." She made an expressive gesture of her hands to imply what I was, and her bracelets jangled.

"Ma'am," I said. "I am willing to concede, as one confidante to another, that I find Colonel Grant very attractive—what woman of any sensibility would not?—but if I am in love with him as you believe I am, then I am all unaware of it."

Again that pointing finger, the searching glance, the gently persistent tones. "This attraction you feel, my dear, be sure that it is love—the love that a mature woman feels for a man who is eminently endowed, in all respects, to make her a proper spouse."

At that moment, the train passed through a dark tunnel, rendering—by reason of darkness and an intolerable clattering and reverberation of sound, coupled with the stink of smoke—any conversation impossible. We emerged into the daylight again, coughing and spluttering with the smoke. The maid Hortense, having opened a window and wafted most of it away with her patchwork, I responded to the princess' assertion—for I had had time to think it out.

"Ma'am," I said, "with respect, you are mocking me."

She threw up her hands in horror. "Miss Herbert, my dear Miss Herbert, surely you would not think . . ."

"Ma'am, you mock me unknowingly," I said. "Unknowing of the true disparity between Colonel Grant and myself. Even supposing that my attraction to Colonel Grant is indeed, as you surmise, a manifestation of true love, what hope for me as far as he is concerned? No—wait, let me finish, ma'am! Colonel Grant is an officer and a gentleman. In my country—as, surely, in your own—that designation is *carte blanche*. It conveys upon the bearer a *cachet* that separates him from all the rest. I am part of all the rest. My father, ma'am—and I am not ashamed to tell you this—was a commercial traveler in corsets."

To my continuing amazement, the princess was not at all put out, but lightly tapped me on the cheek again and smiled serenely, like someone who holds the key to a great truth that will refute all doubts, all arguments.

"No matter, my dear," she said. "Your humble antecedents are no barrier to your suitability for Jack Grant. As I will presently prove to you."

I shook my head, bemused. "Ma'am, I don't understand."

"There is no reason why you should," she replied. "But I am going to tell you a story that will make it all plain.

"Now, you must appreciate that, while still a young gel impossibly infatuated with this English officer at the Imperial Court, I took the trouble to find out everything there was to know about him, to which end I wheedled out of the *chef de cabinet* of the secret police the confidential dossier on Jack Grant. Oh, you may look surprised that such a thing existed, but you do not know our Russian mentality. No person would be allowed close access to the Tsar whose background had not been investigated in the most minute particulars. From that dossier I learned all there was to know about the man I loved—all the things that, added together, made up the whole man. And here is one part that will touch your heart and give you hope . . ."

I remember Princess Natasha's words as if it was only yesterday that I sat with her in that swaying carriage, with the iron wheels rattling over the north European plain in the springtime; and the story she told then, the details heightened, I do not doubt, by the love of deep emotional drama that characterizes her race. The facts, however, needed no embellishment. They existed on their own, stark and poignant.

Jack Grant's father, she told me, like his own father before him had been a soldier. Jack's grandmother was a widow. Daughter of a duke, she was an imperious matriarch and chatelaine of a great country mansion and estate that she held in her own right. When she died, her son Harry—Jack's father—would succeed to the palatial seat, those boundless acres. Meanwhile, Harry must distinguish himself in the army and marry—not too soon, for there is no worse bar to a subaltern's career than an early marriage, however suitable—some nice girl whom Mother herself would choose. A daughter of the nobility, like herself. It scarcely mattered if she was without fortune for Harry would have fortune and to spare. What mattered was blood and birth. The right sort of stock, to breed heirs who would, in their turn, succeed to the inheritance.

Alas for Mother's hopes. Serving with his regiment in Aldershot, Harry suffered an accident while riding on Salisbury plain, when his horse, frightened by an adder, reared up and threw him against a dry-stone wall. A young woman driving by in a governess cart saw the stunned man and, after tending to him as best she could, helped him into her cart and drove him to the infirmary at Salisbury.

On the way, they talked, as a young man and woman will; each searching out the other. From his manner only—for he was not in uniform—she gleaned that he was in the army and undoubtedly an officer. He received a less clear impression of her, reckoning her to be gently reared, a parson's or a doctor's daughter perhaps. They parted at the hospital. He to have his broken leg put right, and she gave her promise—eagerly sought by him —to visit him soon. She did so the next day.

They spent some hours together, that summer's day, while he lay with his broken leg. What passed between them will never be known, for all the expertise of the Russian secret police was not privy to the confidences exchanged between those two young people whom fate had thrown together. At the end of that time, Harry's mother arrived, having been summoned from her broad acres in the north country. She saw the girl and formed her own opinion of her, was scrupulously civil, and with devastating courtesy even accompanied her to the door and saw her on her way before returning to her injured son's bedside.

Some of the words that then passed between Harry and his mother were actually noted down verbatim in the secret dossier, for there were witnesses present—a nurse and a doctor. In a matter of hours, those words were all over the hospital. Within days, they were being laughed at in every mess within the Aldershot garrison.

Harry's comment when his mother returned from seeing the young woman off the premises:

"Jolly fine gel, that, Mater. Hadn't been for her, I might have stayed out there all night."

Lady Alice's reply:

"Yes. A very decent creature. I gave her a sixpence for her pains."

"I say, Mater, that's rather thick. A dashed insult."

"My dear boy, she's nothing but a common private soldier's daughter."

And Harry's reply:

"That's as may be. I know it, Mater. But I'm going to marry her for all that!"

There is no record of Lady Alice's reaction, but it does not greatly tax the imagination to picture her horror. The first shock over, it must have occurred to her that her son had suffered some passing injury to the brain—a temporary aberration that, like his broken leg, would swiftly heal. Alas for Lady Alice. When Harry returned to his mother's stately home a month later on sick leave, his resolve was unchanged. He would marry his Mary come what may.

The mother must have pointed out that he would be committing social suicide. He would have to resign his commission for a start. He would be blackballed from the Cavalry Club. Hostesses in London and the Shires, to whom, as one of the most eligible young bachelors in the country, he had been a heaven-sent adornment for their guest lists, would drop him immediately—had, indeed, already consigned him to a limbo, pending the outcome of the astounding rumors that were circulating about him.

And when he said that, notwithstanding, he was going through with the marriage, Lady Alice threw down her trump card: Marry that gel and I disown you!

Harry left his mother's stately home within an hour of entering it. He never returned.

The following day, he resigned his commission. A month later, he and his Mary were married in an obscure South London church, and the bride wore white. The Russian dossier noted that, despite his resignation, despite his blackballing at the Cavalry Club, despite the fact that it was not at St. Margaret's, Westminster, that the nuptials were held, half a dozen of his former comrades-in-arms journeyed down to Camberwell and made an archway of their sabers for the happy couple to walk under. Married at last, they went to live in a tidy little terrace house, and Harry Grant, sometime cavalry subaltern and darling of the

Society hostesses, got himself employment as a coal merchant's clerk at the wage of seventeen shillings and sixpence a week—the very figure was recorded in the secret police dossier and faithfully remembered by Princess Natasha.

Alas for good intentions. Nothing happened to mar the love that bound Harry and his Mary. The little house in the quiet back street remained a heaven on earth, all the misfortunes that fate might have heaped upon the young couple could never have changed that. But when a man has known the wild joy of feeling a cavalry charger between his knees, and has worn the uniform of the Queen in company of brave men, everything else, however desirable, can never be better than second best. And poring over dusty ledgers and cash books in a coal merchant's yard was far from second best.

Mary must have seen the canker of wanting and needing in him, and it must have been almost with relief that she met the inevitable blow. He must go back to the army. To the cavalry. Not as an officer—that was quite out of the question—but as a private soldier, a trooper of horse. Not, of course, in his former regiment—that also was out of the question.

So it was Trooper Harry Grant, gentleman ranker. And his Mary gave up her little house in the quiet back street and followed her man, living in barracks as she, a common soldier's daughter, had lived for so long. And it was in the barrack infirmary—the place and date faithfully recorded in the dossier —that she gave birth to a man child and named him Jack.

Soon after that, the British Empire became embroiled in yet another of the far-flung wars that flare up like forest fires—no sooner stamped out in one place than to begin elsewhere—throughout the possessions upon which the sun never sets. This time it was India. And Harry's regiment of hussars was ordered out there to ride against the Sikhs who had dared to take arms against the Queen.

It is certain that Mary and the baby were on the quayside when the great troopship sailed away, decks scarlet and blue with massed soldiery. They never saw him again. A few months later, in his first affray with the rebels, Trooper Grant was killed in what was described as "glorious circumstances." When his colonel was struck from his horse, the gentleman ranker, in complete disregard for his own life, dismounted and, throwing the wounded officer across his own mount, slapped its rump with the flat of his saber blade and sent it galloping to safety. The incident was witnessed by the whole regiment, who also saw the gentleman ranker cut down, still fighting.

Mary herself was summoned to Buckingham Palace to receive her dead husband's medal—a stamped-out disc of metal and a scrap of watered silk in exchange for a beloved life—from the hand of the little woman who ruled over half the earth. Nor was that the only token of regard for Harry's gallantry. The officers and men of his regiment banded themselves together to be surrogate fathers to Harry's boy. Little Jack was adopted as a child of the regiment. Showing early promise, no expense was spared in his education, and he was sent to the same famous school that his own father—along with the highest born in the land—had attended. After school, the Royal Military College at Sandhurst, there was a year at the prestigious Prussian Academy of War in Potsdam ("Which is where he achieved the dueling scar on his cheek, my dear. The badge of *un vrai beau sabreur, n'est-ce pas?*"), and after that a commission in the regiment to which his hero father had brought an undying glory.

At this point in her story, the princess broke off, her baby-blue eyes soft with compassion.

"My dear, I have made you cry," she said. "Here, take my handkerchief. There's a clean bit, see? Ah, my dear, you are so gentle hearted. And so much in love, that is certain. Well, what do you think of him now, eh? Do you think for one moment that, with a mother and father like his—a couple who gave everything for their love—what you call the disparity between you could ever weigh in his considerations?"

I dabbed my eyes. "I—I don't know what to say, ma'am," I told her in truth. "It was a beautiful and sad story. I am sure that, remembering his parentage, Colonel Grant will be entirely free of any prejudice when he comes to marrying the woman of his choice. But—I have to admit that I don't see myself in that role. For, despite what you say, I have no real knowledge of my true feelings for him. And I am quite sure that he thinks of me as nothing but a piece of furniture."

She seized my hands and squeezed them companionably. "Let

time tell, my dear," she said. "A week, a little more, when you have come to know him better, you will know the workings of your own heart better also. And I will help you and advise you all I can, for not only am I a Romanoff, with a Romanoff's prescience, but I am also a woman of the world, having been wedded, bedded, and widowed before I was twenty."

"You are very kind," I told her.

She embraced me lightly, kissing me on both cheeks. "From today, you are my friend," she declared. "And I will call you Clarissa, for that is your name, is it not?"

"Or Clarrie," I said. "That is the pet name my family gave me."

"Clarrie it shall be, then."

She embraced me again.

"And I will call you Natasha," I said.

She shook her head. "No, my dear, you will continue to address me as 'Princess,' 'Princess Natasha,' or 'ma'am,'" she replied. And not by so much as a flicker did her eyes cease to express warmth, nor did the friendly smile diminish. "And now, I think we will have some champagne. Hortense—the champagne!"

I was a newcomer to the business of having a princess for a friend—but learning fast.

Hortense produced from a cooler an enormous bottle of champagne, which she proceeded to open.

"This will be an excellent *apéritif*," declared the princess. "I am presuming that we shall arrive in Cologne for a late luncheon, and I see that the time"—she consulted a jeweled watch that hung from a slim gold chain about her neck—"the time is one o'clock. How pleasantly the hours have flown. How diverting it has been to speak of *amours* and forget for a while my grief at the passing of my poor darling little Pepé. Do we have any caviar remaining, Hortense?"

"A little, *Madame la Princesse*."

"Then serve it also, when you have finished struggling with that cork," she said, adding as an "aside" to me, "That I should be blessed with that creature as a lady's maid! *Quelle folle!*"

"You never finished the story," I reminded her. "Having

brought me to the part where Jack Grant gained a commission in his father's old regiment, you broke off, leaving me in suspense. What happened after? Is his mother still living? And what of the grandmother? Was Lady Alice ever reconciled with them?"

The princess looked arch. "I am able to answer all those questions, my dear Clarrie," she informed me. "Which I will proceed to do over a glass of champagne and some of that excellent ikra caviar. Hortense! Have you still not managed to remove that cork? Push harder at it, stupid creature! Use your thumbs!"

"*Oui, Madame la Princesse,*" whined the unhappy woman, struggling hard to force out the recalcitrant cork. "But it is very . . . aaaaah!"

With a tremendous report, the cork was ejected from the neck of the bottle, to strike the wall immediately above my head with considerable force. Immediately after, I was sprayed from neck to waist by a cascade of foaming, ice-cold liquid that drenched my blouse.

"*Stupide!*" cried the princess.

"Mam'selle, I am sorry . . ." wailed Hortense.

"It's nothing," I said, dabbing at my blouse.

"Get mam'selle something dry to wear," commanded the princess. And when the maid looked at her, open-mouthed, "From my luggage, you silly woman. Don't ask me from *which* trunk or suitcase. *You* are supposed to have packed them, not I. Produce a blouse, or a coatee. Something that mam'selle can wear till we reach Cologne and she can get to her own baggage. Hurry, do!"

I shrugged out of my wet blouse, which, fortunately being a dark color and patterned, was not likely to be harmed from being sprayed by the light-colored wine. And, after a few moments' consideration of the princess' formidable pile of luggage (which was all of matching crocodile skin, each piece embellished with a discreet coronet and the initial "N"—and there was more of it, much more, in the luggage van), Hortense opened the lid of a suitcase and recoiled with a shrill cry of alarm.

"What *is* the matter?" demanded the princess.

"The clothes—all your clothes!" cried the maid.

"What of them?"

"They have all been—disturbed!"

"What *are* you saying?"

Rising, we both crossed the compartment to where Hortense stood staring into the opened suitcase. One glance was enough to see that something more than bad packing, or clumsy handling, had caused the jumbled chaos within. It was as if the suitcase had been upturned so that the contents had fallen out onto the floor, and had then been screwed up and roughly crammed back in again.

As if—the word came into my mind, and with it a shudder of sudden unease—as if it had been *searched*. And by someone in a hurry.

"Open the others!" Princess Natasha snapped the order in a voice of ice.

"*Oui, Madame la Princesse.*" With trembling fingers, the maid laid the rifled suitcase on the floor and addressed herself to the one underneath. It presented the same story of brutal disarray. So did a third. And a fourth and last. All of the cases were unlocked. One container only—the princess' jewel case—had remained locked during the journey.

Upon examination, we found that the hinges at the back of the jewel case had been wrenched off, as if by a sharp instrument. The lid opened to the princess' touch. Inside, a veritable Aladdin's cave in miniature: diamonds, pearls, rubies, sapphires, emeralds—all in abundance—set in bracelets, necklaces, tiaras, brooches, earrings. And the velvet-lined interior was brimming full.

"We will soon see if anything has been taken," said the princess in a tight voice. "Do you have the inventory, Hortense?"

The maid had the inventory in her reticule: a square plaque of ivory with a three-column list penned upon its smooth surface in a tight, clerkish hand. I read out the list, while Princess Natasha delved into the Aladdin's cave and produced each named item, laying it upon the sofa, side-by-side with the next: a growing row of glittering toy soldiers.

". . . Tiara—diamond and emerald, with St. Andrew's cross surmounting."

"Yes." Her acknowledgment.

"Ring—oval, with diamond surrounded by pearls. And earrings to match."

"Yes."

"Gold necklace and pendant of a single sapphire, plain."

"That was my grandfather's wedding present to my grand-mama. She was wearing it for the opera when he died in her arms. His blood was never washed from it. I thank God that it has been spared."

"Another pendant. A brooch bearing an enameled representation of St. Basil, set in a border of alternate diamonds and rubies."

"Yes. That is the last. Nothing is missing. Nothing." The princess laid the last of her jewels with the rest and met my gaze. Her lovely eyes—so often brimming with gaiety—were curiously cold, almost cruel. I thought that I saw the long roll call of Romanoffs reflected there, and seemed to hear the screams of tortured men and women, the hiss of descending knouts upon bare flesh, the thud of an executioner's axe.

"Why?" she asked, simply. "Will you tell me why?"

"I can't begin to imagine," I replied. "Why a thief would rifle that treasure chest and go away empty-handed. It—it beggars all belief. Unless . . ."

"Unless—*what?*" Again, the hiss of the knout.

"Unless whoever searched your baggage—and when could that person have done it, Princess? In Paris, before you went into your compartment, or while we were breakfasting in Liège?—unless that person was no thief, but a spy."

"A spy?" she shrugged her shapely shoulder. "We Romanoffs are beset with spies. Spies in our own employ, and that of our enemies. Spies and assassins. But why *me*, of all the Romanoffs? I am not what you call a 'political.' My Uncle Alex loves me very dearly, but, despite what I have said to Jack Grant, my influence with the Tsar will permit me to accompany him and the Emissary Extraordinary to the threshold of Uncle Alex's study and no farther. I am known to the world as pleasure-loving Princess Natasha Bibescu, my dear Clarrie. I will tell you my haunts. My haunts are these: In the spring, as now, I make a brief visit to Russia to see Uncle Alex in St. Petersburg and my brother at our estates in the Ukraine. Summer will find me in Biarritz, which I adore. In the fall, I take the waters of Baden-Baden or your English spas of Bath or Cheltenham. Winter, for me, is Monte Carlo —always. My *pied-à-terre* in between traveling is a pretty little château in Nantes that I inherited from my late husband. That is my life. What possible interest could a spy—or his employers —have in a woman such as I?"

I had no answer for her. Hortense began the daunting task of repacking the tousled mess, after handing me a patterned silk blouse to put on. The rest of the journey was punctuated by the maid's quiet sniveling as she went about her work. Nor did Princess Natasha rebuke her and command silence, but sat with her gaze directed out of the window at the passing landscape, lost in her own thoughts.

I did not make any attempt to draw her out—no repetition of my request for the remainder of Jack Grant's story—but puzzled my mind about the strange occurrence of the rifled baggage, which seemed all of a piece with that other disquietening incident in Liège, the killing of the dog.

What was it, I asked myself, that Grant had muttered half to himself?

"A warning! My God—it's begun already!"

I was still puzzling over the uneasy enigma when our train clattered into Cologne and drew to a halt in a vast and busy station. Taking leave of the princess, I alighted and went to my own quarters next door to fetch a clean handkerchief, and was immediately assaulted by the blazing eyes and accusing voice of Augusta Scrase, who stood in the center of the compartment, arms akimbo, hands upon her slim hips, bosom heaving with emotion.

"My luggage has been interfered with!" she blazed. "Do you know anything about it?"

Chapter Five

BEFORE I COULD ASSEMBLE MY THOUGHTS, BEFORE I COULD EVEN summon up a fury of indignation at the woman's grotesque insinuation, her cry had summoned others: Jack Grant, Orwell, and the Englishman Martin peered in through the door.

"What's amiss, ladies?" demanded Grant.

Miss Scrase pointed. "Look at that!"

Her cases and trunks lay open on the floor all around her. And their contents were in the same jumbled mess that we had found in the princess'.

I said, "Miss Scrase is trying to tell you that her luggage has been opened and rifled. And I think she has some notion that I had a hand in it."

"I said no such thing!"

"You implied it!"

We faced each other, eye to eye.

A discreet cough from Jack Grant disturbed the unnerving tension. "Hem! Ladies, let us retain our sense of proportion. I am quite sure that Miss Scrase implied no such thing, though it is likely that, upset as she is, she might have given that impression."

"Was anything stolen, ma'am?" This from Ralph Orwell.

"I think not," said Augusta Scrase, eyeing me up and down. "It appears that the—person concerned—was merely satisfying his —or her—curiosity about my belongings. Everything has been picked over, handled, examined. My letters taken out and read, my diary riffled through, I don't doubt." Her aristocratic nose twitched with distaste. "I feel as if I have been—soiled!"

"And you, Miss Herbert—have your belongings been similarly interfered with?" asked Grant.

His reflective gray eyes upon me, I looked away. "I—I don't know," I faltered.

"I think you should find out," he said quietly.

I guessed my ill-luck, and would have given anything to have opened my humble carpet bag and my worn old suitcase, to reveal the telltale mess. But there they were—the few possessions that I had managed to assemble in a lifetime—the clothes all neatly folded and sprinkled with dried lavender, a slim bundle of letters tied in ribbon, my new diary lying untouched at the bottom of the pile. I felt the color mount in my cheeks, and would have wished myself anywhere else but within the scope of their probing eyes.

"The princess' things have been disturbed also," I said in a voice that did not sound like my own.

"Humph!" was Miss Scrase's comment.

"Is that so?" said Grant. "Well, I don't like it. Enquiries must be made. But first, Miss Herbert, there is a more immediate problem which calls for your excellent and idiomatic command of the German language."

"Yes?" I said, relieved at the abrupt change of subject, though unpleasantly conscious that Augusta Scrase was still glaring at me with undisguised hostility.

"Immediately upon our arrival," said Grant, "and without a word of explanation, the locomotive that had drawn us all the way from Paris disappeared from sight, along with the two coaches ahead of us. At present, this *wagon-lit* and the luggage van in the rear are standing all alone. My enquiries have brought forth no coherent explanation, for there is a fellow out there in fancy attire who does not appear to understand his own language, or at least not in the turn of phrase that I picked up as a cadet at Potsdam. Would you please be so kind as to request him to give us back the rest of our train at once, or in time for us to resume the journey immediately after luncheon?"

"Colonel, if I may interject?" said the English journalist, blinking nervously at Grant through his thick pince-nez.

"Yes, Mr. Martin?"

"Ah, this carriage, number fifteen, was built by the makers Waggon Fabriken, of Vienna, and not for the German service," said Martin in his pedantic manner. I saw Jack Grant's fine eyes glaze with boredom. "I am not so sure that number fifteen could work through to Berlin, due to technical reasons of couplings, etcetera, and I would suppose that . . ."

"Most interesting, Mr. Martin," interrupted Grant. "You must tell me all about it some time." He turned his back on his fellow countryman. "Miss Herbert, will you please ask that fellow to bring back the rest of the train?"

"Yes, Colonel," I said. And went to do his bidding.

My quarry was standing some distance off, dressed, as I have always understood Prussian official functionaries are, in uniform of most elaborate and military-looking splendor: frogged and bemedaled, with white gloves. His moustache was drawn out to two fine points of waxen magnificence. Marking from whence I had approached him, and dismissing me as another foreigner, this lofty personage was disposed to be totally unco-operative. My first question was met with a brick wall of ambiguous officialdom at its worst: Yes, the locomotive had gone; on the other hand, it had not gone—or words to that effect. Happily, his dismissive response was delivered in that same Berlin argot in which I lay some modest claim to be an expert. I repeated my question, and embellished it in the Berliner's manner. The effect was instant and electrifying. His moustaches fairly quivered with pleasure at the compliment I had offered him by not being, after all, a stupid foreigner who could scarcely declaim by rote the standard phrases from Mr. Thomas Cook's phrase book for Continental travelers, but a highly intelligent lady who had had the good sense to learn the German language as it *should* be spoken.

Briefly, then, and unequivocally, my new friend gave me the position regarding the special train, and would have extended our conversation to gossiping about life and times in the Prussian capital, had I not cut him short by offering him my hand to kiss, and taking my departure.

"Well, Miss Herbert?" asked Jack Grant, upon my return to the *wagon-lit*.

I savored my reply for a few moments and met the anxious eyes of Mr. Martin. Forgetful of the unpleasant incident with Miss Scrase, I was disposed to be amused.

"It seems that number fifteen carriage was not built for the German service, Colonel," I said. "Accordingly, they are transferring us to another. It's a matter of the couplings, you see. They don't match."

"Is that so?" said Jack Grant in very flat tones.

"What number *wagon-lit* are they transferring us to, Miss Herbert?" asked Martin.

"He didn't say."

"And where is this other carriage?" demanded Grant. "How long before the change is effected? I have promised Lord Audubon that we shall stay in Cologne for no longer time than it takes to eat luncheon."

"There appears to have been some confusion in the arrangements," I told him.

"The devil there has! What confusion?"

"The station authorities here in Cologne were not informed till last night of our approach, and had to telegraph to Berlin for the replacement *wagon-lit,* which is coming with all speed." I paused for a moment, so disturbing was the fury that flared up in those commanding gray eyes. "But it won't be here for another three hours."

"Three hours!" he rammed his fist into the palm of his other hand. "Three hours, and we are already behind schedule. Where's this Prussian efficiency they flaunt at every turn? They can't even run a railway!"

"The fault, I fancy, was not with the railway people, but with the British Embassy in Berlin," I told him. "My friend the stationmaster said that they neglected to inform him about us till we were well on our way from Paris."

"Did they, then?" snarled Grant, and he drove his fist into his palm again. I had it in my heart to feel sorry for the staff of the Berlin Embassy. "Then I suppose we must resign ourselves to kicking our heels in Cologne for three hours!"

He turned on his heel and strode toward the open door of his own compartment, but had not gone half a dozen paces before he turned, looked back, flashed the sort of grin that, had I been a soldier under his command, would have nerved me to ride into the very cannons' mouths.

"My apologies, Martin," he said. "I had no idea of the extent of your railway expertise. A most useful accomplishment. I must bear it in mind in the event of future hitches during our journey."

We would have luncheon together, said the princess, whose capacity for recovering her habitual gaiety was quite beyond belief. She had changed from her day gown into an afternoon dress and coat of peach-colored velvet edged with black fox fur, and a bonnet trimmed with a fox's mask and tail. A diamond pendant of enormous size was suspended across her *poitrine*. She took my hand in hers.

The hotel to which the party had been directed lay only just beyond the confines of the great station.

"I know it well," said the princess. "My Uncle Nicky always declares it to be one of the finest in Europe. We shall *à la carte* together, my dear. Come."

The hotel, which was heavy, pillared in the Classical manner and somewhat resembling engravings I had seen of the Acropolis of Athens, had been apprised of our coming. The director himself greeted us in the vast, chandelier-hung hallway and, bowing low over the princess' hand, opined that it was a great honor, and would Her Highness and friend graciously permit him to guide them to the dining room? He swept ahead of us, turning to bow at every other step, gesturing us through vast doorways and down carpeted corridors of inordinate length, till we presently emerged in a circular chamber with a domed glass roof that looked up to blue skies and scudding fat clouds. And then I saw Augusta Scrase.

She was sitting alone at a table by the curved wall and was reading a book. She had witnessed our entrance, and I saw her eyes swiftly return to the pages when I looked her way. At the other side of the room, Orwell, Martin, and Charlot were sharing a table. The three journalists rose and bowed in our direction. There was no sign of Colonel Grant and the Emissary.

"Why, there is the so charming Miss Scrase," trilled the princess. "Let us go and sit with her, Clarrie dear." And waving aside the obsequious director, who was endeavoring to usher us to a prominent table in the center of the room (so that his clientele could enjoy the edifying view of a real Russian princess?), she swept over to the Englishwoman. "My dear Miss Scrase, pray may we join you at luncheon? You look so absorbed in your novel that one is disinclined to intrude. Are you quite sure? So very kind. Be seated, Clarrie dear. Ah, here is the menu. I shall begin with *Weissbiersuppe*, which is rather naughty of me. For fish, I will have carp cooked in beer. Heavens—how I shall sleep this afternoon! And what will you have, Clarrie dear? I see that Miss Scrase is being very austere—a little lamb cutlet only. What noble self-denial. No wonder her figure is so *svelte*." All this in a voice that filled the total stillness of the crowded dining room.

I scarcely knew where to turn my eyes and resolved the problem by hiding myself behind the oversized menu. I had not told my friend about Augusta Scrase's insulting insinuation that I had had some part in the rifling of her luggage, and now it was too late. There was nothing for it but to sit through what promised to be a thoroughly embarrassing luncheon, and hope that I could think of a pretext to make an early departure, to which end, I chose only one course of lightly done fish and a salad, answering the princess' protests with the explanation that I was not hungry.

Upon the arrival of my fish and the princess' beer soup— which she drank noisily and with great relish—Augusta Scrase, who had made no attempt at conversation since our arrival, let her gaze wander back, by easy stages, to the pages of her book. The princess, observing this, laid down her spoon, mopped her shapely lips with her napkin, and smiled amiably at our table companion.

"What is your novel, dear Miss Scrase?" she asked. "Is it a romance, perhaps? Or one of those Gothic tales that are so much the vogue at present, full of inexplicable happenings in bat-haunted castles in Transylvania?"

Augusta Scrase put aside her lorgnette and book with the air of one who knows—and regrets—the code of civilized behavior.

"It is not a novel of any kind, Princess," she said. "It is not a work of fiction, but a true account."

"A true account of what, pray? What is its title, Miss Scrase?"

"It is called *Scrambles Amongst the Alps*," replied the other in a frigid voice.

"*Scrambles Amongst the Alps!*" repeated the princess, and her eyes sparkled mischievously.

"By Edward Whymper," said Augusta Scrase, "the eminent mountaineer who conquered the Matterhorn three years ago. Mr. Whymper is a dear friend of my family," she added, with a touch of pride.

"May I see the book?"

"Certainly." The book was handed to the princess, who opened it and riffled through the pages, pausing from time to time to examine the illustrations within, and commenting loudly, "Ah, those astounding peaks, they fill me with awe and dread. Surely the good Lord did not intend the foot of man to stand upon those remote and solitary cathedrals of ice. It is against all nature, all belief." She paused. "Upon my word, would you believe it? Clarrie, my dear, I beg you to look at this and appreciate in what distinguished company we are sitting."

She passed me the book, which was open at the title page. Written in a flowery and artistic-looking hand under the printed matter were the words:

> *To Dearest Gussie,*
> *in fond recollection*
> *of the many happy days*
> *we have spent climbing*
> *together in the Alps.*
> *—Edward Whymper, Aug. 1872*

"Is this true, Miss Scrase?" cried the princess. And, surely, the very few people in the dining room who were not already savoring her every word paused in their eating and inclined an ear. "Are you, indeed, the 'Dearest Gussie'—what a delightful pet name, Miss Scrase—referred to in Mr. Whymper's dedication? And have you actually *climbed mountains*? You—a *woman*?"

An English lady of the upper class to her fingertips, Augusta Scrase was in no way embarrassed by her public interrogation (though I did notice a slight dilation of her finely chiseled nostrils and a sudden flaring of those haughty green eyes at the mention of her—no doubt jealously guarded—pet name), but replied in an equally loud voice, for the benefit of all who cared to listen,

"I have climbed since I was a young gel. Together with Whymper, Kennedy, Matthews, Moore, Stephen, and others, my father was one of the pioneers of Alpine mountaineering. Accompanied by my father and Edward Whymper, I climbed Gross Glockner, the Fletschhorn, and the Wetterhörner before I was twenty years of age, and have done so on many occasions since."

The princess shook her flaxen head in wonder. "You greatly resemble my maternal grandmother, Miss Scrase," she declared. "I see the resemblance plainly. Grandmama swam in the River Neva regularly, no matter what the weather, till her death at the age of ninety-seven. She also did calisthenics. Do you do calisthenics, Miss Scrase?"

Augusta Scrase colored slightly. The princess' by now quite blatant teasing had slipped under the guard of her upper-class imperturbability.

"On occasions, one performs various exercises to strengthen the muscles employed in climbing," she said stiffly. "In the Alps, one exercises daily, when not actually engaged upon tackling the peaks."

"You don't suppose—no, it would be an intolerable intrusion upon your good nature, and, besides, you have not yet finished your little lamb chop—you don't suppose you could give us a little demonstration, here and now, of some of your less-sensational exercises, Miss Scrase?" asked the princess, her lovely, pink-and-white face totally devoid of mirth or mischief. Despite my feelings about her victim, I could have smacked her, as one would smack a naughty child.

"I think not!" grated Augusta Scrase.

"What a pity," said the princess. "Don't you think it a pity, Clarrie dear? I mean, watching Miss Scrase doing her exercises, one could almost have pictured her up there tackling the peaks, could one not?"

I was saved from any response by the arrival of a bevy of waiters bearing the princess' fish course and its attendant sauces, vegetables, spices, etcetera. The princess threw up her hands in delight.

"My dears, I beg you to regard the condition of the flesh," she said. "This is a carp that has been stewed with loving care. Before immersion in the beer, a little salt was rubbed into it, and the liquid was afterward strained off with great care, leaving the flesh dry and flaky. Not too much lemon juice, my man! Yes, a dash of cayenne! As to my next course—listen to this, my dear Clarrie, and you, my dear Miss Scrase—I will have—let me see —the roast goose stuffed with apples, chestnuts, and raisins, the whole mixed with liver and giblets!"

Augusta Scrase picked up her book and lorgnette. "You will excuse me, Princess," she said, "but I have things to attend to before we depart."

"Of course, of course, my dear Miss Scrase," said the princess. "But—you still have not finished your lamb chop. Oh dear, she's gone. Do you suppose I've offended her, Clarrie dear?"

"You are very naughty," I told her. "I've no brief for that woman, but you deliberately set out to make her look absurd in front of everyone."

She made no attempt to look contrite, but smiled gaily. "We are cruel, we Romanoffs," she said. "And we defend our friends with ruthless passion. Oh, yes, my dear, I have heard how Miss Scrase accused you of rifling her baggage. That nice American gentleman told me."

"You *knew* all the time?"

"Of course," she purred. "Why else would I tease her so cruelly and at the risk of spoiling my appetite and digestion? I assure you, my dear, that I do not make a general habit of such behavior. Even with persons so transparently obnoxious as our Miss Scrase." She stabbed a large piece of her fish and transferred it to her mouth with relish, heedless of the melted butter that trickled from a corner of her lips and fell upon her jabot.

I digested her confession and decided that, on balance, I was grateful to her for championing my cause.

Presently, I said, "But what a remarkable person she is, don't you think, ma'am? I mean, who would have believed that a woman could have climbed those Alpine peaks? How would she manage her skirts, let alone her bustle? You don't suppose?—no, it would be too scandalous to contemplate—you don't suppose that she wore . . . *men's pantaloons* for the purpose?"

Princess Natasha laughed and almost choked on her fish. When she had recovered her composure, her pretty, pink-and-white countenance was strangely grave.

"I would believe anything of Miss Scrase," she said. "Anything at all. She is a very curious woman. Many-sided. And a woman who would not allow her mask to fall and reveal the person within."

"But surely you can discern what lies behind the mask, ma'am," I said, adding teasingly, "you—a Romanoff, with a Romanoff's prescience."

She accepted my teasing as a compliment, acknowledging it with an elegant gesture of her plump, beringed hand.

"That's true," she said. "And Miss Scrase has revealed much of herself to me in this late encounter. More than you would believe, my dear Clarrie."

And, try as I might, I could not persuade my friend to enlarge upon that cryptic utterance.

Having disposed of all her carp but a neat skeleton, the princess tackled a heaped dish of roast goose lying in a sea of sauce and accompaniments; and gave orders for her third course. I, who had brought my fish and salad to an inconclusive end, begged leave to be excused. In the two hours remaining, I wished to see the famous Cologne cathedral. Princess Natasha, accepting this as a no doubt typically English eccentricity comparable only with climbing Alps, gestured with a goose leg for me to depart, with an admonition not to be late for the train's departure.

Outside in the streets, the afternoon had taken on a sullen darkness. The sky above the towers and rooftops was packed with tumbled storm clouds, and the broad River Rhine that flowed close by was steely gray, save for the flecked whiteness at the bows of long barges that nosed their ways up and down stream with fussy tugboats straining at the ropes. The cathedral seemed very close at hand: twin, spiky towers soaring above the gabled houses, almost brushing the fast-moving clouds with their lofty pinnacles. I set off to walk.

The distance was deceptive. It was a piece farther than I had judged, and the sky was already spotting rain by the time I had won my way through a labyrinth of tortuous alleyways and emerged before the great west front of the cathedral, where pointed windows rose tier upon fretted tier to the bases of the towers. I ran the last few yards over the cobblestones, and gained the great arched doorway with my face damp with droplets.

There was a screen door beyond, time-blackened and pitted with the touch of many hands. It creaked open to my touch, and admitted me to a place of scented silence and a gloom that was relieved only by shimmering pinpoints of massed candles at each aisle, to left and right of the wide sweep of nave. There was not a soul to be seen. I was alone in that great building, alone with the stillness and the cloying tang of burned incense.

I released the door, and it closed with a bang that reverberated to the vaulted roof high above me, echoing and re-echoing to silence in the high clerestories. Disquietened by the sudden sound, I addressed myself to a printed notice in German, French, and English, which gave me the opportunity both to reassemble my nerves and acquaint myself with the cathedral's history. It was the largest Gothic church in Northern Europe, I was informed and, though begun in 1248, was still unfinished. Generous friends, pleaded the notice, would greatly assist in bringing the vast design to full fruition by the year 1880. And, it concluded, persons wishing to be shown around the cathedral, including the ascent of the north tower, should contact the sacristan. I slipped an English shilling into the coin box provided and went to seek out the sacristan.

The left-hand aisle, along which my footsteps led me, was lined with tombs of long-dead knights and clerics. The carved, mute faces slid past me. One, a figure in chain mail and surcoat, the features youthful and unformed, the dust of centuries lay in the alabaster crevices of his ears, looked like a grubby schoolboy and not unlike Daisy Marchmain's brother Ned.

I began to giggle—and was shocked by an unexpected note of nervousness in the tones.

There was a carved bishop lying with his hands folded around his pastoral staff, tiny, neatly shod feet resting upon a tasseled cushion, plump face relaxed in sleep. He looked uncommonly like Bishop D'Arcy of St. Errol, and I was wondering what had become of the indomitable Mrs. D'Arcy, when, looking down into the arcaded space beneath the recumbent figure, I saw its counterfeit in a carved skeleton—grim reminder of death's dissolution. Shuddering as if someone had walked over my own grave, I went on.

Reaching the far end of the nave, I looked around me for signs of a door leading to a vestry, or some such place where the attendant sacristan might while away his time on a rainy afternoon. There was such a door in the transept, and it was open, disclosing a shaft of daylight, as if from a window. I was about to approach it when I heard the street door creak slowly open, and then very quietly close.

Someone was in the cathedral with me, someone I could not yet see because I was in the transept, which, like the horizontal part of a massive cross, lay at the top end of the broad nave. Another visitor to the dark cathedral.

Someone from the train? A fellow passenger? Someone who had followed me here?

I had an impulse to retrace my steps back to the street door. Walk swiftly past whoever it was, giving him or her a brief nod and emerging into the daylight. My thoughts flew to the rifled contents of the princess' and Miss Scrase's baggage. That, and the appalling recollection of a tumbled scrap of blood-dabbled fur lying in the grass . . .

Before I could steel myself to make a move, the newcomer began to walk down the nave, slowly and as if on tiptoes, so that his shoes squeaked. It was a man's footfall. Slowly and with deliberate menace—*toward me!*

Too late now to escape through the street door; the newcomer's manner of approach precluded any hope of a brief nod suiting the case.

I looked in anguish about me, left and right. I was trapped in that end of the transept. To emerge from the concealing angle of the wall was to put myself in the sight of the intruder.

I backed away against the stonework, and something touched my shoulder. Turning with a scream mounting to my lips, I looked into the carved, lowering face of an armored knight. He stood upon a low plinth, one arm extended, supporting a lance. I exhaled a shuddering breath.

The footsteps paused. In my dread imagining, I thought I could hear *his* breathing. And then it stopped. Only the thud-thud of a vein in my head marking off a passing lifetime.

And then the squeaking footsteps began again.

They were very close now. I felt myself beginning to die.

Only the open door into what might be a vestry offered me chance of life. There might be no other way beyond it, no means of gaining the world outside. But there might be a lock or bolt on the innerside, something to bar the advance of my murderer. I was already thinking of him as a would-be killer.

Swiftly, I crossed over, and darting inside the part-open door closed it shut behind me. Too hard and too noisily! I caught my breath in horror, to hear the noise it made. Surely *he* could not have missed hearing it.

My fingers sought for a key in the lock: no key. I groped in the half-light for signs of a bolt: no bolt. I looked about me for something to wedge, or jam, the door against him. By the thin light from a narrow window set with a pane of grimy green glass, I saw nothing that suited my purpose.

I was indeed in a vestry. At the far end, facing me, a row of half a dozen headless dummies clad in richly embroidered copes stood like mummers in some grotesque pantomime. Apart from a huge, iron-bound chest, they comprised the entire furnishings of the chamber. They provided my only refuge—and a slender concealment at that. I crept behind the central figure, cowering there like a dumb animal tied up in a slaughterhouse, awaiting the killer's knife. Waiting for the man who had—surely—followed me into the cathedral and was now searching for me.

Crouched with my hot cheek against the smooth silk of the ecclesiastical robe, I addressed my mind to a feverish calculation of my chances if and when—as was almost certain—my pursuer would open the door. Let him enter the chamber, I told myself, and let him cross over to the line of dummies, either to left or right, giving me a clear run to the open door.

But what if he came straight toward me, toward the central figure, behind which I was crouching?

And what—mindful of his terrible designs—if he closed the door, to muffle his victim's cries?

Dear God, I shuddered. Let him leave the door open!

How near was he now? Very close, for sure. He must be in the transept. Perhaps, having heard the vestry door close, he had just located it and was even now approaching it, hand extended.

I must be ready for him, ready to take my chance at flight if the chance was offered. I must watch the handle of the door, to see its first move. The horror of it was not to be thought about, but it had to be done: watch, poise myself in readiness, and when the chance came—run!

Slowly, I raised my head; dragging my reluctant gaze across the embroidered silk, slowly over the curve of the dummy's shoulder.

The door stood immediately opposite, its ringed handle in quite clear view. And, as I watched, it moved.

Slowly. And with undoubted menace.

My fingers tensed against the silk robe, gathering up a handful of the rich material. Staring, I watched for the instant when, the latch being fully lifted, the door would begin to open; a thin sliver at first, then wide—to disclose the face of the man who had sought me out.

Clutching, still, and all unaware of what I was doing, I was suddenly aware of an imbalance. Too late, I realized that I was overturning the dummy figure. It fell back, toppling with monstrous dignity upon me, bearing me down to the flagged floor with it, shrouding me with the folds of the heavy silk robe, shutting out my screams, covering me when, having struck my head with stunning force, I knew no more.

I was back in my narrow little room under the eaves, at Mrs. Mount's School for Young Ladies, during the time when I had had the influenza. I felt very ill, and Daisy Marchmain was sitting with me. I could smell the sweet lavender water that she always used. If I opened my eyes, I would be able to see her, but my eyelids were heavy with the torpor of sickness.

The doctor would come again today. He came from the other side of St. Errol. He came in a trap with a hairy black dog on the seat beside him. Daisy always said that the dog was his assistant doctor.

Someone was bending over me now. The doctor? Not Daisy, certainly, for whoever it was smelled intolerably of stale tobacco and spirits.

"Fräulein!" The voice was harshly insistent, and it was not the doctor's voice. "Arouse yourself! This is a sacred place. And see what a mess you have made of the bishop's cope, which he must wear on Easter Sunday. I have a mind to summon the police. Why, this is sacrilege . . ."

I opened my eyes to see a cross-looking old man in a rusty black cassock. He was stooping over me, having restored the fallen dummy and its rich cope to their former upright position. Still chiding me, he was dusting down the latter with his gnarled hand.

I slid my gaze, fearfully, toward the door. It stood open. With a sudden and glorious feeling of release, I realized that all my terrors had been of my own imagining. The man who had entered the cathedral, who had walked down the nave (and paused in doing so, surely, to attend to some small task like picking up a scrap of rubbish), and who had followed me into the vestry was none other than he who had a perfect right to do so— the crotchety old sacristan who stood before me.

The realization, the surge of relief, lent me an assurance that— considering my embarrassing and undignified position upon the floor—I could not otherwise have summoned. Getting to my feet with some difficulty (my head throbbed intolerably where I had struck the hard flagstones, but it seemed unlikely that I had been senseless for more than the few moments it must have taken for the old man to enter, see the fallen dummy, and discover me beneath it), I summoned up a smile for him.

"I am very sorry, sacristan," I said. "You see, I was looking for you in here, when, noticing these beautiful robes—they really are in most exquisite condition. I suppose it is you who looks after them, and with what loving care—I could not resist touching the beautiful material, and, in doing so, I overturned . . ."

I rambled on, gushingly. It was relief and release that moved me to dissemble with such assurance.

The old fellow heard me out, and slowly thawed. Discerning from my slight accent that, notwithstanding my fluent German, I was some kind of foreigner, and therefore fair game, a calculating look came into his pouchy eyes. He informed me that it would take him some time to clean away the results of the cope's contact with the dusty old floor. And did the Fräulein require the short, or the extended tour of the cathedral? I informed him that I did not, after all, have time for a tour, long or short, and gave him a shilling for his pains. He bit at the coin, and finding it to be true gold, slipped it into his cassock pocket. I had reached the door and was about to go through it when he delivered a parting shot that carved away all my newly won relief and left me in terror again.

"Your friend, Fräulein," he said. "The Englishman, who passed me out there in the transept, I expect he'll be wondering what happened to you, eh?"

Without answering him, I fled, racing out, and down the long, echoing aisle, with the prickling sensation upon my skin that, with every step, a hand might reach out and take me. I burst through the screen door, leaving it to slam behind me, out into the clean air and the overcast.

"Hello, there, Clarissa, Clarissima!"

Ralph Orwell was walking across the open space toward me. His eager, quirky grin faded to concern when he saw my expression, but he said nothing as he reached out and, putting his arms about me, pressed me tenderly to him, waiting for me to unburden myself when I chose.

I told him all that had happened from the time I had entered the cathedral, omitting nothing of my fears and speculations, numbly aware of my cowardice, my unworthy behavior.

It never occurred to me for one instant that it was he—Ralph Orwell—who had pursued me with such stealth and menace in the silent gloom of the great building. I knew instinctively that he could never, ever, have wished to do me harm. A woman knows these things, and she does not need to be a Romanoff, with a Romanoff's prescience, to do so.

He instantly divined the connection between the mysterious and brutal slaying of the princess' little dog, the searching of the women's luggage—and my terrors in the cathedral.

"You're right, Clarrie," he said. "It's all of a piece. There's someone on that train, some person—or persons—with a malevolent intent. Someone who"—he looked down at me keenly—"who isn't maybe, quite what he or she appears to be. Let's start with you and me, Miss Herbert. Are *you* really the pretty schoolma'am from the county of Cornwall who came to tutor Lord Audubon's little daughter and was transmogrified, like Cinderella herself, into an agent of the British Foreign Office? Or have you always been an agent of the British Foreign Office?"

We had left the cathedral precinct and were walking slowly along the road that bordered the river. It had stopped raining. A promising patch of blue sky was gracing Cologne, its rooftops, towers and pinnacles, with the benison of spring sunshine. I liked Ralph's directness and was in no way offended. I watched a trio of small boys fishing at the river's edge. Barefoot and chattering, casting their lines into the slowly moving flow, one of them turned and grinned at us both.

"I am Clarrie Herbert," I said. "And no one—nothing—else. I think something very disturbing is happening on this journey, but am puzzled to know why. And, for your information, Mr. Orwell, Cornwall is not a county, but a duchy. The Prince of Wales is also the Duke of Cornwall."

"I stand corrected on the latter, Clarrie," he replied.

"Nor am I pretty!"

"Upon that point," said he, "the defense rests. Gentlemen of the jury, we will rely upon the evidence of your own eyes."

"Can't you be serious for once?" I snapped, and was immediately sorry.

"I *am* serious, Clarrie," he murmured, and I slid my gaze away from the intense look he gave me. "As to your other point," he continued, "as to why any person, or persons, should be working to disrupt the intention that lies behind our journey to St. Petersburg, I would have thought you had heard enough to realize that there are plenty of people who want Britain and Russia to start a shooting war in Constantinople."

"The Jingos!"

He shrugged. "Call 'em what you like, Clarrie," he said. "They come in all sorts and sizes, depending on the country of origin. France, Germany, England, the Russians, and the Austrians— they all have an axe to grind in the Balkans. And in each of those countries there's a pro-war and an anti-war party."

"In America, also?" I asked him.

He hunched his shoulders. "The Constantinople affair," he said, "raises not a ripple of interest in Washington or elsewhere in the United States. Compared with such disparate issues, even, as this year's output of cereals from the Midwest, or who's to be the twentieth President in two years' time, the possibility of a general European war stemming from the Constantinople affair is like—well, I just can't begin to express what a dead issue it is. Clarrie, two thousand-odd miles of crawling gray ocean separates the New World from the Old World, and until the unlikely day that man can span that void as easily as a bird flitting from bough to bough, none of my countrymen is going to spend any sleepless nights over an issue like: Who fires the first shot in Constantinople—the British or the Russians?"

"Do you care?" I asked him.

"I happen to think it's pretty damned important that no one fires that shot," he replied in his quiet, unhurried voice, and his amber-colored eyes, usually so brimming with puckish humor, were somber as he looked out across the slowly moving waters of the broad river. "But one thing's for sure—I wish like hell that you weren't mixed up in this business we're on, Clarrie."

I had no reply for that.

We came to the station, and met crowds of people massing, one supposed, to catch the early evening trains to the suburbs: Herr and Frau Schmidt, bustling and thrustful after their day's work or an afternoon's shopping. Our train, which now boasted a complete set of new carriages, one of them a *wagon-lit*, had been moved to the extreme end of the station and its precincts guarded from the common run of folk by a roped enclosure and a pair of heavily whiskered railway officials. The locomotive was gushing steam promisingly, and though it still needed half an hour to our revised departure time, several of the passengers were already aboard. I saw Miss Scrase sitting primly in our new compartment reading her book. The English newspaperman, Mr. Martin, was engaged in an animated conversation with the train driver. And Princess Natasha waved to me gaily from her window.

"Let's take a turn as far as the end of the station yard and back, Clarrie," said Ralph. Somewhere between the cathedral and the train we had both slipped into addressing each other by our first names.

"All right, Ralph." I tucked my hand into his proffered arm, and we walked on in silence, in and out of the moving throngs of people, dodging carts piled high with luggage and farm produce, skirting a small group crowded about a sad-looking gypsy who was playing a violin for a moth-eaten bear who slowly and dolefully pranced to its wavering strains. I hate the thought of poor dancing bears.

Presently we came to the end of the station buildings, and were about to retrace our steps when Ralph's arm tensed on mine.

"Well now!" he exclaimed. "There's one member of the Fourth Estate who isn't playing the game by the rules!"

Opposite us, and partly screened by a tall iron column supporting the station roof, was a window, already lit up against the evening gloom. Upon it was engraved the word:

Telegraf

Inside, standing at a counter and engaged in conversation with a functionary in shirt-sleeves and a green eye shade, was the French journalist Jules Charlot. As we watched, he passed a slip of paper to his companion, who took it and nodded.

"He—he's sending a telegraph message," I exclaimed, remembering Colonel Grant's explicit forbidding of any such action.

"That's what he's doing, all right," said Ralph. "Stealing a march on the rest of us. Well, if anyone broke his trust, it would have to be Charlot. In the phrase greatly beloved by my fellow countrymen, Jules is a 'go-getter,' and a go-getter, furthermore, of the deepest and darkest dye. To be first with a story, that fellow would make his own mother run barefoot through snow and ice bearing the message in a forked stick."

"But—if he's revealed the secret of Lord Audubon's mission, won't that put the whole thing in jeopardy?" I asked.

Ralph shook his head. "Even Jules daren't stick his neck out quite so far," he said. "If *L'Observateur de Paris* ran that story before Lord Audubon gives us clearance, Jules would never get another official exclusive in all Europe for so long as he lived."

"Then, what . . ."

"What he'll have done, what he's doing right now," said Ralph, "is to alert his paper that a big story is on its way. He'll have told them to await a code word, which will warn them at a moment's notice to hold the presses and tear down the front page. With any luck, *L'Observateur* could be on the streets with the news of the Audubon mission a whole day ahead of the rest. That's typical of Jules's methods. *That* is go-getting."

"He's coming out," I breathed. "Shall we . . ."

"Duck out of sight? I don't think so, Clarrie. No, let's face him out. I've an idea we'll not greatly embarrass Monsieur Charlot, who, in addition to all the other qualities of a good newspaperman with which he's endowed in such generous amounts, has a hide like an elephant. Smile sweetly, Clarrie. Here he comes."

The Frenchman emerged from the door of the telegraph office: a dapper figure in tailcoat, spats, a fresh buttonniere in his lapel, a gleaming tall hat set at an angle on his carefully waved hairpiece. Tucking his cane under one arm, he paused for a moment, drawing a pair of pale gray gloves over his podgy, beringed fingers. Then he observed us—and, though it must have been transparently obvious to him that we had both seen where he had been and for what purpose, not by so much as a flicker of his clever eyes did he betray any sign of dismay. Instead, having drawn on his gloves, he raised his hat and gave us a small, neatly fashioned bow from the waist.

"*Bon soir, mes amis,*" he purred sibilantly. And, replacing his hat, tapping it in place with the silver head of his cane, he swaggered on his way back to the train.

I stared at Ralph. He grinned down at me.

"You've got to hand it to old Jules," he said. "He's all sorts of a rat, but he's got a lot of style." Then the smile faded and the amber eyes clouded.

"What is it?" I asked him.

"I was just thinking," he said, "that of all the people on the train, Charlot is the most likely to have searched that luggage. It suits his style of journalism."

I drew breath sharply and felt my skin crawl. "And the man who followed me to the cathedral," I whispered. "Do you think that he, also . . ."

"Perhaps."

"Ah, but then," I said, "the old sacristan was quite adamant that it was an Englishman. 'Your friend the Englishman'—that's what he said."

Ralph shrugged. "What does that signify, Clarrie?" he asked. "Plenty of Englishmen look like Jules Charlot. Come to that, among Continentals, I frequently am mistaken for a Limey."

The replacement *wagon-lit* was numbered 25—a fact that Mr. Martin pointed out to me as if a matter of considerable significance.

"Built in Berlin, in seventy-five, Miss Herbert," he said. And by way of enlargement upon this momentous theme. "By Eisenbahn Bedarfs-Aktiengesellchaft."

He had buttonholed me close by the open door of Princess Natasha's compartment, looking down at me like some elongated bird, through his pebbled pince-nez. Was he, I wondered, the nameless "Englishman" who had terrorized me in the great cathedral?

"What a mine of information you are, to be sure, Mr. Martin," I murmured.

"And, being of newer construction than our old number fifteen, is likely to be more comfortable and smoother-running," he said.

"That will indeed be a blessing!" Princess Natasha broke in. She was seated in an armchair in all the glory of a pale pink housecoat with a feather boa collar that shimmered like innumerable small snakes with her every movement. She was holding —inevitably—a glass of champagne. "I must say I have found it extraordinarily difficult to sleep while the train is in motion," she went on. "I would have thought that one would have been more comfortably accommodated in hammocks, after the manner of sailors at sea. Will you take a glass of champagne before we depart, Clarrie dear?"

"No thank you, ma'am," I said.

Mr. Martin, taking his cue from the fact that he had not been included in the invitation, raised his hat and moved away.

"We shall not arrive in Berlin much before luncheon tomorrow," said the princess. "In consequence, Colonel Grant has seen to it that there is ample provender in every compartment, to serve for supper and breakfast. It is to be hoped that the train will stop from time to time, however, so that one can get out and stretch one's legs. What a pity, my dear, that you are not traveling with me instead of the odious Miss Scrase. I would suggest that Hortense went in with her, but you see, I am helpless, quite

quite helpless, without a lady's maid. I can't even button my own shoes." She laughed and took a long sip of her glass. I bade her sleep well, and turned to meet the eyes of Colonel Grant, who was watching me from the next carriage.

He bowed, came toward me. Immediately, I felt my heart increase its beating in a most treacherous manner. Little fool, I told myself, this would never have happened if you hadn't listened to the silly prattling of Princess Natasha. What is this man to you—or you to him?

He was wearing a Norfolk jacket and breeches, and looked every inch the English officer in mufti.

"Miss Herbert," he said, "I hope you are finding the journey agreeable."

"Quite agreeable, Colonel, thank you." I gave him the guarded answer.

He glanced significantly toward the compartment in which we could both plainly see Miss Scrase bowed over her book.

"I much regret the unpleasantness over the rifled luggage," he said. "You must not think too ill of Miss Scrase. She is, perhaps, a trifle—impetuous—in her reactions."

"That she is, Colonel," I said. "That she is, indeed."

"But good at heart, I assure you. Once one has penetrated her reserve."

"I take your word for it, Colonel."

He looked relieved, seemingly quite unaware of the tart note in my responses.

"Then I wish you a good night, Miss Herbert," he said, "and look forward to meeting you at luncheon in Berlin. Our Embassy there, as I understand, have absolved themselves from their mix-up over the carriages by arranging a reception and official luncheon for our party. Till then." He bowed and left me.

I turned to enter the compartment, resolving to make a real effort to ingratiate myself with Augusta Scrase, putting behind me my resentment of the way she had treated me thus far. If she was as good-hearted as Jack Grant said, I would give her every opportunity of showing it.

Alas for my noble intentions!

She started upon me even before the train had set off again.

"I myself shall not require anything else to eat tonight," she

said, glaring at me over the top of her book, lorgnette poised.
"There is a hamper yonder. I am led to understand that it con-
tains food and drink. If you must eat, I beg you to do so before
the train leaves the station, because the smell of food, combined
with the motion of the carriage, can be quite nauseous. And
please be so good as to masticate quietly."

I felt my redhead's temper rise with the inexorable force of
boiling milk—and quenched it as best I was able.

"I am not hungry, either," I responded, when I could trust myself to speak. "I shall need nothing else today."

"Humph!" was her comment upon that, and she went back to
her reading.

I took a seat opposite her, in an armchair. The appointments
in the new carriage were a considerable improvement over the
other, for there were two extremely comfortable armchairs, and
the two bunks, which were already made up, appeared to be
wider. There was a deeply-piled Turkey carpet on the floor, and
a properly fitted handbasin instead of a washbowl and water jug.

Whistles were sounding in the station yard outside. Our locomotive emitted a monstrous gush of steam.

"I think we are about to leave," I ventured.

"So it would seem," was her reply.

And I thought to myself, to blazes with the wretched woman!
She had virtually deprived me of my supper, and am I now to sit
here in silence while she reads her confounded book?

"The cathedral is very fine," I said firmly.

"Yes, it is."

"And the waterfront," I persisted. "We walked back to the station by way of the river. The views were excellent."

There was a few moments' silence. And then she lowered her
book, and her lorgnette also. The look in her large green eyes
was compounded of such loathing and contempt as to deliver an
almost physical shock of impact. I caught my breath.

"Will you kindly understand," she said, "that I have not one
scrap, one remotest scintilla, of interest in your doings, and do
not wish to hear about them, now or later.

"Add to that," she continued, "it is not by my wish that I have
to suffer your companionship during this journey, and I see no
reason why the distastefulness of your presence should be compounded by the fatuity of your small talk. If your empty-headed

compulsion for prattle is irresistible, please address it to yourself."

"You are excessively rude!" I blazed, all thought of ingratiating myself with that woman now cast to the winds. "You are the most appalling, stuck-up creature that it's ever been my misfortune to come across!"

"And you," she said flatly, "are a common little nobody."

At that moment, the train started with a jolt and a rumble, and a cloud of steam that quite obscured the view from the window. By the time it had cleared, we were rolling gently, and with gathering speed, out of Cologne station.

Augusta Scrase and I, having each expressed our opinion of the other, did not exchange another word that evening. When it grew dusk, I lit the oil lamp. A little later, she opened the food hamper, took out a bottle of mineral water and, filling a tall glass, carried it back to her seat. I responded by delving inside the hamper and finding a nice rosy apple, which I proceeded to eat—and with no great regard for doing so silently. And the train rattled serenely on through the encroaching night.

At about eight o'clock, she put aside her book and went behind the curtain to prepare herself for bed, a protracted performance, as on the previous occasion. She re-emerged in nightcap, peignoir, and white-lead cream, and disposed herself upon the lower bunk. It was as she stooped to do so that I noticed a small pendant hanging from a piece of pink ribbon about her slender neck. I was still puzzling over this when, an hour later, having performed my own, more vestigial, ablutions, I climbed up into my cot and pulled Colonel Jack Grant's military cloak over me.

For the pendant that Miss Augusta Scrase wore secreted about her neck under her clothes was—a plain gold wedding ring!

PART
TWO

Chapter Six

WE ARRIVED AT THE PRUSSIAN CAPITAL SHORTLY BEFORE ELEVEN o'clock next morning, having tarried on the way at a small station outside the historic city of Magdeburg, where we were able to obtain fresh coffee and new bread at the station buffet, and the locomotive took on more coal and water—a proceeding about which I was given careful and detailed instruction by Mr. Martin. He was the only one of the journalists to put in an appearance during the halt, and gave me to understand that the others had again partaken of the brandy bottle in the dark hours. Jack Grant and Lord Audubon were up and about. They were taking coffee together when I entered the buffet. Both acknowledged me and then returned to their conversation—though I noticed the Emissary's eyes straying in my direction several times. His lordship, I was by now convinced, was very much a ladies' man. I never saw Princess Natasha till we arrived in Berlin.

Our reception at the capital was almost royal in its lavishness. Firstly, there was the stationmaster, who far outdid his colleague in Cologne both in matter of uniform and hirsute appointments, being bemedaled like a general and possessing a flaxen beard that encompassed all of his chest that was not covered in decorations. And there was the First Secretary from the British Embassy, who, after abjectly apologizing to Lord Audubon for the Ambassador's absence (His Excellency had been recalled to London on high affairs of state), conducted us to a file of waiting landaus that were to convey us to luncheon. There was even a station band, of the military sort, that gave a sketchy rendition of "God Save the Queen" as we were driven off. The entire proceedings—considering that Lord Audubon's mission to St. Petersburg was supposed to be highly confidential—were of an ostentation that puzzled me greatly, and I remarked as much to

Ralph Orwell, with whom I shared a landau during the drive to the hotel where luncheon awaited.

"The ways of higher diplomacy will forever remain a mystery to me," was his comment. "And I'm not to be persuaded that a shrewd fellow like Grant—who is organizing this journey like a military operation—has overlooked the fact that half the chancelleries of Europe must by now have realized that something big is in the wind. No, I think Grant and Audubon are playing it like a complicated game of chess, or like a stage illusionist with a rabbit up his sleeve—now you see it, now you don't; where does the truth really lie? And, by the way, Clarrie, our friend Charlot was first off the train when we arrived in just now, and made straight for the telegraph office."

"Did he make any mention, when you were with him last night, of our seeing him hand in his message at Cologne?" I asked.

"He boasted of it," said Ralph. "That's his style. Mind you, after having been caught red-handed, there was nothing much else he could do. I was right. He frankly admits that he's alerted his paper to a very big story. And there's something else . . ."

"What?"

Ralph frowned. "He wouldn't say. And by that time we had both gone a long way down the cognac bottle, so I wasn't disposed to press the matter. But he did hint that he'd requested his office for information. And that he expected an answer to be awaiting him when we reached Berlin. Hence, the dash to the telegraph office."

"Information?" I asked. "About what?"

"About what—or about whom? He didn't say. Ah, here we have the Brandenburg Gate, Clarrie. Erected by King Frederick William the Second, who was more successful in matters cultural than in matters fiscal. And, beyond, we see the justly famous Unter den Linden with the lime trees, alas, still not in blossom. Nor will they be till May or June, despite all my efforts. Though I have sent representations to the good burghers of Berlin and made burnt offerings to all the named Germanic gods, it has all been in vain. No one has made the slightest effort to bring the lime trees to flower in this unseasonal April. Not even for the fair, the redheaded and ravishing Clarrie, Clarissima."

"You," I said, "drank much too much cognac last night."

"Guilty, Your Honor!" declared he, removing his hat and laying it across his breast in the attitude of *mea culpa*. "But alcohol does not blind me to beauty, nor to the appreciation of beauty."

To change the subject as much as for any other reason, I said, "Miss Scrase wears a wedding ring on a ribbon around her neck. Hidden."

He cocked an interested eye. "Does she now? Is she, perhaps, a widow?"

"She calls herself, 'Miss.'"

"Divorced?"

"Unlikely," I said, having thought all this through in the dark hours before sleep had taken me. "I don't know about America, but in our country divorce is only granted to a woman—and no English gentleman would *dream* of sueing his wife for divorce, any more than he would shoot a fox or cheat at cards—by reason of adultery coupled with desertion, together with other causes I don't wish to mention. For any of these reasons, there are not many women who would so revere the memory of their broken marriage that they would wear a token of their former state around their neck, day and night."

"If she's not a widow and not divorced," said Ralph, "what then? She doesn't have many other options."

"It could be her mother's wedding ring," I ventured. "Worn as a memento."

"It could." He sounded doubtful.

Our eyes met.

"She could simply be a married woman," I supplied, "traveling incognito. Under her maiden name, perhaps."

"Mmmm. As I have said before," he mused, "there's someone on that train who isn't quite whom he or she appears to be. And our mysterious Miss Scrase could fit the role, don't you think?"

Before I could compose a reply, the head of the line of landaus turned off the broad boulevard and glided to rest in the forecourt of a resplendent building. We had arrived.

In glory of ostentation and sheer richness of ornament, the Berlin hotel outdid even the Cologne establishment. A small army of frock-coated directors, managers, under-managers, and under-managers' assistants met us at the head of the steps and bowed us through echoing corridors of veined marble, under vast chandeliers shimmering with cut glass, over Persian rugs worth an empress' dowry, to a private chamber where a large, oval-shaped table was set for nine.

Lord Audubon took his place at one end of the table, Colonel Grant at the other.

"Ladies and gentlemen," said the Emissary, "you will find place cards with your name inscribed thereon. Princess, I shall be honored to have you on my right, and Miss Herbert"—he smiled at me masterfully, stroking his silky moustache—"on my left."

We took our places, which had been arranged to meet the somewhat disparate social positions of those present. Augusta Scrase, I was glad to see, was two places away from me, on Jack Grant's right, with Ralph Orwell sitting between us. I looked across the table, and exchanged a smile with the princess. My friend was in all the glory of a full-length leopard-skin coat, which, having been removed by a flunkey and draped over the back of her chair, revealed an afternoon gown of lilac silk. Her hat was a confection of black velvet trimmed with bird-of-paradise feathers, and she wore for ornament the gold necklace and pendant of sapphire that I had observed when we had checked the inventory: the wedding present from her grandfather to her grandmother that had never been washed of his life's blood.

"I am hungry," declared she. "What is on the menu?"

The First Secretary from the Embassy, a porcine young man with an extremely smooth manner and a pointed beard, answered her,

"Your Highness, in deference to His Lordship's nationality, the management of the hotel have prepared a luncheon of the sort that one might enjoy at any table in Mayfair. In short, the cuisine is very largely French." He sniggered at his little sally.

Menu cards were handed to us. I have preserved mine: a memento of a meal that I shall remember, in shocking clarity of detail, for the rest of my life. The meal, notwithstanding the management's professed deference to the Emissary's nationality and the French cuisine, was carried out in a manner that I later learned to call, "the Russian manner." That is to say, a large number of waiters and servers supplied each guest's requirements from side tables, instead of the normal practice of setting the dishes of each course on the luncheon or dinner table for the gentlemen to help the ladies and themselves.

The meal began at the stroke of one o'clock, and should have occupied us for all of three hours. But fate had ordained that the major part of those rich and varied dishes—some of them named in delicate compliment to our Queen and the more distinguished members of our gathering—was never to be tasted by us.

MENU—à la Russe

Soupe à la Reine Victoria   Spring Soup

Curried Lobster Audubon   Salmon & Dressed Cucumber
Fillets of Mackerel   Soles à la Creme   Shrimp Sauce
Fried Filleted Soles   Stewed Eels   Lobster Cutlets

Filets de Boeuf Princess Natasha Bibescu   Oyster Patties
Chicken Cutlets   Grenadines de Veau
Boiled Tongue with Broccoli   Larded Sweetbreads
Saddle of Mutton   Boiled Chickens and Asparagus Peas
Roast Pork   Ducklings   Croquettes of Leveret
Roast Fillets of Veal   Boiled Bacon-cheek
Sweetbreads   Ham

Guinea Fowl Colonel Grant
Charlotte à la Parisienne   Lobster Salad   Blancmange
Compôte of Apricots   Rice Fritters
Pastry   Iced Pudding
Dessert and Ices

Lord Audubon was giving all his attention to the princess at the commencement of the soup course, so I was able to look around the table. Ralph Orwell, on my left, had engaged

Augusta Scrase in what looked like a very one-sided conversation. I had the notion that my American friend's cheerful brashness would butter no parsnips with the aloof Augusta. I also guessed that question her as subtly and obliquely as he might, he would never get any nearer to the mystery of her hidden wedding ring—supposing that that was his intent. At the other side of the table, sitting between Mr. Martin and the First Secretary, Jules Charlot was addressing himself to his soup like a horse at a trough; scooping huge mouthsful and spilling a very great deal of it down the napkin he had tied about his neck. In between swallows, he carried on a loud and abrasive conversation with the porcine young man from the Embassy. So wild was his manner, and so loud his voice, that I received a clear impression that the correspondent of *L'Observateur de Paris* had by no means recovered from the quantity of brandy he had imbibed the night before. Nor was he content with past excesses, but, between spoonsful of soup, he took long drafts of claret wine. His all-pervading voice, his unpleasing manner, and the matter of his discourse, caused all other conversation around the table to falter and fall away. And I saw two vertical lines of anger appear between Jack Grant's eyebrows.

"Berlin, I know well. Intimately," said the Frenchman. "Here, I reigned for many years as the dean of the foreign press corps. As such, I received many confidences, learned many secrets. I tell you, young man, that there are personages around this very table who would be very surprised to hear how much I know of their private lives."

All conversation had died by then. The only sound was the rattling of plates and dishes over by the serving tables where the staff were preparing the fish course.

The young man from the Embassy said, "Is that so? 'Pon my word." And looked embarrassed.

Not so Princess Natasha. "Monsieur, you intrigue me greatly," she cried. "I simply dote on scandal. Do you think one could persuade you to unburden yourself?"

Grant coughed. "With respect, Princess, I hardly think this is the occasion . . ."

"Fiddle-de-dee!" said the princess, silencing him with a flourish of her small plump hand. "Come, Monsieur Charlot, you must prove your boast. What do you know of our private lives that would surprise us?"

"Princess! I beg you . . ." Grant made another attempt, but was again gestured to silence.

Charlot drained his wineglass and refilled it from the decanter at his elbow, leering sidelong at the princess as he did so. His wig had become slightly awry, giving him a clownlike appearance—a very sinister and malevolent clown, I thought.

"The princess likes to play games," he said. "But perhaps, if the game became—shall we say?—rough and unpleasant, and fingers got burned, the princess would conveniently forget that she urged me on to play. Poor Charlot would be a target for her obloquy, and everyone here would say he is what the English call a 'cad'—which is the opposite of being a gentleman."

"The fellow's right, ma'am," said Lord Audubon. "I think we do not want to hear any of his secrets about us. Ah, here come your lobster cutlets, ma'am. And very fine they look too."

But Princess Natasha was not to be put off either by Lord Audubon's persuasion or by lobster cutlets. Pushing her plate to one side, she leaned forward, elbow on the table, so that she had a clear view of the Frenchman, past Mr. Martin.

"There will be no repining on my part, monsieur," she said. "No matter what is said. Let us play your game."

"No!"

The new protest came from Augusta Scrase. I saw her hand go, almost protectively, to her bosom where the wedding ring lay hidden. And I thought I gleaned the reason for her concern.

"Oh, but why not?" drawled Ralph Orwell. "For my part, I challenge Jules, here, to provide one fact about *my* private life that isn't common knowledge from here to Baltimore. Like all newsmen, our friend greatly exaggerates the scope of his inside knowledge. Such evocative phrases as 'I received many confidences' and 'I cannot reveal the source of my information' —phrases that trip so lightly off a correspondent's tongue—are merely smoke screens to hide the paucity of real hard information, as opposed to blind speculation. Go right ahead, Jules."

I knew he was deliberately inciting the other to indiscretion, and Charlot was responding to his gentle scorn. The Frenchman's sly, dark eyes flared in anger, and a livid spot appeared on each of his sallow, puffy cheeks. He took another long drink of his wine before replying.

"Very well, my dear Ralph," he said. "I accept your challenge."

"Bravo!" The princess clapped her hands and bounced up and down in her seat like a little girl who has been promised a treat. "Me first, Monsieur Charlot. I insist that you begin with me."

Charlot eyed her sidelong. Speared a large piece of stewed eel from his plate. Leered.

"Are you quite sure, Princess?" he asked.

"Quite sure," she affirmed. "Begin. Shock me! Shock everyone!"

"You are—a widow, ma'am," he said in a voice that was scarcely above a whisper.

The princess hunched her shoulders, spread her hands, looked around the table.

"For such resounding news he was called the dean of the foreign press corps!" she declared.

"Your husband was Count Paul Bibescu, who departed this life in Monte Carlo in eighteen seventy-four, eighteen months after your marriage."

The princess' gaze faltered. She delved into her reticule and produced a handkerchief.

"That is so, monsieur," she said, "as everyone knows."

"But your marriage—as a marriage—had finished well before the count's death," said Charlot. "The count was not living with you in Monte Carlo."

Her blue eyes opened wide, and the color fled from her cheeks. "How—how did you know that?" she whispered.

"Charlot! This has gone far enough!" Jack Grant's stentorian voice from the other end of the table.

"No, let him finish!" The princess' gaze never left her interlocutor. "Is there more, monsieur?"

"Count Bibescu was living with another—lady—at the time of his death," purred Charlot. "To be precise, an actress, a soubrette from the Paris Opera. Her name—Josette Heuseux."

At that, Lord Audubon leaped to his feet and threw down his napkin.

"Damn you, Charlot!" he cried. "I demand that you instantly withdraw that vile slur upon the honor of a dead man in the presence of his grieving widow. And, furthermore . . ."

"No, my lord!" Princess Natasha laid her hand on the Emissary's arm. "There is no need for Monsieur Charlot to retract a word. It is all true, you see."

"'Pon my word, ma'am. I . . ." The gallant Lord Audubon might be a diplomat, but his diplomacy was not equal to the sight of a beautiful woman in tears, who, nevertheless, did not forget that she was a Romanoff and kept her head high.

"And now, since the game has become unpleasant, I shall be called a cad?" asked Charlot, smiling thinly.

"Not by me, monsieur," said the princess. "I entered into the game with my eyes open. I have to admit that my intention—it is not a very worthy intention—was to hear scandal about other people. I never guessed, never dreamed"—her voice wavered, and I thought she would not find the fortitude to go on, but find it she did—"that anyone else in the world knew of my broken marriage. I have my Romanoff pride, you see. I allowed my husband his mistress, and in return I demanded—and got—complete discretion."

"Discretion can be bought and sold, Princess," said Charlot. "Every man—and woman—has a price."

"So it seems," she whispered.

There was a long silence. The Emissary had resumed his seat. The German waiters and servers stood around in some dismay, no doubt puzzled as to why the distinguished company were completely ignoring their succulent fish course. The table talk, which was being carried out in English was obviously lost on most of them.

Presently, Jack Grant said, "This business never should have begun, and I now suggest that it instantly cease. And I'm sure you will all agree."

"I disagree entirely," said Ralph Orwell.

"The devil you do!"

We all stared at Ralph, who smiled blandly around the table, quite unperturbed by the immediate wave of hostility that his interjection had drawn from most of the people present.

"Yes, I think the game should continue," he said. "If only out of deference to Princess Natasha, who—though it could be said with some justification that she has got only herself to blame—has not only suffered a public humiliation but, true to the rule that was made, has not repined and has borne her ordeal with seemly dignity."

"All the more reason to end it now!" growled Lord Audubon.

"Not so," said Ralph. "You all let it happen. Oh, there was some protest here and there, but no one made any *real* attempt to prevent the game from starting. We've all had our little thrill of excitement over the princess' secret being uncovered. I think we owe her some small pleasure in return. Who's next, Jules? Do you really know something about me that I'd rather have kept dark? Some scandalous escapade from my Oxford days, perhaps? Out with it, man."

The Frenchman took another sip of his wine, rolled it around his mouth appreciatively. Inebriated—yet in complete control. He looked the very personification of sly malice.

"I know plenty about you, my dear Ralph," he said. "So much, indeed, that I can scarcely decide where to begin. In such an embarrassment of richness, the mind turns to more simple fare. There springs to the recollection stories that are stark and uncompromising in their pattern of light and dark, of evil and good. Such a story came my way in the late summer of eighteen sixty-five, when my paper dispatched me to a remote village in Switzerland to test the *bona fides* of a certain person—a crude peasant, scarcely literate—who had sent an ill-penned letter to *L'Observateur de Paris* containing a very odd allegation. The name of that remote village was—Zermatt. Did you make some exclamation, Miss Scrase?"

Augusta Scrase had certainly cried out at the mention of the place name, and was now staring at the Frenchman in breathless fascination.

"What do you know of Zermatt?" she breathed.

Charlot leered. "The village of Zermatt—and you know this as well as I, Miss Scrase, and who better?—lies within the very shadow of that awesome alpine peak which has fired the imagination of man since time immemorial. I refer to the Matterhorn. The jutting fang of towering rock and ice that was conquered for the first time, in the summer of sixty-five, by Mr. Edward Whymper, the justly renowned English mountaineer—and your good friend. Correct?"

She nodded. "Yes." She continued to stare at him.

"You will bear with me, Miss Scrase, if I refresh the memories of the others here who will not be so familiar as you—or I—with the details of that historic ascent. How on the seventh attempt, upon the Swiss ridge of the peak, Whymper and his six companions gained the summit—only to have their triumph crowned with disaster. Yes, my friends, it happened during the descent. Seven men, all roped together for their mutual aid—or mutual destruction. One of them slipped, lost his footing. Fell, dragging three other men after him; leaving Edward Whymper and two guides perched perilously on that awesome crag of rock, with the weight of four helpless men threatening to tear them from their slender hand and foot holds, so that all seven would fall, still roped together in life—and death.

"How it was that Whymper and the two guides were saved by the providential fact that the rope supporting the four doomed climbers broke. Or was deliberately cut!"

"It's not true!" screamed Augusta Scrase.

"Our informant, the Swiss peasant, was willing to swear it under oath," said Charlot. "He claimed that one of the surviving guides confessed to him in his cups."

"He was lying!"

"Possibly. But he was very specific. He claimed the guide said it was Whymper himself who cut the rope. He would say that, of course. It is to be expected."

Augusta Scrase, now that the outrageous allegation had been made, seemed to regain her habitual fortitude. She rose to her feet, kicking back her chair, so that it fell with a clatter to the parquet floor. The menfolk—Charlot excepted, who remained seated, leering at his victim—got up from their seats and started forward to offer support and comfort to the distraught woman. But she was in need of no such support and comfort, and was far from distraught. Blood and breeding had reasserted themselves. Miss Scrase was all upper-class Englishwoman confronting a mere foreigner.

"That foul *canard* against Edward Whymper has been repeated on other occasions," she said, "but never before in my hearing, though I was aware of it, and my friend—to his bitter anguish—is also aware of it. That such an entirely unwarranted and unsupported allegation against a man of honor should be repeated in polite society, instead of in the haunts of gutter journalism from which it emanated, is, in my opinion, a matter for considerable regret. Lord Audubon, I beg to be excused. Will someone please obtain a conveyance to take me back to the railway station?"

Audubon was entirely at a loss. "Er—dear lady, Miss Scrase—" he looked for succor from his aide-de-camp.

"I will escort Miss Scrase back to the railway station, sir," said Grant, and he shot a savage glance at Charlot. "It is to be hoped that this so-called game is now finished."

Charlot slopped another measure of claret into his glass, shrugged his plump shoulders. "I have not transgressed against the rules of the game," he said, "and there is plenty more to be told. But"—he smiled—"that can wait for another occasion."

"Your arm, ma'am," said Jack Grant, addressing Augusta Scrase. And together they walked out of the chamber: two splendid creatures, perfectly complementing each other in looks and dignity.

"I suppose we had better continue luncheon," said Lord Audubon, "although I must confess that these upsets have taken the keen edge off my damned appetite. What about you, ma'am?" —addressing Princess Natasha.

The princess' appetite seemed in no way impaired. She had quite finished her lobster cutlets and was dabbing up the sauce with a scrap of bread. Knowing her little ways by that time, I had the notion that she had thoroughly enjoyed Augusta Scrase's discomfiture and that it had served as a perfect antidote to her own.

She said, "I am a trifle upset, certainly, not to have heard the end of Monsieur Charlot's story." Her baby-blue eyes slid sidelong toward the Frenchman, and in a very provocative and kittenish manner. "What was the outcome of your journey to Zermatt, monsieur? You did not print the peasant's story in your newspaper—at least, I do not recollect hearing of it."

Charlot sat back in his chair, twirling the wine in the bottom of his glass. He seemed pleased still to be holding an audience.

"The peasant—our informant—was clearly insane," he said blandly. "He even went so far as to claim that Whymper never

reached the summit on that occasion, but that, having been reduced to sacrificing the lives of four of his companions, had then
connived with the two guides to deceive the world that they had
been the first to conquer the mountain. No, we did not print the
story, and the wretched man, upon not receiving the ten thousand francs that he had demanded for our doing so, hanged himself from a roof beam. No doubt out of pique." He laughed.

"How did Edward Whymper come to hear of this allegation?"
It was Ralph Orwell who put the question. He leaned forward,
elbows on the table and stared fixedly at his colleague.

Charlot shrugged. "As I perceive you have guessed, my dear
Ralph," he replied, "it was I who sent Whymper a complete account of the allegations and invited his comment. For reasons
best known to himself, he did not reply."

"And after that, you made no particular attempt to keep the
story a secret," said Ralph. "As today, for instance."

The Frenchman beamed and spread his hands. "We are not in
the secret service, we of the Fourth Estate—are we?"

Ignoring the question, Ralph said, "Surely you have considered, from time to time, the effect that the calumny must have
had upon Edward Whymper?"

Charlot chuckled. "I should think, a very bad effect indeed. By
all accounts he possesses a very severe and forbidding personality. I would not think it has been greatly improved by my little
story. So much the worse for him. And his friends." Again, he
laughed.

There was a stir at my side, and Lord Audubon rose to his
feet. His pale and aristocratic countenance was set in a mask of
scorn and loathing as he regarded the small, stout figure lolling
at the opposite end of the table.

"Sir," he said, "I have not subscribed to the so-called rules of
the so-called game with which you have defiled this luncheon. So
I will tell you what you are. You are a blackguard, sir. A confounded blackguard! I ask you to withdraw immediately and
request you to take your meals apart from the rest of the party
for the remainder of our journey."

Intoxication, conceit, or sheer uncaring—any or all of these
may have accounted for the effect that the Emissary's words had

upon Charlot. He merely sneered, poured himself another helping of wine from the decanter at his elbow, rose, and pledging us all with the raised glass, addressed the company in mocking tones.

"Your health, ladies and gentlemen—your pardon, I should have begun: 'Your Highness, my lord' "—he laughed, went into a paroxysm of coughing, so that his puffy face turned an unhealthy puce and I thought he would collapse. But he recovered himself and went on, "We will meet again, though, by his lordship's request, not around the same table. However, you will hear from me, all of you, during the coming days. I have many, many more secrets to tell."

With that, he drained the glass in one swallow.

We sat silent, waiting for him to quit the room. But he did not move. Instead, he stood there, with a wide-eyed stare, the hand still holding the wineglass at the level of his flowery waistcoat's breast.

The sound of the glass as, falling from his suddenly convulsed fingers, it crashed down upon his plate and flew in wine-flecked shards across the white napery, brought a shrill scream from the princess.

"Great Scott! What ails you, man?" cried Lord Audubon. "You there, Martin—take a hold of him!"

With a long drawn-out, shuddering intake of agonized breath such as I hope never to hear again in all my life, Charlot lurched to one side and fell heavily against the lightly built Englishman, who nevertheless made a manful attempt to catch his colleague. But in vain. Expelling the breath in a howl like a drowning man, Charlot spun right around, seized a handful of tablecloth with one flailing arm and toppled to the floor, dragging napery, dishes, epergnes, a clatter of silverware, and the cloying detritus of the soup and fish courses with him. He lay there, writhing in agony and drumming the heels of his neat little elastic-sided boots upon the highly polished parquet.

By this time, we were all on our feet and rushing to attend him.

"Loosen his collar," advised the princess. "The man is choking."

"Get a doctor!" ordered Audubon. "And summon Sergeant

Gumble. He'll be outside the door. Gumble's a capital fellow in an emergency."

Menfolk rushed to do the Emissary's bidding, and in due course came Sergeant Gumble, who, seeing the prostrate man, knelt by his side and placed ear against his chest. He looked up, his florid, homely face set grave.

"Milord," he said, addressing the Emissary. "I ham of the opinion that this man is dead."

"Dead?" cried Princess Natasha.

I felt a finger of dread trail its way down my spine.

"By jove, you don't mean it, Gumble!" exclaimed Audubon. "Why, the fellow was alive and sneering not a minute ago."

The sergeant picked up a napkin, opened it out, laid it over Charlot's face. I had a last glimpse of staring, astounded eyes, open lips rimmed with a purple tinge. And I knew with a sudden certainty that Gumble was correct.

"Permission to speak, milord?"

"Certainly, Gumble, certainly. What is it?"

"The police should be sent for, milord."

"You think there has been—*foul play?*"

"Milord, I saw such signs on the face of an officer what died by his own hand, o' taking poison in Peshawar. Captain o' the Bengal Lancers he was, milord, and no gentleman in India played a finer chukka o' polo, nor danced an eightsome reel so sprightly . . ."

"*Poison!*"

The word passed from mouth to mouth of that circle surrounding the still figure. I met Princess Natasha's eyes. Like me, she seemed not to have come to full realization of what had happened. The circumstances—the disrupted meal, the scattered dishes, silver, and napery, Sergeant Gumble's lugubrious tale—held a touch of grotesque comedy. Surely, at any moment, Jules Charlot would leap to his feet, laughing at our discomfiture, and would dance a mocking little jig, his neat boots tap-tapping on the parquet.

"Carry him out of here, some of you," said the Emissary. "You there, waiter, is there a nearby room containing a sofa?"

A hand on my arm. It was Princess Natasha.

"My dear, I think we both stand in need of a nice glass of

champagne," she said. "Come, sit with me and let us compose our thoughts till the police arrive."

The police came within the half hour. We watched their arrival from windows of the luncheon room. They came in a flurry of uniforms, long cloaks, plumed hats, much heel-clicking and saluting. Two by two, they marched up the steps to the main door of the hotel, behind the officer who appeared to be their principal.

"Major von Berg of the Berlin Police Department!"

It was Jack Grant who introduced the leader of the newcomers. The colonel must have arrived back at the hotel just before them. I wondered how he had fared with the indomitable Augusta Scrase.

"Ladies and gentlemen!" The major bowed and clicked his heels. He was impressive, the way Jack Grant was impressive, but blond where the other was dark, with pale blue eyes. His thick neck was banded by a tall, uniform collar, and his hair—he carried his helmet in the crook of his stiffly held arm—was cropped close enough to reveal a saber scar that ran from temple to crown. Another duelist.

"Ladies and gentlemen, pray give me your attention." He spoke English without a trace of accent. "It is necessary for me to question each of you individually concerning this matter. Will you then please vacate this room, and you will be called in one at a time. Sir, you have a question?"

Lord Audubon did indeed have a question, as did we all. Five minutes before the arrival of the police, we had seen a tall-hatted gentleman alight from a cab outside the hotel, carrying a bag and looking uncommonly like a physician—a guess that was confirmed by one of the waiters soon after.

"Major, is the man dead?"

"He is dead."

"And the cause?"

A moment's hesitation, but no flicker in the cold blue eyes. "The doctor has determined death by poison. Prussic acid."

We were all ushered out of the luncheon room to the wide, carpeted corridor beyond, which was amply furnished with sofas and armchairs. I looked around for Jack Grant, but saw, with a wayward pang of disappointment that I tried instantly to quench, that he had buttonholed the Emissary and was walking with him up and down the corridor, addressing his superior swiftly and vehemently, and gesturing with his hand. Princess Natasha was making for one of the more comfortable-looking of the armchairs.

Someone came up behind me and touched my elbow. "Come and sit down, Clarrie. We've got things to talk about, you and I." It was Ralph Orwell.

We took facing seats by a long window that looked out across the Unter den Linden, where a pretty girl in a nursemaid's veil walked past, in and out of the sunshine, pushing a wicker bassinet from whose hooded confines a small pink fist was flourished in her direction.

I met Ralph's gaze.

"Well?" I asked. "What happened?"

"I see it this way," he said. "I see Charlot picking up that telegraph message from the office on Berlin station, and reading it through over and over again on his way here for luncheon."

"You think it contained the information he requested?" I asked.

"Maybe. Maybe not. In any event, it cost him his life."

"Oh, no!" I breathed, and seemed to see again the blood-dabbled scrap of fur lying in the grass; seemed to hear sinister footsteps coming down the echoing nave of the great cathedral. . . .

"That charade he played in there," said Ralph, "that game of telling tales out of school, that was Charlot's way of letting someone know that he was on their trail. The stories he told—the item of scandal about the princess' late husband, the rumor about Whymper—they were just to whet the appetite. You remember the last words he ever uttered?—'I have many, many more secrets to tell.' It's possible that if Audubon hadn't silenced him in the way that only an English aristocrat can, he would have read that telegraph message out loud, and we'd have known . . ."

"Ralph," I broke in. "The message—surely it will be in his pocket, still, and the police will find it."

He shook his head. "Gone!" he said.

"But—how do you know?"

And then I remembered that it was he and Sergeant Gumble who had carried the dead man from the luncheon room to a small ante chamber beyond. We had seen them through the open door, laying the still form upon a sofa and covering it over with a tablecloth.

"I searched the dead man's pockets after making some excuse to Gumble about looking for a suicide note," said Ralph. "But the killer had been there before me."

"But—when? How?"

"While everyone was crowding around him," said Ralph. "While someone was smacking his cheek to revive him and someone else was unfastening his collar. Nothing would have been easier."

"You'll tell the police immediately?" I said. "About your suspicions regarding the telegraph message?"

He shook his head.

"But—why not, Ralph?"

"The more the Berlin police know," he said, "the more suspicious—unexplained—facts they stumble upon, the longer they're going to keep us here. And I happen to think, Clarrie, that it's pretty important for this mission to get under way again. And save the peace of Europe by stopping those guns from opening up in Constantinople."

A waiter was trundling a trolley ladened down with tea things: dainty cups and saucers, paper-thin sandwiches, cream cakes, and a samovar. It seemed that cosmopolitan Berlin had adopted the English afternoon-tea habit. Princess Natasha saw it, and called the man over.

A thought came to my mind, "I remember your asking, Ralph—it was during the reception at the Gare du Nord—if there were people who might attempt to prevent the mission from reaching St. Petersburg. Do you now think that one, or more, of those people is traveling with us?"

"Yes, I do, Clarrie." The amber eyes were very serious.

"But—who?" I asked.

He looked at me very straight. "I don't exclude anyone," he said. "Well—Lord Audubon?—yes, maybe. But no one else. Not Martin, or Miss Scrase. Not even the princess. Or Grant himself, who's organizing the whole thing"—his eyes softened—"and if you've any regard for your safety, Clarrie, you'll suspect everyone, too. And, in your case, that also includes me."

I held his gaze, hoping to fathom what lay behind those subtle, amber-colored eyes.

"And, in your case, am *I* a suspect, Ralph?" I asked him.

He shook his head. "I doubt it, Clarrie," he said. "And now, if Princess Natasha has left us any tea, I suggest we make the most of our opportunity. We could be here all afternoon, for it's certain that the likes of you and me will be among the last people whom that very stiff-looking Prussian police officer will summon."

In the event, he was wrong. And I never got any tea. Just then, the door into the luncheon room was thrown open, and one of the major's men stood to attention there, looking left and right.

"Fräulein Herbert?"

Someone had cleared the wreckage away. Major von Berg was seated at the far end of the oval-shaped table, where Lord Audubon had been, a sheaf of papers lying on the table—now denuded of a cloth—before him, with a pen and pocket inkwell aligned precisely by his right hand. He got up when I entered. Bowed. Waved me to a seat—the same one that I had occupied during the fateful, unfinished meal.

"Miss Herbert," he began, referring to the top sheet of paper, "you are English? Accompanying Lord Audubon's party in the capacity of interpreter. What languages do you interpret? German, perhaps?"

"Yes."

"So? That is interesting." He had switched to his own tongue, and the cold blue gaze flickered over me, taking in the details of my clothing, my hair, my fingernails, so that I felt peeled and vulnerable before him. "How long have you followed this occupation?—and you, if I may say so, a woman and so young."

I felt suddenly trapped.

"Since—since we left Paris," I said in a small voice.

"So? This is your first assignment as official interpreter to a high official of the British Foreign Office? And what did you do before taking up your present occupation, Fräulein?"

"I was—a schoolteacher."

"A schoolteacher?" The eyes, the perfectly controlled muscles of his strong face, gave nothing away, but I sensed his mind trying to make the connection between schoolma'am and interpreter to an Emissary Extraordinary—and not succeeding.

"At a prominent academy in St. Errol, in the duchy of Cornwall," I said. Adding hastily, "St. Errol is a city. With a cathedral."

"A cathedral? So?" He made a note on the sheet of paper, dipping the pen precisely, writing with a swift hand, replacing the pen alongside the inkwell. "Your German is excellent, Fräulein. You studied over here, no doubt?"

"No, I learned from my father," I said.

"Your father was, perhaps, of the British Foreign Office—a member of the diplomatic corps?"

Father a diplomat? I thought of poor Papa, trudging the towns and cities of Europe, from emporium to emporium, weighed down with his carpet bags all swollen with samples of modestly priced corsets for ladies and gentlemen both; eating in cheap taverns, listening to the buzz of talk all around him, retaining the lilt and cadence of an *argot* in his keen mind, scribbling down a word, an unaccustomed phrase; responding, perhaps, to someone who addressed him, revealing that warm and lively intelligence which so curiously opened the inner eye of everyone who encountered him, a brilliance that should have won him a place in the great councils of the nations if only that brilliance had not been flawed (or enhanced?) by his quite genuine humility.

"Yes, my father was—a sort of diplomat, Major," I replied.

"Diplomat—ah!" The precise pen made another squiggle on the sheet, and was returned to its rightful place. The pale blue eyes encompassed me again. "Now, Fräulein, let us speak of this murder."

The abrupt change of mood and delivery, from plodding bureaucracy to incisive assault (Major von Berg matched the question by leaping to his feet and striding swiftly to the window, where he turned and treated me to a basilisk stare, pale eyes oddly bright against the bronzed face that was part silhouetted against the light), left me almost incoherent.

"M-murder?" I echoed.

"Herr Charlot was murdered," he said. "It is unlikely that his death was encompassed by any one of the very large number of servants who waited upon the party—though I do not entirely overlook the possibility, and my subordinates are closely questioning these men at this very moment. It follows, then, that one or another of the members of Lord Audubon's mission, or the First Secretary from the Embassy—the eight other people sitting around this table—placed the poison."

"In Monsieur Charlot's glass?" I breathed. "While none of us was looking?"

"The poison—the prussic acid—was placed in the last of the wine contained in the decanter from which Herr Charlot supplied himself," said Von Berg. "According to the doctor, there is still enough remaining in that now almost empty decanter to kill yet another man. Or woman."

In desperation, I said, "Perhaps he committed suicide."

"Not very likely, Fräulein," responded Major von Berg. "Consider—and you are a woman of intelligence—Herr Charlot's circumstances. Here is a journalist, a very distinguished man of his profession, as well known in Berlin as he is in Paris. He accompanies an eminent English diplomat on a mission to St. Petersburg, presumably in order to add further luster to his fame as a political correspondent. Would such a man, with such an intent, come all the way to Berlin merely to destroy himself—albeit in the distinguished company of a Russian Princess of the Blood and a Peer of the British Realm. And that without explanation, or justification? Without even a suicide letter?"

I flinched inwardly at the mention of the suicide letter, and nervously murmured my agreement with Von Berg's thesis. There really was no logical reason why the Frenchman should have killed himself that day.

"Furthermore," went on the major, "death by prussic acid is, though swift, far from easy. It would take a brave and desperate man so to destroy himself. No, Fräulein, I think I have to look for someone sitting around this table during that luncheon. Someone who found the means to introduce the poison into the decanter—during some minor disturbance, perhaps—in the knowledge that Herr Charlot would drink it. Tell me—had he, the victim, been drinking heavily during the meal?"

"Yes," I said.

"He was—perhaps—intoxicated?"

"He had control of his speech, and of his thoughts," I said. "But his manner was very—irrational."

"So! You interest me, Fräulein." Von Berg walked slowly back from the window, the spurs of his highly polished tall boots ringing with every step; paused close by my chair, looking down at me from his great height, hands clasped behind his back; disturbingly male, infinitely masterful. "He was intoxicated and irrational. The intoxication explains why he did not perceive the prussic acid in the wine when he raised it to his lips. Being drunk, he would not realize before it was too late, before he had taken a mouthful—and a mouthful would have been sufficient. More than sufficient."

I remembered Jules Charlot in the last few moments before death struck him down—standing with the wineglass still in his hand. And I shuddered. Von Berg noticed, and I thought I saw a wry smile momentarily ruffle the gravity of his mouth.

He went on, "The irrationality—that interests me even more. I am looking for some clue as to a minor disturbance of the kind that would have given the murderer his opportunity. Now, did Herr Charlot's irrational behavior provide such an opportunity, perhaps? Answer me, Fräulein."

I felt trapped. This man had led me into a trap. I saw its open maw lying in front of my feet.

"I—I don't know," I whispered.

Silence for a moment—in which I seemed to hear Ralph Orwell's words: *The more suspicious, unexplained facts they stumble upon, the longer they're going to keep us here.*

"He did not, perhaps, fall about—the way a drunken man will?" demanded my interrogator. He was all interrogator now.

"No."

"Spill his soup?"

"No."

"Make some indelicate suggestion to one of the ladies present, thereby bringing down upon himself the anger of his host Lord Audubon? He was, after all, French. And Frenchmen sometimes feel obliged to live up to their somewhat exaggerated reputations for gallantry."

"No—nothing like that!"

He was so close to me that I caught a tang of well-kept leather and cologne water.

"Then—like *what*, Fräulein?"

"I . . ."

My hesitation betrayed me. Again I seemed to hear Ralph's urgent declaration: ". . . *it's important to get this mission under way again . . . save the peace of Europe . . .*"

"What did he do, Fräulein?"

"He . . ."

"He did *what?*"

"He—suggested a game. A game of telling secrets." I was extemporizing wildly in my mind, for I thought I saw a way out. I had to tell him something, for had not Ralph also said that it would be suspicious and *unexplained* facts which would prompt the police to keep us in Berlin?

"What secrets were these?" demanded Von Berg.

"Oh—silly things. Small scandals that he had picked up during his career as a correspondent. Nothing at all, really. But, as I said—it was an irrational thing to do."

Had I said enough to satisfy his curiosity, quieten his suspicions? I had not . . .

"Small scandals—about *whom?*"

Again the trap yawned wide . . .

"Oh—well-known people."

"*Which* well-known people?" Then he added quietly, as if he knew the answer; knew that I was teetering on the brink of his trap and all he had to do was to give one small push, "People who were sitting around the table, perhaps?"

Clutching at a straw, I cried, "By no means! Why, one of the people concerned—the mountaineer Edward Whymper—was a stranger to everyone save . . ."

"Let us leave aside the mountaineer Edward Whymper, who was not present," said Von Berg implacably. "Let us speak of the people present about whom the dead man revealed these secrets, these small scandals—as you describe them. Names, Fräulein!"

"Princess Natasha Bibescu," I whispered, lowering my eyes.

"Ah, so! The princess. And who else?"

"No one else," I said.

"And what was this secret concerning Princess Natasha Bibescu that was revealed across the luncheon table, before all?"

I was trapped, and there was no going back. Any lies, half-truths, subterfuges, he—such a practiced interrogator—would uncover in very short order when he came to cross-questioning the others.

"It concerned the princess' late husband," I said.

"Specify the small scandal concerning this gentleman."

"At—at the time of his death, he was living apart from the princess," I breathed, feeling myself to be betraying my friend. "With an actress."

"Aaaaah!" He stepped back and folded his arms. "Now I think we are arriving at the truth. This *small scandal*"—he gave full value of irony to the words—"do I take it that this *small scandal* was unknown to anyone but the princess till the intoxicated Charlot blurted it out before the company?"

"Yes," I admitted. "But I know she wouldn't—couldn't . . ."

"Do what, Fräulein?" he demanded. "Murder Charlot for revealing what for a proud woman was the shameful truth of her husband's infidelity—a secret which she may have hoped had died with him? I can assure you, Fräulein, that in my not inconsiderable experience as a police officer, I have encountered women who have killed, in a moment of passion, for far less."

Having betrayed my friend, I knew that I must now defend her, and this I then proceeded to do. With more vehemence than caution—as it turned out.

"Not the princess!" I cried. "You don't know her character. Yes, she was upset when her secret was dragged out and displayed around the table. She even wept a little. But Princess Natasha is not a person to repine for long. She is all sunshine and shadows. One minute she was crying. Next minute, she was eating her luncheon with every appearance of enjoyment. Full of life and gaiety. Why, she was just the same when her little dog was . . ." I stopped, suddenly appalled.

The pale blue eyes narrowed. His head flicked up.

"When her little dog was—*what*, Fräulein?" he demanded.

And then I had to tell him about the killing of Pepé. And when he interrogated me further, demanding to be told of any other odd or unusual occurrences that had taken place during the journey, I was constrained to recount the incident of the rifled baggage. Thinking the event in Cologne cathedral too insubstantial to be of significance (and, in any case, it had probably been all my imagination), I said nothing of that.

And when I had finished my betrayal—for that is how I saw it —he dismissed me.

Chapter Seven

WHEN I CAME OUT OF THE LUNCHEON ROOM, RALPH ORWELL WAS sitting where I had left him. He sprang to his feet and came swiftly over to join me, hands extended.

"Clarrie, how did you get on? Did you . . ."

And then he saw my tears, though I had dabbed most of them away and had practically composed myself from the effects of the last, hideous ten minutes of my interrogation, when Major von Berg had wrested everything from me.

"Please, Ralph," I pleaded, freeing my hands from his. "Not now. Later."

"Sure, Clarrie," he said, backing away. "But if there's anything I can do. Just as soon as you want me . . ."

"I know that, Ralph," I told him. "And thank you."

I went down the corridor, looking to left and right, into the open doors of richly furnished chambers and into curtained alcoves. Of Princess Natasha there was no sign, but it was not she whom I sought. Grave though the betrayal of my friend, I had committed an even graver betrayal. And there was only one person to whom I must make my confession.

And then I saw him.

Jack Grant was standing in an alcove of the corridor, looking out into the ornamental garden that lay at the rear of the great hotel: a place of fountains and gesticulating statuary, of high flowering rhododendrons as splendid as those of Cornwall, and whispering cypresses. He turned at the sound of my approach.

"It went badly with you, I think, Miss Herbert."

"Yes," I answered. "Is it so obvious?"

I felt the power of his eyes, and was conscious that here was a man of a different quality from Major von Berg. He was as masterful and domineering as the German, but there was something else, and I could not for the life of me determine what it was.

He said, "Your face, Miss Herbert, is very—expressive. I think, if I were your interrogator, I would rejoice to know that at last I had found someone who could never lie convincingly, whose motives were perfectly transparent."

"How right you would be!" I said bitterly.

"Von Berg is a very shrewd man," he said. "I had some conversation with him, and will shortly be interrogated like yourself. I think it will be useless for me to dissemble."

"Quite useless," I said. And I dropped my gaze. "You see, Colonel Grant, I have already blurted out everything to him."

"Everything?"

"All the strange things that have been happening. The dog who was killed. The baggage that was searched. About the horrible game that was played over luncheon. I think I may have cast suspicion on Princess Natasha and Miss Scrase."

"He would have found out in any event," said Jack Grant. "Either from one of us alone, or from all of us, piece by piece. He is a policeman trained in his craft. A person like yourself, Miss Herbert, has as much chance of success in trying to deceive such a man as a rabbit of evading a stoat."

I looked up into his gray eyes and saw only compassion there; no sign of anger or disappointment. But I could not, would not, accept his forgiveness so easily or so soon.

"But I've ruined everything!" I cried. "Now, after what I've told them, the police will hold us here. The mission is finished. And I swore an oath to carry out my duties no matter what the hazards. I should have lied to him. Deceived him. Denied everything to the bitter end. I should have . . ."

He took me by the shoulders. I trembled at his touch.

"No," he said. "It would have availed you nothing and almost certainly made things worse for the mission and for all of us. The truth was bound to get out, Miss Herbert. Von Berg was certain to deduce that we have a murderer in our midst." He turned away, releasing his grasp, and looked out of the window. "God, I should have known better than to bring so many people with us. I should have insisted that only the Emissary and I . . ." He muttered something under his breath that I did not catch.

"Herr Oberst Grant!"

It was Major von Berg's man. He stood to attention at the entrance to the alcove.

"I am summoned?" asked Jack Grant in German.

"Yes, Herr Oberst."

He left me with a nod, a smile. And a ringing in my ears like all the bells of Heaven, a chorus of angels shouting for joy, and —high above in the clear sky—one small bird singing his heart out.

The next hour—or it may have been two—have passed beyond my recollection, since I spent the time in a blissful state between awareness and daydreams. I seem to remember that I found a way out into the sunlit garden behind the hotel; that I walked among the mute statues and felt wisps of fine spray from the fountains cool my heated cheeks, and listened to the whisper of the cypresses and the water as it gushed on high and murmured in its rills. Someone must have sought me out there, for I was presently summoned to return to the luncheon room.

All of them were there—all save Augusta Scrase. The major was seated at the head of the table as before. The others were disposed about the chamber, some sitting, some standing. I met Princess Natasha's eye. She smiled and waved. I could not bring myself to look directly at the tall figure by her side.

"Major, I should be obliged if you would make known your intentions concerning my party," said Lord Audubon, who was sitting at the opposite end of the table from the German police officer, in the place formerly occupied by Jack Grant. "The delay has been considerable, and may seriously jeopardize the outcome of my mission to St. Petersburg. You have, I presume, taken evidence from all persons present. What else remains?"

"I must tell you, Major, that we have made representations to your government," said the porcine First Secretary from the Embassy importantly. "The strongest possible representations, to protest against Lord Audubon and his party being subjected to any further unnecessary delay."

Von Berg treated the latter speaker to a glance of such utter contempt as would have quenched a man of stronger will. The First Secretary turned bright crimson, opened his mouth as if to say something else, and thought better of it.

"What is your answer, Major?" Jack Grant's deep voice cut through the silence like an axe. "Do we go—or do we stay?"

The battle line was drawn, and it was between the two men who faced each other across the table: the one so dark, the other so fair; both men of iron resolve; men's men, both scarred with steel, and steely within.

"Colonel, a murder has been committed," said Von Berg.

"As yet unproven."

"My enquiries will continue."

"The urgencies of international diplomacy must take first place before your enquiries."

"I do not accept that, Colonel."

"You may be obliged to accept it, Major."

Like two fighting cocks! I glanced from one to the other, entranced. And my gaze lingered upon Jack Grant, and stayed there. By what grace, I wondered, had such perfection been fashioned? The breadth of shoulder, the set of head, the way in which his hands remained in perfect repose (Von Berg was drumming a tattoo upon the table with his fingertips), the cool grayness of his steady gaze, the manner in which the dark curls clustered at the nape of his neck. My pulse quickened . . .

Von Berg was talking. Despite the seriousness of the issues involved, I was scarcely attending. While he droned on about the evidence with which he had been presented, the circumstances of Charlot's death, the requirements of Prussian law, I could only stand and wonder at the thing that had happened to me, the revelation that had struck from out of nowhere with the touch of a man's hands upon my shoulders. How my life would never—could never—be quite the same again.

A knock upon the door broke through my blissful reverie and silenced Von Berg.

"Come in!" he rasped.

It was Sergeant Gumble. He stood to attention, saluting his officer and the Emissary.

"You have the reply to my message, sergeant?" demanded Lord Audubon.

"Yes, milord."

"Give it to me."

The sergeant produced from his sabretache a paper, folded and sealed, which he placed in the other's outstretched hand. The seal broken and the paper unfolded, the Emissary read the contents and passed it on to Jack Grant, who did likewise and slid it across the polished table top toward the mystified Prussian.

"I think that resolves your dilemma, Major," he said quietly, "and without offending your admirable sense of duty."

Von Berg took up the paper, unfolded it and read it, displaying as he did so first amazement, then disbelief, followed by wonderment. And then the expressionless mask was assumed again. He sprang to his feet. Clicked his heels.

"My lord. Colonel Grant," he said. "You are free to proceed upon your journey. And I shall deem it an honor for me and the police officers under my command to escort you to your train."

"Thank you, Major," responded Lord Audubon.

The man with whom I had so suddenly and disturbingly discovered myself to be in love (are we so naked and vulnerable, we women, that the mere touch of a man's hand upon the shoulder can so completely and irrevocably set its seal upon one's half-formed speculations about him, or am I different from all the rest?) nodded to Von Berg and took up the paper, which the Prussian had laid down upon the table. I experienced an inexplicable feeling compounded of panic and inexpressible joy as he came toward me.

I was not meeting that gray-eyed gaze (how could I, without betraying the helpless, hopeless feeling within me?), but had fixed my gaze upon the paper in his hand.

"As official interpreter to the mission, Miss Herbert, I think you should see this," he said. "Take charge of it, please, will you? And pass it on to Miss Scrase, who, as Lord Audubon's secretary, will place it in her records. It is, as you will see, a communication from the Chancellory of the Prussian Empire."

"Thank you, sir," I whispered, taking it from him.

"A very satisfactory outcome." The far-off voice of Lord Audubon. "Major von Berg, we will take champagne with you before our departure. Do you not agree, princess?"

"Champagne," declared Princess Natasha, "soothes all ills, resolves all animosities." I supposed that she was smiling her wonderful smile at Major von Berg, but I was all uncaring. My only thought was for him who stood before me—tantalizingly, disturbingly close to me. And how could he not notice that my hand was trembling as I gazed blindly down upon the words that my mind could not piece together?

"Well, what do you think, Miss Herbert?" said the man who had become all my world. "Impressive, eh? We are not without influence in Prussia, wouldn't you think?"

"What?—oh, I'm sorry, Colonel."

"The note, Miss Herbert. Bismarck's note."

Then I read it:

The Right Hon.	The Imperial Chancellery,
the Lord Audubon	Berlin.

April, 1878.

My Lord,
I beg you to direct my wish to any Person or Persons concerned within the borders of the Prussian Empire, which is this: that you and your party are to be afforded every assistance in speeding you on your way to St. Petersburg, and are to suffer no let or hindrance. My respects, Lord Audubon,

Von Bismarck
Chancellor

And I realized that what I held in my hand was nothing less than a passport from the great Bismarck himself, the "Iron Chancellor," founder of the Prussian Empire, second only to the Kaiser, and infinitely more impressive.

The mission to St. Petersburg had powerful friends indeed!

I was addicted to novels of romance when younger, and considered myself thoroughly versed in the habits and mannerisms of those smitten by love. Victims of cupid's dart, as I well knew, were given to swooning and the vapors. In the presence of the loved one, the sufferer grew tongue-tied, incapable of even the simplest of responses, liable to bump into and knock over rare and expensive pieces of ceramic, or upset tea all over maiden aunts. While paying lip service to these beliefs, I had privately reckoned them to be literary conventions, bearing no real connection with true human behavior. I am now able to aver that everything that has been written or spoken about the state of being in love, no matter how far-fetched or bizarre, is entirely possible. The poets were right all the time.

In that grand hotel in the Unter den Linden, newly finding myself in love, I was as bemused and bewildered as any heroine of fiction; totally incapable of rational decision, with only one thought in my head—to seek out my loved one and be with him, alone, even if only for a few brief moments.

After champagne had been drunk and parting civilities exchanged with Major von Berg and his aides, a general movement was made in the direction of the exit. Ralph Orwell, assuming that we should be returning together to the station as we had come, offered me his arm, but I made some excuse that I wanted a word with the princess, and hung back, asking him to wait for me at the carriage. I made a circuit of the room, putting down my reticule and picking it up again, examining myself in the ornate mirror over the chimneypiece, patting my hair in place, setting my bonnet straight, putting it a bit askew again, and all the time hoping and praying for my wish to come true; silently begging that, in return for every good action I had ever performed in my life, Jack Grant would be the last of them to go out of the door and, pausing to see that I still remained, would come back and address a few words to me in private. A modest enough prayer, and one which, considering the number of people in the room, would probably not be granted. But I was in love—and opportunity was everything.

I remained at the mirror, fiddling with my bonnet ribbon, my back to the door. The volume of sounds diminished as, one by one, they went into the corridor. Last of all, I heard the voices of Lord Audubon—and Jack. And then, I was alone in the room.

But not alone. The door closed, and a click-click of male footfalls crossed the parquet toward me. He said not a word. I closed my eyes and fought to control my quickening breath, waiting for the moment when I would have to turn and confront him; certain that my looks would instantly betray me.

He stopped close by me. I gave a swift, shocked intake of breath, as his hand softly insinuated itself at my waist in what was very near to a caress.

I spun around, an endearment already framed on my lips, and looked into the smiling, confident face of Lord Audubon.

"You're looking very fine today, m'dear," he murmured. "The alarms and excursions of the last few hours appear to have enhanced your beauty. I do declare that there is a fresh bloom on your cheeks, a new luster in your eyes."

Gaping foolishly, I stammered, "Th-thank you, my lord."

"No call for thanks," he replied, adding cryptically, "I think we have an understanding, have we not—Clarrie?"

His approach, the manner of my turning to face him, had so positioned us in relation to one another that I was standing at the angle of the chimneypiece, with its marble molding blocking my retreat in one direction, and the paneled wall shutting off my escape to the rear. There remained only one way out. And this he effectively blocked by placing the palm of his hand firmly against the wall at the height of my shoulder, so that his arm was touching mine. I was hemmed in completely. And he was looking down at me from his great height, his other hand still resting gently against my waist, on the hip.

"I really must go," I murmured. "The carriage . . ."

"Do we not have an understanding?" he asked.

"I don't know what you mean," I replied. And, I wondered, what would he do if I ducked under his arm? Would he then seize me with both hands? The risk was too awful to contemplate. Having committed himself to take hold of me, what other liberties might he not attempt?

"Come now, little temptress." Relinquishing the hold upon my waist, he took my chin between finger and thumb and directed my gaze upward to his faintly mocking eyes. "You have led me on far enough."

"My lord, I have done no such thing!" I exclaimed, shocked.

There was no shaking his overweening self-confidence, nor quenching his assured smile. He became indulgent, as one is to a small child who denies—very winsomely and charmingly—that it has stolen jam.

"Very well, my dear," he murmured. "In deference to your sense—your entirely proper and commendable sense—of the proprieties, we will continue the fiction of my being the pursuer and you the pursued. I the hunter and you the poor little frightened doe."

"It is no fiction, my lord!" I retorted with some heat.

"What? Oh, come, my dear, my winsome little Miss Herbert." He was all mockery, now. "Can you deny that you have led me on?"

"Sir, I deny it utterly!" I cried.

"Very well, very well." He raised his finger and wagged it. "We will stay with the proprieties. We will pretend that your subterfuge in remaining behind in this room—so charmingly and convincingly done, the manner in which you made an interminable *longueur* of adjusting your hair and bonnet before the mirror would have fooled anyone but he who had the eyes to see—was contrived for no particular purpose."

I was rendered speechless and helpless by his words, my shield of chastity struck from me on the instant. Lord Audubon had, indeed, discerned the reason for my dalliance. But he had got the wrong man!

"One of us contrived a little *tête-à-tête*," he murmured, and his hand had fallen to my waist again. "Shall we, for propriety's sake, say that it was I who did the contriving? And not that little temptress I see before me."

His hand tensed at my waist, began to encircle me. I felt a sudden surge of something like panic.

"Please, Lord Audubon," I whispered. "I must go. I . . ."

My words were choked off when, swiftly stooping, he kissed me full upon the lips as I had never been kissed before; with moist, brutal sensuality that entirely enveloped me, stopping my breath, preventing the scream that rose to my lips—for how could I bring myself to scream into his very mouth? Both his arms were now imprisoning me, and the hand that had encircled my waist was slowly mounting toward my bosom . . .

And then, the door opened.

"My lord. Oh—so sorry!"

I froze with dread to hear the voice.

With no great show of haste, Lord Audubon took his lips from mine, his hands from my body; turned with a lazy smile to regard his aide. The man to whom I had so recently given my heart stood in the open doorway. His eyes were on me, though his words were addressed to my companion. And what I saw there was—contempt.

"The carriages are ready to depart, my lord."

"Very good, Grant. As you see, I have been slightly delayed."

"Yes, my lord."

Nostrils pinched with distaste, he turned abruptly and went out, shutting the door quietly behind him. Did he think, then, that the Emissary and his scarlet woman were further intending to protract their amorous dalliance? I closed my eyes and shuddered, feeling myself to be soiled.

Lord Audubon patted my cheek.

"Don't cry, m'dear," he said. "'Pon my word, but you are a susceptible little thing, and no mistake. Don't fret. 'Tis a pity that our charming *tête-à-tête* has ended so quickly, but there'll be other times, other places, other opportunities, never fear."

And before I could reply, cry out, or evade him, he had dropped another swift kiss upon my lips and was gone, with one last admonition that I should not tarry any longer, but go to my carriage.

We drove back to the station in great style: clattering through the growing shadows of that spring evening; a line of open landaus escorted by mounted police officers in caped coats and plumed helmets, rising and falling to a sharp trot. We must have looked like a State procession, and the evening strollers under the lilac trees paused in their perambulations to watch our passing. But in that, probably the most impressive journey I have made, or will ever make in my life, I found no delight. All I could think of was the man who sat with the Emissary in the leading carriage—the man who had been witness to my shame, and who now despised me for a loose woman.

Ralph Orwell, with the perceptiveness that I was already learning to appreciate in him, obviously guessed my mood and, no doubt attributing it to the shock of Charlot's murder and what had come after, attempted to divert me by pointing out the places of note as we passed them.

I let him ramble on for a while, then I interrupted him,

"Ralph, how much further is it to Russia?"

"To the Russian border at Eydtkuhnen—about four hundred and fifty miles," he said. "After that, five hundred and more to St. Petersburg. Why do you ask, Clarrie?"

"I think," I said, "that I want to turn around and go back home. To Cornwall."

"Why? Because of Jules Charlot's murder? Are you scared? You should be. I am."

Did I want to cut the ties and flee? Was my new love, so unexpectedly and beautifully granted to me, to be cast aside and forgotten? (As if, by merely distancing myself from Jack Grant, I *could* forget him!) That certainly was my first inclination: to save myself from further hurt, so as not to see the contempt in those fine gray eyes, nor to earn his further disapproval when the Emissary resumed his attentions—as most surely he would.

But—would I ever be able to wrench myself away from Jack Grant, however hurtful his attitude to me, the scarlet woman? Would it not be better to suffer and be with him than to eat my heart out away from him? I wished I knew.

Better, I decided, to keep an open mind. Wait till we reached the station and wait for a sign from him. If his looks were harsh, I would quit the party and return home. If (the wonder of it!) he looked kindly upon me, perhaps realizing that I had suffered Lord Audubon's embraces against my will, I would stay.

The decision made, there remained only the agony of waiting. For no other reason but to occupy my thoughts, I quizzed my companion,

"Ralph, why did Bismarck so readily allow us to go on our way? After all, murder is a very serious matter and is not usually hushed up and thrust under the carpet the way it seems to have been today."

"Always the newspaperman," replied Ralph, "I ascribe the worst possible motives to politicians and statesmen, even—I should say, particularly—statesmen of Bismarck's stature. He's obviously been informed of the purpose of Audubon's mission, or he wouldn't have released us. That means he either approves of the peace plan, or he disapproves. If the former, it means that he sees some profit for Prussia if those guns don't open up at Constantinople."

He paused. Unfortunately, I had been listening to him only with half an ear, registering the words but scarcely the meaning. Alas for distracting my mind from my problems, my real attention was directed toward the back of Jack Grant's head in the leading carriage.

"You are now going to ask me," said Ralph, "what if Bismarck disapproves of the peace plan—why is he then allowing the mission to continue on its way? Or weren't you listening to a word I've been saying, Clarrie?"

We both laughed, I despite myself.

"All right, then," I said. "Tell me."

His sensitive, puckish face grew serious. "That's the alternative I like far less," he said. "If Bismarck wants the guns to open fire on each other and bring the risk of war in Europe, his inclination should be to halt the mission right here in Berlin."

"Then why didn't he, Ralph?"

"Maybe he's figured that a member of our party is traveling with us for no other reason but to prevent Lord Audubon from reaching St. Petersburg," said Ralph, "and that Charlot was killed because he had evidence that would unmask that person—and was unwise enough to show his hand, because of which he was murdered."

"In that case . . ."

"In that case, Bismarck's interests correspond with those of the murderer," said Ralph. "If the plan is to assassinate Lord Audubon before he reaches the Tsar, then Bismarck approves—providing the assassination doesn't take place in Prussia. That would cause a diplomatic row to end all rows. And so . . ."

"And so?" He had all my attention, now.

"The Emissary and his mission is one hot potato that Bismarck wants to drop in a hurry, and right outside Prussia's back door. Mark my words, Clarrie, we're going to be hurried on our way along that four hundred and fifty-odd miles to the frontier, and Bismarck isn't going to be happy till our train pulls into Eydtkuhnen." He paused. "But then, you say you won't be with us, Clarrie. You say you're going home."

"I haven't made up my mind," I told him. "Ask me again, when we reach the train."

In the noise and steam of the vast station where our arrival, heralded as it was by the police outriders clearing our way through the crowds, caused a tremendous stir, I quite lost sight of Jack Grant, and it was not till Ralph and I reached the waiting train that I saw him again. Hatless, he was stooping to listen to a small boy—an urchin in too-small knickers and a too-large cap—who had pushed his way under the rope that kept at bay the crowds and was gravely addressing the tall Englishman in officer's regimentals, pointing to a medal ribbon that Jack wore on his left breast. Gravely, also, Jack replied to the boy's question, patted him on the shoulder as one man to another, and gave him back to the care of his mother.

He never looked my way, either with contempt or with approbation, but turned and strode immediately to the luggage van, where Sergeant Gumble was supervising the loading of what looked like fresh provisions. But the incident with the little boy had touched my heart, and I knew that, come what may, I could never go away from him.

Almost as if he had divined my thoughts, Ralph asked me if I had decided to carry on or to go back.

"I think it's too late to turn back now," I told him.

"You'd have left a gaping hole in my life if you'd decided otherwise, Clarrie," he said. And his amber eyes were disconcertingly tender. Then his mood changed. He looked away. "Well, well," he said. "Not only are we going to have the continued pleasure of your company, but two officers from the Berlin police department are also joining the train. That is going to limit the accommodation in the men's quarters even more. Although, of course, we don't have Charlot any longer . . ."

I entered the *wagon-lit* compartment. Augusta Scrase was seated in one of the armchairs, reading her book. She did not look up or give any sign of being aware of my presence. The atmosphere of hostility and tension in that small space could have been cut with a knife.

I took Bismarck's letter from my reticule and held it out to her.

"Colonel Grant asked me to give you this to put with your records," I said. "You will find it self-explanatory. You know that Monsieur Charlot is dead?"

"Yes," she replied, taking the letter.

"They say he was murdered."

"So I understand."

She unfolded the letter, scanned it, refolded it, placed it behind the flyleaf of her book, and resumed her reading. Not another word passed between us.

Before we left the station, I went next door and saw Princess Natasha. She was in good spirits. The maid Hortense was brushing her mistress's glorious wealth of shining flaxen hair, stroking it gently, handful by handful. "A hundred strokes a day, night and morning, dear Clarrie. Oh, do not be so rough with me, you clumsy creature! Ah, *quelle folle,* my dear!" She pooh-poohed the notion that I had either betrayed her embarrassing secret or laid her open to suspicion of having murdered Charlot.

"Not to protect my own feelings, but only the honor of the Romanoffs, did I countenance my husband's liaison with that vulgar little actress, provided they kept their *affaire* out of the public eye," she declared. "One grows sentimental with the passing of time, remembering the small tendernesses, overlooking the large assaults upon one's sensibilities. I confess that I wept a little when that common little Frenchman bruited the story of the count's infidelity—it was the actress woman, surely—what was her name again?—Heuseux? Heureuse?—who sold my dread secret to the common little Frenchman, don't you think?—but that was mere sentimentality. As for killing the creature, even a policeman would realize that a Romanoff would never descend to the vulgar occupation of executioner. Not when for over three hundred years it has been necessary for us to do nothing but nod —and the sentence is carried out."

The locomotive gave a screech and emitted a cloud of steam that obscured the view onto the platform.

"I think we're about to leave, Princess," I said. "I had better return to my compartment and Miss Scrase."

"That one!" exclaimed Princess Natasha. "Now, I would not be surprised if she had not murdered the Frenchman. Her excessive regard for the climbing gentleman I consider to be quite unwholesome. Ah, yes, I think we are about to move. You must return to your abominable Miss Scrase, my dear Clarrie. It is to be hoped that we shall be stopping for breakfast and to stretch our legs. *Bonne nuit, ma chérie.* Sleep well."

As I left the compartment, she was upbraiding the patient, uncomplaining Hortense for tugging at her hair.

Our train gushed and clattered out of the Berlin station at seven o'clock in the evening, having been there for about eight hours—

hours that had encompassed the termination of a man's life and a revelation of love granted to Clarissa Herbert, spinster, formerly of the Parish of St. Errol in the Duchy of Cornwall.

I stood at the window and watched as we circled the suburbs of the Prussian capital and passed through wooded environs, till at length there were neither trees nor houses and we were speeding, like a ship through an ocean, over a featureless plain in the gathering darkness.

Augusta Scrase was still buried in her book. Ignoring her and her proclivities (memories of, "If you *must* eat . . . please be so good as to masticate quietly"), I delved into the hamper that had been provided for us, where I found fresh bread rolls still warm from the baking and each wrapped in a napkin, a large pot of caviar, and a glass jar of pickled cucumbers. Exploring no further into the gastronomic richness that lay farther down the hamper, I addressed myself to supper and a flagon of a very tolerable white wine also provided. For, despite the torments and rigors of that day, I was hungry, having missed all but the soup and fish courses of the fateful luncheon. Miss Scrase showed her distaste by shifting in her seat and giving a loud sniff, raising her book so that it shielded her view of the "common little nobody" devouring her supper. And what did I care? I had other and more pressing problems on my mind than the distaste that I inspired in my traveling companion.

What hope, now, of my chances with Jack Grant? Men being what they were (and my experience of men, it had to be said, was confined to an inconclusive attachment to the Rev. Richard Neale and what I had gleaned through the medium of literature), they found it easy to countenance loose and flirtatious behavior in persons of their own sex, while unreasonably condemning such behavior in womankind. Munching hard and noisily on a pickled cucumber, I glumly decided that what he undoubtedly regarded as my loose conduct quite put me beyond the pale.

Not even Princess Natasha's story about his own mother and father consoled me. That star-crossed couple, though distanced from each other by reasons of birth, rank, and wealth, had never suffered an instant's doubt about each other's chastity. They had met, they had fallen in love, and they had together remained constant and trusting to the end. Without even a declaration of love, fate had already dashed any hope of Jack and me achieving such a record.

It grew darker. I finished my supper, and Augusta Scrase, making no move toward lighting the lamp, put aside her book and went behind the curtain to perform her ablutions. I sat back in my armchair, rocked by the gentle motion of the train, and closed my eyes.

I do not think that I slept. Rather, the events of the crowded day, and my unquiet heart, kept me in a state between dreams and wakefulness, where the mind wanders freely over the realms of fact and fantasy, darting from one to the other—as in true dreaming—but constantly being brought up short by an effort of will.

I wondered about the end of Princess Natasha's story, which events had prevented her from recounting. Did Jack's mother, the patient and devoted Mary, ever get to be received by the matriarchal Lady Alice? The father having gained so much glory, and his son having become an officer, had the old lady relented and taken her grandson back into the fold? I thought of the derisory sixpence that the duke's daughter had given to the poor soldier's daughter "for her pains," and realized on the instant that there was more to it than forgiveness on the grandmother's part. Mary, also, would have had to swallow a lot of pride in order to cross Lady Alice's threshold.

At this point in my mental ramble, I was aware that Augusta Scrase, having finished her toilette, was going to bed. The expensive tang of her scent wafted to me as she passed, and the wide sleeve of her peignoir brushed my hand. I heard her lie down, sigh, and turn over to face the wall. While waiting to hear the snoring that would betray her sleeping state, I drifted off into a fantasy where Jack Grant and I, having overcome all our differences, were at last about to be married. In the cathedral of St. Errol. And who should be officiating at our nuptials but the aristocratic Archdeacon de Tracey?

I heard the chords of the great pipe organ rising to the carved and painted angels high in Mr. Butterfield's roof; heard the voices of the choir—trebles, altos, tenors, and basses all—swelling in a great, joyous sound. I was dressed in white silk, with a chaplet of orange blossom binding my veil, and a posy of white roses—to tell of my chastity. My lover, my groom, was waiting for me at the altar rail: tall in his dark blue regimentals frogged with dull gold, and Sergeant Gumble his best man at his side.

The bliss, the unimaginable splendor of the fantasy, grew ever more protracted, so that my wedding march up the great nave of the cathedral to the sound of the "Wedding March" stretched out to an infinity of time and space, and I may indeed have slept part of the way through it. I only know that, somewhere between waking and sleeping, and still not having reached my bridegroom standing at the rail, I was rudely aroused by the jolting motion of the train coming to a halt, the squeal of brakes, the hissing of steam, and then silence.

I sat up and looked out of the window. There was nothing to be seen but a thin plume of white steam dissipating itself into darkness.

"What's that—what's happened?" Augusta Scrase sat up in bed. It was too dark to see her face, which was a pale patch against the whiter bed linen.

"It's nothing," I said. "We've just stopped, that's all."

"Have we arrived?" She was more than half asleep.

"No."

"Then what station are we at?"

"No station," I replied, peering out again. "I don't see any lights or buildings."

"Then why have we stopped?" Her voice—usually so well-modulated, cool, and controlled—was whiny and petulant, like that of a small child who has awakened in the night from a bad dream.

"Miss Scrase, I really don't know," I said. "But I'll open a window and look out. Perhaps we have to wait for another train to cross in front of us, or something."

I never opened the window. At the moment of rising from my seat, I saw a dark figure flit past: shadow against blackness. It was gone in a brief instant. The vision so unnerved me that I froze in midmotion, and all at once, I seemed to hear again the steady approach of footfalls up the long nave of Cologne cathedral . . .

"Why don't you find out what's happening?" cried my traveling companion.

I said, "There's someone outside the window, and I think . . ."

My voice was punctuated by a loud report from close at hand, from the front end of the *wagon-lit*, where the other two compartments were.

"Oh, my God—that was a gunshot!" exclaimed Miss Scrase. She knew better than I.

A scream—long drawn out and wavering to silence—sent a prickle of horror from the nape of my neck to the base of my spine. It was a woman's scream.

"Princess Natasha!" I cried.

Concern for my friend spurred me to activity from which blind terror could have held me. I wrenched at the door of the compartment, fighting with it fruitlessly for some moments before I remembered that it was locked. The descent to the railway track was farther than I had imagined: I landed on my hands and knees, and saw the tall figure of Jack Grant loping toward me. There were others behind him. Men were shouting. I scrambled to my feet, and the hand of the man I loved reached out and assisted me to rise.

"Miss Herbert, are you all right?"

"Yes," I replied. "But what about the princess. Wasn't that a shot?"

"It was indeed," said Jack. "We thought it came from . . ."

"Grant! It's here!" Lord Audubon was in a light-colored dressing gown that stood out against the dark livery of the *wagon-lit*. "Great Scott—I hope no one's been hit!"

He was pointing to a small round hole in the window of the compartment, low down. A spider's web of fine cracks radiated from it.

"Open up the door!" From Jack Grant.

"It's locked on the inside, sir!" Sergeant Gumble. He was in shirt-sleeves.

"Get a crowbar from the guard's van."

"Yessuh!" Gumble raced off.

"Princess Natasha!" I cried out, pounding the door. "Are you all right?"

There was nothing to be seen inside the darkened compartment. Only a faint rectangle of lesser darkness betrayed the window at the far side. Of the two women within—not a sign.

Jack Grant and one of the police officers were wrestling—fruitlessly—with the door handle. Beyond them, Augusta Scrase, a pale wraith in her flowing peignoir, looking like Lady Macbeth stalking the castle of Inverness by night, stood with hand pressed to her cheek, eyes staring. The rest of the party was grouped around.

"You'll never open it by hand!" declared Lord Audubon. "Where's that confounded fellow Gumble?"

"'Ere, milord!" The good sergeant bore the load of a massive iron crowbar with a sharply forked end which, being prised into the jamb of the carriage door and the weight of three strong men having been levered against the long shank, presently caused the door to fly open with the crunch of pulverized wood and tortured metal.

"Bring a lantern in here!" shouted Jack Grant. "It's as black as Hades!"

I entered immediately after Jack and the Emissary, Sergeant Gumble standing aside to let me pass. It was he who took the lantern from someone's hand and brought it into the compartment, revealing to my horrified gaze the scene enacted there.

Princess Natasha lay in the middle of the floor, her unbound hair spread like a pale shroud around her head. One outflung hand was frozen in the act of scrabbling at the edge of a rug, which was clenched between her nerveless fingers.

"Princess!" I fell on my knees beside her, and was smoothing the tousled hair from her cheeks when she gave a faint moan.

"She's still alive, at any rate," said Jack Grant at my elbow. "But has she been badly hit?"

"Bring the lantern over here!" cried Lord Audubon, who was crouched by the lower bunk.

Princess Natasha stirred, relinquished her grip upon the rug and made to raise her head. My joyful hope that she might not, after all, be gravely hurt was banished by an exclamation of horror from Lord Audubon:

"Good God! This woman's dead!"

"*Dead?*"

As Jack went forward, and before he obscured it entirely, I

saw the figure lying on the lower bunk, and recognized the mousy hair of the lady's maid, though her face was turned to the wall. One skinny shoulder briefly emerged from the neck of a coarse calico nightdress. The pillow was stained with a wide patch of bright redness.

"Shot clean through the head and died on the instant!" rasped Lord Audubon. "And done with a pistol, by the sound."

"It was an expert shot," said Jack, glancing toward the window. "Six yards, if it's an inch, and into a darkened compartment." He caught my eye. "Don't come nearer, Miss Herbert. Tend to the princess, if you will."

"Yes, Colonel," I whispered. "Of course."

By then, Princess Natasha was sitting up and holding her head in the dazed manner of someone who has suffered a grave shock from which the kindly balm of nature has so protected the memory that the sufferer cannot yet comprehend. As I discovered by a brief examination, she was unhurt in body.

And then, memory having returned, she began to scream.

The special train to St. Petersburg upon which, according to Ralph Orwell, the peace of all Europe depended, was steaming on again through the dark plains of Northern Prussia.

I was with the princess, she having somewhat recovered from her awful experience. She had begged me, clung to me, prayed for me not to leave her to travel alone in the death-compartment, and I was happy to accept; pausing only to go next door and fetch the carpet bag containing my night attire and toilet requisites. Augusta Scrase had gone back there and was sitting in darkness; silent, withdrawn. We did not exchange a word. On the way back, I saw, by lantern's light, the two Berlin police officers and Sergeant Gumble carrying a blanket-wrapped form into the luggage van. Poor Hortense's last journey on earth was fated to end less luxuriously than it had begun . . .

"Who could have done such a thing—*who?*" The princess must have asked me for the tenth time. "Hortense, she was *folle*—yes. But who would destroy a useless, helpless creature such as she? Why, Clarrie, it would be like killing a marmoset for chattering too much, or a canary for singing too persistently."

"Or a little dog," I said.

Her china-blue eyes opened wide. Her soft mouth formed the letter "O."

"Clarrie, *chérie*, you do not mean? No—it is insupportable. Unthinkable!" she whispered.

And then I told her, "Princess, it's all of a piece, don't you see? The things that have been happening since we left Paris: Pepé's death, the business with the baggage, Monsieur Charlot's murder. And now—Hortense."

She closed her eyes, beat her small fist upon the arm of her chair in an agony of mind, the bitter tears streaming down her smooth cheeks. Despite the lateness of the hour, neither of us, by some unspoken resolve, desired to woo sleep. The lower bunk, where Hortense had perished, had been stripped of its blooded linen and freshly remade. Nothing on earth would have driven me willingly to lie there that night, and I knew without asking that the princess felt the same. So we sat in the armchairs, facing each other, she still in nightgown and peignoir, me in a day dress. And the compartment gleamed with light, the oil lamp being lit and all the candles. But all that brightness could not dispel the overtones of recent death, nor the oppressive sense of unspoken perils.

The princess wiped her cheeks. "Life is so *stupide*," she said. "Here am I, a Romanoff. I might have married into any royal family of Europe and become a queen. Poor Hortense Haquin— pfui!—they will bury her and forget her. And yet, the hand of an assassin strikes down the poor maidservant when it could so easily have struck down the Romanoff and . . ."

She broke off. Her eyes flashed up to meet mine, and saw the idea mirrored there.

"Princess," I whispered, "all the way from Paris and till we left Berlin, *you slept in the lower bunk!*"

She did not answer for a while. Realization grew into certainty, and certainty into a new horror. I saw it all in her eyes.

Presently, she said, "It was Hortense's suggestion. She knew I found it difficult to sleep in the train. Poor she, who could have slept on the branch of a tree, declared that I would do better on the top bunk, where she claimed the motion was less. She was so wrong, but in the end I humored her. Clarrie, do not dissemble with me—do you think—do you think that? . . ."

"Princess, I—I don't know!"

She closed her eyes. "I heard the shot," she said. "I was trying hard to sleep, but to no avail. There was a rush of sound, an explosion, a crash, and a thud—all together. The train had been stopped for some little while. I thought that, perhaps, something had bumped into us. I sat up. Called to Hortense. There was one candle still lit. I lowered myself out of the bunk and took the candle from its holder, thinking that I might look out of the window and see what was amiss. 'Hortense,' I said. 'What has happened? Get out of bed, you idle creature. Open the window and find out what . . .'"

She broke off. I reached out and put my arm around her shoulder.

"Don't think of it," I murmured. "Not now."

"When I saw—what had been done to her—I screamed and dropped the candle," she said. "And then I swooned. Next, I remember looking up into your dear, anxious eyes, Clarrie."

She was trembling. I held her close, rocked her to and fro as one would a fretful babe.

"Ssssh! Don't dwell on it," I whispered. "We'll talk about it tomorrow."

"It was meant for me," she said. *"That bullet was meant for a Romanoff!"*

"Why, Princess—*why?*"

An hour had passed. She was in somewhat better spirits. I had found champagne in the compartment's hamper, and two brimming glasses had done their work. She was able to answer me without flinching or glancing away.

"My dear," she said. "It was intolerably presumptuous of me to ask a favor of an old friend, and highly imprudent of Colonel Grant to agree to my coming on this train. For myself, I can only offer the excuse that I positively detest traveling by road, and only the new *wagons-lits* have made railway trains in any way supportable to civilized persons, so that the opportunity of going to visit Uncle Alex in a private sleeping car was quite irresistible." Her blue eyes twinkled. She had recovered, also, a modicum of her habitually bubbling good humor. "But I can think of no excuse for Colonel Grant. He should have refused me —knowing the hazards, the darling man."

"The hazards?" I echoed.

She took another draft of her glass and waved for me to replenish it, which I did. I was not drinking.

"The first I knew about the nature of Lord Audubon's mission was at the reception at the Gare du Nord," she said. "At the time, it seemed an entirely laudable enterprise and quite devoid of any peril. Though I do seem to recall that the American gentleman—I forget his name, if I ever knew it, but I think you have enlarged your acquaintance with him, my dear . . ."

"Mr. Orwell," I supplied.

"Quite so. The American Mr. Orwell suggested that there might be some hazard involved. How right, how very right he was! I think, after what happened in Berlin and what has happened tonight, Colonel Grant will request me—Uncle Alex or no Uncle Alex—to quit this train tomorrow and make my own way as best I can to St. Petersburg, in order to save Lord Audubon's mission."

"But why?" I asked.

"Consider, my dear," she said, "that someone aboard this train —and it may be anyone . . . any of those sitting around that luncheon table in Berlin, or even the amusing Sergeant Gumble, or one of the faceless functionaries from the Paris Embassy who travel with us but have no social congress with us—desires to bring Lord Audubon's mission to naught. What better means than to assassinate Princess Natasha Bibescu?" She gave a dramatic pause, wineglass raised as if to pledge her nameless would-be killer.

"Princess, you mustn't even consider such a thing," I pleaded.

"If I were assassinated," she said, "on this train, and while under the protection of the British Diplomatic Corps—I, the favorite niece of Tsar Alexander the Second, Emperor of Holy Russia—it would mean war. Upon receipt of the news, my Uncle Alex would immediately order his troops to open fire upon the British squadron. That is the size of it, dear Clarrie. And tonight, but for the imperfect light from one small candle, which guided the aim of the assassin and brought about the death of a poor lady's maid, I think it would have happened."

I thought so too, and saw it quite clearly. But I did not wish to dwell upon it.

"Well, we'll see what Colonel Grant says in the morning," I murmured. "Would you like some more champagne, Princess?"

She held out her by now empty glass. "Dear Clarrie," she said. "At the very mention of his name, you cannot help but betray your love for him."

It was then that I confided in her about the love that she had, in the mystic way of the Romanoffs, been able to discern even before I had. And then I asked her to tell me the rest of the story about Jack's mother and the matriarch Lady Alice.

Chapter Eight

THE PRINCESS TOOK ANOTHER SIP OF HER CHAMPAGNE, ROLLED IT around her mouth appreciatively, set down her glass, and made herself more comfortable in her armchair, tucking her tiny, bare feet under her. Like a child, like a small kitten, she had again demonstrated her ability to turn from shadow into sunlight.

"You must realize, dear Clarrie," she said, "that the secret police dossier, which I devoured when I was out of my mind with love for Jack Grant, though unbelievably detailed in many particulars, was not able to record private conversations, nor the intimate thoughts of those concerned. Such details one must piece together with one's own sensibility and imagination. And that I will do, as best I can, during the course of my tale . . ."

She told it exceedingly well, and I listened to her in silence, fearful that the slightest interruption on my part would break the spell of her narrative. She resumed where she had left off, at that part where Jack, after having been adopted by his father's old regiment, had passed through his military education with honors and had been granted a commission in the regiment.

Not a week after his commission had been gazetted (the secret police dossier was quite specific: five days later), Jack and his mother received a summons which took them both to Yorkshire, to the great mansion on the edge of the moorland, with its rolling acres and tended parkland, where the old matriarch, Lady Alice Grant, was mistress of everything that could be espied from the highest point of the great gabled roof—a domain that stretched from the foothills of the Pennines in the west to the shores of the crawling, gray North Sea in the east.

There is no way of telling what manner of summons brought them, but one must suppose that Mary paid for the journey in the hard coin of injured pride, with the memory of how her beloved husband had been cast from his mother's home and fortune, ruined in his army career and in high society—and all for love of her. But however summoned, and no matter at what cost in pride, Mary took her son to see his grandmother.

One can picture it (helped, as I was, by Princess Natasha's evocative description, for all her life had been spent in such surroundings): the scene which greeted the dowdy, middle-aged woman and her son, the boy-officer in his coat of blue and gold. I imagined a house like Buckingham Palace, only set upon the crest of a sweeping escarpment overlooking heather-covered moorland, with a wide carriage drive snaking up the slope to the noble portico, where obsequious servants greeted the arrivals and guided them through pilastered halls and marble-tiled corridors to the old woman's drawing room. And Lady Alice herself: eighty-seven, stricken with part-blindness, and confined forever to a chair (so detailed in the dossier) alone in that great mansion with an army of servants to perform her every whim—yet still alone, living her memories through, perhaps tortured by bitter remorse for what she had wrought upon her son and his family, yet offering herself the defense that it was only out of respect for the code of her blood and her class that she had cast them off without a penny.

And then—presented to her—the bright-faced boy in his regimentals, and the dowdy woman whose faded beauty was made beautiful again with love and pride.

How to guess the old woman's reactions? One statement in the ponderous police report offers the clue: On the evidence of portraits of Lady Alice's dead son, it recorded, Cornet-of-Horse J. Grant of the Wessex Hussars bore a remarkable resemblance to his father when young.

What greater joy for an old woman nearing her end to find that all her tears and all her mistakes, her grief and her remorse, had all been rewarded with a reincarnation of her dead son in the living flesh?

The dossier is vague upon what followed. All we are told is that the lights burned in the great hall of the mansion that night, as Lady Alice broke the long tradition of her widowhood and dined formally with her daughter-in-law and grandson, and that they both departed on the morrow. The mother never returned to that stately home; the son only once more during his grand-mother's lifetime.

A second summons came a few weeks later, and this time Jack traveled alone. His grandmother was dying. He arrived in time to hold her hand while she slipped from life to everlasting sleep. Lady Alice's last action—so the story went, put about by ser-vants who watched from a distance, and all faithfully recorded in the dossier—was to place something in her grandson's hand, though what it was has never been told . . .

"And yes, Clarrie," concluded Princess Natasha, "Jack suc-ceeded to his grandmother's lands and fortune, and is now master of a very considerable part of northern England. If he were to marry you, my dear, you would suffer the embar-rassment of becoming a very grand lady indeed."

"I don't give a fig for his wealth," I told her in truth. "I love the man, and not the shadow he casts. But it could never hap-pen, ma'am. Not now." And then I told her about the incident at the Berlin hotel, where Jack had surprised me in the act of re-ceiving Lord Audubon's unwanted caresses.

"That man!" cried the princess. "I told you, did I not, Clarrie, how he insinuated his foot against mine at breakfast in Liège? I know his sort"—she lowered her voice, and looked conspira-torially to one side and the other, and behind her, as if for all the world we were in some crowded room where there might be an eavesdropper, instead of our sitting alone together in a train that rattled over the plains of north Prussia. "Such a one as Lord Audubon was my late husband, Count Paul. Women! My dear, I once left him alone in a room with a maidservant for five min-utes. A week later, the butler comes to me: '*Madame la Princesse*, may I have a word with you, please?' 'Yes, what is it?'" She spread her hands and rolled her expressive blue eyes.

"And what was it?" I asked, intrigued.

"The butler tells me that she—the maidservant—has been stealing from my jewel case. And well he might. When I have summoned the police, and the girl's quarters have been ran-sacked, and she is standing there, sobbing into her pinafore, they find"—she ticked the items off on her hand—"a diamond brooch worth a thousand louis, a pearl necklace worth two, and sundry jee-jaws. All from Cartier. *Alors*, the Commissaire of Police—

thinking that he is on the verge of solving the crime of the nine-teenth century—calls upon the maidservant to confess that she has stolen them from me."

"And did she?"

The princess screwed up her pretty face in a comic resemblance of a tearful little slut that was quite remarkable in its sharp evocation of character.

"No, monsieur," she whined. "These were given to me by Count Paul."

"No-o-o-o!" I breathed.

"Before the Commissaire of Police," said the princess, "and his minions, and my butler, the truth was laid bare. A fortune in jewelry from Cartier—and for what? For a kiss! That, and a tissue of promises! Do not speak to me of men, Clarrie."

"Men—some men—are quite awful," I declared.

"But not Jack Grant," she replied. "Not the man of your choice, my dear. He is all perfection. *Le chevalier sans peur et sans reproche*. But the others—some of the others—pfui!"

"Your marriage must have been a great heartbreak to you, ma'am," I said. "All the hopes and dreams you must have had, and you being so young."

She reached across and took my hand, and her eyes were brimming with tears.

"There was sunlight and shadow, my dear," she said. "The days of our betrothal, the days and nights of those first few months after our wedding in St. Isaac's cathedral—bliss! But then I became with child, and all that was changed. Count Paul sulked in his study or rode out most of the day, returning home only for meals, and spending the nights playing cards or carousing in the town. It must have been about that time when he met that creature, the actress Heuseux, or Heureux—I can never remember her name. That is men for you, my dear. Some men."

"Princess, I never knew about the child, the baby," I said. "What happened? Did you . . ."

"She lived for just one lovely summer's day," said the princess. "And she was perfection. And then, when night fell and the sun went down, that small life departed with it. And all their medical skills, all my prayers to Saints Andrew and Gregory could not save her."

"But—Count Paul—surely the tragedy of losing his child made him mend his ways," I cried.

She shrugged. "By then, he had established the actress creature in a villa in Menton," she said. "He did not attend the funeral, but he sent a monstrous wreath of flowers: arum lilies, red roses, and orchids—he was ever the vulgarian, my dear; the Bibescus are *arrivistes* and their heraldic quarterings date only from the sixteenth century and the reign of Nikolaos Mavrokordatos—which I snatched from my baby's catafalque and hurled into the face of the courier who had brought it."

"How awful!" I declared, conscious of the inadequacy of my comment. "That any man could behave so!"

The princess took another sip of her champagne.

"As I have already observed," she said, "my late husband, Count Paul, and Lord Audubon are two of a sort. They are a sort, dear Clarrie, who cannot be trusted alone with a maidservant for five minutes without afterward being constrained to load her with *bijoux* from Cartier, as if she were a duchess instead of a sly young trollop with a pretty face and complaisant ways—" she paused in alarm, observing my expression. "Dearest Clarrie, do not for one moment think that I place you in that category . . ."

I gave her a wry smile. "I am sure that to Lord Audubon I am nothing more than the creature you described, Princess," I said. "But it's depressing to be brought face to face with the truth about the impression one makes upon others."

She squeezed my hand.

"My dear," she said, "you are entirely mistaken about my meaning. These men of whom we speak, apart from being addicted to the pursuit of maidservants, actresses, and the like—and who, I ask you, are more available to the predatory male than such women?—are quite without discrimination. Trollops and honest women—they are all the same to such men."

"I would have thought that Lord Audubon might have behaved better," I said, "being a nobleman and the father of a motherless child."

"Widowers are among the worst," declared the princess. "Show me a widower and I will show you a libertine." She looked pensive for a few moments. "And fathers-to-be are somewhat the same, as I know from my own experience. I suppose that being a father-to-be is rather like being a widower, *n'est-ce pas?*"

I could not keep pace with her airy flights of logic, no more than I could match her vaster experience, so I held my peace and made no comment on that.

In my dream, I had reached the end of the aisle at last, white and shimmering in my white silk, my veil bound by the chaplet of orange blossom, and my groom, my tall hussar, was reaching out his hands to receive me. The great pipe organ, rising to a thrilling diapason, was counterpointed by the unearthly shrillness of the treble voices as they took up the words of a canticle.

And the aristocratic Archdeacon de Tracey, splendid in his robes of saffron yellow, scarlet, and white (but why, I asked myself, was he *already* wearing a viscount's coronet, with his father still alive?) began to intone the marriage service.

My glance stole to the man with whom I had chosen to pledge my life. Our hands were entwined, he looked down on me with an expression of such ineffable tenderness as to melt my heart and turn my knees to water.

"I require and charge you both, as ye will answer at the dreadful day of judgment when the secrets of all hearts shall be disclosed, that if either of you know any impediment, why ye may not be lawfully joined together in matrimony . . ."

Our hands remained clasped, our glances unwavering. We had no fears for the outcome. Alas for brave hopes,

"I declare that this marriage is illegal!"

Consternation among the congregation. I half-swooned, but was caught in the arms of my intended.

"Who *is* it?"

"Who has *dared* . . ."

A tall figure strode up the aisle. Clad in black broadcloth, with the star and ribbon of an order of knighthood, hair smoothed sleekly down behind his ears, pale-complexioned face unmoved by passion. Lord Audubon, Emissary Extraordinary to the Imperial Court of St. Petersburg.

"Who speaks?" From the archdeacon.

"Magnus Verity, Baron Audubon of Monsfield, widower and libertine."

"And what the proof and burden of your accusation?"

"The woman is already married."

"To whom, sir?"

"Why, to *you*, sir!"

I was back in the Music Hall at St. Errol, with the hot and rumbustious audience, all reeking of hot pasties and stale cider. I was the poor mute upon the limelit stage who had earned their raucous disapproval, and they were throwing things at me—so that I awoke with a start, to the sound of squealing brakes and the hissing of steam.

The princess jerked awake also. The candles had burned out and the oil lamp was no more than a guttering stub of wick. It was almost dark in the compartment. I shuddered.

"We've stopped again, Clarrie," she said. "Oh, pray God that . . ."

"Hush!" I whispered. "Listen!" Impulsively, my hand reached out for the reassurance of a friendly touch, and was met by hers halfway.

The sound that I had heard was almost immediately followed by another. Near at hand, a carriage door was closed stealthily. Someone was alighting from the *wagon-lit*. Princess Natasha's grip tightened in mine.

"Look!" she whispered. "Look who it is—and coming out of *that* woman's compartment!"

We both saw him quite clearly in a patch of shifting light, as when the moon drifts briefly out from behind a bank of cloud and is almost immediately swallowed up again. He paused at the door of Augusta Scrase's compartment, hand still resting upon the latch, looking up and down the length of the halted train. He was hatless and in shirt-sleeves, with his tunic carried over his arm. Apparently assured that he had not been observed, he moved swiftly past our window and, gaining the compartment on the other side, opened the door and went in, closing it behind him.

Princess Natasha gave a sharp intake of breath. Our eyes met in the gloom.

"What—what has he done?" she whispered.

Terror and despair fought for mastery in my racing mind. Again, I seemed to hear the ominous footsteps tracking me down the great nave of Cologne cathedral, and I saw, again, the huddled figure in the bunk that was not five paces from where I stood, the pillow saturated with life's blood . . .

I reached for the lock of the door, which had been roughly repaired. There was no evading the demands of conscience, no matter what the outcome.

"I—I must go and see what's happened to her," I cried. "To Miss Scrase."

"No, no!" cried the princess. "The train will start again, you will be left stranded!" She barred my way, wrenched at the fastening of the door's window and lowered it to look out. "I will call to her," she said. "If she is all right, she will look out and answer me."

The compartment which I had lately shared with Augusta Scrase was fully illuminated. Three rectangles of light were cast upon the ground in clear view of where we stood. As the princess and I put our heads out of the window, we saw something move in the center patch of light: the silhouetted head and shoulders of a woman.

"She is alive at any rate," whispered the princess. "Wait—she is opening the window!"

Even as we watched, a hand appeared at the now-open window next door. And then Augusta Scrase's white face emerged to regard us, eyes and mouth three dark and expressionless patches against the paleness. She stared full at us for a few moments—and then withdrew. In the center patch of light cast upon the ground, we saw her arms raise up to shut the window again, and the head and shoulders moved out of sight. Almost immediately afterward, the locomotive gave a sigh, gushed steam, and noisily moved forward at gathering speed.

"Well!" exclaimed the princess. "I take back everything I said about the gallant Colonel Grant. 'Le chevalier sans peur et sans reproche!' Indeed! Mind you, my dear, there was a certain amount of gossip surrounding him at Tsarskoye Selo in the old days. Nothing that had any meaning to me at the time, of course, for I was only a slip of a gel. But I do recall my Aunt Olga whispering to Uncle Basil—and you know how young people deceive their elders by pretending to be absorbed in a book, while all the time their ears are reaching out?—some talk of

Lieutenant Grant and a baroness, a married woman. But, Clarrie dear, you are crying!"

"It's nothing," I whispered, fumbling in my reticule for a handkerchief. "I shall be all right in a minute. It's simply that—that . . ."

"The shock has been considerable," declared the princess. "I weep for you, also, my dear. Oh, what devils men are! The English upper classes, they are quite the worst, of course. I have always said so. I wonder if Lord Audubon knows what is going on? Of course, he must. Probably conniving in the affair. Encouraged Jack Grant to sneak into that woman's compartment just as soon as you had vacated it."

"She's married," I said. "At least, I'm convinced she's married, for she wears a wedding ring on a ribbon around her neck."

"Does she now?" said the princess. "Well, I must say I'm not one bit surprised. Any woman who would so fly in the face of all that is decent and reticent as to climb mountains is capable of any excess. I wonder that she troubles to hide her wedding ring while in the course of an *affaire*, when it would be more in keeping with her style to flaunt it openly."

"Please, ma'am," I pleaded, "can we just not speak of it any more?"

"Of course, of course, my dear," she said, gently embracing me. "You have suffered a very grave disappointment. The man you thought you loved, the man who so recently rode into your life like a knight of old, has turned out to have feet of clay. You have . . ."

"Please, Princess!"

"Enough. I have said enough! Make yourself comfortable in the chair, my dear. Try to get some sleep. There, is that better? Will you have your cloak—*his* cloak—draped over you? No, perhaps better not. Here—you shall have my leopard-skin coat. Close your eyes, little one. Sleep."

I lay back in the chair, the perfumed warmth of her fur coat covering me, closed my eyes, and looked around inside my head.

Jack Grant and Augusta Scrase were lovers! And so in need of each other that each was willing to jeopardize their reputations by taking the risk of discovery that they had taken that night.

And now, surely, she must know that the princess and I saw him leave her . . .

The princess was prattling on,

"Believe me, Clarrie dear, I know exactly what you are suffering. How shall I ever forget the day—it was over the breakfast table, and I was eating kedgeree—when the count calmly announced that he was leaving me for the Heuseux or Heureux creature and that they would be residing no farther from Monte Carlo than Menton. Menton, I have always averred, is not smart, and I have never liked the place. But, do you know, ever since then, I can barely abide to hear its name spoken, or see it written. Ah, how we women suffer . . ."

The endless tide of her voice, perhaps, more than the turmoil of the day and my weary heart, sent me to sleep.

I awoke with a throbbing headache to the sound of the locomotive's whistle. We were slowing down. It was daylight. Indeed, the sun was high up on our right, and my fob watch told me it was nearly nine. The train was making a slow, curving passage across a barren flatness of marshland. Away ahead in the distance, I could discern the towers and steeples of a sizable town or city, and beyond it the steely glint of a horizon of sea. Closer at hand, about a quarter mile away, was a small station with a weatherboarded roof and tarpaper walls. We gradually slowed, till it was clear that this unprepossessing place was our immediate destination. As the train squealed to a halt, Princess Natasha stirred in the chair opposite, stretched herself like a kitten, and smiled across to me.

"Where are we, Clarrie?"

"I don't know," I replied, "but there's a rather important-looking place in the distance over there."

She followed my pointing finger, and gave a glad cry.

"Ah, it is Danzig! And there is the dear, dear Baltic! Now, at last I feel that I am nearing home. I always say, my dear, that once Danzig is behind, St. Petersburg cannot be far away. Do you know, I feel quite hungry. Danzig will do us well, I promise you. There are some quite excellent hotels in the city. I must advise Colonel Grant. The Hotel Pomerania or the St. Nicholas are both highly cosmopolitan and provide English breakfast. But why are we stopped here at this poky little wayside halt?"

"I fancy, ma'am, that we are breakfasting here," I told her dryly. "At least, here comes Sergeant Gumble with what looks like coffee and rolls."

And so it proved to be. Upon our unlocking the door and admitting him, the good sergeant placed upon the table a tray bearing coffeepot, cream jug, sugar, and a plate of rolls and butter.

"Best we can manage in the circumstances, Your 'Ighness and miss," he said. "I brewed up the coffee over the guard's stove at the back o' the luggage van."

"But why—why?" demanded the princess, indicating by a dismissive wave of her hand that the fare on the tray was far from her idea of an adequate breakfast. "Not, I hasten to add, that one does not appreciate your devotion and your expertise, sergeant. But why are we not proceeding to Danzig?"

"The orders o' the Berlin police who're still wiv us, Your 'Ighness," replied Gumble. "This train ain't to stop at any main station till we're crost the Prussian frontier. Them's the orders."

I remembered Ralph Orwell's prediction that Bismarck would ensure that the mission left Prussian soil with all haste. He was also ensuring that we would come into contact with as few people as possible.

"Very well," said the princess with a sigh. "Thank you for your trouble, sergeant."

"No trouble, Your 'Ighness," responded the other with a stiff little bow. "We shall remain 'ere for an hour, which will give everybody time to get out and stretch their legs, like. And I 'ave a message from the Colonel for Your 'Ighness and miss."

I felt my heartbeats quicken.

"What is this message, sergeant?" asked the princess, cocking a significant look in my direction.

"The Colonel would like to call upon Your 'Ighness and miss at your convenience afore we depart," was the reply.

I held my breath.

"By all means," said the princess. "Tell Colonel Grant that we will receive him in a half hour."

"Yes, Your 'Ighness, miss. Much honored." Another bow, and he was gone. At least, as far as the door, where he paused. "'Tis the Colonel's intention to press on to the frontier wiv all speed," he said. "In time for supper as soon as we're over into Russia. That's been arranged in advance."

"How nice," murmured the princess. "Thank you, Gumble."

"Your 'Ighness!" The door closed.

"Well, my dear Clarrie," said the princess. "We had better address ourselves as best we may to the good sergeant's exiguous breakfast, and pray that there is still plenty of food left in the hamper over there. For one thing we can be sure of in this uncertain world is that there will be no supper waiting for us in Mother Russia, arranged in advance or not arranged in advance. I know my Russians better than *that!*"

With which cryptic remark, she gestured to me to pour coffee for us both.

With the complete unconcern for events of the recent past that was her characteristic, the princess enlivened breakfast with a running discourse upon Russia and things Russian, enlarging upon the theme that she had opened with regard to the promised supper. And I, burdened with the horrors of the previous day and night, sick at heart with despair and jealousy, was glad of the diversion.

"All Russians," she declared, buttering the last piece of bread roll, "and I exclude the Romanoffs, for we are a race apart and the standards of the common ruck of the Russian people do not apply to us, are at once industrious and idle, philosophical and crass, intellectual and commonplace, generous and totally uncaring. They are also congenitally incapable of punctuality. And, despite Jack Grant's pious expectations, they do not go to the trouble and expense of preparing supper for an entirely theoretical group of unknowns who will almost certainly not arrive on time to eat it."

I laughed at her drollness. "Your uncle the Tsar," I said. "Surely, he demonstrated the generosity, and not the uncaringness, of the Russian people when he liberated the serfs?"

She shrugged. "Much good it did them," she said, "for many

were happier and more secure in serfdom than ever they have been since. What is serfdom? We are all slaves to someone, those of us who have loved. You know that as well as I, dear Clarrie."

That, her first reference to the final and devastating episode of the previous night, brought tears to my eyes. I bowed my head. She was not to be put off, but reached out and took my hand.

"*Chérie*, you must not despair," she said. "Now, I have given much time to thinking about your problem, for it kept me awake long hours last night. And I have come to the conclusion that you must not give up. You must fight for him. Who is Miss Scrase? Pfui! I have seen the look in her eyes when she speaks of this man who claims to have been the first to climb the Matterhorn, this Edward Whymper. I will tell you what she is. She is one who hero-worships. First it is the mountain climber, now it is the gallant and dashing Colonel Grant, who looks so fine in his regimentals. I tell you, Clarrie, there is no depth to her passion. As we say in Russia, no 'stomach.' Let her but cast her eyes upon some of the officers of my Uncle Alex's *Chevaliers Gardes*—and I will see to it that she does, my dear, never fear!—and she will be off again with stars in her eyes, chasing uniforms and decorations. How will you feel then—if you have abandoned him to her?"

"You—you think there's still hope?" I faltered. "Still hope that I—but, no! I couldn't bring myself to look twice upon a man who would . . ."

"Who would have an *affaire?*" she interposed. "My dear, where is your charity? You say that he surprised you in Lord Audubon's arms. Now, let us suppose for one moment that you had succumbed for a brief moment to an irresistible temptation—and who does not do so at least once in their life?—and were, in a sense, guilty. Would you not then have wished Jack Grant to overlook your little peccadillo? Come now, be honest with yourself, Clarrie."

"Well—yes, I suppose so." Grudgingly.

"Then how much more readily must you be prepared to forgive him, my dear?" she said, squeezing my hand encouragingly. "He, who is only a man. One of the inferior breed, slaked with dark, animal passions against which the foul nature of his sex prevents him from offering resistance. Not refined in delicate sensibility as we women are. You must forgive him, Clarrie. You must prepare your heart and your mind for the moment when, the abominable creature Miss Scrase having found yet another figure to hero-worship, he can be yours. Now, what do you say?"

"We-e-el, I suppose you're right," I said. "About forgiving him in my mind, at least. As to him ever being mine . . ."

"It will be so, Clarrie," she declared. "Mark my words! And now, having finished our meager repast, let us make ourselves presentable to receive the gentleman in question." She ran her fingers through her wealth of flaxen tresses. "What I would not give for a bath like the one I enjoyed in Liège. Ah, well, one must do what one can. The teeth. The complexion. The hair. Where, I wonder, did that absurd girl, that *folle*, put my toothbrush—" She broke off, put her hand to her mouth and stared at me, round-eyed with horror. "Oh, what have I said? To speak ill of the dead like that!"

In the event, she found her toothbrush standing in a small vase by the washbasin. She picked it up, looked at it in blank puzzlement, as one will regard an unfamiliar species of flower.

"What's the matter?" I asked.

"Clarrie," she said, "I am rather perplexed."

"About what, ma'am?"

"Well now," she said, turning the toothbrush over and over. "I have cleaned my teeth twice a day and after every meal for as long as I can remember, but do you know, I have never before set eyes on a toothbrush that was not already provided with exactly the correct amount of tooth powder for use!"

I smiled. "You mean—by a servant?"

"Of course," she said. "Formerly by one or another of my nursemaids, and later by my lady's maid."

"But, it's perfectly simple," I said.

"To you, perhaps!" she snapped. "But not to me!"

"You simply put on the amount you require."

"From where?" she cried. "And by what means? And how *much* do I require."

"I'll show you." I could not find it in my heart not to indulge her, for her anger was only a hairsbreadth from tears of pure humiliation at her plight. I found the container of tooth powder, shook out an amount onto the brush, and handed it to her.

"Thank you," she said.

"You do know how to brush them?" I asked. "Your maids don't have to do that for you?"

"Of course not!" she snapped. "Do you imagine that I am help-less?"

That was only the beginning. I had much to learn about the particular state of helplessness to which a royal upbringing re-duces a grown woman even in this latter half of the nineteenth century. The princess was still clad in night-shift and peignoir. It was necessary for me to dress her completely. She could not lace her own stays, nor button her boots. And when it came to her hair . . .

"One hundred strokes," she said, handing me the silver-backed brush. "I have a hundred strokes, night and morning. And not too vigorously, Clarrie, I beg you. My hair is rather fine and tends to tangle. And will you please count aloud? I trust you implicitly, of course"—her lovely blue eyes looked up into mine, and entirely without guile—"but, you see, *they* always do, and it wouldn't be the same."

"Of course, Princess," I assured her.

"So kind, so kind," she responded.

"One, two, three," I began, stroking the lustrous pale tresses with the soft brush, easing the bristles through them with my other hand.

"I wish, I so dearly wish, that I had hair like yours, Clarrie," she murmured.

"Why, ma'am?" I enquired.

"Oh, it is so beautiful," she said. "The color—now, I have never seen that particular tint of auburn before. There are red deer in the forests that fringe Lake Ladoga—such gorgeous crea-tures whose coats resemble your coloration—but they do not possess the subtlety of tint. And the texture of your hair—neither too fine nor too coarse, so that you have only to shake your head and the locks fall back out of disarray. I have seen you do it often. Particularly when you are angry. You have quite a temper, I think."

"Yes, I have," I admitted. "It goes with the red hair."

She laughed. "Well worth it," she said. "To suffer the smaller burden of a swift temper, in return for the larger blessing of such beautiful hair. Please don't stop."

"Fifteen, sixteen, seventeen," I intoned.

"Mmmmm—such heaven!"

"Perhaps," I said, "when I've finished brushing your hair, ma'am, you'd like to brush mine?"

A long silence, during which I must have counted—silently— at least half a dozen strokes. And then that blue-eyed gaze was directed up to me, the expression changing from surprise to affront, from affront to indulgence, afterward—swiftly—to for- giveness. Nothing needed to be said. I had transgressed. For the second time in our friendship I had sought to let my toe stray over the line that separates the royal from the non-royal, the—in Princess Natasha's own phrase—Romanoffs from the common ruck. I accepted the premise because I liked—and accepted—the woman in her entirety.

After tending to her hair, I helped her to choose the jewelry for the day: spreading out the rings, brooches, earrings, and so forth for her appraisal. She consulted me at every turn, and ac- cepted my suggestions, nodded approvingly at my affirmations, and ignored my dissensions. I then pinned the brooch, attached the earrings, placed the rings upon her fingers. And all with a good grace. It amused me to think that, by the alchemy of an odd friendship, I had been translated from schoolma'am to inter- preter to lady's maid. And all in the compass of a few brief days.

Nothing having been said about my lapse from good taste, we waited in pleasant amity for the arrival of Jack Grant. Thanks to her curtain lecture and in some ways bemused by her wayward philosophy concerning the relationship between the male and fe- male sexes, I was curiously at ease when the tall figure of Jack Grant strode purposefully toward our compartment.

"Good morning, ladies. I trust you slept well. And my apologies for the quality of the coffee."

He was wearing a dark blue broadcloth suit, and I was sur- prised to notice in his manner an air of something like gaiety. My thoughts immediately flew to Augusta Scrase, and I bit my lip and looked away.

"I hear we have been forbidden Danzig," said the princess. "A great pity."

Grant looked serious. "That is so, ma'am," he said. "Not unnaturally, the police have no wish to embroil the general public in our—affairs. So we are to be kept incommunicado while we remain in Prussia. I have to say that I am entirely in agreement with the decision. Which brings me to the reason for my requesting this interview."

"We will have champagne," declared the princess. "There is a bottle left in the hamper, Clarrie, and it will serve to take away the quite appalling taste of the sergeant's coffee. Will you join us, Colonel?"

"Thank you, no, ma'am," responded Grant. "I never touch wines or spirits before noon."

"What a quaint conceit," said the princess. "I have heard it before, particularly among the English. What is there about the climate of the forenoon, one wonders, that makes them think it an unsuitable time for drinking? My great-uncle, the late Tsar, had a sizable *flacon* of vodka with his breakfast tray every morning, and would have considered it a very odd caprice to have left a drop remaining. Thank you so much, Clarrie. I do declare that you open a champagne bottle in the manner born. Are you not taking a glass, dear?"

"Thank you, no, ma'am," I said. Grant had made as if to take the bottle from me and open it—as if I were some kind of helpless chit of a thing. I had refused him, and rather brusquely. To my added annoyance, he seemed amused by the incident and was watching me with a slight, quizzical grin.

The princess took a sip of her wine and nodded approval. "Well then, Colonel," she said, "to what do we owe the pleasure?"

"Ma'am, I think you may be in some considerable personal danger should you continue on this journey with us," he said.

Princess Natasha did not turn a hair. The hand that carried the glass to her lips once more did not waver by so much as a hairsbreadth. Not for the first time with her, I wondered at the marvel of a royal upbringing when it comes to instilling the qualities of resilience and fortitude.

"Why do you say that?" she murmured.

"Ma'am, I can think of scarcely anything that would utterly destroy the intent of this mission more surely than if you were to suffer harm while under our protection," replied Grant.

She smiled. "And you think that an attempt upon my life has already been made? Pray do not trouble to dissemble, my friend. It is written all over your face. Add to that, Miss Herbert and I have already so decided. That poor creature and I changed bunks, and because of that she died instead of me."

Grant looked relieved. "Then you are in agreement, ma'am, and you will leave this train and proceed to St. Petersburg by another?"

The princess replaced her empty glass on the table before her and smiled sweetly at him.

"No, Colonel, I will not," she replied.

"Why, Princess?" His tone was glacial.

"In the first place," she said, "to embark in a normal train will cause me the most hideous inconvenience. I cannot abide the enforced company of strangers and cannot exist without the services of a lady's maid. My friend Miss Herbert, here, performs the duties of temporary lady's maid to perfection."

"Ma'am, I . . ." began Grant, but she silenced him with a flourish.

"Secondly," she continued, "I am a Romanoff, with all a Romanoff's passion. We are used to living with the threat of assassination, we Romanoffs. The bomb, the pistol, the knife, poison—they are the constant companions of our nightmares. Well, now I have been threatened. Someone in this assembly has tried to kill me and may well try again. But next time I shall be more watchful. Do you know why, Colonel? I will tell you. I want to stay alive, and I want to remain with this train, because my dearest wish is to see the culprit unmasked." She paused, and her smooth, pink-and-white countenance was as hard as marble. "And I pray that the unmasking takes place in Holy Russia, so that the culprit will suffer the fate of common murderers there: to be flogged and afterward broken on the wheel!"

Her terrible declaration hung in the silent air for several moments. Grant looked put out and embarrassed by the vehemence of her delivery. Perhaps he had never heard a woman speak so.

Presently, he cleared his throat and said, "Princess, you are welcome to remain with us if that is your wish. Before you finally decide, however, I should tell you that Miss Herbert will also be asked if she wishes to leave. So you may be able to persuade her to accompany you to St. Petersburg. What do you say to that, Miss Herbert?" He gazed steadily at me, and I felt again that treacherous weakness of the legs, and hated myself for it. "In my opinion, in Lord Audubon's opinion, all the ladies of this party should be invited to leave if they so wish. What of you, ma'am?"

I fixed him squarely with a look of defiance. "If the princess stays, I stay!" I replied.

He nodded. "So be it," he said. "And now, ladies, I will take my leave of you. There remains ahead of us some two hundred miles to the frontier at Eydtkuhnen, which we hope to reach by six o'clock this evening. We depart in half an hour, during which time I do not anticipate any trouble. The Berlin police officers will be patrolling the vicinity of the train, and they are both armed. You need have no fear while we are here. Similarly, if the train is obliged to halt due to traffic ahead, the police will alight and keep guard, to ensure that there is no repetition of last night's tragedy." He bowed briefly and turned to leave the compartment.

"Colonel Grant!" The words were out before I could check them.

"Yes, Miss Herbert?" He looked back at me over his shoulder, one hand on the door latch. Did I see amusement in those usually so stormy gray eyes?

"You mentioned *all* the ladies of the party," I said. "May I take it that you also asked, or are going to ask, Miss Scrase?"

"That is so, ma'am," he said. "I have already asked her."

"And what was her decision?"

He smiled broadly. "The same as your own and the princess', Miss Herbert," he said. "It seems that you are all ladies of a very gallant sort. Veritable Amazons."

He left us.

"So now we know why he was so odiously cheerful," I said. "Like a tomcat on the tiles. Glad and happy that his mistress isn't taking fright and leaving him unconsoled."

"Tch, tch!" The princess gave me a look of mock disapproval

and shook her head. "I am surprised to hear you carry on so, particularly after what I have told you. La belle Augusta is in the throes of a hero-worship, and any lady who has scrambled in the Alps with the no doubt impressive Mr. Whymper is not to be deflected from her purpose at the first sign of danger. No, my dear, I am afraid you will be burdened with Miss Scrase to the bitter end—or until I have displayed the pick of Uncle Alex's *Chevaliers Gardes* for her delectation."

I laughed. "Princess, you are incorrigible."

"I am," she admitted. And then, more seriously, "It was very nice of you to opt to remain with the train, Clarrie. And I persuade myself that your decision was not entirely due to your passion for Jack Grant."

I shrugged. "Someone has to brush your hair and put powder on your toothbrush, ma'am," I said.

She reached out and squeezed my hands.

Princess Natasha and I went for a stroll in the thin sunshine before the train set off again. We passed Ralph Orwell and the Englishman Martin coming the other way. They were deep in conversation—or, rather, Martin was deep in what sounded like a dissertation on railway matters. Ralph smiled questioningly at me and raised his straw boater. That was the sum of the encounter. Five minutes later, the train drew away from the small station in the middle of nowhere, and in the hour we had rested there not another soul had put in an appearance. The last to board were the two police officers from Berlin. Both carried heavy pistols at their belts.

The next eight hours passed in a kaleidoscope of grays and muted blues, as the coastland of East Prussia slid past our windows. The princess was a fount of information and unconsidered trifles about the district. We passed within sight of Königsberg, seaport and base of the Prussian navy, founded by the Teutonic knights and formerly residence of the grand master of that order. She and Count Paul Bibescu, she told me, had spent some of their honeymoon in Königsberg, when the count's yacht had called there during their cruise of the Baltic. They had stayed one night only at the castle of the Teutonic knights. The plumbing had driven them back to the yacht.

Beyond Königsberg, we followed the course of a slow river that meandered idly across a vast plain black with pine forest. From time to time, between gaps in the trees, one would catch a tantalizingly brief glimpse of some splendid castle: all turrets, soaring roofs, pinnacles, and aged stone. These were the country seats of the Prussian Junkers, said my informant; feudal estates ruled over by the Prussian military aristocracy who were the backbone and sinew of the new empire of the Kaiser and Bismarck. The Junkers were, next to warfare, most addicted to hunting, said Princess Natasha, and she and Count Paul (whose interest in the chase was limited to pursuing young women along the Boulevard des Anglais) were once inveigled by a Junker host into joining a wild-boar hunt in the forest, during the course of which enterprise the count was found to be missing, whereupon the host and his guests—the princess included—called off the chase and set to search for the missing man. Princess Natasha, a bride of only four months, was in a state of mind that can well be imagined, for the forest teemed with savage wild boar and predatory wolf packs, it was a hard winter, snow was falling, night was closing in, and the effete and pampered count had scarcely the constitution to survive the perils and rigors of a long winter night in the open. Come midnight and he was still not found. By the light of their flickering *flambeaux,* the entire party repaired to a remote hunting lodge, to take a brief repast and a rest before resuming their heart-breaking search. And it was there, in the hunting lodge, that they found Count Paul, where he had been all afternoon. In company with a pretty Danish baroness!

Half-laughing, half-crying, the princess told me how—notwithstanding her lofty royal connections—she and the count were asked by their host to leave the following morning—which they did without question, such was the power and authority of a high Prussian Junker.

Gazing upon the passing scene through the windows of our speeding train and listening to Princess Natasha's anecdotes whiled away the time till past midday, when we delved into the hamper and found a pot of *pâté de foie gras,* a jar of black olives, a drum of English Bath Oliver biscuits all the way from Fortnum & Masons, an unpromising German sausage, and a bottle of hock,

upon which we lunched sketchily. Which done, the princess nodded off to sleep, leaving me to the passing scene—and my own
thoughts.

Uppermost in my mind, I discovered, was fear and a premonition of disaster. Though with every passing mile, the princess
seemed to have lightened in spirit, anticipating the arrival in the
safety of her homeland, my own terror increased. Prussia I had
seen, and found to be bright, well-scrubbed, orderly, and
efficient. Russia was known to me only by fable and speculation:
a country ruled over by a tyrannical emperor who had power of
life and death over his subjects—subjects who, though of his
own race and not dark-skinned aliens, had but a few years
previously supplied a vast army of slaves for the rich aristocracy
—a country, moreover, which staunch Britons regarded with the
deepest suspicion of planning to carve a path to the east and
overrun our Indian Empire. No Jingo I—but I could not imagine
that the peril in which we all stood would be lessened in dark
and backward Russia.

I was tired after a bad night. And the human mind, when
tired, shies away from disturbing thoughts and is attracted to
easeful and pleasant topics. Soon, I drifted into a waking fantasy
about Jack Grant, where he had repented of and forsworn his
wicked ways and had come begging my forgiveness and asking
for my hand in marriage, in the contemplation of which delightful eventuality I drifted from daydreaming to deep sleep.

When I woke, the train was slowing down. Though by my
watch it was only just past six, night was falling, and a flurry of
snow all but obliterated a notice board that slid past the window.

EYDTKUHNEN

The last outpost of East Prussia. Somewhere out there, close at
hand and only just beyond the compass of my vision, was Russia.

Chapter Nine

HALF AN HOUR PASSED. THE TRAIN STOOD STILL IN THE DESCEND-ing snow, its locomotive hissing steam. We saw Jack Grant walking swiftly back from a group of dark buildings at the far side of the track. With him was a stranger in a flat cap and an ankle-length greatcoat. Both were talking animatedly and gesticulating. The princess laughed.

"I think the Colonel has been to look for our supper and found the cupboard bare," she murmured.

A few moments after, Sergeant Gumble knocked at our door.

"Compliments from the Colonel, Your 'Ighness and miss. Will the ladies join him and 'is lordship in their compartment, please?"

It was cold outside, so I put on the cloak—his cloak—to alight, and the princess wore her leopard skin. To my surprise, the Emissary's compartment was already well filled. In addition to Lord Audubon and Jack Grant, Ralph Orwell and Mr. Martin were there, together with the man in the long coat, who, on closer inspection, proved to be wearing the uniform of the Prussian State Railways. He clicked his heels upon our arrival. We were no sooner inside than Augusta Scrase arrived, and I could have sworn that she had recently been crying.

"Please be seated, ladies," said the Emissary, indicating the two armchairs and the lower bunk made up as a sofa.

The Scrase woman plumped unhesitatingly for an armchair, the princess did likewise. I took my place demurely on the bunk. The men remained standing.

"Ladies and gentlemen," said Lord Audubon, "this is a council of war. I will not conceal from you that we have run into certain —difficulties. Did you say something, Princess?"

"No, my lord," replied the princess, smothering a laugh and translating it into a cough. "Pray continue."

The Emissary frowned and went on, "I—that is, Colonel Grant and I—thought it best to call upon your combined expertise to attack the various problems. The Colonel will now address you." He sat down on the sofa beside me, crossed one leg over the other and gazed up at his subordinate. "Carry on, Grant."

He had gone back to wearing his dark blue uniform tunic, with the romantic, fur-trimmed hussar's dolman slung jauntily over his left shoulder. The dueling scar on his cheekbone stood out lividly against the rugged darkness of his skin. My heart moved in the contemplation of him.

"Firstly," he began, "with regard to our guest"—he nodded toward the Prussian—"this is the stationmaster of Eydtkuhnen, and he does not understand a word of English, so we may speak quite freely, and address him in German only when we require information. That will be your department, Miss Herbert."

I gave a start. "Oh! Yes, Colonel," I whispered.

"Problem one," said Jack. "I have been across the frontier. The Russians are obviously not expecting us tonight. We come as a complete surprise."

"*They* may be surprised," drawled Princess Natasha. "*You* may be surprised. But *I* am not surprised." Having delivered herself of that homily, she took from out of her reticule a jeweled box from which she extracted a jujube and popped it into her mouth.

"Needless to say, there is no supper awaiting us," continued Jack. "Nor is there any connecting train to take us on our way to St. Petersburg. The sole representative of Holy Russia"—he gave the princess a cold, sidelong glance, to which she responded by smiling sweetly in return—"is a Mongolian sentry who does not even appear to speak Russian."

"Pardon me, sir." The speaker was Ralph Orwell. "Is there no telegraph office on the other side of the frontier?"

"There is, sir," was the reply. "But it is closed one half of the year, from October to Easter."

"Surely, there is a stationmaster over there?"

"Yes there is. But he quit work for the day two hours ago."

"That is Russia for you," said Princess Natasha, adding inconsequentially, "when in Russia, do as the Russians do."

Ignoring her, Jack said, "The immediate problem is that our Prussian friend here has instructions to dispatch this train back to Berlin without delay. And that means we shall all be turned out into the night. There is no accommodation here at Eydtkuhnen and nothing across the border. However, he assures me that, unpromising though the situation may appear to be at the other side of the frontier, the Russian State Railways *are* aware that we exist somewhere between heaven and earth, and a train is on its way. He calls it 'the Kiev train.' Does that convey anything to you, Mr. Martin?"

Henry Martin colored up quite becomingly, and the mild eyes behind the thick-lensed glasses gleamed with the light of true zeal, delighted to be called upon—and in such respectful tones— to give an opinion on the subject so dear to his heart.

"The Kiev train!" he cried. "Ah, yes. Built in sixty-four, and arguably the only *wagon-lit* possessed by the Russian State Railways. I must say, as foreigners we are extremely fortunate in obtaining such a train, for the Russians are most averse to easy access to their country. It speaks well for his lordship's prestige, and, of course, of Her Highness's position . . ."

"I never heard of the Kiev train," said the princess flatly.

"Nevertheless, our expert's knowledge of its existence adds weight to the stationmaster's statement that it is on its way," said Jack. "It only remains for us to plead with him to keep this train here till its arrival. Miss Herbert, how are your arts of persuasion this evening?"

"Me?" I cried.

"Who else, Miss Herbert? You are the official interpreter."

And so, nervously, I addressed myself to the Prussian, who swiftly unbent when he grasped that I could speak German as fluently as he; who went to patient lengths to explain that orders were orders, and that the Prussian State Railways were not in any way responsible for the crass inefficiency of their colleagues over the frontier; but who unbent considerably when I invoked the name of Chancellor von Bismarck, and whose pale blue eyes widened with awe when he read the chancellor's letter (which, at my prompting and to her fury, Augusta Scrase was sent to fetch). In the end, he agreed to hold the train at Eydtkuhnen till the morning or till the arrival of the Kiev train, whichever was soonest.

"Well done, Miss Herbert," said the man I loved. And his approving smile made my poor heart cry out for joy and hope.

They steamed the train slowly to the very end of the line, to within yards of a striped pole that marked the boundary between Prussia and the land of the Tsars, the better for us to see the Kiev train when it arrived.

The snow had ceased to fall, and lay in a deep carpet all about. A small soldier in a large overcoat stood just beyond the barrier, hands thrust deeply into pockets, tall rifle and bayonet slung over his shoulder. Guardian of Holy Russia. Beyond him, the beginning of another stretch of railway line that led to St. Petersburg, down which the Kiev train would come. Away to the right, the edge of a forest, a canopy of whiteness under the full moon, stretching to the far distance. To the left, a small hamlet, with a tiny church surmounted by an onion-shaped dome, a cluster of thatched cottages, a few winking lights.

It was eight o'clock. The remaining food on the train had been gathered in by Sergeant Gumble and meted out by him at the orders of his colonel. For the princess and me there was a cup of tasteless soup, some dry bread, a spoonful of caviar, and a half bottle of champagne. The latter I bequeathed to the princess in its entirety since I felt her need to be the greater. She complained that the caviar was past its best.

We had run out of candles. With no source of heating, it was cold in the compartment, so we were huddled in our outdoor clothes. We sat facing each other in the armchairs, and even Princess Natasha had run out of anecdotes, so we sat in silence, each with her own thoughts.

And then it came to us: faintly at first, then rising in crescendo, the sound of a violin hesitantly sketching the fabric of some wild air. It was then joined by a plucked string instrument whose sound was alien to my ears.

"The gypsies!" cried the princess. "My dear, what a stroke of good fortune. The gypsies are here!" She sprang to her feet, and seizing a shawl, she put it over her head and knotted it under her chin.

"I don't understand, ma'am," I said. "You surely don't mean that you're going to . . ."

"*We*, my dear, are going to the gypsies," she declared. "So put

on a shawl or a bonnet, and also your gloves, for it will be a cold
walk to the village."

"But . . ."

"You will love every moment," she said. "There will be music
and dancing of an almost inexpressible gaiety and abandonment.
There will also be food. Coarse food, but hot and spicy. And
drink. Heavens, is there anything more depressing than luke-
warm champagne on a cold night?"

"But, do you think we should, ma'am?" I cautioned her. "Go
out there in the dark? After all that's happened."

"No danger will come to you, Clarrie," she said. "Not while we
are in the Russian countryside. Not while you are with me. Oh,
we are far from the intrigues and malcontents and revolutionaries here, my dear. This is not Moscow or St. Petersburg.
You will meet only hospitable peasants and gypsies who live for
nothing but music and the dance. Come!"

"But we'll let Colonel Grant know that we're going?"

"If we do, he will forbid it," she said with simple logic.

"All right." To tell the truth, I was intrigued by the prospect.
The small village looked so bland, a collection of dolls' houses,
each with its snow-covered bonnet of thatch. And the wild,
strange music was a sirens' call to my senses. "I'll come with you,
Princess."

With Jack's cavalry cloak wrapped about me, and shawled like
the princess, I descended with her, and we stole, hand in hand,
toward the frontier gate. No one called after us. We were not
followed.

The sentry beyond the striped pole reacted to our approach by
taking his hands out of his pockets, but made no effort to prevent
us as we circumvented the striped pole and entered Russia. As
we drew abreast, Princess Natasha addressed him in their own
tongue, and the effect upon the soldier was quite extraordinary.
Snatching off his cap and pressing it to his breast, he commenced
a pantomime of bobbing bows, replying in answer to her remarks
with what could only have been the most servile acquiescence.
Clearly, we were going to experience no difficulty in entering
Russia. But the princess had accomplished far more than that.

"He's not the most prepossessing of Uncle Alex's soldiers," said
she, "but he will serve his purpose. Come, my dear."

We set off for the village. And the Russian soldier came after us, trudging uncomplainingly through the snow with his rifle and bayonet, abandoning the frontier to any who chose to come or go, and all at the behest of a goddess in a leopard-skin coat.

He had been appointed our personal bodyguard. And I marveled at the power of the Romanoff name.

The music came from a long, low building that had the familiar look of a Cornish barn, being constructed of daub and wattle, with a thatched roof. The princess said that it must be the village hall, where feudal justice was no doubt summarily dispensed by the local lord of the manor, and where such rare events as a visit by traveling gypsies were translated into a night of festivity.

Our bodyguard took up his post at the door of the barn, and his hands did not return to his pockets. The princess opened the door, and we were met by a blast of sound that one could almost reach out and touch, a blaze of color that bemused the eye and sent the senses reeling, a rich odor compounded of roast meats, spices, hot cooking oil, herbs, and packed humanity that was so overpowering as to leave one breathless and yet so subtle as to beggar description. And, at our entry—at the sight of the magnificent creature in the leopard skin with her acolyte in the dramatic cavalry cloak—the music was abruptly silenced as if a door had slammed upon it, the very colors faded, and the myriad odors dissipated. A hundred pairs of eyes were turned to regard us.

The princess was equal to the occasion. With a regal sweep of her bejeweled hand, she uttered one word in Russian which could only have meant, *"Continue!"*

The violin took up the air where it had left off, and the other strings joined in. Two dark-eyed youths who had been turning spitted meats over a roaring fire at one end of the great barn resumed their work, but their dark eyes never strayed from us. A man and a girl in gypsy costumes—bright and flamboyant, with glitter of tinsel and silver-gold—blended their lithe bodies to the jangling rhythm of the air, circling each other, snapping fingers, leaping and stamping. And no one, not even the dancers, stopped watching us for an instant.

A portly middle-aged man in an embroidered hat approached us and bowed deeply to the princess, doffing the hat and holding it to his breast the way the soldier had done. He waited for her to speak first, which she did. I had no way of telling how much of her rank and station she divulged to this man who was presumably some kind of village elder, but what she said was enough to win his abject fealty. Hatless, still, and bowing low with every backward step, he guided us to two chairs—hastily vacated by their former occupants—that stood at the edge of the dance floor. Two tall glasses were brought, the bearer polishing them on the sleeve of his tunic as he came. A clear liquid was poured into each glass and handed to us both. I sipped at mine, encouraged by the princess. It resembled the apple spirit that Cornish farmers secretly distill in defiance of the excisemen, and it burned my throat and set me coughing. Princess Natasha laughed and drained her glass, holding it out for more.

"Drink deeply and forget, *ma mignonne*," she murmured in my ear. "You are in Russia now!"

They brought food for us, the two gypsy boy cooks carrying slender spits on which were skewered pieces of succulent-looking meats and vegetables, all aflame, which they forked from the spits onto wooden platters.

"I'm afraid one eats with one's fingers," said the princess. "But it's very rewarding. No one can do it like they can. My Uncle Basil tried with all his might and main to persuade a gypsy to accept a post in his kitchen, but to no avail. They will not be tied down, you see? The gypsies do not come to one; one goes to the gypsies. Are you enjoying it, Clarrie? Think of our friends back on that horrid, cold train. Think of the abominable Miss Scrase. Of Lord Audubon, a shame upon the English aristocracy, as my late husband was upon the Rumanian aristocracy. Think of poor Colonel Grant. On second thoughts, considering your proclivities, you had better not think about Colonel Grant, or your appetite will be ruined."

"What will they do if they find us missing?" I asked her. "Imagine the consternation it will cause, and you the niece of the Tsar. Really, ma'am, I think we should have left some message."

She smiled. "Messages, my dear, are even now winging through the night, and in all directions. The unprepossessing soldier whom I inveigled from his duties, told me he is to be relieved at midnight, and you may be sure that he will return to his post and hand over his duties to his relief, afterward going back to barracks, where he will wake his comrades and tell of his encounter with a woman of the aristocracy, a *boyar* who treated him as he had never been treated since Uncle Alex released him from serfdom and he was compelled to enlist or starve. By morning, or earlier, the story will reach the ears of his officer. Similarly, the headman of this village, who received us, was so impressed as to send a messenger to the local lord of the manor —did you not observe him whispering his news, and did you not see the messenger slip out of the door?—with information that a lady of quality had arrived, along with others, on the train from Berlin? I promise you, Clarrie, if our friends on the train miss us, they will not have far to look. Every finger in the district will be pointing here. Ah, here comes the chief musician. I must reward him."

He was a swarthily handsome fellow with a mop of tousled, blue-black hair that reminded me uncomfortably of Jack Grant's. Instrument tucked under his arm, he bowed low to the princess, who took from her reticule a gold coin and tossed it to him. He caught it in midair, white teeth flashing a grin of pleasure. There then followed a conversation between them, at the end of which he handed her his instrument, which she took with a grimace in my direction.

"It's an age since I played a balalaika," she said. "And only sheer conceit prompts me to attempt a piece. I doubt if I can even remember the words. Ah, well!"

Diamonds glittered in the torchlight, as her beringed fingers struck a chord across the strings. There was a concerted murmur of approval from the watching people, gypsies and villagers alike. Clearly this was the introduction to a well-known air.

She sang the first few words unaccompanied, and her voice was as clear and strong as any boy treble, with a husky overtone that lent color and expression. The language, of course, was Russian and incomprehensible to me, but it was obvious that she sang of love—sad and unrequited love at that.

The refrain had a heart-rending quality of melancholy, and she accompanied it with brilliant fingering upon the balalaika.

Not a sound interrupted her, no one moved. She had total mastery over her audience. The end, when it came, was a riot of glissading chords, a shouted invocation. Silence.

And then they applauded her, and no one more than I.

"Princess, you are wonderful—wonderful!" I cried.

"Do you think if the Romanoffs were ever deposed from the throne of Holy Russia, I might make an honest living in the British Music Halls?" she asked, blue eyes dancing with quiet pride.

"You would be a sensation!" I assured her.

She was the heroine of the hour. The goddess who had descended upon them from Mount Olympus and touched their simple lives. Presently, the crowd parted, and a woman came forward leading by the hand a small, barefoot boy, who, by his pitiful thinness, by the blaze of unhealthy color on the tautly-stretched skin of his cheekbones, was manifestly far advanced in the consumption. The woman—clearly the mother—knelt to Princess Natasha and weepingly made some request of her.

"What is it, ma'am—what does she want?" I whispered.

"I told you that news of our coming here was winging through the night, Clarrie," she replied. "This woman, by the means known only to the peasantry, heard that a Romanoff was in the village, and she and her child have come through the snow to see me."

The tearful mother was now pushing forward the boy, who hung back nervously.

"What does she want of you, ma'am?" I repeated.

"She wants me merely to touch him," replied the princess. "You see, they believe implicitly in the healing power of the royal touch, and who is to say that they are wrong? In the phrase of your national poet, Clarrie: 'There are more things in heaven and earth . . .'"

She reached out and laid both hands on the boy's shaven head, whereupon the mother burst into heartrending sobs of relief and joy, clutching the child to her breast and rocking him to and fro.

Princess Natasha took a jujube from her reticule and gave it to the boy.

"Perhaps he will live," she said. "And that would be nice."

More singing and dancing. And the princess drank several more glasses of the fiery spirit, but I demurred. She did not perform again, but sat and watched, serene and reposed as a sleek cat in a basket, flashing me a smile whenever our eyes met.

We had been in the village hall for perhaps an hour when a newcomer silenced the music in a hubbub of muttering and side-long looks, as he walked forward and bowed deeply to the princess. He was a man of middle years, with a cadaverous countenance of Asiatic cut, eyes of incredible paleness, and a completely bald skull. Dressed from head to foot in black, with a long caped carriage cloak, I took him—correctly, as it turned out —to be a coachman.

He addressed the princess in heavily accented French, a language which, as I had learned, the Russian aristocracy prefer to their own.

"Gracious lady, I bring an invitation from my master, the Count Orloff. Hearing of your arrival, the count extends the hospitality of his castle to you and your party."

"That is very kind of the count." She looked at me, adding in English, "What did I tell you Clarrie? By now, we are the talk of the province."

"Does the gracious lady please accept?" asked the messenger in sibilant tones.

"You have a coach, fellow?"

"A *charabanc*, gracious lady. It will carry nine passengers comfortably and is waiting outside."

"Then I think we will accept the count's generous offer," declared the princess. She tapped my wrist. "My dear, you can forget that cold and cheerless *wagon-lit*. This night, we shall repose in warmth and comfort. These provincial noblemen do themselves very well, with armies of servants, massive fireplaces that burn whole trees at a time, kitchens and wine cellars that would not disgrace an emperor."

"Princess, do you think we should?" I was dubious of the messenger, who struck me as a most sinister individual.

But she had already decided, and was impervious to argument.

"How far to Count Orloff's castle, fellow?" she demanded.

"Less than a league, gracious lady," replied the other.

She tapped her cheek. "Count Orloff, Count Orloff? Surely we have met, your master and I. Was he ever at the Imperial Court?"

Did I see a shifty look come into the fellow's face as he replied? In that moment, I had an impulse to beg the princess to have nothing to do with him or his master.

"I believe so, gracious lady," he replied. "But that was before I had the honor to enter the count's service."

"M-m-m-m, I am sure I know the count, or know of him," said the princess. "It will come back to me. Now, listen, my good fellow—this is what you will do. You will drive to the train that is waiting at the frontier, and you will give a message to Colonel Grant. Do you hear that? Colonel Grant. You will tell him . . ."

Useless to protest; the princess was in full command.

They arrived within half an hour: Lord Audubon, Ralph Orwell, Mr. Martin, Augusta Scrase (magnificent in a black sable cloak, and eyeing the assembled villagers and gypsies with detestation), and Jack. With them was Sergeant Gumble. Obedient to the princess' demand, he had brought her valise containing her night attire and toilet items, together with my humble carpet bag. The *charabanc* was a four-wheeled coach driven by six horses, with a rear entrance to the interior that contained three rows of forward-facing seats. It must have been a hundred years old if it was a day.

Jack handed the princess into the vehicle.

"I will not conceal from you, ma'am, that Lord Audubon and I were of two minds about this enterprise of yours," he said. "It was only Miss Scrase's plea that turned the scales."

"I could not have abided another hour in that train," cried Augusta Scrase in a voice that teetered on the verge of hysteria. "The darkness! The cold! And I crave a cup of tea. Will there be tea?"

"Come, Miss Scrase, where is the intrepid lady who scrambled in the Alps with Edward Whymper?" said the princess, giving me an elfin wink. "Yes, I am sure there will be tea. We Russians are almost as addicted to the stuff as you English. Now, I wonder where I have met our host Count Orloff?"

I thrilled to the touch of Jack's hand as he assisted me into the *charabanc*, and was emboldened to ask him about the remainder of the party.

"You need not repine for their comfort," he replied. "The stationmaster has so far relented as to put at their disposal a small bothy with a hot stove. They also have what remains of the rations. Your hand is very cold, Miss Herbert."

But, if you only knew how warm my heart, I thought . . .

A ragged burst of handclaps from the assembled villagers and gypsies graced our departure. Princess Natasha waved graciously to them, and the huge vehicle lumbered slowly through the crusted snow and up a wooded incline beyond, the horses straining hard, leaning forward in their traces, their plodding hooves kicking up feathers of snow with every tread. It was a dry, chill, and enchanted night. Inside the coach, all was warmth and comfort, thanks to a charcoal stove that glowed redly in the center. Outside, a fairyland of pine and whiteness, with the great dome of blue-black sky splattered with stars surmounting all. And, by joyful chance, the man I loved was seated beside me, his shoulder close to mine, so close that I could feel his warmth and smell the maleness of his well-kept leather and the macassar oil with which he dressed his dark curls. I could have willed that journey to last an eternity.

After a while, the princess exclaimed, "I have the gravest doubts about our host. It comes to me that he may be the Count Orloff who disgraced himself during the feast of Saint Eudoxia by falling drunk at the feet of the Archimandrite Boris in St. Basil's cathedral in Moscow, as a result of which my aunt, the Tsarina, who is a woman of most daunting piety, caused his banishment to the provinces. On the other hand, another branch of the Orloff family produced a young guards officer who had all the matrons of Petersburg and Moscow exhibiting their marriageable daughters in a quite shameless manner." She nudged my elbow—she was sitting on my other side. "I do so hope that it is the latter Orloff whom we shall encounter tonight. I expect you agree, Miss Scrase."

No reply from Augusta Scrase.

"Certainly, one trusts he is not the gentleman who fell down in church," commented Lord Audubon. He was sitting in front of me, next to Augusta Scrase, and from time to time kept turning to ogle me. "Shocking bad form, that."

"Indeed yes," said the princess. "And you have not heard all. It was rumored in Court that this particular Count Orloff was quite mad, and that he slept in his own destined coffin."

"How disgusting!" said Augusta Scrase.

"But very, very Russian," said the princess serenely.

We journeyed in silence for a while, and I could not have been more grateful for it. The motion of the vehicle as it swayed on its springs brought me and the object of my love into occasional close contact. A particularly violent jolt, as one of the wheels descended into a pothole, caused him to put his arm around my shoulders and steady me. I almost cried out with anguish when he removed it. Almost immediately after that, the *charabanc* reached the crest of the incline that led out of the village, and we were able to see a deep valley beyond, with a river snaking through it and the dark hump of a castellated building rising like a craggy rock from an islet in mid-river.

"By jove!" exclaimed Lord Audubon. "I take it that must be our destination. A most impressive pile, I must say. Quite dwarfs *my* family seat. The fellow must be incredibly rich."

"The Orloff family, as I recall, own estates here in the west and also in the Ukraine and the Crimea," said the princess. "However, that does not resolve the question of the moment, which is, who resides here—the handsome guards officer or the madman? I await the answer with lively interest."

"It's still quite a distance," said the man at my elbow. "A mile at least."

Let that mile take forever! cried my blissfully contented heart.

"I'm sure you ladies would be more comfortable if I moved back into the rear seat with Orwell and Martin," said Jack.

"No!" I almost shouted the word. "There—there's really ample room, and you needn't bother," I added lamely.

Augusta Scrase turned around and gave me a cold glance.

"So cozy, so very cozy," said the princess, nudging me.

And so, we came to the castle of Count Orloff.

How to describe the place? I am not well instructed in matters architectural, so I had no means of telling its age and style. To me it seemed incredibly ancient, almost as if it had risen of its own volition from the rocky islet upon which it stood, during the cataclysmic eruptions which, so we are told by the scientists, took place during the formation of our planet. As we descended the valley and drew closer, so did the bulk of it loom higher above us: three tall towers surmounting sheer walls with blank-eyed slits of windows and a dark gateway. A single narrow bridge connected the islet to the river bank, and there was a lowered drawbridge halfway across.

Presently, the iron-tired wheels of the *charabanc* were sounding a new note over the woodwork of the bridge, and the full moon was reflected in the rippled waters of the dark river.

"Oh, how I yearn for the ecstasy of a hot bath!" cried Princess Natasha.

"I see no sign of life," growled Lord Audubon. "If, as you say, the fellow keeps an army of servants, ma'am, they are uncommonly economical with candles. Not a light anywhere. Wait—there's one in the window above the gatehouse. And I do believe they are opening for us."

As we approached, indeed, vast double gates swung open to receive us, and the *charabanc* swept into a high-walled courtyard beyond. The inside of the castle, as opposed to the dark exterior that it displayed to the world, was tolerably well lit. *Flambeaux* spluttered their rosy light from sconces set at each side of a deeply recessed doorway into the main building, and the loom of candles within described a line of stained-glass windows depicting—as well as one could discern—haloed saints and angels. But no army of servitors stood ready at the foot of the steps to greet us; only a woman in black, whose gray hair was drawn back in a plait over each ear and whose eyes were secret. She bowed deeply as the sinister coachman handed we ladies down and motioned us to follow her up the steps into the building. She then muttered something to the coachman, who replied gruffly. Princess Natasha was by my side and close enough to hear the burden of their exchange.

"They're man and wife and his name is Ivan," she murmured. "I think Ivan is married to a shrew. She wants to know what took him so long. Apparently the count is restless for his supper."

"Supper?" I cried. "After what we had with the gypsies—not to mention what we had on the train!"

"Pfui! Mere *hors d'oeuvres!*" was her comment.

We entered the main doorway, which, despite the massive stonework of its construction, was low enough to cause the menfolk to stoop, and found ourselves in a cavernous vault of a place whose dimensions were impossible to determine by reason of a misty darkness that entirely obscured the roof and the farthest wall, which was well beyond the scope of a single chandelier hanging by a chain from the mysterious heights. That, and the whole main part of a massive tree that glowed redly in a vast open fireplace, provided the only illumination. I was instantly put in mind of the great hall of the ecclesiastical Palace in St. Errol, except that Bishop D'Arcy's hall could have fitted inside Count Orloff's, roof, chimneypots and all, and still left room to spare.

But it was the appointments of the monstrous chamber that astonished the eye and assaulted the imagination. Every inch of wall space was taken up with trophies of the chase, stretching in serried ranks, one above the other, till the highest rows were lost in the darkness above. The heads of deer, bison, and wildebeests; lion, tiger, leopard, and jaguar; tusked elephants, rhinoceros, and hippopotamuses; doe-eyed gazelles and similar creatures whose timid beauty alone should surely have spared them from the hunters' bullet. But pride of place—the longest and lowest rank that ran at eye level as far as one could discern—was given to the wild boar: hundreds of the fierce, tusked heads, all with eyes that reflected the candlelight and seemed to follow one.

"My friends—such a pleasure and an honor. Do I address the Princess Natasha Bibescu?"

A short, bearded man in a smoking jacket and tasseled cap stepped almost from nowhere, and I realized with a jolt of surprise that he was directing his attentions to me, bending slightly at the hip, one plump hand poised as if to receive my proffered fingertips.

"No—no, this is the princess," I faltered, indicating her.

"Aaah! I should have recognized the Romanoff profile. Quite unmistakable. Your servant, Highness. I am not known to you personally since my affairs keep me away from St. Petersburg and Moscow, and may continue to do so indefinitely."

"How do you do, Count?" The princess gave him her hand, and glanced sidelong to me, one eyebrow raised.

So—our host was the less desirable of the two Orloffs: not the handsome and dashing guards officer, but the mad inebriate who was reputed to sleep in his own coffin. I had to admit that the mantle of an eccentric ill-fitted the *bourgeois* little man who stood before us, but perhaps he had hidden subtleties, I thought.

Introductions were effected, and the count, calling for Ivan's wife to bring a candelabrum, entreated us to follow him to the supper table, which was in the far, shadowed end of the chamber, and which was revealed by candlelight as a buffet of most elaborate conceit, being raised, tier upon tier, to the apogee of a whole boar's head, apple in mouth and richly decorated with glazing and piped sugar icing, which stood upon a plinth in the center. In inferior positions were, in descending order, poultry, game, and fish; dishes of salad and vegetables, bowls of cream; cucumber and pickled cabbages; and the inevitable caviar. There was also a plethora of beverages, including champagne on ice.

"Count, what a magnificent repast," said Lord Audubon. "You have done us a great honor—and at such short notice."

"It is the simple fare upon which I sup nightly," was the bland response. "I live quite frugally, with only Ivan and Galina to serve my needs, residing in only this wing of the castle. In Papa's day, we kept open table, but times have changed, alas. Princess, can I tempt you with *zakuski* of any kind? No? Then do essay the *piroshki*, which Galina does to perfection. And a little sour cream, perhaps."

Ralph Orwell sidled up to me, took two glasses of champagne from a tray proffered by Ivan, gave one into my hand.

"I've a notion that our new friend the count is trying to win himself a ticket back to Court through the good graces of Princess Natasha," he murmured.

"He seems a very civilized little man," I said. "So far."

"A very luxurious introduction to Russia," he said, "though a trifle barbaric for my taste—all those stuffed heads! By the way, the Berlin police have departed, having seen Lord Audubon safely out of Prussia. They went back to Berlin on a train that arrived in Eydtkuhnen just after ours. Taking with them the body of Hortense."

"What will happen—about Hortense's murder?" I asked. "There'll be an enquiry, of course?"

He shook his head. "Not in my opinion, Clarrie," he said. "This is high international politics of the very worst and most ruthless kind. The fact that a poor little maidservant got caught up in it is of interest only to her relations, if any. You may take it from me that the Prussian government won't want it widely known that not one but two murders have taken place while the Audubon mission was within their frontiers. No, I'm afraid it's going to be an unmarked grave and quiet oblivion for Hortense."

I clutched the stem of my untouched champagne glass more tightly. "It's so—*unfair!*" I breathed, surprised at the intensity of my fury.

"Clarrie, Clarissima," he said. "Do I discern from your looks that you would seek to avenge poor Hortense, and maybe my late colleague Jules Charlot?"

"Vengeance?" I took the word out and examined it from all sides. "Do I believe in vengeance? Yes, perhaps."

He took a deep draft of his wine. It occurred to me that he had been solacing himself in the cold train with the brandy bottle.

"Then look about you, Clarrie, Clarissima," he said, "for you may be sure that the object of your proposed vengeance is right here with us. Oh dear—and now you've gone and dropped your glass and broken it!"

From that moment, the supper party—already grotesque in its setting of decayed magnificence—turned into a nightmare. Even the presence of the man I loved (who took not the slightest bit of notice of me after we alighted from our conveyance, but stayed at Lord Audubon's elbow) could not dispel the feeling of deep unease that Ralph Orwell's words had inspired in me. I gazed around at their faces—some animated, some in repose— and asked myself who, *who* was behind it all?

Our host was leading forth. The party being largely composed of English people, he turned to the subject of the Constantinople affair. He was, he averred, a man of peace.

"Lord Audubon," he said, "I would give a million roubles—ten million—for our army to withdraw from the gates of Constantinople, for I have no wish to see more war between our two peoples. My papa fought under Prince Menshikov in the Crimea

and had his foot carried away by a British shell. 'Ivan Danilo-
vich,' said Prince Menshikov to Papa, 'you will never waltz at
Tsarskoye Selo again.' To which Papa replied, 'Nor I ever shall,
Alexander Sergeevich.' And that's a true story as I live and
breathe." He hiccuped loudly. I had not seen him touch a morsel
of the richly assorted food, but his glass, though constantly
recharged by the ever-present Ivan, was nearly always empty.

Princess Natasha came close by me, squeezed my arm. "My
dear, I am quite tired," she said. "I think, before the count gets
too maudlin, I will declare myself ready for bed. Would you
greatly mind sharing a room with me? The matter of the tooth
powder I have quite mastered. But the hundred strokes of the
brush . . ." She shrugged her shapely shoulders eloquently.

"Of course, ma'am," I said.

"So kind, as always, my dear Clarrie." She drifted away.

The cadaverous visage of the servant Ivan swam past my vision. Beyond him was a long line of boars' heads, jaws agape,
tusks bared. The glazed and sugared boar's head atop the buffet
table had already had several large slices cut from it. I felt nau-
seated, though I had barely sipped at the second glass of champagne that Ralph had pressed into my hand. And I prayed for
the day to end.

Princess Natasha had buttonholed Ivan and was apparently
giving him instructions about our sleeping arrangements. She
pointed to me and smiled. The man's hooded eyes followed her
gaze, and he nodded.

Mr. Martin the railway enthusiast sought me out. His gait was
unsteady, and there was a rime of sweat on his brow and around
his mouth. His eyes still burned with the light of fanaticism
behind the thick lenses.

"The hour approaches, ma'am," he said. "Yes, the hour approaches."

"What hour, sir?" I asked nervously.

"The arrival of the Kiev train," he said. "That will be something to see, will it not, ma'am?"

Behind my back, Augusta Scrase was talking in a very loud
voice to Ralph Orwell,

"Your assertion is absurd, Mr. Orwell. There is no impediment, either physical or intellectual—only the impediment of prejudice —to prevent a woman from entering public life. By the end of the century, women will have seats in the British parliament."

"Will you be among that number, Miss Scrase?"

"If I am called, Mr. Orwell."

I closed my eyes to shut out the sight of the menacing boars' heads. And I opened them at the unbelievable sound of a man weeping. It was the count. He stood close by the buffet table, drink spilling from the brimming glass that he held in a trembling hand. Tears were streaking down his pudgy face to lose themselves in his beard. His words—punctuated by sobs—were addressed to the princess, who gazed at him in mingled compassion and disbelief.

"If you could but whisper into the ear of your aunt the Tsarina, ma'am. One word would suffice. I am dying of boredom. You cannot imagine the life I have lived. Papa hated me. I keep his trophies to remind me of what might have been. My only happiness was at Court. Whisper that word, I beg you . . ." Another outburst of sobs, and the little man lurched unsteadily toward the princess, stooping as if to kneel at her feet. She drew aside her skirts in distaste, as with a last, despairing cry, he tipped slowly forward and fell face-downward on the cold flagstones.

The man Ivan placed a tray of glasses on the buffet table and strode forward—none too hastily—to his master's aid, picked him up as if he had been a child, and bore him away into the gloom at the far end of the great chamber.

"At least," declared Princess Natasha, "one can now go to bed without incurring the possible displeasure of one's host."

The servant Ivan soon returned carrying two candelabra, one of which he handed to his wife.

"It appears that all of us save Mr. Orwell and Mr. Martin have been given rooms at the head of the main staircase," said Princess Natasha. "You two gentlemen, as I understand it, have rooms in the east tower, which, though perhaps not quite so grand, are sure to be warm and commodious. The woman will escort you there. She speaks only Russian, but then, she is not a sprightly conversationalist even in her own tongue. Good night, gentlemen. Come, Clarrie. Come, all."

We took our leave of the two newspapermen, who crossed the hall at the heels of the woman Galina. The princess and I followed Ivan up a wide and intricately carved stone staircase that ascended from opposite the fireplace. Jack Grant, Miss Scrase, and Lord Audubon came after.

Up, up, till, by the wavering light of the candles, one could pick out the massive beams of the ceiling, which were clustered with what appeared to be dark carvings.

"Do you see the bats?" said the princess, pointing upward.

"*Bats?*" From Miss Scrase.

A few more steps up and we saw them all too clearly. They hung like bunches of dark grapes from the beams, heads down, tiny eyes watching us, pink mouths working silently.

"How appalling!" cried Augusta Scrase.

"They congregate in my brother's place in the Ukraine, also," said the princess, "and no one makes an effort to remove them because they are quite harmless and perform the useful function of devouring insects of all kinds."

"Quite disgusting!" cried Miss Scrase.

At the head of the staircase, we came to a wide corridor lined with blackened pictures in tarnished gold frames, and a row of doors. Ivan stopped by the first door, opened it, and bowed low for Jack Grant to enter.

"Good night, all," said the man who owned my heart, with not a glance in my direction. The door shut behind him.

The next room was for Augusta Scrase. She gave us a brief nod only.

Next was Lord Audubon, while the princess and I were apportioned a room immediately across the corridor from his.

"Good night, Princess Natasha," he said. "Sleep well, Miss Herbert." Fervently hoping that the princess had not intercepted the hot-eyed look he threw at me, I hastily closed our door.

"Ah, Clarrie, suddenly I am so *fatiguée*," she cried, lowering herself fully dressed upon the silk counterpane of a massive double bed whose hangings of dusty purple velvet reached ceiling high where they were supported in the plump hands of gilded cherubs.

"I will brush your hair and help you undress," I said.

"You are such a comfort, my dear," she murmured.

Our overnight baggage had been brought up. I rummaged in her valise and found her hairbrush, and took it back to where she lay.

I said, "Perhaps, in view of the late hour, fifty strokes only will —oh!"

She was fast asleep, one shapely, plump arm out-thrown, and a stray curl of her unbelievable flaxen hair trembling with every expiring breath. Carefully, I stooped and took off her dainty button boots, loosened her bodice.

"Good night, Princess," I whispered.

Though it was past midnight, I could not bring myself to rest, but by the light of the single candle in the room, sat down at a writing desk and took out my diary.

Where to begin? Nearest to my heart was the thought that the past day had provided confirmation of Jack Grant's affair with Augusta Scrase, but I could not bring myself to set the words down upon paper. Of what then should I write? There was the peril that overhung us all: the faceless killer, who, if Ralph Orwell was to be believed, was among us. I caught my breath in alarm. The door! I raced on tiptoe and turned the heavy key in the lock, pausing there to listen. As I did so, I heard the creak of a floorboard somewhere out in the corridor and felt every hair of my head stiffen and prickle.

The sound was not repeated. The prowler had paused out there, waiting, perhaps, to see if the uncautious tread would bring discovery. In a few moments, if I did not throw open the door and confront the creator—and I would as lief have cast myself down from a high window as do such a thing!—the footsteps would continue. I pressed an ear to the panel, my senses straining to pierce the thick oak and reach out to whoever was waiting there.

And then there came the sound of a door being quietly closed. Nothing more, though I waited several minutes. Unnerved, I returned to my diary. Almost immediately, my pencil moved across the page:

> Thursday 18th April: I am afraid. I know that something dreadful is going to happen, and it seems that there is no escape. No matter where we go, in a dark-

ened train, in a busy hotel in full light of day, the
killings go on . . .

Princess Natasha's gentle breathing sounded unnaturally loud
in the stillness, and the scrape of my pencil seemed an intolerable intrusion upon the night. I paused in my task and passed
a hand across my brow. Heaven knows, I was tired, but there
would be no sleep for me that night, not with every nerve in my
body drawn to screaming pitch. What time was dawn? Not that
daylight would bring any relief from the peril we were in. Had I
not better drag one of the heavy pieces of furniture—an armchair, or even the writing table—and place it against the door?
Yes, I would do that.

As I rose to my feet, the silence was shattered by the deafen-
ing sound of a shot. And then another.

From somewhere far off, the sound of the princess' horrified
awakening reached my ears as I struggled to unlock the door.
The key was stiff and would not yield.

"Clarrie, don't go out there! For God's sake stay where you
are!" cried the princess.

The key turned. Next moment, I was out in the corridor. The
door opposite—Lord Audubon's door—was ajar. Oddly, I recall
no sense of danger, only of the most pressing urgency, as I
pushed through it and entered the darkened room, where my
nostrils were assailed by an acrid, alien reek that I took to be
burned powder.

There was a flood of light from the other side of the room, and
a communicating door flew open, revealing Augusta Scrase in
her night attire, a candlestick held on high. By its light, I picked
out the humped shape of a figure sprawled, face-downward,
across the bed, whose white sheets were darkly stained . . .

"Lord Audubon!" The cry was on my lips as I went over to
him. Augusta Scrase was there before me. The closer proximity
of her candle picked out the details in greater clarity. There was
more blood than I had ever seen before. He was still dressed, but
in shirt-sleeves, and barefoot. But the head that lolled slackly
over the edge of the bed was not the sleekly-barbered head of
the Emissary Extraordinary to the Court of St. Petersburg. I
stared in disbelief, willing it not to be happening, while guiding

my unwilling hand to reach down and touch the crisp dark curls that were sticky to my fingertips.

It was no illusion, no waking nightmare. It had happened, it was happening, and it would continue to happen. The killer had struck again—and Jack Grant was the victim.

Someone was screaming. It may have been Augusta Scrase, but it was more likely Clarrie Herbert herself!

Chapter Ten

LORD AUDUBON WAS NEXT TO APPEAR. HIS LORDSHIP WAS IN DRESS-
ing gown and bedroom slippers, with hair so carefully brushed
that it could scarcely have touched the pillow. He took in the
scene at a glance, met Augusta Scrase's eye and delivered the
cryptic question,

"Well?"

"He is badly wounded," said she, "but perhaps not mortally.
One bullet grazed his scalp, as you see. The other"—she touched
the bloodied shirt—"struck him low in the left shoulder, so low
that I think it may have pierced the lung. I haven't stripped him
yet, but there seems to be no exit hole."

"And so?"

"And so the bullet will have to be taken out. Tonight. Now."

There was a long drawn-out shuddering cry from the doorway.
I, who had been watching in silent dread while Augusta Scrase
had been making a brief and exceedingly workmanlike examination of the stricken man, turned to see the princess standing
there, or, more correctly, leaning there, her face ashen, eyes staring out of her head.

"No-o-o-o!" she cried. "It can't be! Not—him?"

"I am afraid so, ma'am," said the Emissary. "From your knowledge of the district, would you suppose that there is a doctor
hereabouts?"

He had to repeat the question before she was able to take it in.
When she replied, it was in hopeless, despairing tones and a
shake of her tousled head.

"There won't be a doctor for a hundred miles."

"Then I will get the bullet out myself," said Augusta Scrase
briskly. She gave me a steady look. "What about you, Miss Herbert? Can you give me some assistance, or are you another of

these useless females who can't abide the sight of blood? I must say you look close to swooning already."

I licked my dry lips and replied with some spirit. "I will do anything you ask, Miss Scrase."

At that moment, Ralph Orwell and Mr. Martin arrived with Sergeant Gumble—who had been accommodated in the kitchen quarters—all summoned by the sound of the shots. Augusta Scrase, completely mistress of the situation, waved them to go.

"You are no use to me here," she said. "Go and build up the fire in the hall. And when I have done what has to be done, you can carry him down and we will make him comfortable in the warmth."

"Yes, ma'am," said Ralph.

"And Gumble . . ."

"Yes'm?"

"I suppose it's too much to hope that there will be carbolic acid in this benighted place, but summon that woman and tell her to heat water, plenty of water, and bring it up here."

"Yes'm!" The sergeant rushed off after the other.

"And you—my lord . . ."

The Emissary gave a start. "Ma'am?"

"In the adjoining room, you will find my small chest with a melontop lid. In it is a sewing box. Bring it to me, please. Are you ready, Miss Herbert?"

"Yes," I breathed.

"Then help me lift him up. Gently. This needs a woman's touch. Lift his head while I take the shoulders. Lay his head on the pillow. Carefully! He is no longer to be regarded as a man in the prime of his strength, Miss Herbert. Treat him as you would a dying child. Ah, the sewing box, Lord Audubon! Now you can go."

His lordship paused irresolutely. "Ma'am, can I not be of some assistance?"

Augusta Scrase was rummaging in her sewing box. She took out a pair of scissors. "Yes," she said. "You can leave Miss Herbert and me to our task. And take Princess Natasha with you."

"I stay here!" cried the princess.

"As you please," said the other, "but if you faint, you will be entirely ignored." So saying, she ran her scissors up the left sleeve of Jack's shirt from wrist to neck, baring his muscular arm and shoulders, and the upper part of the left breast, which was pierced by a gaping mouth that pulsed bright blood.

"We will need clean linen, Miss Herbert," she said. "Bed sheets will do. Don't disturb the patient, get them from my room next door and tear them up into large squares.

I ran to do her bidding, casting a glance at the princess as I went. She was leaning against the wall by the door, a bemused and tragic expression on her face. And her eyes never wavered in my direction, but remained fixed upon the figure on the bed.

The next-door room was in darkness. Only by the candlelight coming through the open door was I able to pick out the bed, and strip it of its sheets. On my way out again, I all but fell over a chair, and only saved myself by grasping its back firmly. My fingers closed on the material of a garment slung over it. Not a woman's garment. I felt broadcloth and thick frogging. And I caught a familiar odor—much loved.

There was just enough light to see that it was Jack Grant's hussar tunic.

"Do you know what you're about—or are you going to butcher him where he lies?"

The challenge came from Princess Natasha.

Augusta Scrase, scissors poised over Jack's terrible wound, closed her eyes and exhaled. "I have a certain competence," she said, "since I studied nursing at the Nightingale School at St. Thomas's Hospital, where I witnessed many operations. I do not say that I am a skilled surgeon, but I am, by your own declaration, all there is within a hundred miles."

"Not only a mountain climber and a lady diplomat, but a nurse also!" The princess' voice was high-pitched and teetering on the edge of hysteria. "How fortunate for us, Clarrie, that the man we both love has a woman of so many facets at hand in his hour of need. Did you know we were both in love with him, Miss Scrase? Oddly, you don't look surprised. Dear Clarrie, of course, she wears her heart on her sleeve. But I would have thought that my own passions had been well concealed—till now."

The object of her wild mockery took another deep breath and

said, "Be ready to staunch the flow of blood when I cut deeply, Miss Herbert. And let us pray that he will remain unconscious till I have probed the bullet and brought it out."

"Such calmness!" cried the princess from the other end of the room. "How does she manage it? Englishwomen—so cold. Small wonder that they make better wives than lovers."

The scissors descended into the wound. I winced, as she turned them this way, then that, making a wide slash in the flesh.

"Staunch the flow of blood!" she hissed. "Press hard—here! Ah, that is the subclavia vein. The bullet missed it by a hairsbreadth, but did it pierce the lung? I think not. And I think it is lodged against the shoulder blade at the back. We shall see. Will you bring the candle closer, Miss Herbert?"

My hand was trembling, causing the light to waver. Noticing it, Augusta Scrase raised her eyes from her task and gave me a slow, flat stare. I, who had suffered the agony of having my emotions betrayed to the mistress of the man I loved, quailed before her glance.

"Steady yourself!" she snapped.

The princess laughed.

"More light, Miss Herbert!" The scissors probed deeper into the white, oozing flesh, till there was suddenly a glint of metal, which was immediately obscured again by a fresh welling of blood.

"Was that—the bullet?" I whispered.

"Yes! Another clean rag. Quickly!"

She drove the points of the scissors far into the wound and brought them together. When she withdrew the instrument, a blooded lump of lead the size and shape of a fingertip was neatly held at its tip. "All that is needed now," said Augusta Scrase, "is to sew him up. And then, if that confounded woman brings some hot water, you can wash him, Miss Herbert."

"Thank God he's saved," I whispered.

"But not saved for you, dear Clarrie," said the princess.

"Be silent, woman!" snapped Augusta Scrase.

"I will not!" retorted the princess. "It is too late for prevarication. My dear Clarrie, you will observe that this room is provided with a communicating door. Lord Audubon, whose room it was, agreed to change rooms with his subordinate. In the dark, the killer shot the wrong man. Jack Grant nearly died—for love!"

Augusta Scrase's dark-maned head was bowed over the task of threading a length of silk thread through the eye of a fine needle. She gave no sign of hearing the princess.

"Miss Herbert, will you please cut a long strip of linen for a bandage?" she said quietly.

I took up the scissors to obey, still watching her.

"But you must not think ill of them both, Clarrie," came the persistent voice of the princess. "What we have witnessed, you and I, is no clandestine *affaire*. Oh, no. Their union is hallowed. In short, my dear—they are married!"

"*Married?*" I blurted the word full in the pale face, as those large and luminous green eyes came up to meet my gaze—and then returned to her task.

"Not only married, but with his child," said the princess. "Though I think not greatly advanced in that interesting condition. Any woman who, like myself, has had the experience, knows the signs and portents."

It was as if a hole had been cut beneath my feet, and I was falling, falling into nothingness. Again the green eyes were raised to regard me.

"Is it—true?" I whispered.

"Do you deny it—*Mrs. Grant?*" came the challenging voice of Princess Natasha.

"I deny nothing!" was her retort. And taking the threaded needle, she drove the point through the opposing edges of Jack Grant's wound and drew them together as neatly as if she were sewing a seam.

A knock on the door and Sergeant Gumble entered, carrying a steaming pan of water. In answer to his anxious enquiry, Jack Grant's wife (with an agonized pang I realized that I should have so to regard her in future), informed him that his officer was out of immediate danger. Numbly I listened while he told us that of the servant Ivan and his wife there was no sign, and that Count Orloff was far gone in a drunken sleep in a bedchamber along the corridor.

"Thank you, Gumble," said Augusta Grant. "Will you tell the

gentlemen that the patient will be ready to be carried downstairs in about ten minutes. When you have washed away the blood, Miss Herbert, I will bandage him." She knotted the silk thread and cut off the end, then began calmly to roll the length of bandage.

In the act of washing the unconscious man, I drew aside his ripped shirt and disclosed a small silver disc that was hung around his neck on a fine gold chain.

It was an ordinary English sixpenny piece.

Later, down in the great hall, to the crackle of newly laid logs and with Jack Grant—still unconscious—lying on a mattress before the huge fireplace, Lord Audubon addressed us all.

The Emissary, though outwardly impressive as ever by reason of his height and bearing, nevertheless seemed to have lost some of his stature with his subordinate's insensibility. Almost as if—I dismissed the thought immediately as being absurd—he was merely a puppet without a master to control his strings.

"As I see it," said his lordship, "the fellow Ivan and his wife are involved. I think we may take it that Ivan fired the shots, and then the both of them made off."

"Is that the best construction to place upon the attempted assassination, sir?" From Ralph Orwell.

Lord Audubon frowned at the interruption. "Do you have anything more illuminating, sir?" he demanded.

Ralph was seated on the wide step of the fireplace, close by Jack Grant's dark head. His clever, amber-colored eyes took pinpoints of reflected light from the blazing logs as he gazed up at the Emissary.

"Are you suggesting that Ivan and his wife were also responsible for Hortense's death," he asked. "And for Charlot's?"

Audubon made a dismissive gesture. "That is absurd!" he snapped. "Naturally, I imply nothing of the kind. I take it that those responsible for the killings have one thing in common. They are all members of a political organization whose intent is to prevent me from reaching St. Petersburg to secure the peace."

I knew Ralph's next question before he put it, and I met the princess' eyes. She was curled up close by the foot of Jack Grant's mattress. She gave me an encouraging smile.

"Do you then not take into account the possibility—indeed, the very strong certainty—that one of us present here is also a member of that same political organization?" asked Ralph.

"Yes, sir, I do!" came the reply. And the Emissary took from his pocket a pistol. "But I am prepared for any eventuality! Are there any further questions?"

"What—what is going to happen now, my lord?" asked Mr. Martin nervously.

"It is now two o'clock," said the Emissary. "At first light of dawn, we will all make our way back to the frontier, where, it is to be hoped, the so-called Kiev train will be awaiting us. In the meantime, ladies and gentlemen, we will remain here together in the hall. And I would advise every one of you, for your own safety, not to stray into the shadows!"

And so we drifted apart, though remaining within the loom of the firelight; the menfolk to one side, the women to the other—that is to say, the princess and I. Augusta Grant took her place beside the man I now had to acknowledge as her husband, the man I must learn to dismiss from my mind. The princess put her leopard-skin coat down beside me. I was lying on my cloak—*his* cloak.

"Do not weep, little one," she murmured.

"I'm past weeping," I told her. "The only clear thought in my mind is one of gratitude—gratitude that he's still alive."

"That is true love, indeed," she said.

"But you also love him," I said. "You love him still, even though you pretended to me that it was a girlish infatuation that had faded with maturity. Or so you said."

She shrugged. "When we deceive others," she said, "we first begin by deceiving ourselves. Yes, I thought I had put Jack Grant behind me. Now I know that I have not. And it is too late for both of us, *ma chérie*. He is married to another and soon to be a father. Such men as he do not look back over their shoulders."

"When did you guess—about Mrs. Grant's condition?" I asked. "Was it during that luncheon in Cologne, when you said afterward that she had revealed much of herself to you?"

"Of course," she said. "For a woman who had been through it herself, it was obvious. Her irascibility, the nausea with which she contemplated the very thought of overrich food. Oh, and I tried her very hard. Do you remember how I described the roast goose and its trimmings in such loving particulars?" She chuckled. "Poor Mrs. Grant."

"She saved his life up there," I said. "At least, he's out of immediate danger."

"We must be grateful to her for that," she said gravely. "Both of us."

"Princess," I said, "if you knew that they were married and that they were going to have a child, why didn't you tell me before?"

She reached out and touched my hand as we lay there, side by side at the edge of the firelight.

"Clarrie, I was not sure," she said. "Not till tonight, when I saw the connecting rooms that they had contrived so carefully. The incident on the train when he went to her carriage—that could have been pure chance, a mistaken importunity on his part, rejected by her, a woman married to another and already *enceinte*. But tonight—I *knew!*"

"Yes, I understand," I whispered.

"Then sleep, *ma mignonne*," she whispered in return. And our hands were still clasped when I drifted into a troubled, dream-haunted sleep from which I woke to find her gone.

I sat upright, struck with a sickening premonition of disaster. At the far end of the firelight's glow, I could see the humped forms of the menfolk. Augusta Grant was asleep on the step of the fireplace, her dark head resting close to that of her husband.

"Princess!" I whispered the word into the darkness beyond the firelight, but brought forth no response.

My first—and prudent—impulse was to arouse Lord Audubon, who was armed; but mindful of his advances toward me, I preferred to seek the help of Ralph Orwell. I tiptoed over to the men's side of the fireplace. There was Mr. Martin, fast asleep with his head resting upon his rolled-up coat. Beyond him, Sergeant Gumble was snoring quietly, hands folded over his massive chest. Lord Audubon had brought forward one of the dining chairs: uncomfortable and straight-backed in which—and no doubt the reason for him doing so—one would have thought it impossible to doze off, however tired. He was asleep also, the pistol lying on his lap between his hands.

And of Ralph Orwell—not a sign.

Little fool, I told myself, go back!

Treading softly up the dark staircase, with nothing but a thin glimmering of moonlight seeping through the lancet window at the head of the steps, I had second thoughts about the impulse that had brought me thus far, and would certainly have gone back but for the sight of a patch of reflected candlelight on the wall of the corridor above, that had to have its source in the bedroom the princess and I had lately occupied.

Relief! The princess had simply gone up to fetch something from her valise. I ran up the last half dozen steps, and peered in through the open door of our room. And was choked to horrified silence by what I saw there . . .

Ralph Orwell was standing with his back half-turned toward me, bent over a low table upon which stood my carpet bag and the princess' valise. There was a candlestick on the table also. Its flickering flame was reflected from the bright metal of a pistol that lay close by his hand. And he had my carpet bag open, was delving into it, throwing my modest belongings into a pile till the bag was empty. He then picked up—and I felt my redhead's fury rise at the sight of it—my diary, which he must have found on the writing desk, and, opening it at the beginning, commenced to read the innermost secrets of my heart.

Instantly I felt defiled. My anger and indignation overcoming prudence, I took three steps forward into the room, and the thick carpeting muffled my tread. Two steps more and I was able to reach out my hand and snatch up his pistol.

He turned. His eyes flared with sudden alarm to see me standing there with the weapon aimed—inexpertly, awkwardly, but with no doubt unmistakable resolve—at his chest.

And then he grinned—that jaunty grin I had grown almost to like.

"Well, Clarrie, Clarissima," he drawled. "Seems as if you've caught me, as they say, red-handed."

"You deceived me," I said. "But not completely. Not all the time."

"I concede that," he said. "Yes, I have deceived you. As now, for instance."

The recollections came crowding back to me. "And at Cologne," I said. "It was not merely chance that you were walking toward me when I came out of the cathedral—you, who had followed me in there. And the telegram—the one you so ingenuously told me you had searched for in Charlot's pockets after you had poisoned him—that would have betrayed you, wouldn't it? So you took it and destroyed it. Charlot was not playing a game at that luncheon table. He was in earnest. He found out who you really are. Who *are* you, Mr. Orwell?"

"Yes, who *are* you?" A voice at my elbow, and a waft of the princess' soft scent. "Clarrie dear, there's a cord holding back the canopy of the bed. Fetch it, and we will tie his hands."

"*No, Clarrie—no!*" shouted Orwell.

But I had already given Princess Natasha the pistol and was on my way to do her bidding. The sharp urgency in his tone, the manner of its delivery, brought me up short. I stared at him irresolutely.

"Too late," he said.

I followed his pointing finger. Instantly, the black muzzle of the pistol in Princess Natasha's hand, which had been aimed at him, swung to face me.

"Don't, I beg you, do anything imprudent, Clarrie," she said. "I should hate to have to kill you, also."

"No-o-o!" I cried. "Not—*you?*"

"Meet the assassin!" said Ralph Orwell. "I pieced it together in my mind tonight. Jules Charlot searched her baggage and found something that prompted him to telegraph his paper for further information on Princess Natasha Bibescu. For that, he died. It seemed to me that the maid Hortense might accidentally have found the same thing and sealed her own fate. So I came up here to have a look."

"And I followed you, you fool!" snapped the princess. She smiled at me. "There I was, crouched in the shadows, watching helplessly while that man rifled my valise, found the false bottom that hid the pistol . . ."

"And phials containing—no doubt—poison?" He raised a quizzical eyebrow at her.

The princess nodded blandly. "And phials of poison," she confirmed. "As I was saying: There I was, wondering how I could get possession of the pistol—when along came you, dear Clarrie, and did it for me."

"I'm sorry, Ralph," I whispered.

"And I'm sorry I searched your things also, Clarrie," he replied.

"It doesn't matter, Ralph," I said. "Not any longer."

"I just had to satisfy myself that you weren't in league with her. You always seem so—so close to each other."

"We are very close," said the princess, smiling. "We are both in love with the same man, are we not, Clarrie?"

I did not reply.

Ralph said, "So what happens now—you'd like to kill us, wouldn't you? But you can't, because the shots would alert the others."

"Please understand," said the princess, "that I have no personal animosity toward either of you. Indeed, I have lately conceived a genuine affection for Clarrie, since, in the circumstances"—she smiled at me—"I can scarcely look upon her as a rival. On the other hand, my motives are entirely political, and that is to your disadvantage because I will stop at nothing to succeed in my mission."

"Which is to assassinate Lord Audubon," supplied Ralph.

"That bungling fool Ivan!" She spat out the words. "He never stopped even to ensure that he had killed his man, let alone check that it was the *right* man!"

"So what now?" demanded Ralph.

My heartbeats quickened. It may have been a trick of the candlelight, but I could have sworn that something—a shadow? —moved out in the corridor behind the princess . . .

She thought for a moment, and said, "I shall lock you together in here. The door and the walls are thick, and no one will hear your cries. And then I will go and finish the task that was so badly begun by Ivan. I will go to Lord Audubon, and . . ."

"No need to go to Lord Audubon, ma'am! Like Mohammed to the mountain, he has come to you! No—do not turn, ma'am! My pistol is trained upon your back!"

The Emissary stood in the doorway, pistol aimed. Oddly, he

seemed, to my eyes, to have gained in stature. Impressive as ever, there was none of the slight indecision that had been apparent when he addressed us in the great hall after Jack Grant's wounding. He was crisp. Masterful. Soldierly.

"I shall shoot them both!" said the princess. And she aimed her weapon at Ralph Orwell.

"What will it avail you, ma'am?" demanded Lord Audubon. "Neither of them will advance your cause by their death. And you will not live to turn your gun upon me."

"She has another option," said Ralph.

"Indeed, she has, sir," said the Emissary. "Indeed she has."

A pause—and I thought that the princess' pretty face was going to crumple into tears of rage and frustration.

"Curse you, Audubon!" she cried. "Curse you!"

And she let the pistol fall from her fingers, to land with a thud upon the richly carpeted floor.

When we came in procession down the great staircase, they were grouped at the fireplace: Mr. Martin and Sergeant Gumble were gathered about the stricken man on the mattress, and Augusta was kneeling there. They stared to see that the princess was pinioned: At Lord Audubon's instructions I had tied her wrists before her—as gently as I could—with the silk cord from the bed canopy.

Among the clamor of questions and explanations, I stood in complete disregard, uncaring of anything save the sudden and blissful joy of meeting a pair of gray eyes that looked up at me from the beloved face—now heartrendingly pale—framed in the bandage that covered his scalp wound.

He smiled at me. "Still alive, as you see, Miss Herbert," he said. "And I am told I owe that in part to your help. Thank you so much."

I felt tears of sheer happiness prickle my eyes, and averted my glance in case he should see and pity me for—in Princess Natasha's phrase—"wearing my heart on my sleeve."

"I—I'm very glad, Colonel Grant," I whispered, conscious of the utter inadequacy of the remark.

"And now what has happened?" he asked me. "Why are the princess' hands tied?"

"We've discovered that she is the one behind it all," I told him. "The killings—everything."

"I can't believe it!" he exclaimed. "Not the Tsar's own niece!"

Augusta—his wife—was of the same opinion and was stating that opinion with her customary forthrightness, addressing Lord Audubon, who seemed to be diminished again in the bright blaze of her vehemence.

"You are mistaken, my lord!" she cried. "Our intelligence service is better informed than to have overlooked such a possibility. No member of the Romanoff family would ally herself with those people—those revolutionaries who want to embroil Russia in a disastrous European war that will destroy the Tsar . . ."

She was interrupted by a peal of laughter—high-pitched, mocking laughter—from the princess. And she watched with the rest of us while the paroxysm lasted, till it died away as suddenly as it had begun.

The baby-blue eyes scanned us all, and the rosebud mouth was twisted with contempt.

"I fooled you all," she said. "Even the excellent Mrs. Grant, who is so *au fait* with all things Russian—or so she claims. Even the gallant Colonel Grant, who actually met Princess Natasha not so very many years ago."

"Good lord!" came the exclamation from the man in question. "Are you telling us that you are *not* . . ."

With a wild, bright smile, she raised her bound hands to her hair, took out the pins that held in place the piled-up chignon, shook her head, so that the glory of her flaxen-blonde tresses cascaded about her shoulders, and laughed as she did so.

Silence. And then Jack Grant spoke slowly, clearly summoning up his recollection:

"There was not one, but two young girls, at Tsarskoye Selo that summer," he said. "Both were blonde. One was Princess Natasha Romanoff. The other, the quieter one who kept very much in the background and ran away when she was spoken to . . ."

"I was that girl!" came her response. "The Countess Olga Galitsyn, sometime playmate of the Romanoff princesses. Trust a mere man not to recognize a woman again with her hair up!"

Augusta snapped finger and thumb and pointed to the woman who stood defying us all, her magnificent tresses unbound.

"Galitsyn!" cried Augusta. "I have it now! The old Count Galitsyn was implicated in the plot to assassinate the Tsar in seventy-two. Galitsyn was no revolutionary, only a radical, but the secret police made him the scapegoat. The evidence was undoubtedly falsified. Count Galitsyn was banished to Siberia, but died on the journey."

"Shot while attempting to escape! That is the sardonic lie they employ to cover such eventualities!" Her face was ablaze with passion. "And they did not even trouble to hide their amusement, the swine—not even when my mother went insane before their eyes!" Abruptly, her mood changed, as I had seen it do so often. She smiled. "I have been mistaken in you, Mrs. Grant. You are to be congratulated on your knowledge of the secret workings of the Russian state."

Augusta inclined her head in a graceful acknowledgment of the compliment. "And so, Countess—and one will have to accustom oneself so to address you in future—you became a revolutionary," she said. "An assassin, moreover."

The rosebud lips were pinched, and a certain hardness came to the baby-blue eyes. "My father, Mrs. Grant, was an idealistic fool," she said. "He believed that all Holy Russia's troubles could be solved by a few liberal decrees cemented together with brotherly love, and he died still believing that, on the road to Siberia—with a bullet in the back of his neck! I have made no such mistake. The Romanoffs must fall, and three centuries of tyranny be brought to an end."

"And how many must die before your dream comes true, ma'am?" asked Jack Grant from his makeshift sickbed.

"As Napoleon said, Colonel, 'One cannot make an omelette without breaking eggs!'"

"It is a hard philosophy, Countess."

"I would have spared *your* life, Jack Grant," she replied, casting Augusta a significant glance. "As your lady wife well knows," she added.

There was no end to the many-faceted creature who had posed as Princess Natasha Bibescu. At three o'clock in the morning, when the others were trying to snatch a few hours' sleep before dawn, and Sergeant Gumble was keeping watch, she was lightheartedly chiding me as we lay side-by-side in the firelight, while

I, though horrified and repelled by the things she had done, still found in her a curious fascination and could protest only feebly.

"You lied to me all along," I whispered.

"Clarrie, Clarrie, you must not think ill of me," she said. "I have been your true friend and given you much good advice. I may have deceived you in the big things, but not in the small things." She laughed. "Like Princess Natasha, I, also, neither learned to put tooth powder on my brush nor to lace my own stays. And some of the stories of Natasha's disastrous marriage with Count Bibescu, they were true in every detail. The poor creature confided in me often, since I was careful to continue my friendship with her, for the sake of prudence, even after they had murdered my father."

"What did you do with the princess?" I demanded. "Did you kill her as you killed the others?"

"There was no need," was her casual reply, "for she is at present in Venice. All our agents had to do was to remove her spare luggage and some belongings—including a certain amount of her superfluous jewelry and her pet poodle—from her château at Nantes, and I was equipped to play the role of Princess Natasha Bibescu as no other woman in the world is able."

I drew a sharp and horrified intake of breath.

"You killed that little dog!" I whispered. "You did *that*, also!"

She shrugged her shapely shoulders. "The horrid brute did not take very kindly to his new mistress," she said. "The lady's maid, that absurd Hortense creature whom we employed at the last minute, could not understand why darling Pepé only wanted to bite his beloved mistress. I simply had to forego my bath in Lille (which I needed very much) and dispose of the creature."

A log collapsed in the great fireplace, sending up a galaxy of incandescent particles. Sergeant Gumble rose from his seat, went over and settled the log in its place with his booted foot. He carried Lord Audubon's pistol in his hand.

"And you killed her," I said. "That poor, ignorant Hortense!"

"As your friend Mr. Orwell so skillfully discerned, Hortense accidentally discovered that there was a false bottom to my valise," she replied.

"'Hé, Madame la Princesse, look what is here—a pistol! And what are these little glass things full of liquid?'" Her mimicry of the dead Hortense was impeccable.

"And for that she had to die?"

"Hortense had a certain—understanding—with one of the young functionaries who traveled with us," she replied. "Whenever we were stopped and I was away from the *wagon-lit,* this young swain would come around. I could just imagine her telling him that *Madame la Princesse* had a hidden pistol and little glass things full of liquid in her valise. The pistol I might have been able to explain away to Jack Grant, but after the dramatic demise of that vulgar little Frenchman from my emptying one of the phials of prussic acid into his carafe"—she hunched her shoulders—"I had no choice. The revolution cannot await upon the babblings of a fool. She had taken the lower bunk, thereby providing me with a perfect explanation. That night, I lay awake, waiting for the train to stop—it did so very frequently, as I, who slept so badly on the journey, was well aware. When it did, I opened the carriage door and went out . . ."

"You shot her in cold blood!" I whispered. "While she lay asleep!"

"What better way to go?" was her reply. "When your time comes, dear Clarrie, could you pray for a more merciful end?"

I searched her face, seeking for a clue to the woman who lay behind the bland, pretty mask that she displayed to the world, but could find nothing. She was as enigmatic and stylized as the Byzantine image of St. Basil enameled on the jeweled brooch at her bosom, and unmarked by the corruption within her.

"And Monsieur Charlot's end—you consider that was merciful, also?" I asked.

She shrugged. "I was obliged to use the only means that I had to hand. He alarmed me greatly, that Charlot, when he came out with the story of Count Paul Bibescu and his actress. As I have said, the princess confided in me about her disastrous marriage, but I had never heard of the Heuseux woman. I did not know, therefore, whether he was telling the truth, or if he was lying—to test me. I took the chance and acknowledged it to be true. If true, he knew too much about Natasha—more than I did. If false, he knew me to be an impostor. Either way, he had to be eliminated."

I shook my head. "It's not for me to condemn you, but I can't imagine what it is that drives you to such acts, that blinds you to compassion, to mercy."

"And I will not attempt to explain, Clarrie," she said. "For it would be like trying to describe the color of a rose to a blind man. And while we speak of compassion, will you not please loosen my bonds? This cord is cutting my wrists." She offered me her bound hands, pouting as she did so, childlike.

"No," I said.

"Not just a little?"

"No."

"You are harder than you appear, Clarrie. Perhaps harder than you think. Perhaps there is something—some cause, some ideal—for which you would kill without mercy."

"I hope I am never tested," I replied.

"And so do I—for your sake, my dear. And now, let us kiss and go to sleep, for it is nearly dawn. And in the cold light of day you will begrudge even the slight degree of understanding that you have shown to me tonight." So saying, she leaned forward and kissed me full upon the lips—a lingering kiss that, despite myself, I could not reject.

I lay back upon the cavalry cloak and went to sleep almost immediately. It was still pitch black outside the leaded windows of the great hall when I was woken by a turmoil of voices.

The woman I had known as Princess Natasha was gone and her leopard-skin coat with her. The others were clustered around Sergeant Gumble, who was slumped in his chair with his head bowed on his chest. Chill dread struck at my heart as I sprang to my feet and went over to the group surrounding him.

Ralph Orwell barred my path.

"Don't look!" he said.

But I saw it all. The good sergeant was quite dead. Attached to the back of his neck—placed there like a bullfighter's *banderilla* by means of its long, sharp pin—was the jeweled brooch with the representation of St. Basil.

Lord Audubon stooped and picked up from the floor a length of cord.

"How did she get free?" he mused.

I heard myself say, "Sergeant Gumble must have been a compassionate man. More compassionate than I."

It was imperative that we move out immediately, while we still had the darkness for concealment. Stricken low though he was,

Jack Grant was the first to see the point and to put it with his customary forcefulness.

"She won't give up, not while Lord Audubon still lives," he said. "Ivan and his wife are members of her organization. There may be others in the district. We must get out of here. Back to the railway!"

"We'll carry you," said Lord Audubon.

"Lift me to my feet, give me a pair of shoulders to hold onto, and I'll walk," was the response.

This was done. Ralph and Mr. Martin, who were much of a size, supported the wounded man with his arms around their shoulders. We set off, leaving the grotesque castle of Count Orloff to its silence and its shadows. The good Sergeant Gumble lay by the fireplace, sleeping his long, last sleep, wrapped in his cavalry cloak. We left him in the pious hope that someone would have the charity to give him a decent burial.

The hour before dawn was blustery and chill, with a wind that cut through clothing like a saber. Lord Audubon led us, pistol in hand, across the narrow bridge that spanned the river. Somewhere off in the darkness, an owl hooted, and was answered by his mate. Something splashed in the water, and I gave a start to see a rat swimming away into the shadows, trailing a mackerel pattern of ripples behind it.

It was further than I had remembered. An hour passed before we had gained the wooded hillcrest above the sleeping village that lay in darkness below us. A discernable yellowness in the east told of dawn's approach. And it began to snow again.

Beyond the village, two lines of railway track scored the face of the snow and vanished in the Russian hinterland. We could make out the tiny figure of the sentry standing at the frontier gate, and the snow-covered Berlin train, a forlorn white caterpillar just inside Germany. Of the elusive Kiev train not a sign.

"But see there!" cried Mr. Martin, pointing.

There was a small locomotive: a bijou thing with six wheels and a tall chimney standing on a short piece of track that ran parallel to, and was connected with, the main line into Russia. In the thin light of coming dawn, we could clearly see a plume of smoke rising from its chimney. Close by it was a wooden hut, whose chimney also emitted smoke.

"It's a shunting engine," explained our railway expert. "The crew, I don't doubt, will be having their breakfast in the bothy yonder, all ready to start work as soon as the first of the day's trains begin to arrive. I wonder . . ."

"You wonder—what, Martin?" demanded Lord Audubon.

"Nothing, my lord," said the other. "A passing thought, but too fanciful for words."

"Tell me, Martin . . ." Another voice.

We all turned to regard Jack Grant, who was seated on a fallen tree trunk by the edge of the rutted road. His face was pale and drawn with pain and fatigue, but his eyes were as keen as ever, and his mouth set in a firm line.

"Yes, Colonel?" asked Martin.

"Could you do it, do you think? Is it a practical proposition?"

"What *are* you two talking about?" demanded Lord Audubon.

Ralph Orwell grinned. "Can't you guess? Well, what about it, Martin, old feller? Think you could drive that little loco to Petersburg?"

I gasped.

"'Pon my word!" exclaimed his lordship.

Mr. Martin went very pink, and his short-sighted eyes glowed with the light of enthusiasm. He tugged at his lower lip, cracked his bony knuckles, and betrayed every sign of a man torn between prudence and passion.

Presently, he said, "The actual driving presents no problem, for the controls will be of the most rudimentary sort. But remember that it is over five hundred miles to St. Petersburg, and the locomotive cannot carry sufficient fuel, let alone water, to take it such a distance. However, the furnace will undoubtedly be wood-burning and for wood we could always forage. Water would be another matter."

"And what of the practicalities of the route?" demanded Jack.

"That is the other prime difficulty," replied Martin. "At Vilna, which is about a hundred miles from here, we would need to change onto the main Warsaw–St. Petersburg line, and that would almost certainly bring us into confrontation with the railway operators. After Vilna, it is a straight run to the capital, via Pskov.

"We'll make the attempt!" declared Jack Grant. He glanced sidelong at the Emissary. "With your lordship's approval."

"Ah, yes—yes, by all means," responded the latter. "But what of the Kiev train? Do you not think it would be wise to wait a little longer for that?"

"I don't believe in the Kiev train any longer," said Jack. "In my opinion, its non-arrival points to the fact that it has been forcibly detained by the opposition, so that your lordship could be lured to Castle Orloff and assassinated. I think we must take the chance, put ourselves in Martin's capable hands, and get out of this district with all speed."

"And what of the others still on the Berlin train?"

"That small locomotive's footplate is going to be crowded enough," said Jack. "They will come to no harm for the Eydtkuhnen stationmaster will dispatch their train back to the capital this morning." He looked to one and the other of his supporters. "Will you two gentlemen kindly help me to my feet? Daylight will be upon us in no time."

If any of us had ever been in doubt as to who was really in command of the mission, Jack had settled that doubt.

We passed the bothy close enough to catch the coarse aroma of frying food, creeping in a straggling line, Lord Audubon to the fore and the injured man and his supporters bringing up the rear. I walked with Augusta Grant. To my astonishment, she flashed me a smile. It was brief—as if she were paying for it in hard coin—but a smile for all that. I remembered what Jack had said about his wife being warm and human underneath.

"What a blessing that he's made such a good recovery," she said.

"You mean—Colonel Grant?" I faltered.

"Who else?" she snapped. And there the conversation died.

As we drew near our goal, even my own inexpert eye could discern that the patina of many years lay thickly upon the locomotive. Its metalwork showed rust through flaking paint, its brass and copper pipes were tarnished green and brown. But the smoke rose from its tall chimney, and it wheezed steam from every crack and cranny. With a proprietorial air, Mr. Martin swung himself up onto what I supposed was the footplate and gazed about him, in particular at a large brass dial on the end of the boiler, which he tapped, and then shook his head.

"Not enough head of steam to move her," he called down. "We'll have to stoke the boiler and wait."

"How long?" said Jack.

"Hard to say, Colonel. This old thing leaks steam like a sieve. It could take quite a while."

"Then get to work!" ordered Jack. "You—Orwell—get up there and help him."

"Yes—suh!" Ralph gave him a smart, half-mocking salute, winked at me, and climbed up to join his fellow-journalist, who had stripped off his coat and was picking up logs of wood from the rear of the footplate and throwing them into the flaming maw of the open furnace door.

"Your arm, Miss Herbert," said Jack.

I gave it to him with all my heart, and I was still supporting him when, some ten minutes later, Martin reported that, in his opinion, the old locomotive was nearly fit to move. With reluctance, I helped hand the man I loved up to the others, and myself joined them. There was scarcely room for us all to stand there without touching.

"One thing remains," said Mr. Martin. "I can't see it from here, but it's likely that we shall have to shift the points up yonder before the loco can get onto the main line. I'd be obliged, Orwell old fellow, if you would go and do that now. You will see that the upright lever yonder moves to and fro and operates the points. As soon as all's well, wave to me and I will see if this old thing is ready to start moving."

"Sure," responded Ralph, "but one thing I ask—don't leave me behind and steal that story in St. Petersburg all for yourself."

He climbed down and set off. The end of the track on which we stood was marked by an upright lever at the place where it joined the main line some two hundred yards distant. The fact that we could now see it so clearly betokened the rapid advance of the dawn light. I watched Ralph Orwell amble casually down the line, his loose, gangling figure part-silhouetted against the new day in the east. There was no sign of the locomotive's crew, who were still at breakfast in the windowless hut.

And then—*they* came!

We heard them before we saw them: a thunder of pounding hooves in the snow behind us. We all turned, and were in time to see them pouring in a cloud out of the wooded slopes of the hill down which we had come. There were about a dozen of them, all mounted on shaggy ponies. Some had rifles slung across their backs, and at least half of them carried sabers. Not uniformed cavalry, but men in coarse sheepskin coats and fur hats. And they had seen us, as well they might, for our footprints in the snow pointed straight to the locomotive.

"Start up, Martin!" ordered Jack Grant. He cupped his hands around his mouth and shouted. "Run for it, Orwell! Get those points moved and watch for yourself!"

We all joined in calling to Ralph, who turned when he heard the warning shouts, breaking into a run when he saw the mounted men streaming across the open space toward the train. He had about fifty yards to go when, with a hissing and a clanking of moving metal, a sigh and a deep-throated groan, the old locomotive moved slowly forward, paused with her wheels spinning impotently on the icy tracks, went on again at walking pace.

"Go it, old gel!" cried Martin. "Put on some speed!"

Our attackers—there was not the slightest doubt, now, of their intention, for sabers were being flourished and it was a regular cavalry charge—were closing fast at the full gallop, and still the old engine had not progressed beyond crawling pace.

"Can't you get any more speed out of this confounded contraption?" cried Jack. "They'll be on us in no time!"

Mr. Martin was bearing down hard upon a control lever, beads of sweat standing out upon his lean face, for all the icy air.

"There isn't the head of steam there yet, Colonel," he protested. "Wait—now—she *is* responding!"

Sure enough, the tired old engine was gathering momentum, gushing steam in billowing clouds. From the corner of my eye, I saw two men burst out of the door of the hut and stand in astonishment at the sight of their mount being stolen from under their very noses. But the horsemen were still going faster than we. My thoughts flew from our own immediate peril to that of Ralph Orwell. I looked forward along the rusty mass of metal to see that he was tugging on the lever, leaning against it with all his weight. I saw it move. I saw him wave, and then commence running back to meet us.

Oh, pray for this old thing to go faster. Faster! I clenched my fists till the fingernails hurt my palms. Another glance back to the enemy. They were still overtaking us, and no more than twenty strides behind.

"My God!" exclaimed Lord Audubon. "It's she herself! Look!"

She was among the leaders, fur-capped and heavily coated like the menfolk with her, and in place of rifle or saber, she carried a light whip with which she lashed the pony's flanks. Her flaxen hair was gathered up under the cap, but there was no mistaking the pink-and-white complexioned face, the bright blue eyes wide with fierce exhilaration of the chase. I did not need to be told how she would rejoice to see her followers fall upon us with their sabers and guns, and I thought how much better it suited her style, to run us down and kill us like carted stags out in the open, rather than resort to poison and subterfuge.

"Faster, Martin! Give her more steam!" From Lord Audubon.

"She has the steam, my lord, but not the stamina!"

"Well—try!"

"Yes, my lord!"

Another anguished glance forward. Ralph was running hell-for-leather to meet us, and we were closing with him fast. But were we too fast? Having reached him, would it be possible for him to get aboard, or would that kindly and humorous American perish before our eyes in alien snow, hacked down by the cruel sabers?

And now Ralph was as far ahead of us as our pursuers were behind—a matter of ten yards in each case. And we were going too fast, much too fast, to pick him up.

It was then that Mr. Martin bore down upon another lever and we were all but overthrown as the brakes took effect, and, with a new outburst of released steam, the old engine tobogganed back to a walking pace. Jack Grant fell heavily against me, and I had the greatest difficulty in supporting him. Our eyes met—close. My heart pounded. I wrenched my gaze away to see how Ralph was faring.

He stood with his fingers poised to grasp the handholds, one foot extended to leap. If he was conscious of the peril that was descending upon him in flying strides, he gave no sign. His whole concentration was clearly directed upon a leap for life.

"Ralph!—look out!"

I screamed the warning, to see the nearest rider closing down on the helpless man, saber raised on high. I instantly recognized the skull-like, Asiatic features of the murderous Ivan, though his hairless scalp was hidden under a big fur cap. The evil eyes glittered with a savage triumph. Two strides, and Ralph Orwell would be butchered.

A pistol, discharged close by my ear, shattered all other sounds and choked me with the stench of burned powder. I saw the man Ivan drop his saber and pitch sidelong from the saddle of his careering mount. Next instant, eager hands were reaching down to snatch Ralph Orwell up from the very threshold of eternity. The brakes were released. The old engine started forward again, bravely gathering speed.

"Well shot, my lord," murmured the man I loved.

"Vengeance for your own wounds, Colonel," responded the Emissary.

"I am greatly obliged to your lordship," said Jack. "Ah, I think we have the measure of them now. Their mounts are blown, and flagging fast. We outstrip them. Look at her, all of you! Did you ever see baffled fury more eloquently displayed?"

As we clattered over the points and swung onto the main line to St. Petersburg, the woman we had all known as Princess Natasha Bibescu, *née* Romanoff, reined in her mount. Her shaggy pony, after its long gallop, stood in a cloud of rising steam that gave her outline a wavering ghostliness in the dawn light. She sat there for a few moments, her face a mask of cold anger. Then, brusquely, she snapped her whip asunder, and, casting both pieces from her, tugged the rein and turned about.

She never looked back. I never saw her again.

Chapter Eleven

WITH THE COMING OF THE DAWN SUN, THE SNOW SLACKENED AND it became quite unbearably hot on the footplate within touching distance of the boiler and the fire doors, so we disposed ourselves upon the piles of logs at the rear. I sat there with Ralph Orwell, disheveled and unwashed, already blackened with smuts from the chimney, my skirts filthied by rust and grime from contact with the footplate. But I was glad to be alive, and happy to be moving on to our goal.

Scarcely a couple of miles from our starting point, we approached a sizable township and a station. Mr. Martin called to us all to lie low out of sight. He himself had found a filthy peaked cap which he had put on askew, giving him a somewhat jaunty appearance. Clearly, our railway enthusiast, danger or no, was entirely in his element. We flashed through the station at full speed, and if anyone questioned our passing, we were certainly unaware of it. Presently, the danger passed, we were able to sit up again, and found ourselves steaming through a plain that was marked only by clumps of fir trees, occasional thatched hovels, and walled fields where patient peasants stooped low over their tasks, never looking up to regard the passing locomotive.

"I must say that a close brush with the angel of death mightily sharpens up one's appetite for living," said Ralph. "And it's quite true what they say about seeing one's whole past life sweep by in an instant of time. I clearly remember a quite protracted episode —so long ago that I could have sworn it had passed from my recollection forever—concerning my older brother, who dived into a water hole for a bet when we were kids. Dived from the top branch of a tree and was an unconscionable time a-coming up. I saw the whole episode right through—and a lot more—

while that feller was coming at me with the sword. But that's not all . . ."

We were alone—or as near as alone could be under the circumstances—at the rear of the footplate, seated on the log pile.

"Tell me all," I said lightly. Indulgent. Unsuspecting.

I met his gaze, and knew at once what he was about. But too late.

"Like I said, a narrow escape such as I had certainly concentrates the mind and helps one to sort the essentials from the inessentials." He paused, and his amber-colored eyes were eloquent of his feelings.

"Ralph, I . . ."

"No, let me go on," he said. "We'll be in St. Petersburg in thirty hours or so, maybe less if our tame expert can squeeze the last ounce of energy from this broken-down old engine. Once we're there, you will go one way, I'll go the other. We'll be caught up in the movement of events, like folks who meet in trains and go out of each other's lives for ever after. Do you know what I'm trying to say, Clarrie?"

I nodded.

"Any point in my going on?"

I shook my head.

"It's as *she* said, is it?" He pointed back the way we had come. "There's someone else."

"Yes," I whispered.

Jack Grant was seated at the other side of the log pile, deep in a muttered conversation with Lord Audubon. His wife sat with her dark-maned head leaning against the rusty ironwork, eyes closed. Miraculously, she seemed as clean and unbesmirched as if she had just stepped out of her boudoir.

"It's Grant, isn't it?" murmured Ralph.

"Yes. There's nothing I can do about it."

"Quite hopeless? Even though he's married?"

"Quite hopeless, Ralph. I wish it were otherwise. I'm very sorry."

He shook his head. "Sorry?" he said. "Sure, we're both sorry, Clarrie. I suppose there's no use in my parading my family background—which is quite impressive, for I have an uncle who once stood for governorship of the state of Maryland? Nor to recite my prospects with the *Baltimore Advertiser and Exam-*

iner, which, since it is owned by my old man, are about as bright as naked nepotism can ensure? And I could touch upon the way I have with children and animals—some animals. No?"

Half-laughing at his drollery, yet close to tears, I laid my hand on his arm. "It wouldn't be the slightest use, Ralph," I whispered. "Don't you see? I'm lost. You are a dear, kind, and witty man who will make some woman very happy. You could even make me happy—I'm sure of it. But my heart is elsewhere, and it wouldn't be fair to you."

"What if I said I would accept the position?" he asked. "Would you marry me then?"

"Marry you—and love another?" I asked him. "Come, Ralph, you know that would be a recipe for disaster."

Again, he shook his head, and relapsed into silence.

By noon, we were following the course of a river that lay on our left hand. The countryside was bleak and uninhabited. Snow had given way to a swirling mist that closed down upon us without warning, shutting out the landscape and reducing our world to the brief dimensions of the little rusty engine that bore us on. Mr. Martin, as the visibility decreased, prudently and progressively reduced speed till we were traveling at walking pace. Presently, after scanning the various dials, he brought the engine to a halt.

"I'm sorry," he said. "We are almost out of water for the boiler. I daren't risk going any further. Indeed, I should draw the fire for fear of blowing us all sky-high."

We digested the doleful news in silence.

Presently, Jack Grant said, "It was a brave try, and you did well, Martin. We are out of immediate danger and on our way to St. Petersburg. Now we must find other means to continue." He paused, cocked his head sideways, listening. "What was that?"

I heard it above the hissing of steam, and my heartbeats quickened.

"Horses!" I said. "Coming this way!"

"It can't be!" breathed Augusta. "Not after we've come all this distance. Not . . ."

"They are approaching from ahead!" exclaimed Lord Audubon. He cocked his pistol. "By jove! There they are—*look!*"

From out of the shifting white mist, a column of horsemen

cantered down the line toward the engine. They wore white uniforms, and their mounts were black. The vapor from the horses' mouths and nostrils issued forth like cotton wool and was lost in the mist.

"Cossacks!" I gave a start to hear Jack Grant's voice at my ear. "Though whether they're loyal or rebel Cossacks, we shall discover all too soon."

The cavalrymen drew rein close by us. Their leader, a tall officer in a high-crowned cap, with a neat moustache, raised his whip and shouted something in Russian.

"Answer him, Augusta," said Jack.

"What shall I tell him? He wants to know who we are and from where. I think—I gather from what he *didn't* say—that they've had news of us. Possibly a telegraph message from the frontier."

"The troopers are unslinging their carbines," said Lord Audubon grimly.

The challenge was repeated. By now, there was a line of gun muzzles pointing in our direction. The officer was tapping the side of his boot with his whip.

"Tell him everything!" said Jack. "Nothing to be gained by dissembling now. We're at their mercy. Tell them who we are and what we are about. And may heaven help us!"

Augusta spoke in loud, staccato sentences, pausing to indicate Lord Audubon and Jack Grant when, as I supposed, she was introducing them by name. I noticed with—despite the seriousness of the occasion—wry amusement that she appeared not to allude to humble me. When she had done, the Cossack officer barked an order to his men, and the carbines were lowered. With a touch of his booted heels, he brought his mount close to the engine. His gloved hand came up in a salute.

"From England?" he said. "How tremendously interesting. And you, sir, are Lord Audubon? Permit me to introduce myself: Major Kuprin, Seventh Bolensky Cossacks." He spoke English like a gentleman, with the same, drawling, carefully inflected accent as—for instance—Lord Audubon.

"How do you do, Major," responded the Emissary, "Have we met? Your face seems quite familiar."

"I rowed at Henley in sixty-six," said the major. "In the Grand Challenge cup eights."

"I was not at Henley in sixty-six," responded Lord Audubon.

"I think," said the major, "indeed, I am sure, that I had the honor of being presented to the dowager Lady Audubon at Verity House, Piccadilly, in the same year."

"That is extremely likely," said his lordship. "My mother opened the London house for every Season till increasing age and infirmity precluded her from doing so. Have you previously met my aide, Colonel Grant, Wessex Hussars?"

"I think not," said the major. "Though I was at Sandhurst in sixty-six and seven."

"A little after my time," said Jack. "But you must surely have suffered the lectures of Brigadier Hobart, Major?"

"Old 'Bootles' Hobart!" cried the Russian. "Did I not, sir! Was there ever such a bore? Though a three-bottle man of the old school, whose like one does not see often nowadays. More's the pity."

"And very sound on the Punic Wars," said Jack.

"Yes, indeed. The Punic Wars. Very sound."

Out in the wilderness of the Russian hinterland, stranded in a defunct locomotive, with heaven knows what perils surrounding us in the mist—and all they could indulge in was small talk about Sandhurst, Henley, and the London Season of 1866! I felt my hackles rise. I need not have perturbed myself. The network of blood, caste, influence, and past association that binds together the upper classes of all civilized nations was working its potent magic even in those unpromising circumstances.

A little more small talk, and presently the major said, "Well, my lord, I have to tell you that there is great concern, it seems, for your safety. At least, I must presume that it is your safety which is referred to in my orders. There has been a wholesale disruption of the railway lines between Minsk and Vilna due to an explosion on the line that prevented the passage of the Kiev train."

"The Kiev train!" A horrified outburst from Mr. Martin, which drew a raised eyebrow from the Russian. "Don't tell me, sir, that the famous Kiev train has been blown up? That would be too monstrous!"

Major Kuprin, glancing to Lord Audubon and Jack for guidance in dealing with the sort of Englishman it had perhaps not been his fortune to meet before, and receiving only the slightest of shrugs, answered poor Mr. Martin coldly. "No, it is not," he said. "But the dastardly action on the part of revolutionaries has also spread chaos between here and St. Petersburg. All rail services are in suspension and the affected regions are under temporary military law."

"You spoke of your orders, Major," said Jack. "Might one ask the nature of those orders—insofar as they concern Lord Audubon and his mission?"

The major took from a gold case a very fat cigarette and lit it with a lucifer match, drew a mouthful of smoke and exhaled it in the chill air. "My orders, sir, are to locate your party and assist your onward passage to St. Petersburg. Which I will proceed to do."

"You will find us a suitable train, Major?" cried the Emissary.

The Russian's eyes slid sidelong to our rusty old engine. "If your lordship's intent is to reach St. Petersburg with all haste," he said, "I would earnestly advise you to regard your present conveyance as 'a suitable train.' In Russia, I hasten to explain, the truth of your old English proverb, 'A bird in the hand is worth two in the bush' has a very special and pertinent application. And the more so in times of crisis and disruption. No, I beg you to stay where you are, my lord. It is not comfortable, but it will get you to Petersburg." He puffed a large smoke ring and looked wise.

"But, we are out of water," wailed Mr. Martin. "And there is scarcely any fuel left!"

"A little over two leagues down the line," said Major Kuprin, "there is a wayside station which is admirably well supplied with both. Similarly, from Vilna junction to Petersburg, where all the stations are at present under military guard, you will find ample fuel and water. All you have to do"—here, he took from his saddle bag a notebook and from his breast pocket a pencil in a gold holder, with which he scribbled a few lines ending with a flourish—"is to present this *laisser-passer* to the officer in command."

"But, sir, how are we to get to the next station when the locomotive cannot at present raise a head of steam?" demanded our railway expert.

"Why, sir, we will drag you there," said the imperturbable

Russian. He gave a sharp order, and his men, who had coils of stout rope slung from their saddles, attached them to the front of our old engine. And presently, with many a creak and groan, with many a Russian invective, our engine was moving steadily through the drifting mist—dragged by a squadron of Cossack chargers.

Kovno was behind. Vilna was behind. Pskov, we had been told, lay about two hundred and fifty miles ahead, and St. Petersburg could not, surely, be much further on.

We were passing through low-lying land set with necklaces of small lakes fenced in with sedge and reed, from which, at our passing, heron and wild duck rose in alarm. There were a few villages: poor, unkempt huddles of thatch and cob that put me in mind of mid-Cornwall, except that, in place of the church spire, there rose the distinctive onion-shaped dome of the Russian Orthodox faith.

It was past midday, and the mist had cleared, as had the snow. Our Cossack friends, from whom we had parted at the first wayside station, had presented us with their rations of black bread, sausage, and coarse red wine—ample to last us till we reached our destination some time during the following morning.

Mr. Martin, who alone knew the intricacies of working the locomotive, admitted Ralph Orwell and Lord Audubon to the more elementary mysteries of the craft, so that they were able to take short spells at the controls and permit him—who had scarcely slept the night before and who was faced with many more hours of heavy responsibility—to catnap. This he allowed himself to do solely on condition that one man remained on the controls while another person—and the composition of the party dictated that it sometimes had to be a woman—kept a lookout ahead. My alarm and embarrassment were considerable when I drew the first watch with Lord Audubon.

The others were all asleep: Jack Grant, a pale wraith stretched out upon the logs, his bandaged head reposed in his wife's lap; Ralph Orwell and Martin slumped against the rusty sides of the footplate. The hissing of steam and the rumble of the wheels masked all conversation above shouting pitch—oddly effective circumstances for a *tête-à-tête*. I feared greatly that my lord would take full advantage of the situation in which we were placed. He did.

"Miss Herbert," he cried, his head close to mine. "Something I must tell you."

"Please, sir, I beg you—not again!" I cried.

"I have wronged you greatly," he told me.

"Yes, you have, but the harm is over and done with. Let us leave it so, I beg you."

"It has to be said, Miss Herbert!"

"Then let it be said and finished," I responded, grateful, at least, that he had ceased to address me by my pet name.

"Not only did I wrong you by my physical advances," he informed me—with his lips still close by my ear, and shouting quite loud above the clatter—but I also wronged you in my mind at Cologne."

"In Berlin," I said, remembering only too well.

"*What?*" he shouted.

"In Berlin. It was there that you offended me!" I shouted back.

"True, Miss Herbert. But it was in Cologne that I wronged you in my mind."

"I don't understand." I stared at him in astonishment.

"Thinking that your glances had lit upon me favorably, and seeing you walk out of the hotel restaurant alone, I took it that you were leading me to some quiet place of assignation. I followed you . . ."

"You did *what?*" With dawning realization, I gazed into his—surely guileless—eyes.

"Followed you to the cathedral," he said. "Thought you had made a mighty odd choice for a *tête-à-tête*, I must confess, particularly when it was obvious that you had gone into a quiet room off the main part of the building. Very daring that, I told myself. Then along comes this Johnnie in the black cassock, who gives me a disapproving glance, for all the world as if he suspected me of having come to steal the cathedral plate. So I gave him an affable nod and left."

"It was *you* who followed me!" I cried.

"Thought you had contrived it, my dear Miss Herbert," he replied. "Thought we had an understanding between us. But am now persuaded that I was mistaken. Please forgive."

He looked so contrite, so absurdly vulnerable with his pale, patrician face crumpled, sleek hair tousled by the wind of passage, his tall and well-built form sagging with despondency, that I could have hugged him out of sheer relief.

If a cad, then certainly a cad with a conscience.

And a waking nightmare dispelled.

Another encounter. This time with Augusta Grant. Unlike that with Lord Audubon, it was curiously inconclusive.

It took place during the late afternoon, as we steamed steadily northward through the unchanging landscape of lake and plain, of sedge and wildfowl. Jack Grant still slept, weak from the wounds, but with his excellent constitution renewing itself in rest. Mr. Martin was at the controls, with Ralph looking out ahead. The two journalists were talking together, their voices entirely muffled by the sounds of our advance.

Augusta took a swallow from a leather flask of the Cossack wine, and I wondered if she had ever stooped to do such a thing before in her life.

She saw my eyes upon her. "I suffered agonies of nausea on the cross-Channel boat," she said, "and also in the *wagon-lit*. Oddly, I am quite free of it at the moment. Would it be the fresh air, do you think?"

"I'm very sorry," I said, "about taking your cabin on the boat—the one farthest away from the engine and the paddle wheels. I should have guessed the reason for your insistence."

Her green eyes flared challengingly. Not for the first time, I was uncomfortably aware of her pantherine temper.

"Because of my pregnancy?" she demanded. "But that signifies nothing. I am by nature an irascible person. At present, a pregnant irascible person. I assure you that the difference is negligible. Whatever my condition, I would have acted the same."

It was another snub, but at least we were talking. Not that communication with the wife of the man I loved was anything but agony and embarrassment, since she herself knew, from the outburst of Princess Natasha (would I ever be able to think of her by any other name?), of my passion for the man to whom she was married and who had fathered the child that lay beneath her heart.

"I'm sorry nevertheless," I told her.

"Yes, I think you are," she commented. "And I have been extremely uncivil to you, Miss Herbert. For that, I too must apologize. And now, would you be so kind as to do me a favor?"

"Of course," I said.

"I am desperately tired," she said. "And Colonel Grant really should have the bandage changed on his shoulder wound. The head will make do till St. Petersburg." She rummaged in her reticule and took out a clean bundle of linen. "I brought enough from the castle for another bandage. Would you mind awfully? Thank you so much."

And she lay back and closed her eyes.

Not a word on the subject that lay between us like a scream in the dark. No allusion to the fact that I had been declared to be in love with Jack Grant. I marveled at the aristocratic detachment that allowed her to entrust the handling of her husband's body to such as I.

And was deeply disturbed.

Augusta Grant slept soundly at sunset, which was when her husband awoke.

I watched every stage of that awakening, savoring each separate experience, as a mother will regard a beloved and only child; noticing the first, slight restlessness, the flexing of the fingers, flutter of eyelashes, a small yawn, and finally the opening of the eyes, a brief smile of recognition.

"Miss Herbert," he murmured. "Have I been asleep for long? What time is it?"

"Nearly seven o'clock," I told him. "This will be our last night. Mr. Martin says we shall be in St. Petersburg before tomorrow noon."

("Our last night"—in the circumstances, a particularly apt and heart-rending phrase!)

"Is there something to drink?" he asked.

"A little wine. Shall I help you?"

"Please."

I held the leather flask to his lips and he took a draft. His head was resting against my shoulder when he drank. I could have wished it to stay forever.

"And now, I must change your bandage," I told him. "Mrs. Grant's instructions," I added.

"Augusta is a very good nurse," he said.

"Yes," I whispered.

"And a real human being. As you have discovered. As I assured you that you might."

"Yes."

Avoiding his eye, for fear that I might betray myself, I unbuttoned his tunic and revealed his shirtless torso, with the heavy bandaging at the shoulder. And I saw again the silver sixpence on the fine gold chain. As I commenced to untie the blood-caked strip of linen, I said lightly, "Why do you wear an old sixpence close to your heart, Colonel Grant? Is it, perhaps, a souvenir?"

"It is indeed," he replied. "And a very interesting tale hangs upon it. Would you like to hear?"

"Yes, I would."

And so he told me. While I tended the wound, bathing it in a little wine and putting on a clean bandage, he told me the story that I had heard from the lips of Princess Natasha (again that name!), and the same in every particular. I marveled that the Tsar's secret police could have such a near insight into the lives and hearts of people. I heard again of his father's meeting with his mother, the old aristocrat's stubborn refusal to countenance the match, her rejection of the son, and what came after.

Jack's fine gray eyes took on an expression of sad pride when he told of his father's glorious death for Queen, Empire, and Regiment, and of how the same regiment had adopted him and raised him to his true heritage as an officer and gentleman. Only when he came to the end of his account did he betray, by a discernible change in the tone of his voice, the depths of his emotions.

"So, in the end, you were reconciled with your grandmother?" I asked him. "And your mother also?"

"It was Mother's decision," he said. "It was, perhaps, the most splendid and unselfish act of a splendid and unselfish life. She knew that Grandmama would never unbend of her own accord, no matter how much she might desire to be reconciled. It would have to be she—Mother, who had been so wronged—who must make the first move.

"We traveled to Yorkshire," he said. "Grandmama had simply responded with a short note, written by her lady-companion, that she would be willing to receive Mrs. Grant and her son. We found her—very old, very pathetic. Almost blind. She broke down completely when she saw me close. Called me by my father's name. Do you know—she had never lost touch with any of us? Cuttings from *The Times,* from *The Illustrated London News,* about my father's death and the presentation of his medal to my mother at Buckingham Palace, my gazetting as an officer in the old regiment—they all lay on a table close by her hand, and showed the marks of much handling.

"It was a complete reconciliation?" I asked.

"Total," he said. "That night, we dined together in the great hall. One could see that there was something troubling Grandmama. Toward the end of the meal, she said to my mother, 'My dear, I did you a great wrong, but I do believe that the greatest insult I laid upon you was to toss you a sixpence for bringing my son home in your governess cart after his fall from the horse. I knew then, you see, that he was attracted to you. In my jealousy, in my arrogance, I sought to dismiss you with the sort of tip one would offer to a cab driver.'"

"And how did your mother reply?" I asked him.

"She smiled," he said, "and took from her reticule the very coin. 'I have kept it always,' she told Grandmama, 'because in all my life I never was more grateful to earn a sixpence.'"

"'Never more grateful to earn a sixpence,'" I echoed. "What a splendid person she must have been, your mother."

He nodded. "And Grandmama also, after her fashion," he said. "In all humility, she begged Mother to give her back the sixpence. It was a symbol, you see? A symbol of her total contrition. And in the giving back and the receiving, all sealed with a kiss and an embrace, the wrong was righted and an end put to a rift that had lasted for nigh upon twenty years."

"You saw your grandmother afterward?" I asked him, knowing the answer.

"She sent for me on her deathbed," he said.

"And she gave you—the sixpence." Here was the one small detail that had evaded the patient enquiries of the Russian secret police.

"It was her last act in life," said Jack. "And when I am dying, I shall hand it on to my son."

His son! I stole a glance at Augusta, sleeping close by, her breast gently rising and falling, her beautifully kept hands folded on her lap. And a sense of ineffable deprivation surged through my mind, till I could have cried out with the agony of it.

"You have bandaged me well, Miss Herbert," said Jack. "And all done painlessly. Thank you."

How to tell him that it had been a very heaven on earth to touch him and tend for him? That to be crouched by his side in the dusty, dirty old engine was an experience that I should treasure all my life, and that, if I could have willed it, our strange odyssey across the Russian wilderness would have lasted for ever and ever.

"Not much longer," said Jack. "The worst is over. Miss Herbert, I cannot tell you how much I look forward to reaching St. Petersburg."

I closed my eyes and leaned my head back against the rusty metalwork.

"Yes, it will be a great relief to you," I whispered, "to bring the mission to a successful end and have your wife safe again."

He did not reply. I did not reopen my eyes, but drifted through silent tears to a long and troubled sleep in which I saw the man I loved in every imaginable circumstance, but always separated from me by a high pale that I had neither the wit nor the courage to climb. It was the last time I ever dreamed of the unattainable Jack Grant. And in the late morning, when I woke, the towers and domes of St. Petersburg were rising out of the shimmering sea in the far distance.

Upon arrival, we were taken by closed carriages immediately to the British Embassy, which is in a vast square overlooking the cathedral of St. Isaac. There, Augusta, the two journalists, and myself were given tea by pretty Russian maidservants who giggled to each other about our unkempt appearances (all of us, that is, save for Augusta, who miraculously still retained her spotless elegance).

I remember the room well, the room in which they put us. It was long and stately, with the most glorious cut-glass chandeliers and portraits of long dead English diplomats lining the walls. A span of tall french windows gave out upon a wide balcony overlooking the square and a general panorama of what must surely be one of the most beautiful cities on earth.

Jack and Lord Audubon had been absent for an hour, having gone straight to see the ambassador, presumably in the expectation of obtaining an early audience with the Tsar. I found myself unaccountably fretful, and could scarcely abide my companions' presence, but went out onto the balcony and drank in some of the sea air and the sunshine.

A step at my side. It was Ralph Orwell.

"Nearly over," he said. "What shall you do now, Clarrie?"

"Go home to Cornwall," I told him. My mind had been made up on the instant of him asking the question.

"Home being the school for young ladies?"

"Yes," I said.

"You'll not keep the job of looking after Lord Audubon's daughter?"

I shook my head.

"Too many memories, I guess."

"Too many memories, Ralph," I assented.

He reached out and took my hand, which I did not deny him.

"No second thoughts—about the proposal I made you? Don't answer that, Clarrie. It's in your eyes. It's written all over you."

"Does it show so much?" I asked him.

"To anyone with the eyes to see," he replied.

"Augusta must see it, even if she didn't know already. But do you think *he* knows?"

"I should think not," said Ralph. "We're not knowing animals, we men. Not in that sort of way."

"Thank heaven for that," I said. "I couldn't bear for him to feel sorry for me."

There was a discreet cough. Looking around, we saw Mr. Martin at the open window.

"Miss Herbert—Ralph," he said, "would you come in, please? Lord Audubon and the colonel have returned."

We went back into the room. My first impression was of Augusta, who was sitting on a sofa, her eyes fixed upon Jack Grant, her lips parted in a half smile. He looked pale, yet entirely composed. His arm was in a sling, and his blue uniform, despite the rust mold and the oil stains, became him magnificently. The Emissary, from the crown of his sleeked-down hair to the toes of his newly polished boots, looked as if he had stepped out of a bandbox.

It was Jack who—typically—assumed the initiative. He addressed himself to the two journalists,

"Gentlemen," he said, "I have the pleasure to inform you that you may immediately telegraph your papers to this effect: The Constantinople affair is over. Peace is preserved."

"Thank God for that!" exclaimed Mr. Martin.

Ralph looked skeptical. "Upon what terms, might one ask, Colonel?" he demanded.

"The Royal Navy will immediately withdraw from Turkish waters," said Jack. "At the same time, the Russian armies will also withdraw. The entire Turkish question will be settled not by war but by negotiation. A congress of the European nations involved will shortly be called in Berlin."

"At which poor Sultan Abdul Hamid and his ramshackle empire will be carved up in accordance with the interests of Bismarck, the Tsar, and Queen Victoria," said Ralph.

Jack frowned. "I am not a diplomat, sir," he said, "but a soldier. All I know is that Lord Audubon was granted an audience with the Tsar yesterday and that his Imperial Majesty readily assented to the Emissary's proposal. There, as far as I am concerned, the matter ends. My brief is discharged."

As when a pebble falls into still water and there is a sudden disturbance and a flurry followed by a silence that seems greater and more intense than the one that went before, so did we stand and stare and ponder upon the fallacy that Jack Grant had just pronounced. It was Ralph Orwell who broke that silence,

"Colonel, you said that Lord Audubon saw the Tsar *yesterday*," he declared. "Yet, as all here know very well, Lord Audubon was riding the footplate of that old loco yesterday, along with the rest of us!"

Jack and his companion exchanged tight-lipped smiles.

"Do you tell them?" asked Jack. "Or should I?"

"I think the pleasure should be yours, sir," was the reply.

With the air of a man introducing a paradox, Jack indicated

the tall figure at his side. "Miss Herbert—gentlemen," he said, "may I present Major the Honorable Francis Verity, Bengal Lancers. Younger brother to the same Lord Audubon, who did *not* travel in some ostentation by private train from Paris to St. Petersburg, but by sea. And not, as one might have supposed, in a battleship of the Royal Navy, but in an ordinary packet from Harwich to St. Petersburg—incognito."

"You were a decoy!" cried Ralph. "We were all decoys! To draw the enemy fire from the real Emissary!"

"We had hoped," said Jack gravely, "that there would be no violence, but we were prepared for it. Our supposed mission, deliberately contrived as a badly kept secret, was, as you say, a decoy to fool those elements whose interests lie in embroiling Russia in a disastrous war leading to revolution. From the twilight world of spy and counterspy, our people at the Foreign Office learned that their act of summoning from Constantinople our authority on Turkish matters, Lord Audubon, had not passed unnoticed. It was clear that the revolutionaries' best hope was to assassinate the Emissary on Russian soil, and so give ammunition to our own war party, the Jingos. Accordingly, I was given the task—with the aid of Lord Audubon's brother, here—of heading them away from the real mission to St. Petersburg. The rest you know: A distinguished journalist, an innocent maidservant, a gallant non-commissioned officer—and a small dog—paid the price for European peace."

I was speechless with astonishment. So was Mr. Martin, who could only stare at Jack Grant, then at the man we had come to know as Lord Audubon. Nor did Augusta say anything. Not so Ralph Orwell, who was all vehemence.

"Jules Charlot guessed something was odd about this mission!" he cried. "It never looked right from the first. We were the wrong kind of journalists for the assignment. Miss Herbert here" —he indicated me—"a schoolma'am from deepest Cornwall promoted to a diplomatic interpreter overnight . . ."

"Miss Herbert was an embarrassment!" interposed Jack Grant, and he gave me a smile that took the sting from his declaration and set my heart pounding. "Lord Audubon advertised for a governess before he was given his orders to depart, and left no word of her. I, who was summoned at a moment's notice to organize the decoy mission, was obliged to absorb Miss Herbert into the organization, since my military training tells me that it is the loose end, the unconsidered trifle, that betrays the deepest laid stratagem. I may say"—and again he smiled at me—"that Miss Herbert has discharged her duties in a most exemplary manner."

"Colonel, you've been damned lucky!" declared Ralph. "Hell, I give you top marks for audacity, but you never really deserved to win. I ask you"—and he pointed to Augusta—"what kind of a military commander would bring along his own wife on a mission like this?"

I looked toward Augusta. Her face was bowed, and her hidden eyes told me nothing. I looked back to Jack. He was smiling a broad, opened-out smile before which one could have warmed one's hands.

"The lady in question, Mr. Orwell," he said, "was appointed to accompany this mission by the Foreign Office by reason of her considerable knowledge of Russian protocol. And the lady in question is not my wife, for I am a bachelor. It can now be told that she is the wife of my friend and comrade here. I have the inestimable pleasure of introducing—the Honorable Mrs. Francis Verity."

They had all gone their various ways—Ralph with the promise that he would write to me, Mr. Martin with the assurance that he would send me an inscribed copy of a projected monograph on the *wagons-lit* of Europe which he was preparing.

Augusta took me aside to say good-bye.

"I really have behaved appallingly to you," she said, "and on a trifle light as air. I thought, you see, that you were leading Francis on. You told me, in Cologne, that you and someone had walked back together from the cathedral. My dear, I have no illusions about Francis's predilections for pretty women." She shrugged. "And all the time it was Jack you loved. Oh, my heart has bled for you these last days. I would have told you that that woman was mistaken, that I was married to the man who was supposed to be a widower. But the risk was too great. The journalists, you see? One can't trust such people, and you appeared to have adopted Mr. Orwell as your confidant. Why are you crying? Do you have a handkerchief? Here, have mine, it's quite clean."

She left me with her handkerchief. Jack accompanied her and her husband out of the room, and I went out onto the balcony again. My whole world had suddenly become one enormous query. I rested my hands upon the stone balustrade and closed my eyes.

It was the dining room in the Berlin luxury hotel repeated, and I, waiting and hoping against all likelihood or probability . . .

I heard him re-enter the room and close the door behind him; thrilled to hear him unhesitatingly direct his footsteps toward the french windows; pause there for a few moments to regard me, and I with my back turned to him.

He walked quite slowly up to me and placed his hands—those curiously delicate hands—on the stonework close to mine.

"A good fellow," he said, "Francis Verity. You would scarcely tell the two brothers apart, but Lord Audubon was blessed with the brains for the pair of them. Still, Francis has the advantage of an intelligent wife. I shouldn't doubt if dear Gussie isn't our first lady member of parliament. Every evening, you know, the three of us would hold a council of war in which Gussie was unquestionably the master of the situation."

I saw it all quite clearly, then. "That was why you went to her compartment on the train," I said. "To have one of your councils of war!"

"It was all perfectly proper," he said. "The lady's husband was with her, and remained with her after my departure."

"And at the castle," I said, "you took his room because it had a communicating door and you were able to join the two of them in her room for another of your discreet councils of war. And because of that you were nearly killed."

Somewhere out across the sun-dappled city, a bell tolled.

"They are an odd couple," he said. "Francis—well, you have had some experience of his little ways. I am afraid he is prey to certain compulsions, though all the time devoted to Gussie. And I have to say that when I pointed out that you were a lady of virtue and not for him, he responded admirably and promised he would apologize for his behavior at Cologne."

"And that he did," I murmured. "Poor Augusta—poor Gussie —how can she abide such a man?"

"Gussie is well competent to deal with him," said Jack, smiling. "She is—as you must know—a lady of some considerable spirit. I was appalled to learn, when she arrived in Paris, that she was with child, and I forbade her to accompany us. When she gleaned, however, that another lady—and a beautiful lady at that—had joined the mission, she immediately telegraphed London and had her appointment confirmed by the Foreign Secretary. I suppose, knowing Francis, one couldn't blame her."

Silence hung between us. His hand was resting even closer to mine.

"It was very gallant of you," I said, "to speak out in defense of my virtue."

"Gallant?" he said. "Perhaps, but I wouldn't put it higher than —self interest."

There was no longer any use pretending. His eyes told me all. He stood revealed to me as I to him. We faced each other, while on the instant all the bells of St. Petersburg gave tongue together in a clamorous roundelay of joyful sound.

"It's Easter morning, Clarrie," he murmured, taking my hands in his. "And we have played a not inconsiderable part, you and I, in bringing an Easter of peace."

Peace? Yes, he was right. We had done that, but as I looked out over the great city of St. Petersburg under the spring sunshine, I thought of the flaxen-haired woman on the shaggy pony who had broken her whip in fury. Could the Tsar of All the Russias continue to rest easily while she and her followers remained?

Happily, my doleful speculations were instantly dispelled by the sudden delight of Jack's lips on mine and a coming together that was beyond all belief, all previous understanding.